*A Promise Car*

Claire Templeton is drawn to the majestic beauty of the California Redwoods in the hopes of capturing an unexplained phenomenon on camera. What she doesn't expect is to run into her first love, Jed Lafferty, the boy she worshipped as a child, the man she's never been able to forget.

Carefree, fun-loving Jed doesn't believe in fate, preferring to make his own luck. But when he runs into the little girl who used to follow him like a shadow, now an irresistible woman, he can't help feeling the odds are turning in his favor. Letting Claire walk out of his life the first time might be his single biggest regret. But when strange gifts and cards left for Claire turn sinister, it's clear someone else from her past isn't ready to let go . . .

**"Jannine Gallant is an exciting new voice in romantic suspense."**
**—Mary Burton, *New York Times* bestselling author**

**"Well developed, realistic characters. Entertaining family dynamics. Jannine Gallant gives you a satisfying read."**
**—Kat Martin, *New York Times* bestselling author**

**"Check all the windows and doors before you go to bed because the relentless, obsessive stalker in Every Move She Makes will have you looking over your shoulder long after the lights go out."**
**—Nancy Bush, *New York Times* bestselling author**

Visit us at www.kensingtonbooks.com

# Books by Jannine Gallant

*Who's Watching Now Series*
Every Move She Makes, Book One
Every Step She Takes, Book Two
Every Vow She Breaks, Book Three

**Published by Kensington Publishing Corporation**

# Every Vow She Breaks

*Who's Watching Now Series*

## Jannine Gallant

**LYRICAL PRESS**
Kensington Publishing Corp.
www.kensingtonbooks.com

Lyrical Press books are published by
Kensington Publishing Corp. 119 West 40th Street New York, NY 10018

All Kensington titles, imprints, and distributed lines are available at special quantity discounts for bulk purchases for sales promotion, premiums, fund-raising, and educational or institutional use.

Special book excerpts or customized printings can also be created to fit specific needs. For details, write or phone the office of the Kensington Special Sales Manager:
Kensington Publishing Corp.
119 West 40th Street
New York, NY 10018
Attn. Special Sales Department. Phone: 1-800-221-2647.

Kensington and the K logo Reg. U.S. Pat. & TM Off.
Lyrical Press and the L logo are trademarks of Kensington Publishing Corp.

First Electronic Edition: March 2016
ISBN-13: 978-1-61650-655-1
ISBN-10: 1-61650-655-5

First Print Edition: March 2016
ISBN-13: 978-1-61650-656-8
ISBN-10: 1-61650-656-3

Printed in the United States of America

*To my husband, Pat, the inspiration for the hero of this book. May your life always be filled with excitement and fun. Thank you for everything you do.*

# Chapter 1

The scent of burgers and fries drifted through the diner as the swinging kitchen door slapped against the wall. Claire Templeton's mouth watered. With a sigh, she poked through her salad, stabbed a tomato and popped it into her mouth. Given her petite frame, eating fries wasn't an option unless she wanted to look like the portly waitress. Not that the woman, who dwarfed the taxidermy bear in the restaurant's entrance, was doing too badly at the moment.

Her ample bosom swayed as she set a plate loaded with a double-decker cheeseburger and onion rings on the table in front of the customer in the booth across from Claire. *Customer* didn't do the man justice. Supreme specimen of manhood came close. Those naked Greek statues had nothing on this guy. Sun-streaked brown hair crowned a tanned face with bright blue eyes and a killer smile...which he was currently using as he requested extra mustard.

"I'll get it right away, hon." Augusta—if her nametag was to be believed—put one hand on her padded hip to lean in close. "You have to be the best-looking man ever to walk through that door." A jerk of her head toward the bear set graying wisps of hair fluttering around an age-creased face. "If I were thirty years younger—"

"They'd arrest me for soliciting a minor."

A robust laugh drowned the chatter of a family with three young children two booths down. "What a charmer."

The linoleum floor shook as the woman rounded the end of the counter and disappeared into the kitchen.

Claire rolled her eyes. "She didn't move like that when I asked for another slice of lemon in my iced tea."

Her hunky neighbor met her gaze and grinned. "Didn't your mama ever teach you you'll catch more flies with honey than vinegar?"

"I didn't want to catch flies. I wanted lemon."

Something about his smile nagged at the back of her mind.

*Nope. I'd never forget crossing paths with this man.*

Augusta returned and plopped a bottle of yellow mustard on the tabletop. She gave Mr. Ruggedly Handsome a toothy smile. "You planning to be in town long?"

"A couple of days. I want to do some hiking in the redwoods around here."

"Be sure to come back for breakfast. No one makes pancakes like Ralph."

"I'll do that. Can you recommend a campground? I drove by quite a few."

"Take a right at the first cross street heading north and follow the road to the end. Towering Trees Campground has showers. Some of the others don't. Enjoy your meal...er, what's your name, hon?"

"Jed. Thanks for the tip...and the mustard."

Claire's head snapped around. Jed. Memories swirled. A laughing boy with bright blue eyes sliding worms down her shirt, hollering over his shoulder at her to ride faster, licking a triple-decker chocolate ice cream cone—

"Careful of your drink."

She jerked her elbow back and slid the plastic glass away from the table's edge. "Thanks." Surely this man couldn't be—

"Are you just passing through?" He picked up his burger.

Collecting her scattered wits, she shook her head. "Actually, I have a reservation at the campground Augusta mentioned. Uh, you said your name's Jed?"

He nodded and popped an onion ring into his mouth. "Nice to meet you..."

"Claire."

His hand stilled over his plate. "Claire. Maybe we'll run into each other again while we're camping."

She worked her way through lettuce and an assortment of veggies while sneaking glances across the aisle. Jed wolfed down his burger then started on a chocolate shake topped with a cloud of whipped cream. The man might not have weight issues, but surely his cholesterol levels were as lofty as the dessert topping.

His gaze met hers again as he set down the glass. "I swear this isn't some kind of lame pick-up line, but you remind me of someone I used to know. I don't suppose you ever lived in Reno?"

She dropped her fork, eyes widening. "Oh, my God, it is you. Jed Lafferty. I can't believe it. You were skinny and obnoxious, and now you're...not."

His smile stopped her heart.

"Little Claire Templeton all grown up." His gaze swept downward. "Sort of. You're still pint-sized."

"I prefer vertically challenged."

His laugh turned the heads of the two old-timers at the counter who'd been eating blueberry pie and arguing about fishing. Augusta stepped through the kitchen doorway to glance in their direction with raised brows before retreating.

Claire pressed a hand to her chest. "I had the biggest crush on you despite all the nasty bugs and worms you tortured me with. I cried the whole way to Winnemucca when we moved."

"Your parents dragged you off to the middle of nowhere. I'd have cried, too."

"Good point. Not surprisingly, we didn't stay there long. After two more stops, I ended up here—" She spread her arms wide. "—for high school."

"No kidding?" He picked up his shake, crossed the aisle and slid onto the bench seat facing her. "How come you're camping if you're visiting your family?"

"I'm not. They left the area years ago. You remember my dad, always on the go, dragging my mom off to someplace new before she even had a chance to finish unpacking from the previous move. They're currently up in Oregon. How're your parents?"

His gaze dropped. "My mom died of breast cancer a few years ago. My dad's still in the same house, retired from the Reno police force. I see him on a regular basis."

She touched his arm. "I'm sorry. I loved your mom. She always had a smile and a cookie for the lonely, little girl from across the street. What about your brother?"

"Kane's married and has three stepdaughters. They live in the Napa Valley area."

His hand lay on the tabletop, ring finger conspicuously bare.

"You're not? Married, I mean."

He shook his head. "Not even close. What about you?"

"I've been within shouting distance a couple of times."

Leaning back in the booth, his gaze wandered over her face. The smile she remembered from the best time in her childhood grew.

"Those guys must have been crazy to let you get away."

"Augusta's right. You are a charmer." She wadded her napkin and dropped it next to her salad bowl. "How are you, Jed? Tell me all about your life for the last—what—twenty-five years?"

"Sounds about right. I was ten, and you were nine when you moved."

"Yet I still have vivid memories of following you around that summer. Apparently you leave a lasting impression on a girl."

He took a final swallow of his shake. "If you're finished with your rabbit food, let's go somewhere to catch up. The day's too beautiful to hang out in here. No fog or rain is a rare combination in the redwoods."

"It's not even very windy. We could drive through the woods to the beach." She dug her wallet out of her purse then glanced over to smile before dropping a few singles on the table. "I can't believe we met again, here of all places, after all these years."

"Must be fate or destiny or whatever."

Augusta lumbered out of the kitchen and headed toward the cash register. "If you're finished, I'll ring you up."

Jed tossed a five dollar tip next to his empty plate as he led the way through the diner. When her steps slowed, he turned. "What?"

She gripped her purse a little tighter. "You're not a serial killer on the run from the police or an escaped lunatic, are you? Going off alone into the forest with a relative stranger seems like something a dumb blonde in a horror flick would do. I may be blond, but I'm not stupid."

His smile flashed. "Want to call Kane? He's a small town sheriff. His endorsement should ease your mind."

She let out a breath then continued toward the register. "I'll take my chances and go with my gut. My gut tells me you're a good guy."

"That's because I am."

They paid for their meals, thanked the waitress then left the diner. Claire paused beside her compact motor home while he stopped next to an older SUV two spots over.

"Want to lead the way since you're familiar with the area?"

"Sure. There's a terrific beach not far from here. A twenty-minute drive at the most."

He nodded. "See you when we get there."

Claire backed out of the parking spot then turned onto the street. Heart thumping, she glanced in the rearview mirror. His SUV was right behind her. Pressing more firmly on the accelerator, she followed the highway through the tourist area of Shady Bend, past a gas station, a convenience store, several souvenir shops and a burl wood business into a thick grove of redwoods. Only a few rays of sunlight sifted through the trees, casting shadows across the narrow stretch of highway. She turned onto a rutted county road leading to the ocean.

Jed Lafferty—her first love. Not that he'd cared two shakes about the shy, scrawny girl next door. Although he might have felt sorry for her since he'd frequently let her tag along on his adventures. She'd peddled her heart out trying to keep up with him on his bike, endured skinned knees and elbows rollerblading down the steepest hill in their neighborhood and sprained her wrist bouncing off the trampoline in his backyard. Her family had moved to Reno late in the school year, and she'd never fit into any of the firmly established groups of girls in her class. Only when she was hanging out with Jed had she been happy.

A lot had changed in the last twenty-five years. She wasn't a sad preadolescent, and he wasn't an overactive little boy. Still, it would be interesting to see what he'd made of his life.

Turning into the sandy lot adjacent to the beach, Claire set the parking brake. When a thump sounded from the back of the motor home, she glanced over her shoulder and smiled.

"Did you have a nice nap…on my bed?"

Scoop yawned and shook then sauntered over to the door and plopped his butt on the mat in front of it. Leaning across him, Claire opened the door then waited for the dog to jump to the ground. She grabbed a windbreaker off the wall hook beside the table before following. Scoop walked over to a clump of waving sea grass and lifted his leg.

"Good God, what is that thing?" Jed stood next to his SUV, hands stuffed into the back pockets of his jeans, eyeing her dog like he might turn and charge.

"That *thing* is Scoop. Two years and one hundred pounds ago, he was a cute little rescue puppy. The shelter people weren't sure about his breed, some cross between a boxer, a Rottweiler and a hound."

"Interesting. Want to take a walk?"

"I'd love to. I'm stiff from driving all morning."

Slipping on her windbreaker to combat the light, autumn breeze, she strolled beside him down to the damp, packed sand. The tide was receding, leaving salt residue on the beach as the waves surged then retreated. High above in the endless stretch of blue, seagulls squawked and circled. Scoop ran ahead before pausing to sniff a pile of seaweed. Claire took a deep breath of tangy sea air then let it out slowly.

"Looks like we have the beach to ourselves."

She glanced his way. "I used to come here with friends for evening bonfires when I was in high school. The access road is crappy and unmarked, so not many tourists know about it."

Hands stuffed in his pockets, he squinted against the sun. "So, you're here to camp and visit your old stomping grounds?"

"Actually, I'm here for my job. I'm a nature photographer."

"Oh, yeah? Someone pays you to travel around to beautiful places and take pictures?"

She grinned. "Pretty much. I work for a magazine called *Rugged America.*"

"I want to be you when I grow up."

Her laugh set a flock of sandpipers running in all directions. "You look grown to me."

"Naw. I'm just a big kid. Up until a couple of weeks ago, I ran a wilderness camping retreat. Not the most adult job in the world."

"I'm not surprised in the least. The summer I lived across the street from you, you slept in a tent in your backyard most nights."

"Houses are overrated."

She smiled. "I don't know about that. You'll notice I have a motor home, not a tent. Where's this retreat?"

"It is—was up on Donner Summit in the middle of the Tahoe National Forest. Unfortunately, the government chose to revert the land to wilderness, so the camp's closed permanently and will soon be dismantled."

Stopping, she laid a hand on his arm. "I'm sorry."

"It was a good run, ten years, probably long past time for something new. In the winter, I work out of a ski rental shop offering backcountry skiing tours, so I have months before I need to worry about what to do next summer."

"This is your off season?"

He nodded. "I plan to spend the next few weeks hiking and camping along the coast."

"A busman's holiday."

"The best kind. Maybe we can hang out together while you're here photographing trees."

"Maybe."

They stepped across a shallow stream running through the sand then continued down the beach. Up ahead, Scoop wrestled with a giant chunk of driftwood before dropping it to trot back to her side. Claire reached down to rub his ears.

"I'll definitely be photographing trees, but that's not the focus of my story. I got a tip from an old friend who still lives in the area. A member of a research group camping in the woods swears he saw a Bigfoot."

Jed turned and stared. "You're writing a story about a bunch of crazies?"

She shrugged. "Could be. I intend to take a lot of cool pictures in addition to documenting the group's research. I'll let readers draw their own conclusions about whether or not Bigfoot is real or a hoax. To keep the magazine's core supporters happy, I'll mix in plenty of information on the area's flora and fauna along with spectacular photos. The Bigfoot angle is a twist to draw in a new group of readers. The marketing department is all over it."

He grinned. "Claire Templeton, does the heart of a rebel beat beneath that proper façade?"

She glanced down. "What's so proper about jeans and a T-shirt?"

"It's the *look but don't touch* aura you project."

"Hmm. Is that why your hands are jammed in your pockets?"

He nodded. "It helps me resist temptation and maintain my good guy persona. I wouldn't want you to think I grew up to be the sort of man who preys on lone, defenseless women."

"I'm not defenseless. I took classes. Besides, Scoop isn't just a pretty face. If you threatened me, he'd rip your arm off."

"Good to know. I'm in favor of keeping that mutt happy."

"You have something against dogs?"

"Only ones who look at me like I'm on the dinner menu."

Claire didn't blame Scoop one bit. The man was drool-worthy. She licked dry lips and turned when the beach ended at a rock cliff jutting into the water. They started back the way they'd come.

"Do you plan to camp with this research group?"

She glanced over. "Not right away, although I may spend the night out there at some point. I have an appointment with the director tomorrow, so I'll know more after that."

"I'd give my left—uh, arm to see a Bigfoot. Can I tag along?"

Pressing a hand to her mouth, she couldn't hold back a giggle. "You sound exactly like the ten-year-old boy I remember. I'll tell them I have an associate and ask permission for you to join me on any expeditions."

"Hot damn!"

The giggle erupted in a laugh. "You know it's all probably a big, fat farce, right?"

"Sure, but what if it isn't?"

"What if Santa Claus and the Easter Bunny and the Tooth Fairy are real?"

"If you're such a skeptic, why're you writing the story?"

"I'm writing about the process of hunting for a Bigfoot...and photographing a beautiful area of California. Anyway, I have an open mind." She swept a hand toward the forested hills rising away from the coast. "Who knows, any number of things could be hiding out there."

He reached over to snag her hand and squeeze. A tingle shot up her arm then fluttered around in her chest before moving on to heat her southern regions.

"This is great, Claire. Running into you just made my week." His grip tightened. "Unless you want me to take a hike, so to speak? If you'd prefer not to have company, I'll understand."

"I enjoy my dog, but having someone around who talks back is better." When he released her, she hesitated then stuffed her fist into the windbreaker pocket. "Okay, maybe not always better, but I'm looking forward to hanging out with you. Evening campfires should be a shared experience."

He stopped when they reached the trail to the parking area. "You're okay with continuing our get-reacquainted session at the campground? I don't want to be pushy or assume anything."

"You're not. We're both alone, so why not join forces?"

Brushing a strand of hair off her cheek, his finger moved in a soft caress. She held her breath until his hand fell away.

They turned together to walk side-by-side up the path from the beach, their arms touching.

"I like the sound of that. I'm pretty handy to have around camp. I promise you won't regret teaming up."

A hint of doubt crept to the surface. Once before, leaving Jed had broken her heart. She couldn't help wondering how the woman she'd become would fare when they parted ways this time. Looking into blue eyes full of light and laughter, she shrugged. It was a risk she was more than willing to take.

* * * *

*At last!*

He straightened in his seat and started the engine as a motor home rolled through town with Claire in the driver's seat and a big, brown mutt riding shotgun. With a smile stretching his lips, he pulled onto the street behind an older SUV.

She was finally here. As he'd hoped, the pull of a Bigfoot story was too strong for her to ignore. After waiting an eternity, they'd be together the way she'd promised all those years ago.

He was counting on her to keep her word.

Tapping his fingers on the steering wheel, he kept some distance between their vehicles then slowed when the RV pulled off the road into the lot of the supermarket on the far end of town. He edged up to the curb and parked. Turning in his seat, he held his breath as Claire stepped from the motor home and pushed the door shut behind her. Rays of late afternoon sun highlighted her beautiful blond hair.

The smile slipped from his face when she walked toward a man— one of those grunts who spent all his time in the gym from the looks of him—who slammed the door to the SUV that had been following her. *What the hell?* Claire wasn't dating anyone. He'd kept close tabs on her over the last few months as the big day drew closer, and he was one hundred percent positive there was no significant man in her life. Surely she hadn't picked up some guy on the drive to Shady Bend? One-night stands weren't her style.

His hands clenched around the wheel as the two strolled side-by-side into the store. Taking a deep breath, he let it out slowly, practicing the calming techniques his shrink had taught him. No point in panicking until he knew all the facts. No point in panicking, period. He'd simply adjust his plan to deal with any new circumstances.

Long minutes ticked by before Claire emerged carrying a bag of groceries. The stranger was still with her. He smacked his fist against the dashboard then closed his eyes and breathed deep. Opening them, he turned the key in the ignition and slouched lower in his seat when the woman he'd waited for—forever—drove past. Painful emotions churned in his gut as he flipped on his blinker to follow her through town. When she turned down the road leading to Towering Trees Campground, he continued past. Now was not the time to confront her. First, they'd get to know each other again. Maybe he'd leave a few more reminders of her promise.

Everything would have been perfect if the damned SUV hadn't turned toward the campground right behind her. No matter. No one, certainly not some fly-by-night boy toy, was going to stop him from getting what he wanted—the beautiful Claire. Not this time.

# Chapter 2

Jed pounded in the last stake then pitched his sleeping bag, thermal pad and duffle bag into the tent. Stepping back, he stumbled over Scoop and lunged against the corner of the picnic table to break his fall.

"Damn!" He glared at the oversized mutt.

Every time he turned around, the dog was behind him. He couldn't decide if it was a case of canine infatuation or the hound's version of keeping his enemies closer.

Now, if Claire chose to follow his every move the way she had when she was a girl, he certainly wouldn't complain. For a ten-year-old boy, her hero worship had been irritating at times but more often a source of secret pleasure. Even then, she'd been a cute little thing. Now there was an underlying layer of sexy that made his mouth go dry every time she smiled.

Especially when she smiled. He drew in a sharp breath.

There was something special about Claire. Her delicate beauty tugged on his heart...and wouldn't his brother die laughing if he could hear that sentiment.

Letting out a grunt, he shook his head. Jesus, he was thinking like a girl. Time to man up and chop firewood or something.

"Move over, Scoop." Giving the dog a push out of his way, he headed into the trees along the backside of the campground to forage for dead limbs. Returning with an armload, he dropped them beside the open fire ring and snuck a glance toward the motor home. Soft humming drifted through the open window along with an occasional burst of singing. What the hell was she doing in there—he glanced at his watch—for the last twenty-eight minutes and fourteen seconds?

The door opened, and Claire stepped out carrying a bowl in one hand and a plate topped with chicken breasts coated with some sort of marinade in the other.

"I made a salad. Shall we grill these?" She set her load onto the picnic table.

"Sounds good to me."

She'd changed into athletic pants that hugged every curve of her body, along with a soft fleece top. His fingers twitched as he stuffed his hands into his pockets.

*Mind out of the gutter, Lafferty.*

"I have a gas hibachi and propane canisters in my car. I'll get them."

He gave himself a mental slap as he opened the back of the SUV to pull out the covered grill. She wasn't the type of woman you hit on a few hours after meeting, even if they did have a history together.

He carried the hibachi back to the picnic table and set it up. "What else are we having?"

She gave him a blank look.

"You know, to fill up on. Potatoes, pasta, rice, bread?"

"Uh, I'll be full with just chicken and salad."

He patted his stomach. "I'd be starving again before bedtime. I have a stockpile of boxed pasta meals. I live on those things. It'll only take a few minutes to whip one up."

"They're full of sodium."

"Who're you, the health food police? They taste great."

"Knock yourself out. You can use the stove in the motor home if you want."

"I have a camp stove."

After a second trip to the rear end of his SUV, he hauled back a tub full of pots and dishes and another one loaded with nonperishable foods, along with the stove. Minutes later the pasta was bubbling and the chicken sizzling.

Claire sat in a canvas camp chair and stroked her dog's ears. "You seem awfully handy in the kitchen."

"Yep. I'm competent at most everything I do on a regular basis. Sometimes more than competent."

"I bet."

Were her cheeks pinker than they'd been a moment before? Did she think he was alluding to his skill in bed? Or was he the only one with sex on the brain? Heat crept up his neck as he searched for a new subject.

"Where do you live when you aren't driving around the country in search of the perfect picture?"

"Right now, nowhere."

The spoon stilled, suspended over the pot. "Huh?"

"I was renting a little cottage north of San Francisco. When the owner died, his family put the house on the market. It sold in about two seconds."

"They booted you out?"

"Sixty days' notice. I put all my furniture in storage and am living in the motor home for the summer. I should think about getting another place once I wrap up this story. It's already the middle of September...." She shrugged one shoulder. "I haven't decided where exactly I want to live, which is why I'm still traveling around like a nomad. All I know is I'd like to make this move permanent. I've spent most of my life never belonging anywhere, and frankly I'm sick of it."

"Don't you have to be near your work?"

"The magazine has headquarters in New York, Chicago and San Francisco. I only stop by the West Coast office once or twice a month since everything I do is online for the most part. When someone needs to speak to me, they pick up a phone. Occasionally I meet face to face with my editor to go over details or get her approval for a story idea if I feel an in-person appeal will produce better results. Bottom line, I can pretty much live wherever I want."

"Food's ready." He served the chicken and set the plates on the picnic table. "Sure you don't want some pasta?"

She sat down on the bench then heaped salad on her plate. "Maybe a small helping. I'm pretty hungry."

"I'd be half dead if I ate what you did for lunch." He dropped a spoonful of noodles next to her chicken then sat across from her. "So, where are you considering establishing your home base?"

"I imagine I'll stay somewhere in Northern California. Definitely a small town. I've lived in cities before and wasn't much of a fan. I like the ocean."

He glanced up from his meal. "How about mountains? Do you like those?"

"I do in the summer. Winters..." She wiggled her hand back and forth. "I went on a couple of ski trips to the Sierras when I was in college. I spent most of the day picking myself up off the snow."

His gaze roamed from her face downward, and he cleared his throat. "You look athletic. I bet you'd learn fast with a few lessons. Where'd you go to college?"

"Cal Berkeley. How about you?"

"I stayed in Reno and went to the university there for a couple of years before I dropped out. All I wanted to do was spend my time outside. It finally dawned on me that planning a career which would lead to working indoors was just plain foolish. I'd have been miserable."

"Obviously you aren't."

"Nope. I love what I do—or did. I'll figure out something new to keep me busy in the summer. I'm great at thinking outside the box. As for winters, I'm set. I spend my days skiing in the backcountry with other Nordic enthusiasts who want an experienced guide. I've been working out of the same shop for years, and I get a lot of repeat customers. I make enough to meet my needs, and that's all I care about."

"Sounds perfect for you."

"Might be better if I had someone to come home to at night."

She laid down her fork. "I'm pretty sure women stampede when you snap your fingers. You aren't exactly hideous to look at."

He grinned. "Not as fast as they run in the opposite direction once they get a taste of my lifestyle. I live in a two-room cabin with no neighbors within shouting distance. During winter, the place is literally buried in snow."

"Gee, you make it sound so attractive."

"That's what I'm talking about. Most relationships haven't lasted longer than a month."

"You didn't care about any of those women enough to change?"

"Not yet." He pushed back his empty plate and stood. "It's chilly tonight and getting dark fast. I'll start a fire."

"I'll wash the dishes while you're building one."

Turning, he laid a hand on her arm and squeezed. "We make a good team."

"Hmm…the jury's still out. Any man who lives someplace that requires shoveling to get out the front door has to be a little crazy. It's going to take more than good looks to compensate for being snowbound six months of the year."

"Sounds like a challenge."

Her brows shot up. "Oh?"

"By the time you finish your Bigfoot story, my list of sterling qualities will far exceed the negatives. Just wait and see."

\* \* \* \*

Claire leaned back in her chair, propped her booted feet on a rock outside the fire ring and tucked her chilled hands into her pockets. The fire crackled and snapped. Above the dark shadows of towering trees, stars filled the night sky.

"You're sure you don't want a s'more? I'll toast the marshmallow."

*Jannine Gallant*

"Positive."

Jed shook his head. "When it comes to food, you're absolutely no fun at all. It's not like you need to watch your weight. You're tiny."

"I'd like to stay that way. Besides, all that sugar and fat is bad for you."

"I work off the calories, and I'm disgustingly healthy. I have good genes."

"Is that supposed to be a mark in the positive column?"

He pressed a graham cracker down over a beautifully browned marshmallow and slid out the stick. "Why not? You wouldn't want to pass along any wimpy genes to your kids."

"True."

"Enough about me. I want to hear all about the near miss you had with marriage."

She suppressed a smile. "Why?"

"Well, duh. If I'm going to lure you to my snowbound cabin, I need to know what turns you off."

"Is that your goal?"

"Sure. You can cook and clean and…do other things to keep me happy all winter."

Rolling her eyes, she reached for the chocolate bar sitting between them and broke off a square. Popping it into her mouth, she savored the rich flavor. "Are you ever serious?"

"On occasion. Spill it. Who'd you almost marry?"

"Not almost. Remember that ski trip I mentioned while I was in college? My boyfriend talked me into eloping to Reno."

He juggled the s'more, swore then sucked on his marshmallow coated thumb. "Why'd you do something stupid like that? How old were you?"

"Nineteen. He was twenty-three. My parents were living in North Dakota—don't ask why—and I hadn't seen them in nearly a year. Ian was a grad student. I met him when he was a teaching assistant in one of my classes. He was finishing his master's and planned to move to Seattle where he already had a job lined up." She shrugged. "I was feeling a bit lonely and left behind."

"So you actually married him?"

"Yep. I was already regretting it before the Elvis impersonator who performed the ceremony told him to kiss the bride. It wasn't until the next day…" She pressed her lips together.

His warm hand covered hers where it rested on the chair arm. "What happened?"

"For some reason, I insisted he drive by our old house. I told him I wanted to show him where I used to live. Your mom was on her front porch doing something with a bunch of pinecones—"

"She made Christmas decorations out of them."

"I broke down and started crying. All I could think about was how nice she'd been to me and how much I'd missed you after we moved...." She drew in a long breath. "Ian probably thought I was a complete loon. Anyway, our parents freaked when we told them, and I had their full support when I went to court to get the marriage annulled. Everyone but Ian was completely relieved when it was over."

"He wanted to make a go of the marriage?"

She nodded. "He was still pretty angry when he left the Bay Area. I haven't heard from him since, though, so I guess he got over me and moved on with his life."

"Wow. That's quite a story."

"Not one of my prouder moments. I've thought about Ian a few times since I decided to pursue this article. His degree was in physical anthropology, and he had a thing for Bigfoot. His theory was Sasquatch are an offshoot branch like Neanderthals with distinct human characteristics, but the species never went extinct. Not that he was alone in his thinking. When I did some research before driving up here, I discovered there's a whole community of scientists and pseudo-scientists who follow his reasoning."

"So is this Ian guy part of the group camped out in the woods?"

Claire's boot slipped off the rock and hit the ground with a thump. Beside her chair, Scoop let out a snuffling snort and a moan.

"Oh, my God, I suppose he could be. I know he still works in the field. A couple of years ago I ran into an old friend of his who mentioned they'd attended the same conference. Wouldn't that be a trip—first you and then Ian?"

"Are you going to dump me for your first love? I swear you'll break my heart if you do."

"Ian wasn't my first love. You were. Why do you think I cried so hard sitting in front of your house that day?"

Jed sealed the bag of marshmallows with a twist tie then dropped it into the food box before giving her a slow smile. "I'm touched."

"I was nine. My taste in the opposite sex wasn't exactly discriminating at the time."

"Ouch." Ducking his head, he winced then smiled. "And now it is?"

"Let's just say I've learned a few things over the years, but enough about me. Your turn to bare your soul."

"I would, but there isn't much to tell. I've had dozens of short-term relationships. Honestly, I never let myself get involved enough to be hurt when they ended."

"Why not?"

He shrugged. "I don't know. It's not that I'm against falling in love. The problem is most of the women I meet are on vacation. They go home, and I move on to the next one."

"Wow. You should come with a warning label tattooed on your forehead—Love 'em and Leave 'em Lafferty."

"I'm not that bad. I only go for the women who know the drill. I don't prey on naïve innocents."

"I guess that's a point in your favor…an extremely small point."

He grinned. "I can be rehabilitated. Give it your best shot."

"Sounds like a daunting task." She levered herself out of the chair. "Maybe tomorrow. Right now I'm going to bed, but can I help put away the food first?"

"I'll take care of it."

They stood close between the fire ring and the chairs. The dancing flames cast shadows across his face but didn't disguise the heat in his eyes.

He reached out a finger to touch her cheek. "This has been great."

She swallowed. "I agree. Of all the friends I left behind over the years when my family moved on to the next town, you were the one I most wanted to see again."

"Am I living up to your expectations?"

Her gaze slid upward from his broad chest to the pulse beating in the hollow of a strong neck, then over chiseled lips curved in a smile and on to the blue depths of his eyes.

"It may be a little too soon to say. We've made a good start, though."

"I'm a big fan of new beginnings—that initial rush when you're getting to know someone, discovering what makes them tick."

Her toes curled in her boots. "What do you think makes me tick?"

His eyes searched her face. "Emotion."

"You're wrong. I'm all about logic."

"Maybe when it involves your job…."

"No, pretty much all the time. When it comes to relationships, when the going gets tough, I head for the hills. I've learned the hard way that trying to force something that isn't right just doesn't work in the long run."

"Your old college boyfriend?"

She nodded. "Among others."

"Good to know, but I have one thing working in my favor."

His teasing smile heated her more than the fire. "Oh, what's that?"

"When you head for those hills, I'll be waiting at the top. Remember, I live in the mountains."

She let out a small laugh then shook her head and grinned. "Thanks for the reminder. On that note, I think I'll go to bed."

"Good night, Claire."

If she took one step forward, she'd wind up in his arms. *Too soon.* She inched around him. With a groan, Scoop rose to his feet and followed.

"Good night, Jed."

# Chapter 3

Claire slowed as the dirt track narrowed and snaked around a giant redwood. Her teeth clanked together when she hit a rut, and the steering wheel jerked in her hands. Thank heaven she'd accepted Jed's offer to drive his SUV. Her motor home would have gotten stuck at least a mile back. Several bone-jarring minutes later, she pulled into a small clearing where a big tarp-covered shelter stood beside several smaller tents. She parked next to an ATV.

Sliding off the high seat to the ground, she slammed the car door and surveyed her surroundings. A blue jay squawked from the branches of a tree, but nothing else stirred. To ward off the early morning chill, she pushed her hands into her jacket pockets then strolled toward an area set up with a table and chairs. A large map stuck full of colored push pins rested on an easel. The swirling lines and different shades of green that might or might not represent changes in elevation meant absolutely nothing to her. When it came to maps, if there wasn't a big *you are here* arrow, she was lost.

Fog hung in the trees. Not ideal lighting for photos, but it did give the camp a certain eerie quality. If she could get the angle right… She retrieved her camera from the car, adjusted the settings and took several shots.

"Hey, what the hell are you doing?"

Claire swung around, camera poised. The man raised a hand in front of his face.

"Paparazzi out here? Are you freaking kidding me?"

Dropping her arm, she stepped back. "I'm Claire Templeton from *Rugged America.* I have an appointment with Leeland Harper."

Pink colored the man's cheeks as he pushed graying dark hair off his forehead before extending a hand. "I forgot all about our meeting. Sorry. Please, call me Lee."

Claire took his offered hand in a firm grip. "Nice to meet you."

A little on the stocky side and probably in his mid-forties, the scientist's defensive posture eased. "I apologize for my abruptness, but I've had a couple of reporters snooping around. I don't care if they tell the world what we're doing—I'm proud of the progress we've made—but I won't allow any disturbances to the habitat we're monitoring."

"Makes sense to me. I'm here to photograph the area and document your research. I promise to be as unobtrusive as possible."

"Then we shouldn't have any problems." He pointed toward the table. "Why don't we have a seat? The others are out checking the trip cameras, so we'll have a few uninterrupted minutes."

"Great." After dropping onto a chair, she pulled a notebook and pen from her pocket then gave him an encouraging smile. "Let's start with your group. How many people do you have working here?"

"There are four of us, all respected scientists from around the country with a common interest. We aren't a bunch of yahoos floundering in the woods, hoping to scare up a Bigfoot. Individual research led each of us to believe this is an ideal habitat, so we planned something of a retreat."

She grinned, thinking of Jed. "A busman's holiday."

"Exactly. My home base is Cincinnati. Bart Kelton works out of Los Angeles. Margaret Welsh is a Boston native, and from Seattle—"

"Ian Rutledge." Claire let out a breath. She and Jed had talked about the possibility last night, but she hadn't really believed Ian would be here. Seeing him again promised to be…uncomfortable. Or not. Maybe her ex—boyfriend, semi-husband, whatever—was married with four kids and thanked God every day she'd initiated the annulment.

Lee's brows shot up. "How'd you know?"

"Just a guess, but I know he works out of Seattle. Ian and I are old acquaintances."

"Wonderful." He beamed. "I'll let him give you a tour of the area, then. The others should be back soon."

*Terrific.* Worrying about Ian's reaction to her presence wouldn't accomplish a thing. Instead, she'd focus on getting a few answers. "What exactly are you doing out in the forest?"

"We're keeping careful documentation of vegetation disturbances with photographs and video recordings. Like other animals and humans, Sasquatch form patterns of behavior. Over time, we're hoping to identify these patterns, which will make sightings easier. We're also searching for sleeping nests and feeding areas."

"Have you found any yet?"

His face darkened. "There've been a few irregularities that indicate activity."

Claire couldn't help wondering if the activity had been produced by a bear or a deer or a big, fat raccoon, but she kept her thoughts to herself. "Word is one of your group actually saw a Bigfoot—or do you prefer Sasquatch?"

"Either term is fine. Bart saw something, but it was too far away to accurately identify the creature. I'm afraid a careless comment was exaggerated and spread by the locals the way these things are prone to do."

*Well, crap!* She'd been hoping for one spectacular photo. The type of picture that would launch her career as a nature photographer into the stratosphere. *Damn. Damn. Damn.* At least she still had redwoods to photograph. She'd salvage something from this trip.

"Ah, here comes the rest of the group." The scientist rose to his feet. "Let me introduce you around."

Claire snapped her notebook shut. Slowly she stood and turned.

Ian hadn't changed much in the last fifteen years. Same dark blond hair with a hint of wave and hard, compact build. The man wasn't overly muscular, but she knew from experience he was stronger than he looked. His cool gray eyes widened when he met her gaze.

"Claire?" His voice came out in a gasp as he pressed a hand to his chest. "Good God, it is you."

"How are you, Ian?"

"I'm—speechless. Did someone tell you I was out here?"

"Not until about two minutes ago." She nodded toward Lee. "I came to write a story on your project. I work for *Rugged America*. Maybe you're familiar with the magazine?"

"Of course I'm familiar with it, but Lee didn't mention—"

"Slipped my mind, what with the disturbance last night." The man inched backwards. "I'll leave you in Ian's capable hands since I have a few urgent matters to attend to."

Before Claire could protest, he hurried off. Reluctantly, she returned her attention to her ex and gave him a weak smile. "Looks like you're stuck with me." She cleared her throat. "May I ask what disturbance? Your colleague appeared more than a little flustered."

"It doesn't matter." He ran a hand through his hair, his gaze never leaving her face. "Jesus. This is the last place I expected to run into someone I know. I remember you lived around here for a while, but—" His chest rose beneath a light jacket as he drew in a breath. "I don't know what to say."

"How about, 'Good to see you, Claire. You look spectacular.'"

"Very funny, not that you don't—look spectacular, I mean. If I'm in charge of filling you in on our work, I suppose we should sit." He waved toward the chair she'd vacated.

"I'd rather take a walk."

He hunched one shoulder. "Sure. I'll show you around." He turned then stopped as his two colleagues broke off their conversation. "Where are my manners? Margaret Welsh, Bart Kelton, meet Claire Templeton." His eyes narrowed. "It is still Templeton, isn't it?"

"I'm not married."

"Oh." He glanced away. "Not that it matters one way or the other."

Claire grasped the hand of a handsome, blue-eyed blond who looked more like an aging surfer than a scientist, then exchanged greetings with an older woman with short, gray hair and a direct gaze.

The woman's forehead creased. "We won't tolerate a sloppy, sensationalized story. *Rugged America* has an excellent reputation for reporting the facts along with beautiful photography, but I'll admit I wasn't in favor of allowing a journalist into our camp."

Claire kept her gaze steady on the skeptic. "My intention is to photograph and chronicle what I see. I don't embellish the truth."

Margaret looked away. "If that's the case, we'll get along fine, but right now I need to drive into town. I'll answer your questions some other time."

"Not a problem."

Without another word, she strode toward a truck parked at the edge of the clearing, leaving an awkward silence in her wake.

Bart cleared his throat. "Don't mind Margaret. She's crusty but brilliant. I, on the other hand, am happy to cooperate."

Ian scowled. "You can talk to Claire later." Turning his back on the other man, he jerked his head toward a trail that disappeared into the forest. "If you want me to show you around, let's go."

She picked up her camera then looped the strap over her neck before tucking her notepad into her pocket. "I'm ready."

"This way."

Claire followed, increasing her pace to keep up as the giant trees closed in around them. "Where's the fire?"

"What...oh, sorry." He slowed then waited before moving onward. "It's just odd, seeing you again."

"I hope you don't have a problem with me being here."

He let out a huff of breath. "Why would I? We were stupid kids back then. I won't hold the fact that you ripped my heart out and stomped all over it against you."

"Ian—"

"Kidding, Claire." He rolled his eyes. "You should see your face. Our marriage—if you can call it that—is ancient history. I see no reason we can't maintain a professional, even friendly, relationship."

"That's a relief." She forced a smile. "I was more than a little worried."

"Don't be." He turned away then pointed. "There. See the camera positioned up in the tree. That spot below is a prime feeding location. The salmonberries are thick but easy to access. Anything entering the area will activate the equipment."

She lifted her camera, adjusted the settings then took several shots as weak rays of sun filtered through the fog to glimmer on damp foliage.

"We have similar trip cameras set up in a wide radius." His lips firmed. "It's just a matter of time before we capture a Sasquatch on film."

"Nothing yet?"

"Bear, deer, raccoon, skunks…" He shrugged. "We're working on making the equipment less sensitive to smaller animals."

"They all subsist on the same diet?"

"To some extent, but then so did humans indigenous to this area going right back into pre-history. Are you a non-believer?"

The fiery look in his eyes practically dared her to say yes. She took a step back.

"I'm not ruling out anything. At this point, I'm gathering data. I'll hold off on forming opinions and making conclusions until I know a great deal more about the subject."

"You sound more like a politician than a photographer."

She lifted her camera as a squirrel, bushy tail waving, stilled on the trail ahead. After snapping the picture, she answered. "I won't be deterred by insults."

He snorted. "Same old funny Claire. I did miss your sense of humor after we split up."

"My levity provided balance in our relationship since you were always so serious." When his eyes darkened, she rushed on. "Which is probably an asset in your line of work."

They walked in silence for some time before he spoke again. "People tend to scoff when they hear the subject of my research." He scowled. "Frankly, it's irritating as hell."

"I bet."

"I'll prove them all wrong." He kicked a fir cone off the path. "There's another monitoring station up ahead."

His quick change of subject left Claire grasping for a reply. Not that there was much she could say in response to the vitriol in his voice. The intelligent, idealistic student brimming with confidence she remembered was lost inside an angry, resentful man. Regret filled her as she photographed the tiny clearing surrounded by waist-high ferns.

"Is that enough for now?"

"Huh?" She glanced over then lowered her camera. "Sure. I can come back another time."

"Sorry, but there are a few things I need to take care of today."

She ran a few steps to catch up then walked beside him as he took off down the trail. "Anything to do with the disturbance Lee mentioned?"

"Christ, you're like a dog with a bone. It wasn't that big a deal. One of the cameras fell, damaging it. We determined something—or someone— tampered with the straps holding it in place."

"Who would bother your equipment? My friend, the one who notified me your group was out here, didn't mention any problems with the locals."

He shot her a sharp look. "I didn't know you stayed in contact with any of your old high school pals. You never talked about them much in college."

"Just Theresa."

"Oh."

They were quiet as they followed the needle-covered path back through the forest.

Finally, he shrugged. "I doubt it was one of the locals. Most of them are hoping to cash in on a Bigfoot sighting, though there have been a few negative grumblings. The locals seem divided over all the Sasquatch hunters they get around here. Could have been kids, I suppose, but more than likely it was that damned reporter from one of those sensational rags. Lee found him snooping around a couple days ago and told him to get lost. Somehow I doubt we'll get rid of his type so easily."

"I feel honored you agreed to let me interview you."

"*Rugged America* is a reputable magazine. *Nature Exposed* isn't."

She turned and stared. "Wow. Small world. I got my start at *Nature Exposed*."

His head jerked back. "Why would you work for a piece of trash like that?"

"Don't sound so superior. You need experience to land a decent job, so I did what I had to do to get it. Who was their journalist?"

"If Lee mentioned his name, I don't remember."

"Probably some young kid just starting out." She followed him out of the woods then stopped beside Jed's SUV. "Thanks for the tour. When would it be convenient for me to come back?"

"Tomorrow's no good." He frowned. "Maybe the day after. We're planning to expand our working area. I guess you could tag along while we set up equipment."

"Great." She ran the toe of her boot through the thick fir needles littering the ground. "Do you mind if I bring a friend?"

He shrugged. "Why not? As long as she's a decent hiker and won't slow us down, it shouldn't be a problem."

Claire opened her mouth then shut it. He probably assumed her friend was Theresa. At this point, enlightening him that *she* was a *he* would probably only lead to an argument. "I'll see you in a couple of days, then."

"Sure. Take care, Claire." Turning on his heel, he walked away.

After climbing into the SUV, she started the engine and pulled out of the clearing. Steering with one hand, she shook a couple of aspirin out of a bottle stashed in her purse and swallowed them dry. Her head ached with trying to find some resemblance to the youth she'd once loved in the embittered man she'd just spent the last hour with—and failed.

When she'd thought of Ian over the years, she'd pictured him at the top of his field, enlightening a bevy of adoring underlings—much the way he'd enraptured her with his knowledge and enthusiasm. She sighed, for a moment wishing she'd kept her illusions about her ex and never come on what would surely prove to be the quintessential goose chase. Not that she'd expected to uncover the truth behind the legend of Bigfoot. Still, a girl could dream.

"What the hell!" Claire stomped on the brakes and prayed as the SUV skidded to a stop inches from an old van parked smack in the middle of the track. Heart pounding, she threw open the door and jumped off the seat, landing on the ground with a thump.

"Hello! Ever hear of pulling off the road?"

No one answered. Gritting her teeth, she strode to the open driver's side window and glanced inside. A lumpy looking mattress heaped with clothes filled most of the cargo space. Empty fast food containers were piled on the passenger side floor, while a stack of notebooks and folders graced the seat. At least the keys were in the ignition. She'd move the damned thing herself if she had to.

Something crashed through the dense underbrush.

"What in the world...." Hand pressed to her chest, she spun around and flattened against the door. The breath left her in a whoosh when a man—not a bear—emerged from the trees.

"Sorry. I'm sorry. I didn't think anyone else would be on this road."

The speaker rounded the front of Jed's SUV and stepped fully into view. Claire's jaw sagged. "Preston?"

"Oh, my God, Claire?"

A grin spread as she studied warm brown eyes and a broad mouth beneath a mop of auburn hair. As tall and gangly as she remembered, Preston Meyer rushed forward, stumbling over his own feet, to take her hand and squeeze it.

"This is great! What has it been, ten years since I last saw you?"

Claire nodded, flexing her fingers when he released them. "Yep, ten years ago this month I left *Nature Exposed*." She drew in a breath. "Are you the paparazzi Lee Harper mentioned?"

"Guilty." He laughed. "Hey, this could be my breakout story."

"Speaking of break, did you mess with one of their cameras last night?"

He reared back and frowned. "No, why would I do that? I've just been hanging around, hoping to be in the right place at the right time when they find a Bigfoot. What're you doing here?"

"Writing a story. Only difference is, I have an official invite."

His comical mouth drooped for a moment before curling upward. "Not a problem. I thrive on competition. Let the better man—or woman—win."

"You don't intend to leave as they requested?"

"Hell, no! Would you?"

She lifted a shoulder. "Maybe not." Stepping past him, she walked to the SUV and pulled open the door. "It's good to see you again, Preston, but I need to get going." She pointed toward the van. "Do you mind?"

"Oh, of course not. I'll get out of your way."

"Thanks. I'm sure we'll bump into each other again before either of us has enough pictures for a story."

"I'm sure we will." The van door creaked open, and he climbed in before slamming it shut. "See you around, Claire."

She nodded then squeezed the SUV past his old clunker after he backed to the edge of the road. When she glanced in the rearview mirror, he was standing on the track, arms crossed over his chest, a smile curving his lips.

The same old Preston. Ever the comedian. Always ready to cheer her up when she was down. His positive attitude had bucked her up on more than one occasion after her brief engagement to a co-worker ended, leaving her miserable and alone. It wasn't a time in her life she liked to think about.

At least some people hadn't changed.

# Chapter 4

When his SUV rolled into the campground, Jed's spirits lifted. Not that there was anything wrong with his mood. After a five-mile hike with Scoop, he was warmed up and ready for whatever the afternoon might bring. If it brought Claire along for company, even better.

After parking next to the motor home, she opened the door and slid down from the seat then braced herself as the dog galloped toward her. His front paws hit her chest, knocking her back against the hood as he licked her face.

"Yes, I love you, too, but get down." With a shove, she pushed her pet away then glanced toward Jed. "Apparently he thought I'd left him with you for good."

"I'm surprised he still has so much energy. He collapsed after our morning hike."

"Scoop only looks slothful. In reality, he has more stamina than the two of us combined." Her voice held an edge, and the sparkle was gone from her eyes.

When she approached, he slung an arm over her shoulders to squeeze then held on, enjoying the feel of her slim body tucked against his side. "How'd it go with the scientists?"

She relaxed into him for a moment before straightening to pull away. "Remember how we joked about Ian being a part of that group?"

"Your ex? Seriously?" At her nod, he whistled. "Wow. How awkward was the reunion?"

"I suppose it could have been worse. He doesn't seem to be holding a grudge, but he's changed." She dropped into one of the camp chairs by the fire pit. "I'll admit it shook me."

"Balding? Pot belly? What?"

A smile tilted her lips. "If only. No, attitude. My guess is a few too many people have made fun of his Bigfoot fetish over the years. Guarded and sullen sum up his disposition."

He leaned against the picnic table. "That's a relief. You won't be tempted to dump me for a grouch."

The grin flashed again, and he gave himself a mental pat on the back for cheering her up.

"No, I won't be the least bit tempted, but I did run into someone out in the woods who rivals you in the sunny outlook department."

"A happy-go-lucky Bigfoot?"

The last of the melancholy faded from her eyes with his teasing.

"I wish. Actually, someone I used to work with. Preston was a friend of mine when I was on staff at *Nature Exposed*."

"Hey, I've seen that magazine in the checkout line of the grocery store. Isn't it one of those sensationalized papers full of half-truths?"

She nodded. "Actually, it makes sense that someone from their staff would show up, since news of the Bigfoot sighting has spread. This is exactly the kind of story they like to twist into a major news event, ranking right up there with UFO sightings or reports of mermaids. They don't worry much about relating the actual facts. God, I hated working for that rag."

He studied her clouded eyes. "I bet, but you moved on."

"The minute I was offered something better. I guess Preston wasn't as lucky. We lost touch after I quit."

"So he's out here hoping for a career-boosting story?"

"Yes, except the group has made it clear they want nothing to do with him. My old pal, however, is undeterred."

"That positive attitude you mentioned?"

"Or just plain dumb stubborn. Take your pick. Oh, if you care to join me, I asked if I could bring a friend along on an all-day outing planned for the day after tomorrow."

Crossing his arms, he stepped away from the table and leaned back on his heels. "I wouldn't miss it. Please tell me we'll be hunting down and trapping a Bigfoot."

"I hate to burst your bubble, but the group plans to set up cameras and trip wires deeper into the forest. Their immediate goal is to capture a Sasquatch on film."

"Not quite as exciting but still cool. Thanks for including me." He nodded toward the dog stretched out at her feet. "What about your friend there?"

She closed her eyes. "Crap. I forgot to ask. I guess I'll bring him with us. We can always leave him in the car if they don't want a dog roaming around in their research area."

"He does tend to dive into the underbrush every time he sees a squirrel, and he isn't exactly quiet about it."

"He's a total pain sometimes." She pushed up out of the chair. "Have you had lunch yet?"

"No, my food's in a cooler in the back of the SUV."

"You could have raided my refrigerator."

"Except you locked the motor home and took the keys."

She paused to press a hand to her forehead. "Sorry. I'm so used to being on my own, I didn't think."

"Don't sweat it, Claire. I survived. We'll eat then go do something fun. Sounds like you have a couple of days to play before work intrudes."

"I'll spend them photographing the area." She unlocked the door to the motor home and stepped inside. "Lunch is on me. I can offer ham, tuna or peanut butter. Take your pick."

He followed her inside, sat and squeezed his knees beneath the miniscule table. "Ham. Can't you photograph and have fun at the same time?"

"You bet. Want to hike in the woods with me this afternoon, or have you had enough exercise for one day?"

He leaned into the corner, his focus on her upended behind as she pulled bread from a lower cabinet. Tearing his gaze away, he cleared his throat. "Do I look like a wimp?"

She glanced over her shoulder and smiled. "No, you're definitely not wimpy."

"Now that we've cleared that up, where do you want to hike?"

"There's a great trail a few miles northeast of here with some spectacular old-growth trees. Since the whole Bigfoot thing is probably going to be a bust, my main focus is on getting some striking photos of the redwoods. I can salvage a story about the area based on scenery alone."

"Makes sense." He glanced out the window. "The morning fog is finally starting to lift."

"Should be a terrific afternoon." She set a plate topped by a sandwich bristling with lettuce, tomatoes and sprouts in front of him. "Sorry I don't have any chips to offer you."

He rolled his eyes. "Wouldn't want to clutter up your cupboard space with fat and salt."

Dropping onto the opposite seat, she grinned. "You know me so well already. Eat, and then we'll go. Daylight's burning."

An hour later they left the SUV in a parking area and headed up the marked trail with Scoop leading the way. Waist-high ferns lined a path so thick with needles their footsteps were silent, while high overhead moss hung from branches like a lacy green curtain, dimming the sunlight. Claire paused frequently, shooting off pictures in rapid-fire succession.

Turning, she smiled up at him. "I'd almost forgotten how much I enjoyed living in this area. There's nowhere else like it for eerie beauty."

"Today's nice, but the usual rain and fog might get old after a while."

She shrugged. "I'm not particularly fond of the heat, so I don't mind cooler temperatures." She stopped in a shaft of filtered sunlight to gaze upward, her eyes filled with wonder. "You've lived in the mountains for years. Aren't you tempted to try someplace different?"

"Not really. I'm happy with my life the way it is."

She let out a little sigh. "I want that. I want to find a place where I belong and settle down. Most of my friends are married with children." Her lips curved downward. "I guess I'm feeling the pull of domesticity."

"You have plenty of time."

She frowned. "Do I? I'm thirty-four. The clock's ticking."

When Scoop dropped a dead branch at his feet, Jed bent to retrieve it before giving the limb a hard toss. The dog leaped into the underbrush.

"You don't see the whole traditional family thing as a trap that'll eventually suck all the fun out of life?"

She turned and crossed her arms over her chest. "Do you?"

He shrugged. "My work doesn't pay a lot. The idea of being forced into the nine-to-five grind to support a family is about as appealing as a lobotomy."

"Well, when you put it that way…"

He grinned. "Okay, maybe I'm being a bit dramatic. Some people thrive in that environment. My brother is completely happy with his new responsibilities as a stepdad."

"Seems like the two of you had plenty in common when you were boys. Kane was always outside doing something right alongside you."

Jed threw the stick again for the mutt. "True, but he was more serious about everything, from school and sports to a career in law enforcement. He needed to excel. I just wanted to have fun."

"If it makes you happy…" She raised the camera and aimed skyward into the canopy.

"It does." *Doesn't it?* For the first time since he'd dropped out of college an eternity ago, doubt about his choices niggled. Of course he was happy. A little lonely on occasion, but wasn't everyone?

"I'm losing the light."

"Huh?" He jerked to attention.

"The fog's creeping back in. We might as well turn around." Lifting the camera from around her neck, she returned it to its case in her backpack.

"Sure. Let's go."

Neither said much as they headed down the path. When Claire tripped on an exposed root, he lunged forward, grasped her around the waist and hauled her upright, slamming her against his chest. The floral scent of her shampoo invaded his senses, and he breathed deep.

"Thanks." Her voice was breathless. "I almost took a header. That'll teach me to pay more attention…"

When she turned in his arms, he relaxed his hold, but not by much. His blood heated as he met her gaze. Her breath fanned his neck on an exhaled gust as she stared back through wide eyes. His fingers tightened at her waist.

"You okay?" At her nod, he dipped his head. "Good."

He gave her time to pull away, hesitated for a fraction of a second before pressing his mouth to hers. When a tiny noise not unlike the purring of a kitten escaped her lips, the remainder of his self-control vanished. One hand hovered then clasped the seat of her jeans to cup the enticing firmness beneath as he tugged her tight against him to settle into the kiss. She tasted of fresh air and woman, bringing his heated blood to a boil. His body's reaction was instantaneous. Brain cells scattered with the temptation of soft, warm female.

She pulled back, dragging her mouth away from his. "Jed?"

His lips caressed the angle of her jaw then dropped to the soft skin beneath her ear. "Hmmm?"

"We can't do this."

"Kiss? Why not?"

She quivered when he flicked his tongue against the side of her neck.

"Feels like you want to do more than just kiss."

Finally, he drew back. Blue eyes held a touch of panic mixed with desire above cheeks blooming with color. Letting out a long breath, he gave her a few more inches of space but didn't release her completely.

"There's a big difference between wanting and doing. Should I apologize?"

"No, I think we've both anticipated that kiss since we ran into each other in the diner yesterday. Doesn't mean I'm going to take things to the next level."

He touched her flushed cheek. "I respect your feelings, but for the record, I've wanted to kiss you for a lot longer than two days."

"You have?"

"I almost did once, back when we were kids, then I chickened out. After all, I was only ten. Still, I wasn't going to make the same mistake twice." He stepped away, missing her warmth before it was entirely gone. "I also don't intend to jeopardize our newfound friendship by pushing you if you aren't up to it yet. The ball's in your court. Let me know when you're ready to play."

"Are you so sure I'll want to *play*?"

He grinned at the irritation glimmering in her eyes. "Let's just say I like my odds."

"Really." Adjusting her pack, she headed back down the trail.

He had to hustle to keep up.

Jamming her hands into her pockets, she glanced over her shoulder. "Has any woman ever told you no before?"

"Why do I feel the truth will only get me in trouble?"

She laughed, and humor replaced the annoyance curling her lips. "I shouldn't be in the least surprised. You're a hard man to resist, Jed Lafferty, but I'm pretty sure I'm up to the task."

"I guess we'll have to wait and see."

Her smile grew. "Don't hold your breath. I never learned CPR."

"Too bad. I'm pretty sure I'd enjoy having you resuscitate me."

With an eye roll and a whistle to her dog, she broke into a jog and never looked back.

\* \* \* \*

"Do you mind if we stop at the local market before we go back to the campground?" Claire flipped her hair over her shoulder. "I forgot to buy shampoo yesterday when we went to the store, and I need more lunchmeat."

"No problem, especially since I'm the one who ate it all. How can you survive on one sandwich?"

She glanced down. "Do I look malnourished?"

Jed took his gaze off the road for longer than he should have to study her. "No, you look...healthy."

Her cheeks heated. After that mind-blowing kiss, every word out of his mouth sounded like a proposition.

"How can you make a word like *healthy* sound sexual?"

He grinned. "It's a gift. Just tell me where to go."

With an effort, she withheld the comment that sprang to mind. "We don't turn until we get into town."

Following her directions, he made a left at the stop sign in the center of what passed for Shady Bend's business district, slowed in front of the hardware store when a man in overalls jaywalked across the street and then parked in the lot of Hansen's General Store. The mom and pop establishment had apparently survived the encroachment of a big chain supermarket built on the highway.

The car door opened with a squeak, and Claire hopped down. Turning, she dug through her backpack for her wallet before giving Scoop a shove when he pushed between the seats. "You stay here."

"Huh?"

"The dog."

Jed smiled as he walked around the hood of the SUV to her side. "Oh. I thought you were barking orders at me."

"Not out of the question if you push too hard."

His eyes heated. "I promised not to...no matter how tempting you are."

"Jed..."

He held up his hands then dropped them to his sides. "I'll back off. For now."

Elbows brushing, they strolled toward the entrance. A bell over the door dinged as he pushed it open. Inside, narrow aisles were crammed with an array of merchandise, from canned goods to work boots to greeting cards and party supplies.

Claire looked around and sighed. "I always loved this store. Seems like if you dig deep enough, you'll find a real treasure hidden under a stack of towels or buried beneath a selection of fall produce."

Jed lifted a straw hat decorated with pink ribbons off a shelf and plopped it onto her head. His gaze dropped to her mouth. "The place does have its charm, but do they carry lunchmeat?"

"There's a meat counter and deli in the back. At least there used to be."

"Is turkey okay?" At her nod, he turned toward the rear of the store. "Then I'll take care of our lunch needs while you find shampoo in this rabbit warren."

"I'll meet you at the checkout stand in a few minutes." Removing the hat after he left, she turned—and rammed into a solid chest. The breath left her in a whoosh as big hands grasped her arms.

A deep voice rumbled in her ear. "I'm sorry. I should know better than to hurry through this place."

Claire's chin snapped upward. The voice hadn't changed. Neither had the dark, unruly hair or the chocolate-brown eyes. Only the torso she'd slammed against was different, thicker than she remembered. At a guess,

Dallas Simms had gained at least fifty pounds since his glory days playing high school football. Old emotions churned, memories of sitting for hours in his car, planning a future....

"Claire?" His grip loosened as he stepped back. "It is you." The chest she'd pulled away from rose and fell on an exhaled breath. "Theresa told me you'd be in town."

"It's good to see you, Dallas. You look...good." She pressed her lips together on the final inanity, feeling like a fool.

His eyes darkened. "Wow, you look incredible. How long are you staying in the area?"

"A few more days at least."

She edged backward as he advanced to enfold her in a hug. Her nose smashed against a hard button. The yeasty smell of beer permeated his shirt.

"I can't believe how great you look, though I don't know why I'm surprised." When she tugged against his embrace, he released her. "We should get together to catch up. Have dinner or something."

"Uh, maybe, though I am here to work." This was Dallas, her old boyfriend. Just because he was easily twice her size and had her pushed up against a display of brooms and dust mops was no reason to feel nervous.

"Theresa mentioned you aren't married. Did she tell you about my divorce?" His lips flattened. "Mandy took the kids and moved up to Portland."

"I'm sorry about that." She put another foot of space between them. "It must be hard."

On his long sigh, the scent of beer drifted her way. "Yeah, it's been rough."

"Claire?"

She turned quickly then reached to steady the broom display when it swayed. Jed's focus was on Dallas, eyes narrowed.

"Everything okay?"

"Sure. I ran into an old friend." She forced a smile. "Literally. Jed Lafferty meet Dallas Simms."

Both men nodded a greeting. Neither stepped forward to offer a hand. Tension sizzled.

Claire cleared her throat. "It was great seeing you again, but I'm afraid I'm a little pressed for time right now."

Dallas shrugged one broad shoulder. "I understand." His gaze flicked back to Jed. "We'll talk later. Theresa told me you're camping. Are you at Towering Trees?"

"I am." With a hesitant smile, she escaped around the end of the aisle.

Jed followed close behind. "I didn't like the way that guy looked at you. Needy. What's up with him?"

She stopped in front of a shelf full of hair care products. "Nothing. We used to date."

"You dated *that* guy? Do you have a thing for Neanderthals?"

Her back stiffened as she reached for a bottle of honeysuckle scented shampoo. "He's a big man. So what? In high school, he was also kind and open with his feelings. I imagine he still is. Did you get the lunchmeat?"

He lifted a package wrapped in white paper. "Lunchmeat and steaks. They looked too good to pass up."

"Let's go, then."

Neither said anything as they paid for their purchases and left the market. Dallas was nowhere in sight. The silence stretched when Jed stopped for gas.

Leaning back in the seat, she studied his tight lips as he stood by the door, waiting for the tank to fill. "What has your tail twisted into a knot?"

He glanced at her through the open car window, and the lines around his mouth eased. "Your ex-boyfriend reminded me of this bully who used to give little kids wedgies when I was in third grade. I know I'm stereotyping, but the resemblance is scary." He rolled his eyes. "Sorry. I'm sure Dallas is a swell guy."

Her lips curved upward. "*Swell guy?* Are we in Mr. Roger's neighborhood?"

"How about a good dude?"

She held her response until he'd finished pumping the gas and climbed back into the SUV. "You can call him whatever you want. What happened to the bully?"

"He gave me one wedgie too many, and Kane beat the crap out of him."

"Good for Kane."

"So, are you going to tell me about Dallas?"

"Not much to tell." She stared through the windshield as he started the engine. "He was my high school sweetheart."

"Let me guess—the guy played football."

"Captain of the team. We dated for two years and planned to attend the same college. Only problem was, he didn't get in. Dallas wanted me to go to the local community college with him instead."

"You didn't."

She shook her head. "He was hurt, and I felt awful. At one point during our senior year we'd talked about getting married sometime in the future...." A long sigh slipped out. "You know how it is when you're young and think you're in love. Lucky for me, I wised up before ruining my whole future."

"Your ex never left Shady Bend?"

"He married the head cheerleader on the rebound, then went to work in his father's hardware store where he's now the manager."

Jed rolled to a stop at the corner and flipped on his blinker. "You seem well-versed in the life and times of a guy you haven't seen in what, sixteen or seventeen years?"

"That's because my friend, Theresa, the one who told me about the Bigfoot sighting, is overflowing with local gossip. I'm sure you'll meet her sometime in the next few days. We plan to get together while I'm here."

"Don't change the subject. Is Dallas still married to the cheerleader?"

"No, he and Mandy divorced a couple of years ago. She took their kids and moved to Oregon. According to Theresa, Dallas drinks too much and needs a new woman to buck him up."

"Hmm."

"Hmm, what?"

"Good thing I thrive on competition. Sounds like I'll have my hands full fighting off all your old boyfriends. First Ian, and now Dallas."

She did her best to squash a spurt of satisfaction. "Jealous?"

He glanced over. "Should I be?"

"I've never been one to backtrack in my relationships."

"Smart woman."

The emotions churning in her middle eased as they headed toward the campground. When they passed the entrance booth, she waved at the attendant reading a romance novel with a picture of a bare-chested cowboy on the cover. Turning right, the vehicle bumped down the dirt track to their campsite. When Jed hit the brakes, her head snapped back.

"What the hell?"

She rubbed her neck. "What's wrong?"

He pointed toward her motor home.

A string of puffy metallic bells in silver and gold hung across the windshield. Beneath them was a sign with bold, black lettering. *Time's up. You promised.*

# Chapter 5

Claire held her hands closer to the flames and shivered. Despite the mild evening temperature and crackling fire, she couldn't get warm. Those damn wedding bells had chilled her to the core.

Jed kept a steady eye on her from across the fire, a frown etched between his brows. "I suppose we could notify the police, tell them someone's harassing you if you're really concerned."

She hunched into her down jacket. "It's not like he—she—whoever threatened me. What would the authorities do, besides laugh? The mad wedding planner strikes again."

His head jerked back. "What do you mean, again?"

Another chill shivered through her. "A couple of weeks ago I found a package in the post office box I use mostly for work. In it was one of those little wedding favors, a plastic champagne flute with two entwined pink hearts stamped on the front. The accompanying message was similar to this one. *Almost time. Can't wait.* I thought it was some kind of joke sent to me by mistake."

"Obviously you were the intended recipient." He scowled. "Mailing a package is one thing, but those bells were hand delivered. Whoever put them on your motor home is here in Shady Bend."

Her gaze darted toward the dark woods beyond the edge of the campsite, and she shuddered. "This *person* followed me?"

"Unless he was already here."

She turned back to face Jed, dread settling in the pit of her stomach. "What do you mean?"

"I mean, the message is pretty clear. *You promised.* That implies a personal connection. This nut job—let's assume it's a he—wants something you promised to give him. The wedding decorations lead me to believe his fixation is with marriage…to you."

"That's ridiculous. I never promised to marry anyone!"

"I can think of two men who may feel differently. And those are only the ones you've told me about."

She clamped her teeth together then mentally counted to ten. After taking a deep breath, she let it out slowly and managed not to yell. "Are you saying I asked for this?"

His brows shot up. "Huh? No, of course not. I'm saying one of your exes doesn't like the fact that you dumped him."

"I didn't dump anyone. I simply walked away from both of them *years* ago. Why would he—whoever he is—say my time's up now?"

Jed shrugged. "How am I supposed to know how a crazy person thinks?"

"Ian isn't crazy. Well, maybe a little crazy. He's nuts for Bigfoot, not me. Dallas is just lonely, not a lunatic."

He leaned forward to place another piece of wood on the fire. Sparks shot upward. "Personally, my money's on the football player. I already know he bugs me. The jury's still out on good old Ian."

His blue eyes sparkled, and she narrowed hers. *Is he enjoying this?*

"Good God, Jed. We're not playing some kind of mystery game where you follow the clues to uncover the killer's identity."

"No dead body, so of course we aren't. Still, the whole thing does remind me of a good whodunit."

"Since the dead person would probably wind up being me, let's be thankful for small favors."

He stood then stepped around the fire to reach out and draw her close against his side. The contact provided comfort despite her irritation. She met his gaze and gave him a weak smile.

The bright speculation in his eyes dissolved, leaving only concern. "You aren't frightened, are you? I thought you were more annoyed than worried. It's not like the guy left something dead on your windshield."

"Eww. Don't even say that!"

She tugged against his hold, but he didn't let her go. Instead, he wrapped both arms around her. With the solid warmth of his chest behind her, some of her anxiety faded.

"I'm not afraid…exactly. More like unnerved. I'd almost prefer it if the person who left the bells was someone I know rather than a crazy stranger with a possible fixation on me."

"Well, you can start with the direct approach and ask each of your old boyfriends straight out if he's the one leaving you messages. Maybe whoever set this up was just trying to be funny."

"I hope so. Still…" She bit her lip. "I can't ask either of them a question like that. What am I supposed to say? 'Um, Ian, have you been harboring a secret obsession with me over the last decade and a half? Since I insisted we have our marriage annulled?'"

His chin came down to rest on top of her head. A little quiver shot through her as his arms tightened.

"So, you think it's Ian?"

"No, I don't think it's Ian. I don't think it's Dallas, either. This whole theory of yours is ridiculous."

"Do you have a better one?"

She let out a sigh. "No. Maybe if I ignore the bells the way I did the champagne glass, whoever left them will get tired of waiting for a reaction and quit bothering me."

"I guess it's worth a try. It's not like he actually threatened you. I'd be more concerned if the messages contained direct warnings."

"The vagueness is part of what makes it so creepy."

He turned her in his arms. Light and shadow from the flickering flames danced across his face, but his gaze remained locked on hers.

"You don't have to worry about it, Claire. No one is going to harm you while I'm around, and I'm not going anywhere."

For a moment, she relaxed against him then stiffened. "You said you were only staying in the area for a couple of days."

He shrugged. "Plans change. I'm not on a set schedule, and there's nowhere I have to be until snow flies in the mountains. That's two months from now at the earliest."

"Still, you shouldn't have to rearrange your life because of me, though I'm grateful for the offer." Her voice came out a little breathless as his big hands squeezed her waist.

"I do what I want. Right now I *want* to hang out with you. Unless you don't—want me I mean?"

"I want you."

When heat shimmered in his eyes, her cheeks burned. She glanced down, wanting to kick herself for the thoughtless remark. "You know what I mean."

His lips twitched. "I know what you mean. More's the pity." One hand left her waist to cup her chin, forcing her gaze upward again. "I'm serious, Claire. No one will hurt you while I'm around. I promise."

She tried to speak, but emotion clogged her throat. When was the last time anyone put her needs before their own? "Thank you."

"You bet."

As much as she was enjoying the hard arms wrapped around her, after the kiss they'd shared in the woods, this type of closeness would only lead to…trouble. Getting involved with Jed would surely be right up there with rollercoasters when it came to fun and excitement, but she wasn't ready to risk the plummet back to reality. He was the ultimate good time, no strings attached, type of guy. Hadn't he warned her he'd never had a serious relationship in his life? Alarm bells clanged a raucous tune in her head.

"It's been a long day. I should go to bed."

His head dipped, and warm breath fanned her cheeks. "Do you always do what you should?"

She swallowed. "Yes."

"That's the difference between us."

"Oh?" Her stomach fluttered.

"We covered this already. I do what I want."

He closed the distance, and his lips caressed hers in a kiss so sweet she ached with wanting more. His arms tightened for a moment before pulling away. When she stepped back, he released her completely. Already she missed the contact.

He frowned. "You sure you're okay?"

"I'm fine." She fought to bring her breathing under control. "Good night, Jed."

"Claire?"

Taking two steps forward, she looked back over her shoulder. "What?"

"You don't have to be afraid. Honest."

She wondered if he was talking about the wedding stalker or the attraction simmering between them. Either way, she wasn't sure she believed him.

"I'm not." The lie slipped easily from her lips.

"Good. See you in the morning."

\* \* \* \*

Jed forked another bite of pancake into his mouth, making inroads on the giant stack, and wondered if he'd died and gone to heaven. The only thing better than eating Ralph's specialty pancakes was watching Claire savor them. With her eyes closed, she leaned back in the booth and chewed slowly before swallowing with a little moan of pleasure. Heat shot straight to his groin, and he shifted on the seat. He was more than a little surprised at how much he was enjoying her company—especially since she seemed determined not to sleep with him. Platonic relationships with women weren't usually his thing.

"Oh, God, I'm so glad I let Augusta talk me into ordering these."

With a smirk, he licked syrup from one finger. "And you said you don't do sugar."

"Rules were made to be broken."

"You don't have to break them if you don't make any to begin with."

She glanced at him and laughed. "I suppose not, but honestly, you sound like you're still ten years old when you make those kinds of comments."

"Nothing wrong with that. Ten-year-olds have it good."

"Claire?"

The voice came from the direction of the entrance. Jed looked over his shoulder at a tall, thin woman with dark hair and tired amber eyes hovering near the taxidermy bear. The eyes brightened as Claire rose from the booth to rush toward her. The two women rocked together in a long embrace before pulling away.

"Oh, my God, you still look like you're eighteen."

"Hardly." Claire grinned. "Wow, it's so good to see you."

The woman's gaze darted toward Jed then back. "Uh, I don't want to interrupt your breakfast. I didn't realize you'd have company."

"You aren't interrupting. Join us." Taking her arm, Claire tugged the newcomer toward the booth. "Theresa, this is an old friend of mine, Jed Lafferty. Jed, meet Theresa Wilson. We were best buds in high school."

He shook her outstretched hand. "Nice to meet you, Theresa. You're the one who gave Claire the heads-up about the Bigfoot story?"

She nodded. "For years we've been saying we should get together. This seemed like the perfect impetus."

Claire slid into the booth and made room for her friend. "It's a little odd being back here after all this time, but I'm enjoying it. How are you? How's Shelby?" She squeezed Theresa's hand, which was resting on the tabletop.

"Shelby's wonderful and exasperating. Aren't all thirteen-year-old girls? I'm good. It was tough for the first couple of years after we lost Roger, but I'm doing much better now."

"I'm glad." Claire's voice held a soft sincerity that lightened as she picked up her fork. "Order some pancakes. They'll make all your problems disappear. I haven't had one negative thought since my first bite."

Theresa smiled. "I've already eaten, but finish your breakfast. Maybe coffee…"

Augusta stopped beside the booth to set a mug on the table. After filling it from the carafe she carried, she topped off the other two cups without asking. "Can I get you anything else?"

"This is perfect." Theresa reached for the metal pitcher containing cream. "Thanks, Augusta."

"You bet." The waitress smiled at Jed. "What about you, hon? Want me to have Ralph start a second stack?"

Jed shook his head and groaned. "As much as I'd like to, I'll have to pass. I won't be able to move if I eat any more."

"Lightweight." With a parting laugh, she walked away.

Claire kept up a steady stream of chatter while they finished eating. Jed's attention drifted as the two women reminisced about old classmates— until Theresa mentioned Dallas Simms. His hand jerked, slopping coffee. Pulling a napkin from the dispenser, he mopped up the spill.

Creases marred Claire's forehead. "I ran into Dallas at the market yesterday. He's changed more than I expected."

"Not where it counts. Inside, he's still the same, good-hearted man you dated in high school. Having Mandy move his kids so far away has been a tough blow. I know he doesn't see them as often as he'd like. If you ask me, the custody arrangement shafted him. His ex-wife made some allegations about his drinking, and the judge sided with her."

"Were they true?" Claire pushed her cup away and crossed her arms on the table top.

"He has a bit of a problem, but it's gotten worse since Mandy left. Still, he'd never do anything to endanger his kids."

"I'm sorry he's having such a battle. Divorce isn't easy. Divorce with kids involved is worse. I've watched a couple of other friends go through it."

Theresa sat up straighter. "He threw off some of his gloom and doom when I told him you'd be in town. I know he's looking forward to seeing you again, catching up on old times."

"He mentioned something to that effect."

Theresa glanced at her watch. "Damn. I have to go. I'm showing a house in a half-hour. Can we get together again before you leave town?"

"Sure. I'd love to."

She stood then turned back. "I almost forgot. Did some lawyer contact you? I gave him your work address."

Claire frowned. "No, what lawyer?"

"He wouldn't say, which is why I didn't give him your cell number or e-mail. Sounded kind of fishy to me, and I didn't want some shyster harassing you. He mentioned he'd been trying to track you for weeks, but the only addresses he had were your box number in Shady Bend and the apartment you rented in college. Apparently old Mrs. Evans at the post office offered my name and told him I might know where you were since we used to be friends. She isn't above bending the rules."

"That's odd. Why would a lawyer have addresses that old?"

"He said he couldn't discuss it. I didn't want to give out your personal information, just in case he was a fraud or something."

"I appreciate that. If he mailed me anything, I left the Bay Area before it arrived."

Theresa glanced at her watch again. "Gotta go or my clients will beat me to the house. Bye, Claire. Nice to meet you, Jed." She hurried away without waiting for a response, and the door slapped shut behind her.

"Is she a realtor?"

Claire nodded. "Theresa got her license after her husband died. I hope she really is doing all right like she said."

"Your friend seems like a strong, self-sufficient woman."

"She is." Claire was silent for a moment as Augusta cleared their plates and left a bill on the table. After she moved to the next booth, Claire frowned and dabbed at a spot of syrup on the Formica surface with a napkin. "I wonder what the whole lawyer thing is about."

"Can you have someone check your mailbox?"

"I could ask my editor, I suppose." She shrugged. "It's probably nothing. Shall we go?"

"If I can still walk after all those pancakes."

Picking up the bill, he slid out of the booth. Grabbing her purse, Claire did, too. Once they'd paid, Jed held the door for her then followed her outside. Wind swirled, and he zipped his jacket.

Taking a deep breath, she let it out in a white puff. "Cold today, but at least the fog is beginning to clear."

"Tell me again why you like the coast."

She raised her head and laughed. "Because... Hey, that's Preston's van." She pointed toward a heap of scrap metal in the parking lot.

"And I thought my SUV was ready for retirement. I'm drawing a blank here. Who's Preston again?"

"My old buddy from *Nature Exposed*." She glanced around. "I wonder where he is."

As she finished speaking, the rear doors of the van creaked open, and a lanky redhead wearing a puffy, black jacket with a piece of duct tape covering one elbow, backed out. When he turned, his gaze zeroed in on Claire, and a wide smile split his face.

She raised a hand and waved then grabbed Jed's arm to drag him forward. "Come meet Preston. You'll like him. Everyone does."

The guy looked like the amiable sort. Good natured if the broad grin was any indication. When their gazes met, the journalist's held a touch of curiosity.

"Jed Lafferty meet Preston Meyer. It's like a reunion around here, there're so many familiar faces popping up." She fisted her hands on her hips and glanced between the two men with a smile.

Preston's brows shot up beneath his unruly hair as he straightened. "Are you another contender for the Bigfoot story?"

Claire spoke before Jed could answer. "No, he was my next-door neighbor when I was a kid. Haven't seen him in twenty-five years."

The man's stiff posture eased into a slouch. "Well, that's a relief. I'm having a hard enough time getting the inside scoop without more competition. That group sure is tight-lipped. I confronted an older woman in the woods yesterday afternoon and got the feeling she'd rather spit in my face than turn loose of any pertinent details."

Claire rolled her eyes. "Margaret Welsh. She wasn't exactly warm and friendly with me, either."

His easy smile returned. "No matter. I'm not giving up. I'll get a photograph of Bigfoot if I have to settle here permanently to do it. I suppose there are worse places to be stuck for the foreseeable future."

"Personally, I think it's all a wild goose chase." She stuck her hands in the pockets of her jacket and rocked back on her heels. "If nothing breaks in the next few days, I'll write a lovely piece on the mystery and beauty of the redwoods to submit with my photos. You can have Bigfoot."

Preston let out a boisterous laugh. "Thanks. I'll take him." The chuckles ceased, and resolve glowed in his eyes. "Getting this story will be the answer to all my problems."

Reaching out, Claire squeezed his arm. "I hope you're successful. Right now, though, we'd better get moving. We want to hike while the sun is shining, and it may be a brief window of opportunity."

"Sure. I'm on my way to breakfast, anyway."

Jed cleared his throat and stuck out his hand. "Order the pancakes. You won't regret it."

"Thanks for the tip." The man grasped Jed's palm in a firm shake then dipped his head in a nod. "See you around, Claire."

After he walked away, Jed headed toward his SUV. "You're right."

She skipped a couple of steps to catch up. "I am?"

"I do like him. He seems like a nice guy. A little down on his luck, but determined to make something happen for himself. I've been in his shoes a few times."

Claire glanced over her shoulder with a sigh. "Haven't we all? Preston deserves a break, and I hope this is it." Her pensive expression dissolved in a grin. "If there's a Bigfoot or two lurking in those woods, however unlikely, I hope we *both* get the pictures to prove it."

\* \* \* \*

With a few deft movements, he worked the lock, smiling in satisfaction when the mechanism clicked. Humming, he pulled open the motor home's door and stepped inside. Chances were he had an hour or two before Claire returned. She'd taken the dog and her camera when she left with the two-bit bum who'd been attached to her like a friggin' limpet since she had arrived in Shady Bend.

Except at night. Crouching in the trees, damp cold chilling his bones, relief had flooded through him when Claire retired to her motor home. Alone. Whatever the man was to her, she wasn't sleeping with him. *Yet.* Hopefully another reminder of her promise would prevent her from even considering it.

He hadn't waited and watched, kept tabs on her for all these years only to lose her now. He'd see she honored her vow…one way or the other. He'd accept nothing less than her willing cooperation. Surely with a few more jogs to her memory, she'd come around and see they were a perfect match.

Making his way through the tiny RV, he stopped beside the bed. Careful to keep his dirty boots off the spread, he lay down and turned his face into her pillow. Breathing deeply of the floral scent lingering there, his lips brushed over the fabric. His jeans tightened at the crotch. With a moan he sat upright. No time to waste. He couldn't risk being caught.

Standing, he reached in his pocket for the package wrapped in silver tissue and tied with a gold bow. A small card dangled from the ribbon. Oh, how he'd labored over this message, wanting to get it just right. With a quick glance around, he pulled open a drawer opposite the bed. Sweaters filled it, packed in tight, leaving little space for his gift. Pushing it shut, he opened the drawer beside it. Silk and lace underwear and bras in every color imaginable tempted him. After lifting out a tiny pair of bikini panties, he pressed them to his cheek. Pulse pounding, he licked the strip of cotton lining before dropping them back in the drawer. His hand slid down the front of his pants for a few swift strokes. Perspiration broke across his upper lip.

*Later.*

Burying the package under a layer of underwear at the back, he closed the drawer and walked toward the front of the motor home. Taking a deep breath, he opened the door a crack and peered out. Not even a squirrel was around to witness his departure. Making sure to relock the door behind him, he hurried out of the campsite.

Sometime soon, Claire would find his gift and remember her promise. Once she did, he'd have all the time in the world to make love to her.

Together forever.

# Chapter 6

Scoop leaped out of the SUV to tour the unfamiliar surroundings, nose to the ground working overtime, tail trying to keep up. Claire followed with a lot less enthusiasm, wondering if Ian always wore the scowl he had on now or if he donned the glower especially for her. As her ex approached at a fast clip, his gaze darted between the dog and Jed with ill-concealed annoyance.

"I thought you were bringing your *girlfriend* with you. Uh, Theresa wasn't it?"

"Jed's an even older friend—from my grade school years. We bumped into each other a couple of days ago."

Her *old friend* rounded the front of the vehicle and stuck out his hand. After a moment, Ian shook it.

"How're you doing? Hope you don't mind I tagged along. I'm fascinated by your Bigfoot research. Claire tells me you document each step so there'll be no doubt about the authenticity of your findings."

Some of the tension around the other man's mouth eased. "Sorry if I seemed unwelcoming. I was just a little surprised. Nice to meet a fellow enthusiast."

Claire turned away, pressing her lips together to hide a grin. Jed's wide-eyed innocent act was perfect for gaining Ian's approval. He'd always loved having adoring disciples hanging on his every word.

She pointed toward Scoop, tail waving as he thrust his nose into a hole. "Is having my furry pal along going to be a problem? I can always leash him."

The glower returned as Ian rolled his eyes. "You're turning what's supposed to be a routine hike into a freaking circus. We're here to work, for Christ's sake."

"I suppose I can leave him in the car, but he'll be miserable." Her shoulders sagged.

With a snort, Ian turned away. "Bring him, but keep him under control."

"Oh, I will. Where's the rest of the group?"

"Lee and Margaret left a while ago. I waited for you. Bart is—"

"Right here." The other scientist hurried out of the trees, smiling as he approached. "I had a few calls to make, and service out here is spotty at best. Good to see you again, Claire."

"Likewise. This is a friend of mine, Jed Lafferty. Jed, Bart Kelton."

The men shook hands, eyeing one another up and down like two alpha dogs meeting for the first time. If they'd had fur, it would have bristled. With a whistle to Scoop, she followed Ian, leaving Jed to fend for himself.

"I hope you're prepared for a fairly long hike. It'll be close to ten miles, round trip."

Claire patted her backpack. "I brought water and lunch along with my camera. Thanks for being a good sport about Scoop. I didn't want to leave him tied up or stuck inside my motor home all day."

Ian shrugged. "I guess he won't be a problem." His glance slid toward her then away as he held back a limb. "How'd you hook up with that Jed guy?"

"We were both at Ralph's Diner the day I arrived. I almost fell off my seat when I realized he was the daredevil little boy who lived across the street from me when I was a kid, all grown up. We got to talking, and since he was interested in your project, I invited him along."

"Oh." The word fell hard and flat into the silence. With their footsteps muffled by a thick layer of needles, tree branches sowing in the breeze high overhead barely ruffled the stillness. Ian let out a breath. "If we don't discover any new evidence of Bigfoot on our hike, will you leave?"

"I'm not sure. I may give it a couple more days. I took a lot of tree pictures yesterday after the fog lifted, just in case I need to change the focus of my story."

"Typical Claire. Ready with a backup plan at a moment's notice."

She stopped and fisted her hands on her hips. "What the hell is that supposed to mean?"

"Just that you're always prepared. When you didn't want to be married to me after our ill-fated trip to the Elvis impersonator, you were damn quick to start annulment proceedings."

"Because *your* father—the lawyer—told me exactly what steps to take." Her voice rose. "Your parents weren't any more thrilled about our marriage than mine were."

"True. But how about us?" He shrugged. "Don't answer that. It all worked out for the best. Right?"

"Right."

"Hey, kids, no fighting."

Claire glanced over her shoulder and met Bart's curious blue gaze as he and Jed caught up with them. Jed gave her a questioning look but didn't comment.

Bart cleared his throat. "Everything okay? Ian mentioned you two have a colorful past. Care to share?"

Claire glanced from one man to the other. "I need all my breath for hiking. Anyway, I wouldn't want to bore you with ancient history."

Bart's gaze dropped, skimming down her light jacket and running pants before rising again. "I bet I wouldn't be bored in the least." White teeth gleamed. "If you don't want to rattle Ian's cage with personal revelations, let's talk about Bigfoot. That's why you're here, isn't it?"

"You bet." She whipped her notebook out of her pocket. "I'd love to hear your perspective on the project. Ian can keep Jed company while we talk."

With a shrug, her ex dropped back, and Bart walked at her side. "I was just trying to get a rise out of Ian. He's a good guy, and we get along well, but with his uptight attitude, he's an easy target." He shook his head and smiled. "Guess it's my fault I take advantage."

Claire eyed his sun-bleached blond hair and deep tan. "You don't seem the type to spend your days in a lab analyzing DNA samples the way Ian does. What exactly do you do?"

That smile flashed again. "God forbid. I'm a zoologist. My specialty is primates."

"You play with monkeys all day?"

He coughed then let out a laugh. "Something like that, but apes, not monkeys."

"Ah, the Bigfoot connection. Lee mentioned you saw something—"

With a grimace, he held up his hand. "I should have kept my big mouth shut. The locals—" On an eye roll, he let out a sigh. "—blew a single comment made over a beer all out of proportion. I caught a glimpse of something large and brown at quite a distance. It could easily have been a bear standing on its hind legs. They're pretty creative foragers. Unfortunately, it wasn't in an area conducive to gathering prints, and we discovered no collaborating evidence when we searched."

"Now you sound like a scientist."

Bart chuckled. "I may look like a beach bum, but I do have a serious side. When it comes to my work, I can be every bit as staid and systematic as Ian."

"That's great, but staid doesn't translate into an exciting article. I want to hear some fun facts about Bigfoot."

"I have plenty of those. Did you know Bigfoot sightings have been reported all over the world for hundreds of years?"

Stumbling over a protruding root, she jotted notes. "Very cool. What else?"

"Though there've been many, many sightings, we still don't have definitive proof of Bigfoot's existence. Add to that, idiots who plant fake evidence have given the rest of us a bad reputation. Our intention in establishing this retreat was to provide the world with some indisputable facts and photographs."

She glanced up from the notepad. "I hope you do. Even if I don't get a career-changing picture while I'm here, I hope you uncover the evidence you're looking for."

"Every indicator tells us this is prime territory to sustain the species. Bigfoot quite likely migrate in search of new food sources and to mate, but we believe there's a well-established colony in this area. It's one of the few spots where sightings have been consistent during all four seasons."

"So it's just a matter of being in the right place at the right time."

"Exactly." He cast her a sideways glance. "You and Ian aren't…"

"God, no." She frowned. "That came out a little stronger than I intended." She lifted one shoulder. "Ian and I…dated in college. I respect him completely."

"But?"

Claire smiled. "No buts. Our romance died years ago. I'm not here to rekindle it."

"I wondered about that. The guy's been a bear the last couple of days. How about Lafferty?"

"We're…old friends."

"Hmm."

When Scoop leaped into a salmonberry bush, she jammed the notepad into her pack before running forward to grasp his collar and haul him out. "Damn it, Scoop, behave or you'll get us both in trouble." Releasing her grip, she turned toward the grinning zoologist. "Hmm, what?"

He angled his head toward the dog. "Who's the boss, you or him?"

"We both have our moments."

The sparkle in his eyes gradually dimmed. "Did I detect a hint of uncertainty in your tone when you mentioned your…old friend?"

"Probably. Jed's like chocolate. Not healthy in the long run, but still tempting. We aren't involved." She cleared her throat. "Uh, we seem to be off topic."

A fallen tree blocked the trail. Grasping her arm, he steadied her as she climbed over it.

"Not at all. You're an interesting—not to mention beautiful—woman. I'd like to get to know you better. No reason why we can't enjoy each other's company while I work and you take your photographs."

Bracing one hand on the mossy log, she jumped back onto the path. "Not that I don't appreciate the sentiment, but I probably won't be around long enough for that."

"Too bad. What the hell?"

Claire stopped and stared then reached for her camera. Barking furiously, Scoop plunged through the underbrush to plant his paws against a small fir tree. A half grown bear cub scrambled higher through the branches. The tree shook and quivered.

Bart frowned. "That fir doesn't look very sturdy."

Zooming in on the bear's face, she focused and clicked. "Just a couple more shots…"

"Oh, hell!" The scientist gave her a hard push, sending her staggering out of the way.

The tree top bent then snapped, and the cub plummeted to the ground. Scoop's eyes widened as the bear landed two feet in front of him. With a bellow, the cub bounded into the forest with the dog in noisy pursuit.

A piercing whistle stopped him in his tracks. Turning, Scoop galloped back, a canine grin on his face as he plopped down, tongue hanging, in front of Jed.

Jed reached down to pat his head. "Good boy."

Claire stared from the man to the dog. "Unbelievable."

"On our hike the other day, I made certain he knew who was in charge."

*Women probably react the same way when he whistles.*

Ian scowled as he stopped beside them. "At least someone has a little control around here. If you're through terrorizing the wildlife, let's keep going."

They hiked for another hour. Claire was beginning to wonder if they were ever going to take a break, when Ian glanced over his shoulder.

"This is the area we decided on for additional surveillance. Lee and Margaret should be somewhere up ahead."

Minutes later, the sound of voices filtered through the trees, growing louder as the forest thinned. Jed raised one brow, and she shrugged in response. Either the other scientists were having a disagreement, or—

"Goddamn paparazzi!"

Claire jerked to a stop and peered around Ian's shoulder then drew in a breath.

In a small clearing, Preston Meyer spoke in rapid-fire bursts of words, hands flapping to emphasize a point. From the apoplectic color of Lee's face and Margaret's downward twisted lips, he wasn't having much luck convincing them of…what?

"Obviously talking isn't getting our point across to that creep." Ian's hands flexed at his sides as he stepped through a thicket of ferns.

Claire rushed after him to grab his arm. The muscle tensed beneath her fingertips through the sleeve of his shirt. "Preston is a good guy, honestly."

Ian stopped and turned to face her. His gray eyes narrowed. "You know him?"

She nodded. "We worked together at *Nature Exposed*. He's just looking for a story, same as I am."

"You sure about that? The camera he broke was expensive."

"Preston didn't break it. I asked."

With a snort, Ian strode forward. "You think he'd admit something like that?"

"Maybe not, but what purpose would destroying your equipment serve?"

"How the hell would I know?"

At the last comment, flung over his shoulder, Margaret spun around. "About time you got here. We have a situation."

Bart stepped past them and cleared his throat. "Let's not overreact, folks." His gaze shot to Ian, and he chuckled. "No reason we can't settle this without bloodshed."

"Very funny." With another scowl, he turned toward Lee. "What happened this time?"

"Nothing's happened." Preston cast a pleading look toward Claire. "I was simply out for a hike, and these two confronted me with accusations—"

"You were following us." Margaret planted hands on her bony hips. "No doubt waiting for another opportunity to damage our property once we set up new cameras."

"How many times do I have to say it?" Preston closed his eyes and pinched the bridge of his nose before letting out a gusty breath. His Adam's apple bobbed. "I didn't break your camera."

"I believe him. What about you, Claire?"

Turning, she gave Jed a grateful smile. "That's what I've been trying to tell Ian. Preston has no motive for vandalism."

"Even if it was an accident the first time—"

The photographer rounded on Lee before he could complete his sentence. "Not intentionally and not by accident. I didn't touch your damned equipment! Yes, I followed you today. As fast as you were hiking, I thought you were hot on the trail of a Sasquatch." He raised his camera by the strap around his neck. "I came prepared to get the picture of a lifetime. Same as Claire. If you'd simply agree to answer my questions, I wouldn't have to sneak around."

"He has a point."

Ian glared at her. "I don't think we need your input."

She held up her hands. "Sorry."

Bart cast a conciliatory glance around the group. "Maybe we should reconsider our decision—"

"Absolutely not. I won't have my words twisted and misquoted by the likes of him." Margaret pointed one long, narrow finger at Preston. "The sort of story *Nature Exposed* prints will make us all laughingstocks. If you want to talk to him, Bart, that's your business, but I won't have any part of it."

"Don't get into a huff, Margaret. I simply said—"

"Ah, the hell with it. I'm out of here." Without a backward look, Preston disappeared into the forest. Silence followed his departure.

Lee raised a hand to scratch the back of his neck. "Well, that was certainly unpleasant. Let's forget about it and get to work." He turned his gaze on Jed and frowned. "Who, exactly, are you?"

"A friend of Claire's. Ian was kind enough to let me tag along."

When Lee held out his hand, Jed shook it and introduced himself. The smile he turned on Margaret thawed the woman's dour expression a few degrees—until she glanced down at Scoop.

"Is that animal yours?"

Claire cleared her throat. "Uh, he's mine, but he'll behave. I promise."

Brushing her hands on her pants, she snorted. "We've wasted enough time. Bart, I want you to set up the new camera over in the…"

Tuning out Margaret's drill sergeant directives as the men jumped to comply, Claire stepped closer to Jed and lowered her voice. "Maybe I was wrong when I said Ian isn't crazy. Talk about paranoid. I think the whole group is certifiable. Except Bart. He seems normal enough."

"I actually felt sorry for Preston. Doesn't seem like his actions justify their outrage." Lines creased his forehead as he turned his gaze on Ian.

"Possibly I jumped to conclusions about Dallas. Maybe Ian's the one who left the notes and wedding decorations." He rolled his eyes. "I have to say, I'm not very impressed by your choice of men. I'm Prince Charming in comparison to the exes I've seen so far."

Lips tight, Claire shook her head. "They've both changed. And not necessarily for the better. When I dated them, they were a heck of a lot more normal."

"If you say so."

Her hands fisted. "Sarcasm doesn't become you."

With a soft chuckle, Jed squeezed her shoulders. "I'll stop with the teasing. Uh, shouldn't you be taking pictures or something?"

If the other men from her past had changed almost beyond recognition, Jed certainly hadn't. His resemblance to the obnoxious little boy she remembered grated on her nerves—until she looked into his twinkling eyes then allowed her gaze to drift across the breath of his chest and downward....

Letting out a long sigh, she shook her head again. "Or something. I've about given up on the whole Bigfoot angle. Is it my imagination, or does the group as a whole seem a little desperate? Maybe their lack of results is why they're so defensive."

"Makes sense to me. What are you going to do?"

"Change the focus of my story to how Bigfoot hunters affect tourism and the local economy. I can still use the photos I've taken along with some insights from longtime residents to add a personal interest dimension. I'm sure Theresa will give me a quote. Maybe Augusta or Ralph from the diner would like to comment, too."

"What about Dallas? He'd talk to you in a heartbeat."

Ignoring his condescending tone, she grinned. "Excellent idea. There's also Stan Hansen who owns the local market and Phyllis Evans, the postmistress. She'd probably love to chat about the crazies chasing after Bigfoot. I'll get my quotes tomorrow then head out the following day."

"Just like that?"

"I don't have any other reason to stay in the area."

His lips pressed together. Was she imagining the disappointment clouding the bright blue of his eyes?

"Where will you go?"

An aching hollowness filled her. She had nowhere to go. No home except her RV. When Scoop wandered over and leaned against her leg, she dug her fingers into his short fur. No one but *a dog* to care about her. Sure, she could check in at the office and speak to her editor in person, but it wasn't necessary or expected. Phone calls and e-mails were just as effective.

She lifted one shoulder in a shrug. "I'm not sure. I suppose I should get serious about finding a new place to live."

"You could hang out with me for a while longer." His voice deepened. Gentled. He rested a hand on her arm, softly stroking his thumb along the back of her hand. "I'm not ready to say goodbye to you yet."

Emotion tightened her throat. She didn't want to walk out of his life again, either. Despite his devil-may-care attitude—maybe because of it— Jed opened up parts of her heart that had been closed off for years. The problem was, those same parts would be the ones hurting the most when two old friends eventually went their separate ways. She'd be better off finding someone solid and dependable, someone—

"Jesus. Is that what I think it is?" Excitement edged Bart's voice.

Claire's head snapped up. The four scientists huddled together, crouching around a patch of dirt near some bushes. Equipment and backpacks were scattered on the ground around them.

She took a couple of steps forward. "Found something?"

Ian turned, his gray eyes flashing. "A footprint. We found a freaking footprint."

Heartbeat picking up, she took a few more steps. Coming up behind her, Jed grabbed her hand again and squeezed.

"You don't mean—"

"Hell, yes, I mean." Ian's voice rose. "We found a print—from a Bigfoot."

# Chapter 7

"Looked like a bear print to me. Not a Bigfoot." Jed held open the door to the motor home as Scoop pushed past him to head straight for his food bowl.

"Bear paws aren't that long." Claire glanced over as she stepped inside, shrugged the pack from her shoulders and dropped it onto the table. Pulling off her jacket, she hung it on the hook by the door.

"The mother of the cub Scoop chased was probably strolling through the area earlier. Maybe she slid in the mud and sort of elongated the print."

"Good thing you didn't mention your theory to Ian. He was practically orgasmic over that mark."

His gaze drifted from her bright eyes and pink cheeks down across the form fitting T-shirt clinging to her breasts. "I can think of better reasons to get orgasmic. No wonder you dumped the guy."

The color in her cheeks deepened. "I think I'll go grab a quick shower before dinner."

"Take your time. It's my turn to cook, anyway. How do you feel about tacos?" He swallowed then choked as she bent to pull a sweater from the bank of drawers near the bed. "I'm in the mood for something spicy."

"Spicy's good." She opened a second drawer. "Do we have tortillas?"

"I may need to go to the store. What's wrong?"

Hand pressed to her mouth, Claire backed against the bed and turned. She clutched the sweater to her chest as the color faded from her face.

Stepping around Scoop, he grabbed her arm. "You okay?

"Look in there." Her voice squeaked on the final word.

A bright array of underwear filled the drawer. Just thinking about how Claire would look wearing the hot pink number—

"In the back."

Silk slid across his hand as he pushed bras and panties aside. Wrapped in silver and gold, a package was buried beneath something green and lacy. He pulled it out and glanced up. "Someone put this in the drawer while we were gone?"

Face pale, she nodded and sank onto the edge of the bed. "I guess so, though I suppose it could have been in there when I got dressed this morning. I didn't bother turning on a light, and it was still pretty dark."

"You're sure the door was locked when we got back?"

"Yes."

"Anything else out of place or missing?"

She glanced around and frowned. "I don't think so. I had my wallet with me, and it's not like I have a lot of valuables here other than my camera equipment. I had most of that with me, too."

"That's good." He gave the package a toss. Not heavy, but tissue covered something solid. "When was the last time you really looked in that drawer?"

"Yesterday morning before we went to breakfast at the diner. I was searching for—" She stopped speaking, and some of her color returned. "I would have noticed it."

Jed couldn't help wondering what exactly she'd been hunting for amongst her underwear. He cleared his throat. "So the intruder could have left it either yesterday or today. There's a note attached. Do you want to read it?"

"No." The word came out hard and flat. She pressed her lips together. "Can you?"

He pulled a card embossed with silver stars from the envelope, flipped it open, scanned the message then gave her a reassuring smile. "It's not bad. A little creepy maybe, but…"

She let out a long breath. "Read it to me. Please."

He dropped onto the bed beside her, his thigh pressed against the length of hers. She leaned into his side and shivered.

"You sure?"

"Yes."

After hesitating for a moment, he read, *"I'm disappointed, Claire. Have you forgotten your promise? I can't believe you'd go back on your word. Maybe this will help you remember."*

Her troubled gaze met his before she lowered it to hands tightly clasped in her lap. "Go ahead and open the package. Wondering what's in there is probably worse than the reality."

He gave her a long look. Dark lashes brushed her cheeks, and little lines bracketed her mouth. Her bottom lip quivered. "Claire…"

She opened her eyes. "Please. I'm okay."

He ripped off the wrapping and held up two figurines. The female was swathed in a traditional white gown and veil, while the male wore black tails and a top hat. Long noses and drooping ears added charm to the canine cake toppers.

"*Dogs?* I don't get it? Does this mean something to you?"

Claire glanced over at Scoop, sprawled in front of his empty bowl, and shrugged. "Whoever left the figurines must know I love dogs."

"You didn't have a pet when you lived in Reno."

"No, but we did when I was in high school. A beagle named Buddy. I missed him so much when I went to college I talked about adopting a stray. Totally impractical, but—"

"Ian knew about your dog addiction, then. Obviously, so did Dallas."

"I guess so." Her knuckles whitened as she pressed her fists against her thighs.

He slid one arm around her waist. "What?"

"Ross and I bought a puppy together, the most adorable little basset hound...." Her teeth clamped down on her lip. "The bastard took her when we split up. I think I was more upset about losing the puppy than I was about our engagement ending."

He pulled away. "Who the hell is Ross?"

She picked at a loose thread on the bedspread. "My ex-fiancé. Ross and I were engaged about ten years ago. We both worked for *Nature Exposed* at the time."

"Why didn't you mention him before?"

"Why would I?"

He ran a hand through his hair. "I don't know. Maybe because we were talking about men you promised to *marry*."

She frowned as she stared at him. "As I've said before, sarcasm doesn't become you."

Taking a couple of slow breaths, he unclenched his fists. "Sorry. I guess it threw me, hearing you'd been engaged in addition to the aborted marriage and the high school sweetheart who still has a thing for you."

"Dallas doesn't—"

"Let's not argue. Tell me about the fiancé. Where is he?"

When she managed to eye him steadily, he gave her a brief, encouraging smile.

*Exactly why does news of her engagement bother me so much?*

"Ross left the magazine about the same time I did. I think he lives in Arizona now, although I'm not one hundred percent sure about that. He's in advertising."

"How'd you break this one's heart?"

She reared back. "I swear—"

"Sorry. No more sarcasm. I just assumed…"

"Well, you assumed wrong. He broke mine. When I found out he was cheating on me, I called off the wedding."

"Asshole."

"Yeah, he had the nerve to tell me I was overreacting, that a couple of slips didn't mean anything. He said he'd settle down once we were married."

He touched her arm. "You didn't buy that load of crap, did you?"

"I told you once before—I may be blond, but I'm not stupid. The breakup was the kick in the butt I needed to leave *Nature Exposed* to look for a better job."

"You must have loved the guy if you agreed to marry him, so the situation couldn't have been easy for you."

"It wasn't. I was young and made another bad choice. I couldn't see there was no depth beneath Ross's charm. Live and learn. I've been a little more choosey about the men I've dated since then."

"I bet." He tossed the cake topper figurines on a shelf. "I want to know exactly where your ex-fiancé is. Any idea how we can contact him?"

"We haven't exactly kept in touch. He did have a couple of close friends on the staff of *Nature Exposed*. Maybe one of them would have his address."

"I don't suppose Preston was one of those friends?"

She shook her head. "Preston was on my side of the break-up. He thought Ross was a complete jerk. Still, he could ask Ross's old buddies for his contact info if either of them still works at the magazine."

"Sounds like a plan."

"Except I don't have Preston's cell number." She gave him a tired looking smile. "I imagine we'll see him somewhere around town. We've bumped into each other often enough over the last few days."

"I'll keep my eyes open for him." Taking her hand, he stood and pulled her to her feet. His gaze scanned her face, noting the shadows darkening her eyes. "Are you going to be okay if I go to the store, or should we just make do with leftovers?"

"Don't be silly. Of course I'll be fine." She glanced toward her dog, who remained prostrate in front of his bowl. "I'm going to feed Scoop, who looks like he may die of starvation at any moment, and then go take that shower."

He touched her cheek, a brief brush of his fingers.

The gaze she raised to his was so filled with uncertainty, his heart wrenched. Cupping her chin, he kissed her, a slow, gentle caress, then drew away. *No pushing until she's ready.*

"I won't be gone long." With a final backward glance, he left the motor home and headed for his SUV. One hand shading his eyes from the glare of the setting sun, he scanned the woods on either side of the site as he rolled through the campground loop.

No one lurked in the shadows. Other nearby campers consisted of an older couple in a fifth wheel, two guys with dreadlocks from whose tent drifted a suspiciously sweet odor and a family with young children. All very non-threatening.

Not that he was exactly worried about Claire's safety. Her admirer—if that's what this loon could be considered—didn't seem dangerous. Still, the fact that the guy had gotten into her RV while they were gone bothered him. Maybe the door hadn't been locked properly, though it wouldn't take a rocket scientist—or a criminal mastermind—to jimmy the damned thing. They'd just have to be more careful about securing the campsite in the future.

He flipped on his blinker and turned down the street toward the market. If Claire had her way, their *future* here wasn't going to last much longer, anyway. She seemed determined to wrap up her story and get the hell out of Dodge. A dull ache settled in his chest. Having her walk out of his life *again* would just plain suck. Maybe they weren't exactly involved…yet. Fact was he'd give his left nut for a shot with Claire. The right one, too.

A few minutes later, he parked in front of the market and killed the engine. His lips tightened. Karma had thrown them together, and if he'd learned one thing over the years, it was not to turn his back on fate. Now all he had to do was convince Claire to stick around to see where the attraction simmering between them might lead.

* * * *

Claire pushed open the door to the post office as a flood of memories smacked her in the face. The place looked exactly as she remembered. The same bank of little metal doors with gold numbers on them covered the wall to the left. The same high counter manned by a tiny woman with fluffy white hair was on her right. Maybe a few more wrinkles lined Phyllis Evans' face, but she'd swear the cat-eye glasses decorated with blue rhinestones hanging from a chain around the woman's neck were the same one's she'd worn twenty years before.

A hint of confusion in faded blue eyes disappeared as the postmistress's lips turned upward in a smile. "My goodness. Claire Templeton, you haven't changed at all."

"Neither have you, Mrs. Evans." She reached across the countertop to squeeze the woman's frail hand. "It's good to see you."

"It certainly is. Quite fortuitous, as well."

Claire grinned. The woman's vocabulary put most English teachers to shame.

"Oh, how's that?"

"You have mail. I tried forwarding the envelope to your parents' last known address. Maybe I shouldn't have, but..." Narrow shoulders beneath a pink cardigan rose in a shrug. "Anyway, it was returned. Apparently they've moved again?"

"Several times. Theresa Wilson mentioned a lawyer was trying to get in touch with me. Is the package from him?"

She nodded. "He's been very persistent, which is why I bent the rules and mailed the documents to your folks. I was just about to stamp *return to sender* across the front when you walked in. Imagine that." She slid a manila envelope with a series of crossed off addresses over the counter.

Claire glanced at the return address label in the corner. William Hutchins, Esquire of Hutchins, Lehman and Zottola, Attorneys at Law in Fort Bragg, California. Certainly sounded legitimate. Fort Bragg was the nearest decent sized town to the south of Shady Bend, which wasn't saying much. She resisted the urge to rip open the envelope.

"Actually, I stopped by to see if you'd be interested in giving me a quote. I work for a magazine called *Rugged America*. I'm taking photographs and writing a story about the Bigfoot hunters you get in this area." When Phyllis's fine, white brows shot up into her cotton ball curls, Claire mustered up her most professional smile. "As a longtime resident, surely you must have an opinion about their activities."

She let out an unladylike snort. "A bunch of fanatics, although the group out there right now seems brighter than most of the enthusiasts we get. Usually it's a handful of foolish men old enough to know better, acting like little boys. They dress up in camouflage, wave rifles, cavort in the woods and drink like fish. After a weekend of carousing, they go home without having seen any sign of a Sasquatch. Big surprise." She rolled her eyes. "Like I said—fools."

Claire pulled a notebook out of her purse. "Do you mind if I quote you?"

Phyllis's lips pursed. "You may. I stand by my words."

"What about the local economy? Does it benefit from the influx of people hoping to catch a glimpse of a Bigfoot?"

"Well, now, that depends. The bars do a thriving business, and I'm sure the restaurants and grocery stores also profit. However, family groups vacationing in the area often leave for a quieter environment, so it's a bit of a wash. I think you'll find community sentiment divided over the issue." She fiddled with the dangling glasses, and her forehead puckered. "This current group is relatively quiet, mostly staying out at the camp they've set up. I think the locals have gotten used to them. For the most part."

Claire glanced up from scribbling notes. "You sound hesitant."

"There're always a few who see the world in black or white. I think I've said enough."

"You've been very helpful, Mrs. Evans. Thank you."

The hint of worry in the older woman's eyes cleared. "I'm more than happy to be of service to a former resident. Will you be staying in town long?"

"Maybe another day or two. I've taken most of the photos I need and just have to speak with a couple more locals. Ralph at the diner was full of comments when I stopped by after the lunch rush was over. He's highly in favor of Bigfoot hunters."

Phyllis's chest rose beneath her pink sweater. "Ralph Potter is full of bologna. The man likes to exaggerate."

Claire smiled. "Augusta set me straight on a few facts after he went back to the kitchen."

"Good for Augusta." Phyllis glanced toward the plastic bin full of mail on the chair beside her. "I'll be closing soon…"

Claire backed up a step. "I'd better not take up any more of your time, then."

"Heavens, don't forget your envelope."

"Right!" Stuffing the mail into her purse, she turned toward the door. "Thanks again, Mrs. Evans. Take care."

"You, too, dear."

The wind hit Claire when she stepped out the door. Pushing her hands into her pockets, she hurried toward Jed's SUV, hoping he hadn't locked the doors.

"Claire."

Turning, she pushed wisps of hair out of her eyes. "Hey, Dallas."

Her old high school boyfriend hurried up the street. Stopping in front of her, he rocked back on the heels of battered tennis shoes. An old letterman jacket stretched across his shoulders and didn't quite meet over his chest. "One of my employees at the hardware store said you were looking for me."

"He told me today was your day off."

"Yes, but I had business…it doesn't matter." His gaze slid across her face. "I'm glad I found you. Can I buy you a cup of coffee?" He jerked his head toward the small café next to the post office.

She glanced back at the SUV. Jed's errands were taking longer than she'd expected. A cup of coffee might warm her up, though she hadn't planned to talk to Dallas in such a date-like setting. Truthfully, she would have skipped interviewing him altogether if Jed hadn't made such a snarky comment earlier. "Sure. Thanks."

He held open the door of Java Jane's, and the scent of strong, freshly brewed coffee nearly weakened her knees. She glanced up at Dallas as they approached the counter. "I know caffeine is bad for you, but coffee—"

"—was always your secret weakness. Even in high school."

"It was the only thing that got me through our first period econ class senior year." She smiled at the tattooed girl behind the counter. "A large cappuccino please."

She snapped her gum as her gaze darted upward. "For you, Mr. Simms?"

"Regular coffee. Black. None of that fancy crap."

"Got it. I'll have your order ready in a minute. You can pay now."

Dallas pulled a wallet out of the back pocket of his jeans. "I've got it."

"Thanks." Taking a seat at a round table by the window, Claire glanced down the street. Still no Jed. She turned her attention to her companion as he sat across from her.

Dallas ran a slightly unsteady hand through his hair and smiled. "I was afraid you'd left town without saying good-bye. When I talked to Theresa yesterday, she wasn't sure how long you were staying."

"I'm wrapping up my story."

With an eye roll, he leaned back in his chair. "Does that mean the group out in the woods tracked down a Bigfoot?"

Claire opened her mouth then shut it when the barista delivered their coffee. She took a sip of the frothy concoction and sighed. "Afraid not, though they did find a print."

His chair banged to the floor. "Of what?"

"That's still up for debate. How do you feel about the Bigfoot hunters, Dallas? Are they good for business in the area?"

"Hardly." His lip curled. "Mostly they're just a bunch of rednecks looking for some fun."

"The group camped in the woods now are all respected scientists."

One shoulder hunched as he stared down at his coffee. "We've had others like them before. They still didn't find any proof. I wish they'd all just leave us alone."

"Why's that?"

Deep brown eyes darkened as he studied her. "Theresa said you hadn't changed. She said you were still the same sweet girl I was crazy about back in high school."

Claire ran a finger around the rim of the cup. "We all change."

"Yeah, I guess so. For you, it's all about taking pictures for a magazine. I get the feeling anything I say will wind up as a caption beneath one of them."

"Only if you give me permission to quote you."

His brows lowered. "When did you become so hard?"

"I'm not hard. I'm realistic. You don't have to talk to me if it makes you uncomfortable."

He let out a long breath. "I want to talk to you—the old you. Not the woman waiting for a perfect quote."

"Fair enough. Everything we say is off the record." She sat back with her cup cradled in her hands. "Are you okay?"

"Yeah. No." His shoulders rose and fell again beneath his too tight jacket. "Mandy's been badgering me about extra child support to pay for piano lessons and soccer cleats. She also said missing school to see me for long weekends is too disruptive for the kids. If she has her way—and the judge made damn sure she pretty much gets what she wants—I won't see them again until Thanksgiving."

"I'm sorry."

"Yeah, so am I, but I shouldn't have taken my bad mood out on you. You're just doing your job, and I'm sure you don't want to hear my problems."

"Dallas?"

He glanced up.

"I still care about you. I want you to be happy."

The anger in his eyes faded. He sipped his coffee, his gaze never leaving her face. "I saw one, you know."

"Huh?"

"A Bigfoot."

Her cappuccino sloshed over her hand. She set the cup back on the table and reached for a napkin. "You're kidding?"

"No." He shrugged. "It was a couple of years ago, and I never told anyone. I guess I figured people would laugh. It was evening, and I was out in the woods looking for my dog who'd run off chasing something. I was stumbling along in the dark when I saw him—it—whatever from about thirty yards away. The thing just looked at me, and the expression in its eyes was almost sad—or hunted. After a few seconds, whatever it was moved off into the forest."

Claire let out a long breath. "That's some story."

"I never forgot that moment of connection. Anyway, I went home and left the dog to fend for himself. He turned up a couple of hours later." Dallas took another swallow of coffee. "Off the record, Claire. You promised."

She couldn't help wondering how many beers he'd had before he headed into the woods that night, what he'd really seen. Obviously Dallas was a believer. "Sure. Off the record. But can I get your opinion on Bigfoot hunters, for the record?"

"Against. Definitely against. I say leave the Sasquatch in peace. Why do they need to be documented and studied? They've done fine all alone out there for centuries, maybe millennia. Next thing you know, the so-called scientists will want to put one in a zoo."

"You do have a point. Thanks."

She glanced out the window. Jed stood on the sidewalk in front of the post office, talking to a man wearing old jeans and a hoodie. Though she couldn't see his face, only one person she knew shuffled and gestured in that particular way.

"I've got to go." She gulped the rest of her drink. "Thanks for sharing your story with me, even if I can't tell it to the world. It matters."

"Felt good to talk about it." He pushed back his chair and stood. "Will I see you again?"

"Maybe. I'll probably be around for another day."

His chest rose. "If I don't, I'm glad we talked." He reached out to touch her arm. "See you, Claire."

"Bye, Dallas."

The bells over the door jangled as she shut it behind her. When she passed the window, he was still standing, head hanging, shoulders slumped.

Guilt ate at her, but she shoved the feeling aside. She wasn't responsible for Dallas's misery. Still, if he was the one leaving the notes and *reminders*... Claire drew in a breath. She'd call Theresa and ask her to check on him. Make sure he really was okay. It was the best she could do. The only thing she could do.

# Chapter 8

"Thanks, man. I appreciate it." Preston disconnected then typed something into his cell before glancing up at Jed. "According to Doug, Ross McGregor moved from Phoenix back to California last year. He's living in Sonoma now, working for a winery. Doug gave me his phone number and address."

"Hot damn." Jed pulled out his cell. "Go ahead." He recorded the information Claire's former colleague recited then smiled. "If he's the one harassing her, we'll know soon enough."

Preston ran his scuffed boot along a crack in the sidewalk. "I can't believe someone is threatening her."

"Not threatening exactly, but she's worried.... Hey, look who's here."

A little burst of warmth filled his chest as Claire hurried toward them, boot heels clicking on the pavement, tight jeans hugging tempting hips and thighs. With an effort, he forced his gaze upward. Questions brightened blue eyes as she pushed wisps of blond hair out of her face. She looked so innocent—and sexy. He could almost sympathize with the man from her past who didn't want to let her go. Almost.

Claire stopped in front of them. "Hey, yourself." Her direct gaze shifted right. "Hi, Preston. You two look like you're plotting trouble. What's up?"

"Preston tracked down your ex-fiancé's address. It shouldn't be hard to find out if he has an alibi for the last few days."

"That's good. I guess. I still can't imagine Ross had anything to do with the notes."

Preston frowned. "I'm sorry. According to Jed, some jerk has been bothering you. Do you know why?"

"I haven't a clue. The notes are pretty ambiguous. All I can figure is it's someone's idea of a joke." Her eyes clouded. "Too bad I don't think it's the least bit funny."

"If you need any help…"

"Appreciate the offer, but I think we have it under control." Jed stepped back and glanced at his watch. "Thanks for getting that address."

"No problem." Preston's brows drew together. "I always thought Ross was a complete ass, but I can't believe he'd send you notes and gifts. Not his style. He's an in-your-face kind of guy, if you know what I mean."

"I know *exactly* what you mean, which is why I told Jed this is a wild goose chase."

"Hey, you have to look at all the puzzle pieces before you know which ones will fit." Jed cleared his throat. "Uh, don't you have an interview scheduled with—"

She winced. "Riley down at the Belly Up. Is it five-thirty already?"

"Almost."

"I'm sorry. I didn't mean to keep you." Preston's lips twisted into a comical smile. "I never know when to shut up."

She gave his arm a squeeze. "And I still meet myself coming and going. We're quite a pair."

"Always were. See you, Claire."

After Preston left, they walked over to Jed's SUV. He unlocked the passenger door then held it open for her. When she brushed past him, he couldn't resist stroking one hand along the curve of her waist down to her hip. "Maybe we can go get some dinner after you talk to the bartender."

For a moment, heat flared in her eyes as she hiked herself up onto the seat. "Sure, but first…" Pulling an envelope from her purse, she ripped open the flap.

Hurrying around the front of the vehicle, he jerked open the driver's door and climbed in. A frown settled between Claire's brows as she read the top sheet of the papers clutched in her hand.

"What is it?"

"Apparently my great-aunt died."

Reaching across the center console, he laid a hand on her knee. "I'm sorry."

She glanced up, confusion darkening her eyes. "I thought she died ages ago. When the cards and letters I sent her started coming back, I called my dad. He told me the old…witch…was too mean to die. They had this big fight back when I was still in high school, and Aunt Agatha disowned him. If I'd known she was still alive all these years…" She drew in a long breath.

"Obviously you're upset. Do you want to call the Belly Up and cancel your appointment? You're going to be late as it is."

She shook her head. "No, I'm okay, and I want to wrap up this story. Once I get a quote from Riley, I'll sit down and figure out what these documents are all about. I'm not sure why a lawyer would be contacting me. I hadn't seen my great-aunt since my parents moved away from Shady Bend years and years ago."

He started the engine. "Your aunt lived here?"

"On the coast, not far away. She had this cool old gothic house overlooking the ocean. Even after the blowup with my dad over—" She frowned. "I can't remember what it was about, but I still went to visit her now and then. She really was an argumentative old biddy, but she was all alone. Aunt Agatha didn't have any children of her own, just a couple of nieces back east and my dad."

Jed glanced over as he pulled out onto the street. "You're a kind person. It's one of the things I like most about you."

She didn't respond, just stared through the windshield with clouded eyes.

After parking in the lot behind the bar, he set the brake and turned to face her. "You're sure you're up for this."

Her clenched fist jerked. "Yeah, it won't take long. Then we'll go get some dinner." After stuffing the papers back in the envelope, she opened the door and gave him a hesitant smile. "I'll be right back."

"I'm coming with you." Rounding the front bumper, he walked at her side then slipped an arm around her waist. Their feet crunched gravel as they headed toward the bar. "You don't have to act so tough, you know."

"I kind of do. There's been a lot of crap to wade through lately. First getting kicked out of my home. Then the nutcase leaving me wedding paraphernalia. Now this."

His arm tightened. "You can lean on me."

She paused beside the door and glanced up. A dying ray of late afternoon sun highlighted the smooth curve of her cheek and the vulnerability in her eyes. "I know. It helps, honestly."

"Good." He pulled open the heavy wooden door.

Squaring her shoulders, she stepped inside.

\* \* \* \*

Claire's head throbbed from the blare of a football game along with the accompanying shouts from the men glued to the action displayed on the wide screen TV. In the far corner of the bar, pool balls smacked together, and over all of it, a country tune about a man with a cheating wife whined through hidden speakers.

"Thanks, Riley." Claire raised her voice to be heard. "Your insights were extremely helpful." She held out her hand.

The bartender shook it. "Being interviewed was kind of fun. Nice, having someone listen to me for a change." Dark eyes twinkled beneath shaggy brows as the old-timer released her hand and set a highball glass on the polished burl wood bar. "We tend to get a noisy crowd for Monday Night Football. You look like you could use a drink. What can I get you— on the house?"

She glanced across the room at Jed, who stood beside a dart board talking to a tall, curvy redhead. "If I start drinking now, I might not stop. It's been one of those days, but I appreciate the offer."

"Everyone has them once in a while. Did I answer all your questions?"

"You did. Thanks for being so candid." She slid off the stool.

"You bet. Hope your evening improves."

Claire shot another glance toward Jed as he threw back his head to laugh at something the redhead said.

"Doubtful. Seriously doubtful." Letting out a long, slow breath, she headed across the scared wooden floor, boot heels thumping with each step.

A smile curved his lips as Jed turned to face her. "All finished with the interview?"

She met the resentful gleam in the other woman's gaze with a cool look. "Yes, but I can always walk back to the campground if you're...busy."

"Celeste and I were just shooting the breeze. I'm ready to go." The smile he turned on the woman had probably charmed more than one recipient straight into bed. "It was nice meeting you."

Celeste blinked long, mascara-coated lashes and sighed. "I'm here most evenings if you get—" Her glistening lips tightened as she glanced at Claire. "—bored."

Jed backed up a step. "I'll keep that in mind."

"Nice meeting you, Celeste." Claire turned on her heel and stalked across the room, wondering if he'd follow. Jed caught up just as she reached the door and stretched out an arm to hold it open. When his chest pressed up against her back, she hurried outside.

The fog had rolled in while they were in the Belly Up, swirling thick in the air. She plunged her hands into her jacket pockets and shivered.

"Where do you want to go for dinner?"

Stopping beside the SUV, she scowled. "Just like that—dinner?"

"Huh? Just like what?"

She forced herself to breathe. So he'd talked to a woman in a bar. Big deal. It wasn't like they were a real couple. A few kisses didn't exactly constitute a relationship. If seeing him laughing with another woman made her want to rip every dyed hair out of the bimbo's head, then that was her problem. Not Jed's.

"Nothing. Sorry I sounded grouchy. The noise in there gave me a headache."

Resting both hands on her shoulders, he turned her to face him. "We don't have to eat out. We can go back to the campsite and cook something there. I know you're probably anxious to look at those papers."

"I'm not in the mood to cook tonight. Let's compromise and get takeout."

He gave his keys a little toss. "Burgers or pizza?"

"How about Chinese?"

"Sounds good."

"The Golden Dragon is just down the street. Want to walk?"

"Sure." Stuffing the keys back in his pocket, he took her hand. When she tried to pull away, his grip tightened. "Are you mad about something?"

Some of the tension drained out of her as they headed down the sidewalk. "Not mad exactly…"

"Then what? I can't fix it if I don't know what's wrong."

She peered up at him through the gloom. "Are you really that clueless?"

A smile flashed. "Apparently I am."

"No wonder you're still single."

"I should be insulted, but—"

"No woman likes seeing the man she's with—" Claire held up a hand. "I know we're not exactly a couple, but it kind of feels like we are after nearly a week of constant togetherness." She lifted one shoulder in a little shrug. "It stung, seeing you flirt with that woman."

He stopped and tightened his hold on her. "Who? Celeste?"

"Were you flirting with more than one woman?"

"No, I mean, I wasn't flirting with *anyone*. She was waiting for her date and was irritated because the guy was late. Since we were both just standing there, I didn't see any reason not to be friendly."

"God, do you not know the effect you have on the opposite sex? Celeste would have dumped her date in a heartbeat if you'd given her one reason to believe—"

"But, I didn't." He tugged her up against his chest and tilted her chin. Looking into her eyes, he smiled. "Why would I encourage another woman when I could be with you?"

Heat worked its way from deep in her belly upward, curling around her heart and filling an empty void. She clung a little harder and forced her brain to shift out of neutral. "Celeste would probably sleep with you."

"I don't want to sleep with Celeste. I'd rather hang out with you, even if we're just talking. Not that I wouldn't jump at the opportunity to… never mind. I'm a patient man. I can wait. You're worth it."

Standing on her toes, she pressed a kiss to his lips before stepping away. "A few more lines like those, and you'll have me exactly where you want me…but then I'm pretty sure you already know that. You're smooth, Lafferty. Very smooth."

"Hey, I meant every syllable."

"I'm sure you did." Swinging their clasped hands, she pulled him toward the restaurant. "Let's go order. My headache's gone, and I've worked up quite an appetite."

\* \* \* \*

Jed heaped a pile of lo mein onto his plate then slid the container across the table to Claire. "What does it say?"

She glanced up from the documents spread in front of her. Eyes wide, she pressed a hand to her chest and gulped air.

"Are you okay?" Shoving aside the mu shu pork, he laid a hand on her arm. "You're scaring me a little."

"I can't believe it. Aunt Agatha left me her house."

He reared back, thumping his head against the wall of the motor home. "Wow."

"'Wow' doesn't quite cover it. There's some money, too." Tears welled in her eyes. Pressing shaking fingers to her cheeks, she wiped them away. "Why would she do that? I hadn't talked to her in fifteen years. Surely there was someone else more deserving."

"You said she didn't have any immediate family, that she was estranged from your father…."

"She sent back my letters. Why would she return them then leave me her home?"

He tapped the address label on the corner of the envelope. "Maybe the lawyer who mailed these papers will know."

"I hope so." Claire rested her head in her hands. "I feel awful. I should have made more of an effort to find out what happened to her."

"How old were you when the letters were returned?"

"Nineteen. Actually, it was right around the time of my breakup with Ian. Between trying to stay on top of my studies and dealing with annulment proceedings, I was already overextended. Still, it's no excuse for ignoring a lonely old woman."

"You didn't ignore her. She severed communication. Don't beat yourself up over it." He held out a bag of egg rolls. "Eat. The food's getting cold."

"I don't know if I can. There's a huge knot of emotions tangled in my stomach. Part of me is thrilled about the house. The place is beyond cool, or at least it used to be. I'd be ecstatic if I didn't feel so guilty. And sad."

Jed picked up one cold hand and squeezed it. "It's okay to be confused. Finding out your aunt died was a shock. Add to that the house—well, it's a lot to process. We'll figure it all out. Tomorrow. Right now, have some dinner."

She let out a long sigh. "You're right. I tend to obsess over things beyond my control, and there's absolutely no point since I certainly can't change the past." Pulling her hand from his, she lifted the container of lo mein to scoop a helping onto her plate.

Claire was quiet throughout the meal. The pain in her eyes squeezed his heart. When she stopped pushing the food around her plate, he cleared the table and washed the few dishes. After rinsing out the sponge and tossing it next to the sink, he leaned against the short strip of counter and idly reached down to scratch Scoop's ears when the dog pressed against his leg.

"Want to sit outside? I can build a fire."

After a long pause, she glanced over at him. "I'm pretty tired. Do you mind if I pass?"

"Of course not."

Her lips curved downward. "I'm not much fun this evening. Maybe you should have stayed at the Belly Up."

"We've already been through this. I didn't want to stay at the bar, and I don't expect to be entertained, for crying out loud. You're allowed to have an off night."

Stepping forward, he pulled her up off the seat. With the pad of his thumb, he stroked her soft cheek as the honeysuckle scent of her shampoo invaded his senses. Warmth filled his chest before an arrow of heat zinged straight downward. Shifting, he tugged on his jeans to ease the ache. If she didn't look so damned vulnerable...

"Why don't you get into your pajamas then read or something. Want me to make you a cup of tea?" His hands moved to her shoulders to knead tense muscles. "Aren't the ones that taste like bark and berries supposed to relax you?"

She smiled. "Tea and a book sounds like heaven."

"I guess that would make me an angel. I can honestly say no one's ever accused me of being angelic before."

Her eyes drifted shut, and a little moan slipped through her lips. "Don't stop. Your hands are magic. Maybe you are good for me, after all."

He paused before continuing to massage the tight muscles. Her chin tilted down to rest against her chest as he stroked the back of her neck.

"Why would you think I'm not good for you?"

One shoulder moved in a tiny shrug. "You're a lot of fun."

"I won't argue with that." Taking her hand, he pulled her toward the bed and pushed her, face down, on top of the spread. Sitting beside her, he went to work along the length of her spine, thumbs moving down her backbone. "Doesn't answer my question."

She turned her head sideways on the pillow. "Maybe too fun."

"How can anyone be too fun?"

"I'm thirty-four years old, which means I've had plenty of time to play. I told you once before I'm ready to settle down now."

"You're saying settling down and having fun don't go together? Maybe you should reconsider your priorities."

"They aren't mutually exclusive—for me. With you, it's a whole different story. I get the distinct impression *settling* isn't in your genes."

"So you're looking for a boring guy." He dug his fingers into her back. "Ouch!"

"Sorry." He went back to stroking gently and elicited another one of those moans that made him wonder if he should rethink the benefits of a more traditional future…. He shifted uncomfortably on the edge of the bed, his thigh pressing against the length of hers. "You're anything but boring, Claire. Honestly, I think you're all wrong about what'll make you happy."

She rolled over and frowned up at him. "I'm not wrong. Since my breakup with Ross, the few involvements I've had have been casual. In each case, we both had some fun before going our separate ways with no regrets. Because I didn't want to get hurt again, I've been pretty cautious. But—"

"Why does there always have to be a *but*?"

Her brows lowered. "Are you trying to annoy me?"

He held out his hands, regretting they weren't still touching her, and smiled. "Now why would I do that?"

She rolled her eyes. "*Anyway*, fun is, well, fun, but it gets old after a while. I want stability, commitment, a home that doesn't have wheels. You don't."

"My cabin is pretty damn permanent. It isn't going anywhere."

"No, but you aren't in it. You're extremely mobile."

"I can't argue with that either. However, you're missing one big point. Isn't your job all about travel? Going to some new, out-of-the-way location to take photographs for people who never make the time in their lives to visit these places in person?"

"Yes, which is why I want someplace—*someone*—stable to come home to between assignments. Is that unreasonable?"

"I suppose not." He let out a sigh. "So, because I'm fun and like to explore new places, *exactly like you do*, you've determined I'm not good for you."

"When you put it in those terms, I sound like a lunatic, but am I wrong?"

He stared long and hard into her beautiful blue eyes. She didn't blink, didn't look away. Not a hint of playfulness or humor crept into her gaze. She was dead serious.

For once, so was he. "I think you're very wrong. I think we could have something good together if you'd let down your guard. We have caring and companionship and chemistry. Especially chemistry. Don't dismiss all that just because I'm entertaining and unconventional."

She sighed. "I'm not. I'm still here with you, aren't I? Even though I know I should run far and fast to avoid another disastrous relationship, I haven't."

"Why not?"

"Because I like you too much to walk away. But—and it's a big but—I'm not stupid enough to think you're going to change your lifestyle for me."

"So where does that leave us?"

"Same place we've been. Here. Together. For now."

"And afterward?"

"Maybe we'll keep in touch, text each other, send an e-mail now and then."

"Sounds awful." After a moment of silence, he stood. "You're tired and emotionally drained, so I'm not going to push tonight, but you should know I'm not giving up. I don't quit when I want something."

"Even if the *thing* you want gets hurt in the process?" Before he could answer she held up her hand. "Don't make promises you can't keep, Jed."

"I won't. I'm a man of my word. Count on it."

# Chapter 9

"I still can't believe Aunt Agatha left me her home." Claire leaned forward and clutched the dashboard as she and Jed bumped down the long, rutted driveway. Anticipation, along with more than a few nerves, fluttered in her chest as she waited for her first glimpse of the house. Hutchins, the lawyer, had warned her the place needed some work. Still, it was *hers*.

Jed glanced over and smiled then put his hand on her arm. "How many times are you going to say that?"

"Until I don't have to pinch myself to make sure I'm awake."

She'd expected the atmosphere between them to be awkward after everything she'd said the night before. It wasn't. Another damned point in Jed's favor. He didn't brood or hold grudges. Make that two points. He'd whistled while he scrambled eggs for their breakfast then held her hand through a difficult call to her great-aunt's lawyer. If she didn't know better, she'd start believing he was as perfect inside as he appeared on the surface.

The SUV rounded a bend then jerked to a stop. She sat back in her seat and stared.

Jed spoke before she could find any words. "Wow, the place reminds me of something out of a horror movie. All it needs for atmosphere is bats circling instead of seagulls."

Perched near the edge of the cliff, the weathered, gray shingled house was just as she remembered with its round tower and steeply pitched roof—until he shifted into gear and drove closer. Crumbling mortar and a few stray bricks lay in the weedy grass along the side of the building, and the porch was propped up with…

"Cinderblocks?" Claire's grip on the dashboard tightened until her knuckles turned white. "What happened to the front steps?"

"Looks like someone ripped them out, probably intending to replace them. Maybe your great-aunt was planning a few repairs before she had the stroke and moved to a convalescent home." He turned off the engine and set the parking brake.

Taking a deep breath, Claire opened the door to step down. Scoop scrambled out of the backseat and leaped through the opening. Nose pressed to the ground, he ran in circles, sniffing his new surroundings.

"A little work? If this is the lawyer's idea of minor repairs, I'd hate to see major." Her gaze scanned upward. "The roof doesn't look too bad, but a bunch of the shingled siding is damaged. If those bricks are from the foundation…" She let out a long sigh. "Do you think the building is structurally sound?"

"I'll have to take a closer look to answer that question. If you don't want to hassle with repairs, you could always sell the place as is, though you'd probably make a larger profit after renovations. The view is unbelievable."

Behind the house, choppy gray water stretched to the horizon in an unbroken vista. Overhead, seagulls swooped around the tall, brick chimney, their harsh cries an echo from her past. Down the coast, a fog horn blared mournfully as she breathed in the salt scented air.

"I don't want to sell the house. I want to live here."

His brows shot upward. "You're kidding. The place is a wreck."

"Good thing Aunt Agatha left me some cash. I'll hire a good contractor. I'm sure Hutchins can recommend one."

"I'll check the place out first to see what needs to be done."

She turned and stared. "How would you know about structural repairs? A few are obvious, but—"

"I worked construction for several years before I took over the camping retreat. I know enough to make sure you won't get ripped off if you're serious about restoring the place."

"I'm serious."

Skepticism darkened his eyes. "Let's take a look inside. The house has been standing this long. I don't think it'll collapse around our ears during a walk-through."

Taking her hand, he led the way across the sparse grass that had once been a beautiful lawn. Tail waving, Scoop trotted at his side. With a leap, the dog launched up onto the porch. Jed heaved himself up beside him then reached down to give her a hand. His warm palm closed over hers again as he tugged her up onto the wide plank flooring.

"The porch is solid. Looks like it was replaced not so long ago. Where's the key?"

Curling still tingling fingers, she stuck her hand in her pocket. "There should be a lockbox on the door. The combination is six-three-one."

He pushed the proper buttons then removed an old-fashioned brass key. The door creaked as he opened it wide on a rush of stale air.

Jed turned and smiled. "I'll go first just in case there're any…surprises."

She paused on the threshold. Straight across the entry, stairs wound upward like something out of *Gone With the Wind*. She'd always loved that staircase. Her head jerked around as his words finally registered. "Surprises? What kind of surprises?"

"Weak floorboards. Rodents. Snakes. Spiders."

Clasping her arms around her chest, Claire shuddered. "By all means, lead the way. I don't mind mice, but a snake…ugh."

"I remember. You weren't fond of creepy-crawly things when you were younger."

"I'm less fond of them now." As they made their way into the place, she poked her head through the doorway on the left. Sheets covered a large flat surface and miscellaneous lumps. "This is the dining room. At least someone covered the furniture. I remember how shiny Aunt Agatha's dining room table used to be. She went ballistic once when I set a cola can on it without using a coaster."

Jed lifted a corner of the sheet. "Walnut. A little formal for my taste. This room doesn't seem to need any major repairs. The wallpaper is pretty dingy, but you could remove it and paint to lighten things up in here. Maybe get rid of those heavy drapes and put in some blinds. The hardwood flooring is indestructible. All it needs is a good cleaning."

She pulled Scoop away from a pile of mouse droppings in the corner. "Were you also an interior decorator?"

He grinned. "I just know what I like."

"The kitchen is behind this room. I wonder how bad it is."

"Let's find out. Move it, Scoop." He gave the dog a shove then headed through the doorway in the far wall. "Not bad if you like retro. Looks like the last time your aunt remodeled was in the 80s. The plumbing and wiring will have to be checked, and you'll probably want to switch out those florescent lights for recessed. The terracotta tile floor isn't bad."

"Maybe change the handles on the cabinets. I'll have to see if my budget will stretch to new countertops. Formica—double ugh. The kitchen looks exactly the same as it did when I was in high school. The olive green appliances were ugly even then."

A small breakfast nook with a spectacular view of rolling waves completed the south side of the house. Across the short hall behind the stairs, a big living room with tall windows overlooked the ocean. Squeezed between the formal gathering area and the library in the front tower room was a half-bath.

Jed rested one hand on her shoulder and pointed with the other. "See those water stains? Looks like you have a leak behind the sink."

She nodded, her head brushing against his chest. "The vinyl floor needs to be replaced, but I like the pedestal sink. At least the living room and library are in good condition."

"What's upstairs?"

"Four bedrooms and two baths."

"Let's go check them out." He led the way up the staircase, running his hand along the mahogany rail. "The place is a little big for one person."

"Aunt Agatha grew up here. She had two younger sisters and a brother. Her father, who I guess would be my great-grandfather, owned a lumber company. After he died in an accident, the business was sold, but she lived here with her mother until she passed away. Her siblings, including my grandfather, all moved out of the area."

Jed paused in the doorway of the first bedroom and glanced around. "Nice crown molding." His lips quirked upward. "While I appreciate the family history lesson, I meant big for you."

"Oh." She shrugged. "If I get lonely, I could always advertise for a roommate." When Scoop raced down the hall and disappeared into one of the back bedrooms, she followed. "Or adopt another dog. Maybe a couple of cats. Aunt Agatha had a huge, gray tabby that was meaner than hell."

"Is that your plan, to become a crazy cat lady?"

"Maybe." She walked over to the bay window and leaned on the sill. Out at sea, a fishing trawler moved slowly down the coastline. The faint barking of a sea lion on a rocky perch penetrated the single-paned glass window. "You never know. One of these days I might get married and fill the house with rug rats."

"I like kids. What you see is what you get with them." He stepped up behind her, surrounding her with his warmth when he rested his hands on either side of the window. "Of course then they turn into teenagers. Kane's oldest stepdaughter is sixteen." He laughed. "She's giving him gray hair."

"Not the easiest age, that's for sure. What about you? Do you want kids of your own, or are you content being an uncle?"

"I'm not against the idea of fatherhood...when the time is right."

Claire turned slightly to glance up at him. A pulse beat at the base of his neck, and a day old growth of beard darkened his jaw. When his bright blue gaze met hers, she swallowed. The man was too damn sexy for her peace of mind.

"You're thirty-five. How long do you intend to wait?"

"I don't know. I'm not on a schedule."

"Of course you aren't." She ducked under his arm then moved out of reach to stand in front of the brick fireplace. "This was Aunt Agatha's room. I thought it was beyond cool that she had a fireplace in her bedroom."

"It'd be a total pain in the ass to haul wood all the way up here." He followed Scoop out into the hallway. "The bathrooms on this floor need to be remodeled, and the windows should be replaced, but that's about it. The house is in better shape than I thought."

"That's a relief." Claire headed for the stairs, pausing to take a quick peek into the tower bedroom. The small space would make an ideal office—or a nursery. She shook off the second thought. "The lawyer said it won't take long to settle the estate. As soon as everything's legal, I'll get started on the exterior repairs. Best to get those done before the rainy season sets in."

"So, you really intend to stay?" His footsteps were muffled by the dusty wool runner stretching the length of the hall.

"I told you I wanted a place where I belong." Her lips firmed as they came to the stairs. "It makes sense to settle here. I always loved this house, and I like the town. Everybody knows everyone else. There's a real sense of community. And one of the best friends I've ever had lives here. That's a big plus."

His lip curled. "Dallas?"

She paused on the first step. "I meant Theresa."

"Oh."

Scoop's toenails clicked on the wooden stairs. The silence stretched between them as they reached the entry.

She cleared her throat. "No critters. I'm thankful for that."

Jed held the front door open. "Huh?"

"Rodents or snakes. I saw a few cobwebs, though."

"Based on the droppings, I'm pretty sure there are mice, but they haven't completely taken over the place. The sheet covering the big couch next to the fireplace in the living room looked like something had gnawed on it."

"Even if they gnawed the couch, it's not a great loss. The one I remember had big pink roses splashed all over it."

Jed locked the door and returned the key to the box. "Anything else you want to do before we go?"

"Not much point in checking out the garage or the storage shed. Thanks for touring the house with me."

"You bet." He held her arm as she jumped down from the porch, then walked around the side of the building to crouch beside the foundation. "The loose bricks came from the chimney running up the side of the house, not the foundation. The mortar is crumbling in places. You'll need to hire a mason to fix it before you can use the fireplaces."

She came to stand behind him. "So the foundation is sound?"

"I'd say so." He rose to his feet. "The repairs and upgrades shouldn't be too horribly expensive, considering it's an old house that has been neglected for what, twenty years?"

"Fifteen since my aunt had her stroke. I can't believe no one notified my dad even if she stipulated he not be contacted." Her fists clenched. "She lived for years in that nursing home with no visitors. That's just not right."

"She made her choice, Claire." He wrapped an arm around her shoulders as they headed back to the SUV. "Sounds like she was a proud woman in addition to being set in her ways and a little mean. Maybe she didn't want to be pitied. The lawyer told you she had excellent care in the convalescent facility, right?"

"Yes, but still…" She sighed. "I would have gone to visit her."

"I know you would have."

He opened the passenger door then whistled. Scoop raced across the weedy lawn to leap inside. Claire climbed in and waited for Jed to take his seat.

"What would you like to do for the rest of the afternoon? I'm finished taking photos, but we could still go for a hike. It's a beautiful day."

After starting the engine, he glanced over. "I could use the exercise, but I want to track down your ex-fiancé before we do anything else."

She leaned back and pressed her fingers to her temples. "I can't believe I totally forgot about my weird wedding stalker. Maybe he gave up. It's been a couple of days since the last incident."

"Or, he's just waiting patiently for your response."

"The man isn't Ross. I'm one hundred percent certain."

They bumped down the rutted driveway. "You said you were positive he wasn't Ian or Dallas, either. Your stalker has to be one of them…unless you neglected to fill me in on another ex. Are there more suspects we should consider?"

"Really? You want me to tell you about every guy I've ever dated?"

"Only if you promised to marry them."

She scowled. "You're fully informed, then. How are we going to check on Ross's whereabouts?"

"I was thinking we could take a road trip to Sonoma."

"Why not just call him? Didn't Preston give you his number?"

"Yes, but if he's the one leaving messages, he's not going to admit it over the phone. We can ask his neighbors if he's been home the last few days, maybe check at the winery where he works. If he's been there the whole time, we'll check him off our suspect list."

When they hit a bump, she clutched the door handle. "Do you mind stopping in Fort Bragg on the way down? The lawyer said I have papers to sign. I might as well make the trip worth my time."

"I'm in no rush. We can drive your motor home and spend the night there, then go on to Sonoma tomorrow."

She turned to face him as he flipped on the blinker before merging onto the highway.

"Not that I don't appreciate the moral support, but how long do you intend to stick around the area?"

"Trying to get rid of me?"

"No, I just thought, after what I said last night…"

"I'd bail on you if there was nothing in it for me? In other words, if I'm not going to get laid?"

"No." She crossed her arms over her chest and hunched down in the seat. "Okay, maybe."

His eyes crinkled at the corners when he smiled. "You get points for honesty, and I guess I don't blame you."

When Scoop poked his head between the seats and whined, she scratched his ears, taking comfort in the soothing motion. "I'm probably going to regret asking, but why don't you blame me?"

"Your track record. Based on the men you've been involved with in the past, it's understandable you'd believe I have an ulterior motive. Dallas is a pathetic loser, and Ian is a paranoid nutcase. Ross sounds like a complete asshole. You sure know how to pick them."

Anger at his smug tone simmered in her gut. "Wow, that's a relief."

He slowed as they entered Shady Bend. "What is?"

"I was beginning to think I could get past your free-spirited outlook on life since you're so damned perfect in every other way, but this jealous streak isn't pretty."

The wheel jerked, and a horn blared as he swerved back into his own lane. "Jealous! You think I'm jealous? Of Dallas and Ian?"

"Either that or just plain mean."

The tires squealed as he turned down the road leading to the campground then blew by the entrance kiosk with a wave at the attendant. The SUV jolted down the track to the campsite. Claire bit her tongue. Tears stung.

Jed didn't look at her when he spoke. "If the truth about the men you've dated hurts…"

When he stopped with a jolt in front of her motor home, she threw open the door and leaped out. "Go to hell, Jed." Running the few steps to her RV, she stabbed the key into the lock. The door crashed open against the side.

"Might as well." His infuriating voice followed her. "It'd sure be a lot warmer than…"

Claire rocked to a stop in the doorway and pressed her hands to her chest but couldn't hold back a whimper. A white lace nightie lay draped across the bed. Candles burned on the shelf above it near a square, red envelope.

"Claire! What's wrong?"

Backing up, she missed the step and crashed to the ground. Pain stabbed through her ankle as Jed's arms closed around her. With a cry, she pressed her face against his chest and let the tears fall.

# Chapter 10

Jed handed Claire a cup of tea before sitting across from her at the table.

With shaking hands, she brought the mug to her mouth for a sip. "Thank you."

"You're welcome. How's the ankle?"

She stretched her foot, wrapped in an elastic bandage, out in front of her then rotated it slowly. "Better. I think it's just twisted not sprained."

"Good." Regret ate at him. If he hadn't been so damned rotten to her, she wouldn't have stormed into the motor home. God only knew why he'd pushed her so hard. Maybe he *was* jealous. Not of Ian and Dallas. *Hell no.* Maybe he was a little jealous they'd each had a shot with her, but she wasn't prepared to give him even that. After all, he was too *fun.*

Reining in his burgeoning temper, he forced a smile. "We should have someone look at the lock on the door. It must be faulty since I know I pulled it tight when we left. Coming home to these creepy gifts is getting a little old."

"You think making access to the motor home more difficult will stop this guy?"

Jed pushed a hand through his hair and glanced down at the nightgown, wadded into a ball and flung onto the floor—by him. If he'd found the idiot who'd left the damned thing when he searched the campground, he would have beat the shit out of him for making Claire cry. A sneaking suspicion he was responsible for a few of those tears ramped up his guilt, pissing him off even more.

"I don't know if the freak would quit or not. He's pretty persistent... not to mention desperate and pathetic."

Tea slopped onto the table. "He must have left the nightgown *minutes* before we got here. The candles had hardly melted."

"He probably didn't want to chance burning down the motor home. I bet he waited until he saw us coming to light them then bolted. Risky."

Jed gestured out the window. "He'd have about two minutes from the time he saw us enter the access road until we reached the campsite, barely enough time to slip out the door and disappear into the woods. He got lucky. By the time I carried you back into the motor home and went to look for him, he had a decent head start."

"I'm sorry." She leaned against the wall, her hands curled around the mug. "If I hadn't broken down the way I did—"

"You're entitled. Christ, Claire, give yourself a break. You've had a tough few days." He looked down and sighed. "Anyway, I'm the one who's sorry. I was an ass, and I apologize." His gaze rose to meet hers.

Wide eyes held shadowed remnants of pain. "Maybe I was overly sensitive. There's probably a lot of truth to what you said about Ian and Dallas. The thing is, I remember how they used to be." She sipped the tea then set down the mug. "You're right. My judgment when it comes to the opposite sex probably does suck."

Reaching across the table, he took her hand and linked their fingers. "Whatever they are, it isn't my place to criticize men you once cared about, and hurting you was inexcusable. Some of the things you said about me bit a little deeper than I liked, but it was petty of me to lash out in response."

Her grip tightened. "I didn't mean to hurt you, either. It's just that I'm starting to care about you...more than I should. It worries me."

"Claire—"

"Can we not talk about it right now?" Her gaze dropped. "I should read the card he left. I can't put it off forever."

His lips firmed. After a moment, he let go of her hand and stood. "I'll get it." Stepping over Scoop, who lay close beside her feet, he grabbed the red envelope off the shelf.

She took the damned thing from him and ripped open the flap. Her hands shook as she pulled out the card to open it. The front photograph portrayed bare legs—male and female—entwined on red satin sheets.

He leaned down to read over her shoulder. "What does it say?"

She glanced up. Anger flickered in her eyes, darkening the blue depths. "It says, *Think hard. Remember your promise. I can't wait for the honeymoon.*" Slapping the card shut, she threw it down on the table. "That's disgusting."

Jed drew in a deep breath and resisted the urge to put his fist through something. "Well, that's a little more direct than the other notes."

"I guess you were right about it being one of the men I dated. Still..."
She pushed the card away from her. "It's so unlike any of them to play
these kinds of guessing games."

"You said yourself Ian and Dallas have changed. We'll look up Ross.
Maybe he's changed, too. Maybe he's become the type of guy who gets
his kicks out of tormenting women."

"I guess anything's possible. Obviously one of them either morphed
into someone I don't even recognize, or he did a hell of a job hiding his
true personality back when we were together." She swung her legs out
from beneath the table and nudged Scoop out of the way. "Do you still
want to leave this afternoon?"

Jed glanced at his watch. "It's after two. By the time we eat a late lunch
then pack up and get out of here, it'll be too late to stop at the lawyer's
office. They'll be closed when we reach Fort Bragg."

"Let's drive straight through to Sonoma then. We can camp somewhere
around there tonight, check out Ross's alibi tomorrow morning then hit
the lawyer's office on the way back. Whatever it takes to find out who's
doing this to me."

"You think your ex-fiancé might be the one?"

She pushed a hand through her hair. "I don't know what to think
anymore. If it isn't Ross sending these insane messages and gifts, I'll
confront both Ian and Dallas. I don't care if they do think I'm crazy. I
want this to stop!"

Reaching down, he pulled her up off the seat. When she leaned against
his chest without protesting, he stroked the length of her back, rubbing
along her spine. "We'll find out who it is and end his game for good."

Her head came up, and her smile was strained as she met his gaze. "As
long as it isn't for better or worse."

He tilted her chin with one finger. "Good one. You still have your sense
of humor. This lunatic can't keep your spirits down for long."

Her jaw clenched. "No, he can't because I won't let him."

\* \* \* \*

The wipers slapped back and forth, brushing the drizzle from the
windshield. Jed slowed as they entered the Sonoma Ridge Campground.
Rain dripped from the trees. When a gust of wind rocked the motor home,
Scoop pushed his nose against Claire's leg and moaned.

"This is why I don't have a tent." She rubbed the fogged up window
with the edge of her sleeve then peered out. "The weather was beautiful
this morning."

"Well, it's miserable tonight. Sure you don't want me to call Kane? They have a nice, dry house we could stay in, and it's only about a half hour drive from here."

"I'm sure. Your brother might not care, but his wife probably wouldn't appreciate last-minute company on a school night. Didn't you say they have three girls?"

"Yes, but Rachel would just go with the flow."

Leaning back in her seat, Claire raised a brow. "Afraid to get wet in your leaky tent?"

"My tent doesn't leak, and I've camped in worse conditions. Anyway, we can have a relaxing dinner in your wonderfully dry RV." He grinned. "I'm not above making use of the amenities at hand."

"In that case, you can pay for your comfort by walking Scoop in this downpour."

He glanced her way. "Always working the angles."

"You're darn right. Stop. This looks like a good spot. The attendant said we could pick whichever one we want."

"I can barely see through the rain." He turned into the site and killed the engine. "Feels pretty level, at least."

"Good enough for one night." She unfastened her seatbelt and rose to her feet. "If you'll go register us and take Scoop with you, I'll cook. It's getting late."

"Sounds good. I'll hook up the electrical while I'm out there, so we'll have some light." He stood and inched around her.

Claire backed out of his way, but his chest still brushed against her breasts in the tight quarters. A tingle ran through her, starting near her heart and heading south. She drew in a breath. "Is soup and sandwiches okay? I can make chicken salad from leftovers."

"That's why I always cook extra." He rested a hand on her shoulder then squeezed. "Keep it simple. I know you're tired."

She nodded. "I've had better days."

After shrugging into his jacket, Jed flipped up the hood. "We'll both turn in early tonight. Let's go, Scoop."

Thunder rumbled as Claire pulled out a pan and set it on the stove. Searching through the cupboard, she chose a can of hardy minestrone and hoped Jed wouldn't be starving again an hour after their meal. The man ate more than she and her dog combined. While the soup heated, she shredded the leftover chicken, chopped a green onion and some pecans then mixed it with a little mayonnaise. When the overhead vent rattled in the wind, she juggled the loaf of wheat bread and dropped it on the floor.

"Pull it together, Claire." Her heart thudded in the silence. She bent to retrieve the bread then drew the curtain across the window over the tiny kitchen sink.

*No one's out there. My imagination is working overtime.* The internal pep talk didn't help. She was one big nerve stretched to the breaking point.

When the door opened on a gust of wind, she dropped the bread again and swore. The RV rocked as Scoop leaped inside then shook. Jed followed.

Snatching up the bread, she tossed it on the counter before grabbing the dog towel off its hook to dry her soaking wet pet. "That was quick."

"The minute Scoop peed, we came back." After Jed hung his dripping jacket, he took the towel from her to mop the floor and glanced up as he rose to his feet. "He wasn't any happier out there than I was."

"Thanks for taking him. The soup's hot, and your sandwich will be ready in a minute."

"Excellent." He made no move to take out a bowl, but stood inches away, his eyes filled with concern. "What's wrong?"

She let out a breath. "That stupid nightgown got to me. I can't seem to shake a bad case of heebie-jeebies."

One big hand caressed her cheek. "No one's here but us. Let yourself relax."

"I'm trying. The good news is my ankle feels fine, so I can run away from any monsters."

He snorted. "This guy isn't a monster. More like a joke. A real man would come right out and face you. This lame-ass is so afraid of rejection he's playing games instead, probably hoping you'll be intrigued. I honest to God don't think you have anything to fear from him. He's too much of a wimp."

"I hope you're right." She turned away to assemble the sandwiches. "Can we find something else to talk about? I don't have much of an appetite as it is, and speculating about my stalker isn't helping."

"Suits me." Filling two bowls with soup, he set them on the table then slid onto one seat. "Want to discuss the elephant in the room instead?"

Her lips tilted in a smile as she sat across from him then pushed the plate of sandwiches closer. "Are you calling my dog an elephant?"

He glanced at Scoop, sprawled in front of his empty food bowl. "This elephant is even bigger and more awkward. S-E-X."

The spoon clattered in her bowl. She choked on the bite of soup and gasped for air. It was several long moments before she could respond. "You want to talk about sex while we eat?"

He calmly chewed and swallowed. Apparently imagining the two of them heating up the sheets didn't twist his insides into knots the way it did hers.

"Might as well. We're both thinking about it." His gaze dropped from her face to her breasts and lingered. "At least I know I sure as hell am. I also know you have concerns, and I don't want to screw things up between us. So, maybe we should set a few ground rules. That way we won't have a repeat of our earlier—I don't even know what to call it. Discussion. Fight. Pissing contest."

She choked again and dropped her sandwich. Eating obviously wasn't going to be an option just now. "Pissing contest?"

He shrugged. "We both made a few comments we regretted in order to score points. Problem is the only thing we accomplished was hurting each other when all I really want is to make you happy."

"Goes both ways. Seems like you give and give and give—comfort, protection, advice. All I do in return is take. How lame does that make me?"

He frowned and set his sandwich back on the plate. "Is that the way you see our relationship?"

She nodded. "How else would I see it? You're still here because of me, because some psycho is scaring me, and you're too nice to leave me alone and frightened. I know I said your prime motivation in life is to have a good time, but you're also a compassionate and giving man."

"Oh, God, not the nice-guy label."

"Why not? It's true."

"I wasn't nice when I took a few verbal shots at your exes."

She swallowed a spoonful of soup, her appetite returning. "No, you weren't, but overall—"

"I'm a *nice* guy who likes to have *fun*." He crossed his arms over his chest. Muscles flexed.

Her gaze scanned over his chest and arms before she looked away. "That about sums it up." *A super-hot, nice guy who likes to have fun.* She forced the thought aside and took a bite of her sandwich.

"You are *so* off base. I'm not sticking around because I feel the burning need to protect you. That's something my brother would do. Not me. Anyway, as I pointed out, I don't think you're in danger. When this guy finally sucks up the courage to face you, you'll politely tell him to go away, and he'll go. He's shown no sign he's the violent type.

Wedding decorations aren't exactly the tokens of choice left by a serial killer, though the nightie puts a slightly different spin on things." When she opened her mouth, he held up a hand. "Since the whole situation is bothering you, I'm game to end it sooner rather than later by figuring out who the prankster is and confronting him. Anyway, my curiosity's roused. My money's still on Dallas, and I want to see if I'm right."

Lettuce and chicken scattered as she dropped her sandwich. "So, you're sticking around to solve *The Case of the Wimpy Wedding Stalker?*"

If her snarky remark angered him, he didn't show it. "I'm staying because I enjoy spending time with you. Or I would if you'd stop worrying about what I want. I don't want anything you aren't fully ready to give. Which leads me back to the original topic. Sex."

Confusion churned in her stomach. She pushed her bowl away and crossed her arms on the table. "What about it?"

"I think we're both so busy waiting for the inevitable to happen we've created this big cloud of tension. Not surprisingly, the result is an occasional thunderous outburst. In a normal dating situation, we'd get reacquainted in a less intimate setting." He waved an arm. "Spending so much time alone in close quarters..."

Her eyes narrowed. "You think because we're brushing up against each other every time we turn around I'm dying to rip your clothes off?"

White teeth flashed in a broad smile. "Are you?"

She shrugged. "Occasionally, but I have incredible self-restraint."

His shout of laughter roused Scoop from a deep slumber. Scrambling to his feet, the dog went into a barking fit.

Claire clamped both hands over her ears. "Scoop! Stop. You're going to disturb any campers stupid enough to be out in this pouring rain."

Jed glanced over when the dog finally quieted. "If I didn't know you were kidding..."

Standing, she cleared the table then dumped the remains of her sandwich into the trash. The soup bowls clattered into the sink. "I'm not."

"Huh?"

"Kidding. I'd be lying if I pretended I wasn't attracted to you."

"Claire..." When his voice came out in a rasp, he cleared his throat. "Are you saying—"

"No, I'm not. I don't start relationships based on hormones alone. You're right, though. This has been a rather intense reunion." Her chin dropped, and she tightened her grip on the dishrag. "What should have been a couple days of camping and hiking together has turned into a marathon week of emotional upheaval, at least for me."

He rose to his feet and rested his hands on her shoulders. With a deft movement, he spun her around to face him. She tossed the rag on the counter and met his gaze.

"If you're uncomfortable having me around, I'll leave. I never intended to push my way in where I wasn't wanted. I just assumed you were having as much fun as I was getting to know each other again."

Reaching up, she rubbed her thumb across the frown lines bracketing his mouth. "I've enjoyed our time together, probably more than I should have. I'm only uncomfortable because I know saying good-bye to you isn't going to be easy. Maybe I should quit anticipating future heartache and simply live in the present."

His clear blue gaze darkened. "That's not who you are."

"It's who I want to be—just this once."

"Claire…"

"I'm not going to send you out into the rain to put up a tent."

"Then I'll sleep on the floor."

"There isn't room down there for you and Scoop both."

He stroked her cheek, his fingertips rough against her skin. She shivered as a dart of need shot through her.

"Too bad for Scoop. The dog's comfort, or lack thereof, isn't a good enough reason to sleep together."

Her breath hitched in her throat. "You need a reason?"

"God, no. Wanting you has become an addiction. I can't get you out of my head."

Wrapping her arms around his neck, she stood on her toes to kiss him. "For tonight, that's reason enough."

# Chapter 11

They couldn't do it, could they? Claire was exhausted, emotionally and physically. Jed shifted, drawing her closer. She didn't feel tired. Anything but if the way she was kissing him back, her tongue twined with his, was an indicator. Warm. Willing. Woman.

A burning need to take what she offered consumed him. If he didn't do something—either stop while his brain was still functioning or carry her straight to the bed—he was going to self-combust.

With a moan, he tore his mouth away from hers. "We can't."

She nibbled tiny kisses along his jaw. "Want to bet?"

"Well, we *could*. Definitely no problem in that department." He focused on breathing as she nipped his earlobe. "I mean we *shouldn't*."

"Why not?"

His hands molded her firm ass through her jeans. He swooped in for another kiss. "I know there's a reason."

*Lord help me, I'm going to explode.*

He gritted his teeth. "I knew what it was a moment ago."

"We both want this."

"Well, no kidding. I want it so bad I hurt. Wait! That's the reason. You don't want to get hurt, and you're going to hate me in the morning if we do this." He released his grip on her ass and pressed fingers to his temples. "That's the reason we can't."

"I won't hate you." Claire grabbed his hands and held on tight. "I promise I won't. What I need tonight is emotional and physical contact with someone I care about—someone who cares about me."

"I care. You're incredible. If you'd just give us a chance…"

"What do you think I'm doing?"

He pulled one hand from her grasp and tilted her chin to look into her eyes. "Really? You're willing to risk getting involved with me even though I'm—"

"Don't say it." She pressed a finger to his lips. "I'm sorry I called you fun."

His heart thudded in a deafening rhythm. *This is going to happen. I'm going to make love to Claire.*

"Fun isn't all bad." He scooped her into his arms and carried her the entire two steps to the bed. "I'm going to show you the best time you ever had."

\* \* \* \*

Claire didn't doubt it for a moment. Sex with Jed would surely be better than anything she'd ever experienced in the past. If practice made perfect…she wouldn't think about all the practice he'd surely had.

He whipped back the spread and laid her on the bed then sat pressed close against her side. Without speaking, he slipped off her shoes to toss them on the floor. Big thumbs massaged the bottom of one foot then the other. Closing her eyes, she drifted on a wave of pleasure.

"Look at me."

"Hmm." Her lids flickered open.

"I want to see what you're feeling reflected in your eyes."

She was going to melt into the mattress. Could a man get any sexier?

With a minimum of effort, he pulled off her jeans and T-shirt then paused. His gaze slid down the length of her in an admiring sweep. "When we found the cake toppers in your underwear drawer, all I could think about was how you'd look in the pink ones." A long finger drew a line from the lacy strip of fabric between her breasts to the top edge of the matching barely-there bikini panties. "My imagination didn't do you justice."

Breathing was a challenge. When he stood, kicked off his shoes and then peeled his shirt over his head it became a near impossibility. Muscles rippled across his chest and abdomen beneath skin still tanned nut brown from a summer spent outside. When he dropped his jeans, her mouth dried up completely. Long, strong legs stretched upward to a pair of extended blue briefs. She tried to swallow and failed.

When she dragged her gaze up to meet his, he grinned. "Told you *could* wouldn't be an issue."

"I guess not." Her voice came out in a croak. "God, you're beautiful."

"Hey, that's my line." He sat again and caressed the slope of her breast. "Gorgeous and delicate and perfect in every way. I'm afraid I might break you."

"You won't. I'm flexible."

He groaned. "Like I needed to hear that to kick my imagination into overdrive."

Lying next to her, he pulled her into his arms and kissed her until she couldn't think, couldn't focus on anything but Jed and how he made her feel. Treasured. Special. Oh, so sexy.

She blinked twice, and the pink panties and bra were gone. He laid her back against smooth, cool sheets. The man braced above her had everything it took to heat them, and then some. When he tossed his briefs onto the floor, her heart stopped for a moment before racing like a champion sprinter headed for the finish line.

His biceps quivered as he held himself still and looked into her eyes. "You're sure?"

All she could do was nod as he trailed kisses down the side of her neck. When he licked the tip of one breast, she tensed. Was she sure Jed wouldn't smash her heart into little pieces somewhere down the road? No. Did she care? At the moment, not in the least. All she wanted was...

He sank into her, filling her soul. Wrapping her arms around his broad back, she held on, never intending to let go.

His lips touched her ear in a horse whisper. "Oh, God. Protection. I'm an idiot."

"I'm on the pill."

"Then..."

She turned her head and kissed him, her tongue twining with his. He tasted of need, pure and primal. Her whole body pulsed with the same urgent desire.

"We're good," she gasped. "If we were any better—"

He pushed hard then pulled back to surge forward again. Pressing her face against his shoulder she clung tight in anticipation as spiraling sensations carried her toward completion. In a burst of triumph that accompanied his long, low moan, she let herself spin out of control, falling into—love?

Heart hammering, she breathed deeply the musky scent of sex, tasted the tang of perspiration dampening his chest, relished the arms that tightened around her as a long exhale stirred her hair. A mixture of satisfaction and lingering desire fueled by the feel of him still buried inside her enfolded Claire. Was the excitement that brightened every day she spent with him really love? Or just a combination of old memories and compatibility along with a healthy dose of lust?

"You okay?"

She glanced up, meeting a lazy, satiated gaze. "Oh, yeah."

Jed rolled to his side, carrying her with him. "You aren't talking much."

She smiled. "Anything I say would give you a swelled head. Can't have that."

A chuckle rumbled in his chest. "I love your sense of humor…among other things." He surged inside her, and his expression turned sheepish. "Uh, it's been a while, and you are without a doubt the hottest, most irresistible woman I've ever met. Once isn't going to be enough."

Cupping his face in her hands, she kissed him, long and slow and deep. When they both came up for air, she pressed hard against him. "That, my friend, isn't going to be a problem."

\* \* \* \*

From the street, no sign of light showed behind the drawn blinds of Ross's dark gray bungalow style house as Claire stopped the motor home at the curb. A scattering of leaves had drifted across the brick walkway, and a pile of soggy newspapers littered the front porch. Down the block, the clang of metal against metal disturbed the early morning quiet.

"What an idiot. If McGregor planned to be gone for a while, he should have stopped delivery of his paper. Talk about an invitation to thieves."

She glanced over at Jed. "I wonder how long Ross has been away." Leaning out the open driver's side window, she craned her neck to get a better look at the neighboring houses. "The guy two doors down just put out his trash. We could ask if he knows."

"Let's check the papers first." After wrestling Scoop away from the door, Jed opened it then stepped outside.

"No, baby. You can't come." She gave her dog a commiserating pat before shutting the RV's door to follow Jed up the walkway.

Squatting, he sorted through the papers. "He subscribes to the *San Francisco Daily News*. The oldest ones should be on the bottom—oh, wow."

"What?" Putting a hand on his back, she leaned down. Beneath her fingers, muscle flexed as he shifted.

He held up a paper. "Check this out."

Squinting at the wet, faded ink, she frowned. "It's hard to read, but the issue is from early September. He's been gone a couple of weeks at least."

"I meant the lead story." He stabbed a finger at a photo of a young man with a direct gaze and a confident smile.

"*Assassin With Local Ties Pleads Insanity.*" Claire's brows shot up. "He looks more like a college kid than a killer. What about him?"

"This freak tried to kill Kane's sister-in-law. That's her byline."

"Grace Hanover?"

Jed nodded. "Kane helped take him down after the lunatic kidnapped her. Thank God the guy stalking you is someone you know and not a deranged maniac out for revenge."

Claire stepped back as he pushed to his feet. "Poor woman. She must have been scared to death."

A smile curved his lips, and his eyes took on a reminiscent gleam. "Knowing Grace, the assassin was probably more afraid of her than she was of him. The woman is a force of nature."

Something in his smile irritated the hell out of her. Claire crossed her arms over her chest. "I'm happy she made it out of the ordeal alive, but can we get back to business?"

"Huh?" His gaze focused, and he dropped the paper. "Oh, sure. Looks like good old Ross is a prime suspect. He sure hasn't been home in a while."

"Maybe he's on vacation in Hawaii or something."

"Let's go talk to the neighbor." He took her arm as they walked down the steps. "Careful. With all that rain, they look slippery."

Claire rolled her eyes. "I need help on wet steps, and Super Grace intimidates assassins. Perfect."

He stopped and turned to face her. "What the hell are you talking about?"

"Nothing." She bit her lip then forced out a breath. "Is she one of your ex-girlfriends?"

His forehead crinkled. "Who? Grace?"

She glanced away. "Forget it. Not my business."

His hand cupped her chin as he tilted her head upward to meet his gaze. Teeth gleamed in the dim morning light. "Jealous?"

"Should I be?"

"No, but it's nice to think you are. Now you know how I feel, tripping over all the men you used to date every time I turn around." He bent and touched her lips in a slow, lingering kiss. "For the record, Grace and I weren't involved other than a single make-out session at my brother's wedding. Besides, she's engaged, and her soon-to-be husband would probably have no trouble kicking my ass."

Claire smiled, relief washing through her. "Oh, yeah?"

"Yeah, he was a Navy SEAL who's kept in shape."

"Sounds hot."

Jed's laughter roared into the chilled air. He wrapped an arm around her shoulders to squeeze. "Hey, the neighbor's headed toward his car. Let's catch him before he leaves."

They hurried down the sidewalk, passed the RV from which muffled barking issued and turned into the driveway of a tan split-level.

A middle-aged man wearing an outdated suit and a harried expression moved away from his sedan and scowled. "Whatever you're selling, I'm not buying."

Claire stepped forward, giving Jed a subtle elbow. "We aren't selling anything, and we don't want to take up too much of your valuable time." She glanced up at the man through her lashes. "You look like you have somewhere important to go."

The irritation faded from his brown eyes. "I may have an extra minute or two. How can I help you, pretty lady?"

She quelled the urge to bat those lashes. "I'm hoping you can tell me where I might find Ross McGregor. We used to work together, and since I was in town, I wanted to surprise him." She let out a sigh and a self-deprecating laugh. "He's not home, so looks like the joke's on me. I don't suppose you know when he'll be back?"

The man scratched his head. "Ross has been gone for a couple of weeks. He mentioned taking a month's leave from work to deal with some old business. I'm not sure where he went, but I'm afraid you definitely missed him."

"Well, darn!" She ramped up the wattage of her smile another notch. "I guess I'll catch him next time I'm in town. Thanks so much for your help, uh…"

"Frank. You're welcome. Can I give him a message?"

Jed cleared his throat. "Just tell your neighbor his ex-fiancé isn't interested in games—or anything else. He'll understand."

"Uh, sure." He gave his keys a toss. "I have to get to work."

Claire stepped back. "No problem. Thanks, again."

Taking her arm, Jed led her down the driveway. "Old business my ass. Good thing I didn't bet any money on Dallas. Ross is my current favorite for pervert of the year."

She drew in a breath and glanced up as the sedan rolled by them. "I wouldn't have believed Ross was the one. He was always so direct about everything. Even cheating. He never tried to keep it a secret, just assumed he could do what he liked, and I'd sit back and take it." She kicked a branch downed in the previous night's storm and winced. "Jerk."

"I think I'll have a talk with McGregor. Lucky for us Preston gave me his cell number."

"You think he'll answer a call from an unknown number?"

"I'll leave an ambiguous message to rouse his curiosity if he doesn't."

She stopped beside the motor home door. "The one you left with his neighbor was pretty straightforward, even without giving my name."

"At this point, all I care about is stopping his harassment. I'll do whatever it takes to put your mind at ease again."

Warmth filled her despite the chill in the air. Maybe they hadn't vowed their undying love for each other the night before. There was also the issue of their different lifestyles, which had to be addressed if they were to have any kind of future together. Her stomach knotted just thinking about the complications of trying to make a relationship with him work. All she knew for certain was Jed cared. She'd hold onto the tenderness in his gaze when he looked at her and appreciate the way he couldn't stop touching her. It was enough. For now.

\* \* \* \*

The motor home was gone. *Shit!* Had Claire finished her story for *Rugged America* and left the area for good? He'd been counting on her to stick around indefinitely to wait for another Bigfoot sighting. Had he misjudged her on that front as well? At this point, it seemed obvious she had no intention of following through on the vow she'd made all those years ago. She'd ignored the nightgown the same way she'd ignored his other gifts. He lowered his head to his chest and closed his eyes. Knowing she'd forgotten her promise to him broke his heart.

He didn't like having his heart broken.

Giving his door a hard slam, he left the vehicle and strolled into the campground from the woods to avoid the attendant at the kiosk. Lafferty's SUV was still parked in the site they'd occupied, but his tent had been taken down. The man was nowhere around. Maybe Claire had left because she'd finally realized she had nothing in common with a jerk with no ambition and fewer prospects.

His mood lightened at the thought. Still, Lafferty would undoubtedly know where she'd gone. Once he had the information he needed, he'd simply revise his plan. After all, there was more than one way to skin a cat.

He checked the fire pit. Not a hint of warmth in the ashes. Hard to tell when that idiot had left the campsite. Maybe he hadn't bothered with a fire that morning. With a sigh, he headed back toward the woods to wait for the asshole's return. He'd stay out of sight and assess the situation before approaching him. Hopefully he wouldn't have long to wait.

Dropping down onto the rotted remains of a fallen tree, he massaged his temples. He'd thought for sure Claire would respond to the nightgown. She'd joked with him about her love affair with lingerie. He slammed his fist down on the log, and pulpy bark flew into the air. *Why didn't she remember?* Sometimes he wished he could simply forget her promise and move on. *Not likely.* No other woman had ever made him feel the way he did about Claire.

*What was that?* His chin snapped up as he peered in the direction of the road. The engine rumbled closer followed by a flash of blue and white. *Claire's motor home?* As he stood to move cautiously through the trees, relief surged through him when Claire's—*Thank God*—RV paused at the kiosk before turning into the campground.

*She's back.* He rubbed his hands together and sighed, anticipating that first glimpse of his one true love.

The rumble of the engine ceased. A moment later the door opened, and that monster dog shot through to land on the ground with a thump. Claire followed, hair gleaming in the late afternoon sunlight, her laughter echoing in the forest.

He frowned. Surely the dog wasn't that funny—*God damn it to hell and back!*

Lafferty jumped down without bothering with the step. Claire glanced up at him wearing a smile he didn't deserve. The asshole leaned in to kiss her.

Pain ripped through his chest. He couldn't breathe. Doubling over, he focused on drawing in air. After a few quick pants, he forced himself to look. The shithead had stepped away from her and was hunkered down doing something with a jack. Leveling the RV no doubt, so they could go back to staining the sheets. Lafferty stood to move forward then draped his arm around Claire's shoulders.

He closed his eyes but couldn't hold back a moan. The way they looked at each other had changed. The self-satisfied expression on the idiot's face made him want to beat the shit out of him. Claire was sleeping with the asshole now. That had to be it. The love of his life had betrayed him.

Straightening, he clenched his fist at his side. This changed everything! But he refused to be denied. He wouldn't give up. He'd *never* give up. All he had to do was adjust his plan.

Claire wouldn't know what hit her.

# Chapter 12

Jed turned the container of paint to read the label. "*Breezy Blue*. That's even dumber than *Aqua Swirl*. A breeze doesn't have a color."

"I like it. Cool yet comforting." Claire scribbled on the back of a sample card before adding it to the growing pile in her basket. "*Breezy Blue* is my top choice for the master bedroom. I'll try a few of the others, though, just to be sure they look the same on the walls."

He replaced the can on the shelf. "You're the one who's going to have to sleep in a room named after the wind."

"Don't complain. I let you talk me out of *Sunrise Burst* for the bathroom, didn't I?"

"It hurt my eyes, not to mention my sense of dignity."

She grinned as she moved down the aisle of the hardware store to some tan colors with undertones of pink. Thankfully, these didn't make him want to gag. Not that he had any real say in the matter of paint color. It was her house. Soon to be home. He was merely a temporary fixture in her life. Pressing a hand to his chest, he rubbed against the sudden pain.

It was past noon. The gnawing in his stomach must have migrated north. There couldn't be any other explanation for the hollowness behind his ribcage. At least not any he was willing to think about.

"I like *Sand Storm* for the living room. Pretty, don't you think, with that rosy glow?"

"Uh, sure. More weather related colors. You seem to have a theme going."

She leaned back against his shoulder as she held up two different samples in muted shades of green. "I do, don't I? Guess I should go with *Sea Mist* for the tower bedroom then."

A throat cleared behind them. Jed glanced to his left then tightened the arm around Claire and squeezed. "Look who's here. Hey, Dallas."

"Hey." The man took a step back and rubbed his hands down the front of the denim apron covering a gray shirt and jeans. "I was stocking shelves, but my clerk said you'd been back here a while. I was wondering if you needed some help."

When Claire pushed against his arm, Jed reluctantly released her.

"I'm choosing paint colors. Did you hear I inherited my great-aunt's house? I still can't believe it."

"Theresa mentioned it when I ran into her earlier."

Claire's eyes brightened. "She was almost as thrilled as I am that I'll be staying in the area. After we finished jumping up and down and squealing with joy like a couple of schoolgirls, she promised to line me up with a reliable contractor for the major repairs." She waved toward the racks of samples. "I'll handle painting myself."

Dallas glanced toward Jed. "Well, let me know if I can do anything to help."

"Actually, you can." Claire stepped around the cart and touched his arm. "Theresa told me if I set up an account and order the materials myself instead of having the contractor do it, I can avoid some extra costs."

"Sure. We just need to sit down together to fill out the form."

Jed glanced at his watch. "I thought we were going to go get some lunch."

"Do you mind waiting? Since we're here, I'd like to get this finished."

He let out a slow breath, knowing he was acting like a jealous idiot because she was being nice to one of her former boyfriends. *Time to quit being such a moron, moron.* "Of course not. I probably won't starve, though it may be close."

Her smile for him took some of the sting out of the one she turned on Dallas.

"Do you have an office we can use?"

The man nodded with unwarranted enthusiasm for the task at hand. Not that Claire seemed to mind. With his customary bitter expression replaced by one of good humor, Jed could almost see what had attracted her to the store owner when they were teens. Simms had a certain degree of appeal…at least he assumed a woman would find the combination of brawn and ardent fascination attractive.

"Uh, my office is kind of cramped…"

"No problem." Claire glanced over her shoulder. "Jed can pick out some more weather-related colors for me while we take care of the paperwork."

Dallas stared at her. "Huh?"

"Inside joke." She disappeared around the end of the aisle, chattering away to the football hero.

*Terrific.* At least Dallas wasn't the one stalking her. With a sigh, he turned back to the paint samples. Maybe he'd pick out a couple of colors he actually liked.

"Jed?"

Jerking around, he nearly knocked the cart filled with brushes and rollers into a stack of paint cans. Ian and Bart stood at the end of the aisle. Judging by their frowns, neither was thrilled to see him.

"How's it going?"

The beach boy zoologist crossed his arms over his chest. "Not that great. We had another tampering incident. Whoever has been messing with our equipment broke one of the mounts for a camera. We need a couple of new bolts to re-secure it."

Jed glanced between the two scientists. "You didn't catch the guy?"

Ian scowled. "No, but we will." Shoving his hands into the pockets of his cargo pants, he rocked back on his heels. "I'm surprised you're still hanging around the area."

"I'm helping Claire with some repairs to her great-aunt's house."

The man's gray eyes darkened. "I thought Claire finished her story and left for San Francisco. What're you talking about?"

Jed eyed the pair. Both seemed genuinely confused—or their acting skills were superb. Claire's stalker would know exactly where she was. One more reason to believe Ross was the one harassing her, not Ian.

"I guess the news hasn't spread to your camp yet. Claire got word from a lawyer that her aunt left her a house not far from here. The place needs some work, but she intends to move into it soon."

"I thought that old biddy died years ago." Ian's brows pinched. "When we were still...together...Claire mentioned the woman had stopped responding to her letters."

"There was a misunderstanding." Jed edged his cart down the aisle. "Good to see you both. I'll be sure to tell Claire I bumped into you."

"Maybe I'll offer my help with the renovations." Bart's smile flashed in his tanned face. "Since she intends to stick around, there's no reason she and I can't get together."

Maintaining a civil expression took an effort. *Overconfident ass.* "You have plenty of time to spare?" He couldn't resist a little dig. "No Bigfoot sightings?"

Ian grunted. "Not yet."

"Too bad. I'm headed up to the check-out line. See you around."

He escaped to the front of the store. When Claire didn't show while the clerk rang up her purchases, he pulled out a credit card to pay for them then carried the bags outside. Scoop greeted him with an enthusiastic round of barking while he loaded the supplies into the back of the SUV.

He patted the mutt's huge head. "Quite frankly, I'd rather spend time with you than any one of Claire's ex-lovers or current contenders for the title. That Bart guy is a definite player. I have a feeling if I turned my back for two seconds—"

"Talking to yourself or the dog?"

He smacked his head on the lifted rear door and swore loudly. Turning, he frowned at Preston. "Jesus, it's Grand Central Station around here."

"Oh, yeah?" Brown eyes gleamed with humor.

"Ian and Bart are inside buying replacement parts for more damaged equipment. They're pissed, so you may want to make yourself scarce."

The journalist shrugged. "What do I care? I didn't do it."

"Maybe not, but I doubt they'll take your word for it."

"I'm not afraid of a couple of squints." He leaned against the bumper. "Where's Claire?"

"Inside opening up an account. She should be out shortly."

"Did you track down Ross?"

"He's MIA. Interesting, don't you think?" Pushing the dog back into the cargo area, Jed slammed the door.

"You said before this guy is leaving Claire gifts. So, you think McGregor's the one?"

"I do."

Preston scowled. "I wonder why he's pursuing her now."

"I don't have a clue." Jed shook his head. "Neither does Claire. She's still having a hard time believing Ross is responsible."

He glanced toward the hardware store when the door opened. A man with a bushy brown beard carrying a box of nails exited.

"So, when do you two plan to leave the area?"

"Actually, Claire's staying. She inherited a house on the coast just south of here and intends to fix it up. That's why she's opening an account. I'll be around for a while, at least until we confront McGregor and stop his harassment."

"You're kidding?" Preston's brows shot up, disappearing into a mop of red hair. "A house on the ocean? Well, good for Claire."

"Yeah, she's pretty excited about it." Jed straightened as the door opened again and Claire emerged. "Here she comes now."

Preston raised a hand and waved. "Hey, lucky lady. Jed told me the news."

A smile flashed. "I'm still trying to process it. I went from homeless to homeowner in a blink." She met Jed's gaze. "The clerk told me you paid for my supplies."

"I wanted to get out of there. You can pay me back."

She nodded then turned to Preston. "Jed's a bottomless pit, and it's past lunchtime. Would you like to join us?"

"Sounds fun, but I have notes to compile since I'm still working on my story. We'll do it another time."

"Sure."

Preston strolled away, and Jed opened the passenger door for Claire. "Did you see Ian and Bart?"

She hopped up onto the seat then turned with a frown. "No."

"They were inside. More damaged equipment to repair, and they needed parts."

"Wow, Ian must be ready to explode."

"Neither of them was in a good mood…until I mentioned you were staying. Then Bart turned into Mr. Congeniality." Jed cranked the engine and accelerated out onto the street. "I have a feeling he'll be in contact with you soon."

Claire scratched Scoop's ears when the dog pushed his head between the seats. "Great. I'll put him to work painting. The more the merrier."

Whipping around a car trying to parallel park, he pulled up in front of the diner. "I'm pretty sure the only thing he's interested in painting is your naked body with whipped cream and chocolate."

"Jed!"

"What? The guy practically drools when he says your name."

She pushed the car door open, slid down from the seat then slammed it. "I think he has a bit more class than that."

With a snort, Jed walked around to her side. "Yeah, right."

As they approached the diner, his cell phone trilled. Pulling it from his pocket, he glanced at the display. "Hot damn. It's your ex-fiancé. Told you he wouldn't be able to resist responding to the message I left."

Claire's eyes widened. She stepped through the open doorway, paused beside the taxidermy bear then touched his arm. "What are you going to say?"

"I'm going to wing it. Hello."

"This is Ross McGregor. Are you the one who left me a message about an old girlfriend suing me for harassment? What the hell are you talking about? What girlfriend? Are you a lawyer? I swear I never—"

Jed cleared his throat. "Are you harassing more than one woman?"

"I'm not harassing *any* woman. Okay, maybe I shouldn't have told Bambi that when a man buys a lobster dinner and champagne for his date he expects a little something for his time and expense, but she's hardly an old girlfriend. Is that bitch the one behind this? What did she tell you? Jesus, can you blame me? Her name's *Bambi* for Christ's sake."

"You're a piece of work, buddy." His fist clenched around the phone. "What the hell did Claire ever see in you?"

Silence filled his ear as the seconds ticked by.

"Claire? Claire Templeton?"

"Were you engaged to another Claire?"

A long sigh whistled across the airwaves. "I haven't thought about Claire in a while. How is she?"

Bells clanged over the entrance as a young woman wrestled a stroller inside. Jed stepped closer to the bear and held the door wide. With a harried glance, the mother nodded her thanks before moving past them. When Claire took his hand, he followed her into the restaurant and sat at the same booth they'd occupied the last time. The greasy scent of burgers and fries made his stomach rumble.

"She'd be a whole lot better if you weren't leaving her a bunch of cryptic notes and idiotic gifts. What's your problem, jerk? She dumped your ass *years* ago."

"What're you talking about? Is someone threatening Claire?"

Uneasiness slithered through him. The man sounded genuinely bewildered. Either he was lying through his teeth or—

"Who the hell are you?"

"I'm a friend of hers." He lowered his voice as Augusta stopped beside the booth to smile a toothy grin and drop menus on the table. "We know you haven't been home in weeks. Where are you, McGregor?"

"You checked up on me?"

"You bet. Answer my question."

"I'm in Connecticut. My grandfather passed away, and I'm helping my mother settle his estate. It's a mess."

Leaning back, Jed pinched the bridge of his nose. *Shit.* "You can prove that?"

The man snorted. "I've spent the last two days in a courtroom. Hell, yes, I can prove it."

"Sorry to bother you. I guess someone else is responsible. Thanks for answering my questions."

"Don't hang up! Is Claire there? I want to talk to her."

With an eye roll, Jed handed her his cell. "He wants to talk to you."

The half-smile faded from her lips as she spoke. "Ross?"

While she talked, mostly in monosyllables, he pretended to study the menu. When the waitress approached, he dropped it on the table to glance over at his companion. Her hair hung across her cheek as she faced the plate glass window overlooking the street. With a hand that wasn't quite steady, she tucked the strand behind her ear and mumbled something.

Augusta cleared her throat. "You ready to order, hon?"

"Sure. Bring us a couple of burgers and—"

Claire turned with a frown. "No burger. I'll have the broccoli soup." She pushed the menu toward the edge of the table. "And an iced tea with lots of lemon." Her chin dipped. "I have to go, Ross. Honestly, I'm fine. Thanks for your concern, and I'm sorry about your grandfather. You, too. Bye." She clicked the phone off then held it out. Her lips pinched tight.

His gaze held hers as he took the cell before glancing up at the waitress. "I'll have root beer with my burger, cooked medium, and fries."

"Cheese on that?"

"Of course."

"I'll be right back with your drinks." Augusta scooped up the menus and moved away.

He touched her hand. "You okay?"

Claire nodded. "It was strange talking to him again. He sounded exactly the same."

"The guy doesn't have much respect for women. Dumping him was the right move."

"Thanks for not saying what you're really thinking." She sighed. "I know what an idiot I was to get involved with him. At the time, Ross's interest was flattering. I was young and still pretty naïve. It took me a while to realize what a complete ass he was since he was the exact opposite of Ian. Ian may have his faults, but at least he's genuine."

"You figured out McGregor was a user before it was too late. That's what matters." He pulled his gaze away from her troubled eyes and smiled when the waitress delivered their drinks. "Thanks, Augusta."

"You bet, hon. Your food will be ready shortly."

Jed sipped his root beer. "You know what this means, don't you?"

"Hmm." Claire squeezed a lemon slice into her glass then dropped it on a napkin. "What?"

"Ross didn't leave the wedding paraphernalia."

"I told you guessing games weren't his style."

"Which means either Ian or Dallas is guilty."

Her hand jerked, sloshing the tea. "Damn."

"We need to confront them. Individually. It's time to end this."

She lifted her gaze to meet his, piercing and direct. "Past time. Let's go do it."

His nose twitched as Augusta approached carrying their lunches. "Just as soon as I eat my burger."

# Chapter 13

"We missed Dallas by fifteen stinking minutes." Claire pried the lid off the paint can and frowned into the swirling blue depths. "He left for a three-day hunting trip with one of his buddies right before we got there."

Theresa leaned against the window sill with arms crossed. "Good. Dallas needs to have a little fun."

"Not good. I wanted to settle this whole stalker thing, damn it."

Her old friend gave her a commiserating look. "Okay, the timing for the trip could have been better. Did you question Ian?"

Using a flat stick, Claire stirred the paint. Some slopped over the side. "No, he and Lee are camping out in the woods for a couple of nights. After they finish repairing the damaged equipment along the perimeter of their observation area, they're pushing deeper into the forest to look for any signs of Bigfoot occupation. I got the impression it's a last-ditch effort before they admit defeat and pack up to leave." She poured a stream of shimmering blue into the roller pan. "Oh, Bart may be by later today to help. Do I need to give you another rundown on who's who in the Bigfoot camp?"

"I think I can keep them straight. How does Jed feel about Bart hanging around to work on the house? The way you described him, he sounds kind of sexy."

"Uh, Jed missed that part of the conversation. He was chasing after Scoop, who was terrorizing the wildlife. Thank God it turned out to be a rabbit and not something that would have fought back. By the time Jed saved the poor little bunny, Margaret had arrived and was spouting off about something or other, and I forgot to mention Bart's offer."

Theresa snorted. "Forgot?"

"Okay, I chose to withhold that piece of information in the interest of avoiding an argument." She ran a roller across the pan. "Jed thinks Bart has the hots for me."

"Does he?"

"Yep. No doubt about it." Standing, she applied fresh paint to the wall. "Hmm. That looks nice." When Theresa didn't answer, she looked over her shoulder. "Are you going to help me paint or watch?"

"Help." She checked her cell before shoving it into the pocket of her pleated trousers. "I have an hour before I need to leave to pick up Shelby. Do you have another smock? I don't want to get my good blouse dirty. I was showing property earlier and didn't have time to change."

"There should be one in that box." Claire pointed then turned to re-apply the roller to the wall. "Pretty, don't you think?"

"Absolutely. There's a hint of silver in the blue that adds a nice glimmer. Speaking of Jed, where is he?"

"We ran out of tape, so he went to get more. I think he was glad to have an excuse to escape the tedium of masking off windows. He mumbled something about taking Scoop down to the beach for a run afterward."

"I thought you were replacing all the windows."

"Eventually. There are other more pressing projects, and I'm not sure how far my budget will stretch. In the meantime, I don't want to look through paint-splattered glass."

"I don't blame you. Are you staying here now? I noticed your motor home parked outside."

Claire nodded and rolled on more paint, satisfaction mounting as the wall turned from off-white to silvery blue. "We checked out of the campground. No point in wasting money. Plus, this is more convenient. I'm not planning to sleep in the house until we finish most of the interior work, but we can use the shower."

Theresa tucked a strand of dark hair behind one ear as she started on the adjacent wall. "Is Jed a permanent fixture? I didn't realize your relationship was so serious."

Claire's hand stilled. "Permanent is overstating the situation. I'm not sure how long he's staying."

"Aren't you two—"

"Yes." Hunching one shoulder, she painted a little faster. "I knew going in he'd take off eventually."

"Oh, sweetie. I'm sorry."

The sympathy in her friend's voice made her eyes smart. After some rapid fire blinks, she forced a matter-of-fact tone. "My choice, and completely my fault if I get hurt."

"Maybe he'll stay."

"Doubtful. Jed isn't big on commitment."

"He seems to like you more than a little. When you're around, I might as well be invisible for all the notice he takes. In my opinion, the man has some serious feelings for you."

Claire set the roller in the tray then hauled the ladder she'd borrowed over to the wall. After climbing up a couple of steps, she swore before reversing direction to grab a paintbrush. She'd edge around the top of the window frame with a steady hand if it killed her.

"He does care about me, but that doesn't mean he's looking for a long term relationship."

"Is that what you want?"

She drew in a breath then released it slowly. "I guess it is. I'm just not sure Jed is the right man to invest my time in, no matter how good he is in bed."

Theresa sputtered and coughed. "Oh, my."

"That's not the only thing I like about him. He's funny and sweet, and his toleration for my dog has grown into an actual bond. Scoop's going to miss him, too."

"Then why shouldn't you dive into the relationship headfirst and convince him to stay?"

She pressed her lips together. "Honestly, he's kind of a flake about the future. The man lives in the present. Period. I'm a planner, so I fear we'd end up clashing in the long run."

"Compromise is a beautiful thing. You should try it."

"I will—if we ever get to that stage. Right now, we aren't even close. What we have together is more like vacation sex."

Theresa glanced over and frowned. "Are you sure about that? The way he's pitched in to uncover the identity of your stalker shouts serious boyfriend more than casual fling."

After climbing off the ladder, Claire set down the brush and picked up the roller again. "Like I said, he...cares. The L word has *not* been mentioned."

"You have plenty of guts, my friend. Take a risk. If you have strong feelings for this man, tell him. His response just might surprise you."

\* \* \* \*

Jed gave the stick a hard toss then stuffed his hands in his pockets to follow the galloping dog down the long stretch of sand. Drawing in a breath of salt scented air, he turned his face up to the weak sunlight filtering through a layer of clouds. This was why he worked outside. If you could call what he did work. He'd been told by more than one irritated woman that his life was more suited to an adolescent than an adult. What did they know? After spending an endless morning taping off windows, he remembered exactly why he'd quit the construction business. Life was too short to spend half his waking hours doing something guaranteed to bore him into a coma.

Even for Claire. And damned if he wouldn't do almost anything for her. Except get a soul-sucking, nine-to-five job. Not that she'd asked him to, but he could see the direction they were headed.

When Scoop skidded to a stop in front of him and dropped the chunk of driftwood, he stooped to pick up the stick then tossed it with all his strength. He wasn't sure which would be worse, walking away from Claire…or staying. So instead of committing either way, he was doing what he did best, avoiding a hard choice and going with the flow. For now, indecision was working.

When his cell trilled, he pulled it from his pocket and checked the display. Kane. His lips curved upward as he answered. "Shouldn't you be working? Or are you so good crime has taken a vacation in Vine Haven?"

"Smart ass. For your information I spent the morning busting a bunch of pot growers. One of them even took a shot at me. Luckily, his aim was off, and the bullet just nicked my arm."

Jed faced the endless stretch of sea and pushed an unsteady hand through his hair. "Jesus. Are you okay?"

"I'm fine. Rachel was a little upset, threatened to shove a hot poker up the guy's ass."

Snorting with laughter, he reached down for the stick Scoop dropped then threw it. "Good for your wife."

"Rachel insisted I call you and Dad, even though the wound is no big deal."

"I'm glad you did. How is he, by the way?"

"Same as always. Dad mentioned he hadn't talked to you in a while."

"I'll call him. I've been…distracted."

"Why don't you head down the mountain for a visit? Dad would appreciate the company, and I can't get away from work right now."

Up the beach, the dog ran full speed at a flock of seagulls gathered around something dead. The birds squawked their displeasure before taking flight. Jed turned away.

"I'm not at home. I'm still on the coast up in the redwoods."

"Oh? I thought you headed north weeks ago."

"I did. Then I ran into an old friend and decided there really wasn't a pressing reason to hurry home."

"Let me guess." Humor laced his brother's words. "An old *female* friend."

"Well, duh. Why would I stay for a dude? Actually, she asked about you. Do you remember Claire Templeton?"

"Doesn't ring a bell. Wait. The little girl who lived across the street from us when we were kids? That Claire?"

"She grew up feisty and hot. Getting reacquainted has been great."

"Hmm."

"What? Jesus, you sound like your wife when you do that."

"Nothing. I'm glad you're enjoying yourself." There was a brief silence before Kane spoke again. "Have you thought about what you're going to do for work after the winter is over?"

"That's months from now. I'll figure out something."

Even over the noise of waves slapping against the sand, he could hear his brother's teeth grinding.

"It wouldn't kill you to plan ahead once in a while."

"I don't know. It might."

"You're in rare form. What the hell's wrong with you? I'm the one who got shot today."

Taking a deep breath, Jed let it out slowly. "I spent the morning up to my eyeballs in masking tape and paint. Helping out a friend for a few days is fine, but it's not what I want out of life."

"Who said it should be?"

After picking up the stick Scoop dropped, he chucked it into the water then swore as the mutt launched into the waves. Terrific. Now he'd have a wet dog on his hands.

"No one. I don't know. I guess I'm feeling pressured."

The seconds ticked by. "Jed, is this about Claire?"

"No. Yes." He closed his eyes and pinched the bridge of his nose. "Maybe. I care about her, but she isn't interested in a bum like me."

"You're not a bum. Exactly."

He rolled his eyes. "Gee, thanks."

"Back when I was still working in San Francisco, I can't even count the number of times I wished I had your life. Then I found Rachel and made some major adjustments."

"I'm glad. You were miserable, but I'm not. I love the way I live."

"It's been fine up until now, but your circumstances have changed. Don't you think maybe you should change with them?"

Scoop dropped the chunk of driftwood on his foot then shook. Icy drops of water sprayed Jed's face. He winced and swore. The dog was a royal pain in the ass.

"Jed, what's going on?"

His brother's voice intruded on his thoughts.

"Nothing. Absolutely nothing. Look, I appreciate the advice, but I am who I am. I can't change for a woman."

"I guess not. Look, I have to go. Are you going to be okay?"

"I always am."

"Maybe that's the problem."

The phone went dead. With a snort, Jed stuffed it back into his pocket. Kane thought he was so smart just because he had his life together. Maybe he envied his brother's happiness a little, but that didn't mean he wanted what Kane had.

Did it?

\* \* \* \*

"It's okay, Bart. Honestly. I know work comes first." Pressing the phone to her ear with her shoulder, Claire sprayed the paint roller with the hose and eyed the SUV bumping along the driveway.

"I said I'd help, and I meant it. Maybe tomorrow…" His smooth voice trailed off.

"I'm not sure if I'll be painting tomorrow. I have a call in to my editor about a new story idea, and I may need to follow up on that. How about if I contact you?"

"Sure. We should be here for a few more days at least to wrap things up and take down the camp. I'd like to get together again."

The man was nothing if not persistent. "Thanks, Bart. I need to go, but I'll be in touch." She pocketed the cell, dropped the roller into the pan then braced herself as Scoop leaped from the now stationary SUV to race across the weedy lawn. His greeting knocked her on her butt.

"Sorry about that."

She shoved the dog off her and glanced up into Jed's sparkling eyes. "You don't look sorry."

He held out a hand. When she grasped it, he hauled her to her feet. "Shouldn't you call him a bad boy for jumping on you?"

"I tried that for six months. All it did was make both of us miserable, but not miserable enough for Scoop to change his habits." She stood on her tiptoes to give him a kiss that lasted longer than she'd intended. She drew in a ragged breath as she stepped away.

"I guess you can't teach an old dog—or a stubborn, young one— new tricks."

"Looks that way, doesn't it. You were gone quite a while."

"Did you miss me?" He wrapped an arm around her shoulders and squeezed.

She leaned into his side, letting his warmth take away the chill of the encroaching fog. "Theresa kept me company, but yes, I did miss you. With your height, painting the ceiling in the master bedroom would have been a whole lot easier."

He pressed a hand to his chest but couldn't hide a grin. "I'm wounded."

"I bet." Her nose wrinkled. "What's that smell?"

"Probably me. Your dog rolled on a dead fish at the beach, and it was quite a tussle getting him washed off. He still needs a bath, and I need a shower."

"Lucky for you the hose is already out. I'll get you some dog shampoo."

"Oh, joy."

"I'm not the one who took him to the beach instead of painting." She smiled up at him. "Just to show what a good sport I am, I'll make dinner while you get cleaned up. Right after I put away the painting supplies."

"All right. Deal."

Claire took two steps then stopped and turned. "Is everything okay?"

"Sure. Why wouldn't it be?"

She shrugged. "I don't know. You seem kind of quiet. I expected more of an argument over giving Scoop a bath."

"I don't mind."

Little lines radiated from his eyes, and the smile curving his lips seemed strained.

"Look, you don't have to help me paint if you don't want to. This is your vacation, after all. You should spend it having fun."

He shoved his hands into his pockets. "I'll survive a few days of painting."

She took another step then hesitated. "I'm not trying to domesticate you. I'm fully aware it would be a colossal waste of time."

"So, you're not even going to make an attempt?"

Her brows pinched. "Do you want me to?"

"No." He let out a breath. "Don't mind me. I'm in a mood. Kane called a while ago to tell me he was shot."

"What?" Turning, she rushed back to lay a hand on his arm. "Oh, my God, is he okay?"

"Just a flesh wound. Still, it cemented my long held belief that life's short. We should do our best to enjoy the time we have."

Dread filled her, and her stomach clenched. Something in his eyes… she swallowed and forced herself to speak. "What are you trying to say?"

"I don't know. Nothing." He clasped her cheeks between his palms then bent to kiss her. A quick brush of the lips. "I'm no philosopher. Get me that shampoo, and I'll go wash the dog."

The breath left her in a whoosh. Maybe she was imagining problems where none existed. Maybe Jed wasn't regretting that they were still together, or thinking about ending it. One thing was certain, she would ignore Theresa's well-intentioned advice. Now wasn't the time to tell him how she was really feeling because she was pretty certain a declaration of love—or a strong leaning toward that overrated emotion—would push him right over the edge and out of her life.

"Claire?"

"Huh? Oh, right, dog shampoo. I'm going."

She practically ran to the motor home. Anything to escape a possible confession that would surely break her heart.

# Chapter 14

"I have to drive down to San Francisco." Claire set her phone on the table next to her half-eaten breakfast and frowned. "My editor wants to discuss the proposal I e-mailed her."

Jed swallowed the toast he'd just bitten into. "Seems like she did plenty of talking while your eggs got cold."

"We discussed the fact that my last piece was about redwoods instead of Bigfoot. Louise is bummed I didn't get the photo of a lifetime." She picked up her fork. "Not half as bummed as I am. Still, we haven't had a face-to-face conversation in months, and she has some concerns about the scope of the new story. I don't mind a quick trip to the city."

"What exactly is this new project?"

"Creatures from the sea." She pointed out the motor home window toward the gray expanse of ocean. "The view from here inspired me."

"Are we talking seals or mermaids?" Jed took another bite, his eyes bright with curiosity. Leaning back, he wiped his mouth with a napkin.

She tore her gaze away from mobile lips—*damn the man was kissable*—and cleared her throat. "Uh, sea lions, walruses, sea otters... normal sea animals."

"Mermaids would be more interesting."

"Not to mention harder to photograph. I've been down that road once already, and I'm not going back."

"You're no fun."

"That's not what you said last night."

The blue of his eyes deepened. "Those types of comments will get you nothing but trouble."

Heat crept up her neck. "We don't have time for any more *trouble*. I have to hit the road."

"Can I come with you?"

"You'd rather drive than paint?"

He snorted. "No contest. Anyway, the trip doesn't have to be all about work. We can have an evening out after your meeting. I could go for something a little more glamorous than Ralph's Diner for a change."

She glanced up from poking at rubbery eggs. "You mean I get to dress up?"

"Sure. I may have packed something other than jeans and T-shirts."

Standing, she dumped her plate into the sink. "A real date. Imagine that. Go do whatever it is you need to do so I can get ready. Now I'm excited."

He rose to his feet and paused beside the door. "Let's take my car and spend the night in a hotel. It'll be a nice break from the motor home."

Turning, she grabbed him by the shoulders and stretched up to place a smacking kiss on his lips. "Better watch out or I'll start thinking you're civilized."

When barking erupted in the yard, he glanced out the window. "Your dog must have treed another squirrel."

She slapped her forehead. "Well, damn. What're we going to do with Scoop? Hotels don't usually want dogs his size."

"Would your friend take him overnight?"

"Maybe. I'll call her. Go. I need to dress and pack."

His expression turned serious as he ran a thumb across her cheek. "You deserve to be treated like a queen. It's about time I stepped up." Backing away, he opened the door. "I'll go take the mutt for a run. See you in a few."

When Theresa didn't answer her cell, Claire called her home phone and spoke to her teenage daughter who assured her she would love to watch Scoop. Hoping her friend would be half as enthusiastic about the arrangement, she promised to drop him off on the way out of town. After cleaning up the breakfast dishes, she packed, then dressed in a pair of slim-fitting pants and a lilac blouse, added a dash of makeup and smiled at her reflection in the mirror on the back of the closet door. Cool and professional for the meeting with her editor who'd agreed to come in on the weekend, but still comfortable for the drive.

The smile faded. As much as she appreciated Jed's efforts to plan an evening out, something felt a little off. Almost as if he were creating a few special memories to soften the blow when he walked away. She gave herself a mental shake, determined not to second guess his every move. She'd simply enjoy the day and the company.

The door squeaked open as the man she couldn't get out of her thoughts poked his head inside. After a slow perusal, he smiled. "You look really nice. Ready to go?"

*Nice?* With an eye roll, she turned back to the mirror. "Just about."

"I unloaded all the camping equipment and put it in the house. What about the dog?"

"We'll leave him with Theresa."

"Great. I locked up after dumping my gear. I'm ready whenever you are."

Knowing Jed's penchant for driving with the windows down, she took another moment to secure her hair in a gold clip then grabbed her purse, computer case and overnight bag before locking the door behind her. She tossed the luggage in the back of the SUV beside Scoop and moaned. "Damn, I forgot his food and bowl."

"I got them while you were messing with your face. The leash, too."

She hitched herself up onto the seat and slammed the door. "You really are handy to have around. Thanks."

"I do have my uses." He started the engine, lowered the gear shift, and they bumped down the driveway.

"One more expense. Filling in the pot holes. Turn left at the highway. Theresa lives on Elm Street just this side of town." They rode for several minutes in companionable silence. When Scoop pushed his head between the seats, Claire reached up to stroke his ears. "Shelby promised to take him for a walk after she gets home from volleyball practice. I hope he won't miss us too much."

"I think the dog will survive. Is that the right street?"

"Yep, it's the fifth house on the left, the green one with the fenced yard."

Jed pulled into the driveway. While she let Scoop out of the car and opened the gate, he retrieved the food and bowl. "Where should I put this stuff?"

"I guess by the door. Theresa must be working since her car isn't here." Claire gave the dog a hug and was rewarded with a slobbery lick. "Be a good boy. I'll see you tomorrow."

When the latch clicked into place, Scoop barked and lunged against the fence.

She bit her lip. "Maybe—"

"He'll be fine. Let's go."

With a final backward glance, she climbed into the vehicle. "He'd better stop barking, or the neighbors are going to complain."

"They'll get over it." Reaching across the center console, he squeezed the hand clenched on top of her thigh. "Sit back and relax. Today is about enjoying ourselves."

"Yeah, I guess it is." She smiled. "I promise not to stress over my dog."

Once they were back on the highway, he turned the radio on low and picked up speed. "Classic rock okay with you?"

"That's what I usually listen to."

"Good thing. If you'd asked for country, I might have had to kick you out of the car."

Claire grinned. "It's nice to know where your breaking point is."

"I don't live with a lot of rules, but a man has to draw the line about music." He gave her a quick glance before returning his attention to the road. "Let's hear all about your story proposal."

"Mostly it's about making my life easier. With the whole remodel project certain to occupy the majority of my waking hours, I thought I'd try to stick close to home." She waved a hand toward the west. "I can get a lot of photos of the marine animals I'll need right in my backyard, so to speak. For a fresh angle, I plan to incorporate photos of lighthouses into the piece with quirky facts about each. That'll require some travel, but there are several cool ones within a day's drive."

"Sounds interesting. What're your editor's concerns?"

"She wants to discuss a more in-depth story focusing on a single lighthouse. I think my idea would be more visually stimulating. Less writing required, too, and that's always a plus for me." When he rolled the window down a couple of inches, she tucked a blowing strand of hair behind her ear. "Including photos of sea mammals is a no-brainer. Our readers love animals of every shape and size. Louise was ecstatic about the bear cub photo I took. It almost made up for not getting a picture of a Bigfoot—preferably autographed by the creature and certified as authentic."

Jed snorted. "Bet if you'd asked Bart nicely he would have put on a costume and then sworn out an affidavit declaring it the real deal."

She put her head back and laughed. "Now why didn't I think of that?"

"You don't have a devious mind. I do. I imagine the idea of a fake is looking pretty good to your buddy, Preston, about now. His boss must be getting pissed he doesn't have a story yet."

Claire frowned. "Poor Preston. Nothing ever seems to work out for him."

"The whole Bigfoot retreat was a bust for everyone involved." He patted her knee then left his hand on her thigh. "Except for you. You were smart enough to change the focus of your article and make the most of the situation. I admire the hell out of you for that."

A jolt of heat shot straight up her leg to her core then spread outward like molten fire. The breeze coming through the window couldn't begin to cool her hot cheeks. With an effort, she focused on his words.

"Thanks. I may be an optimist, but I'm not stupid. I know when it's time to cut my losses."

The fingers on her thigh tightened. "I'm sure you do." With a final squeeze, he released her. "Do you think you can talk your editor into seeing your point of view about the lighthouses?"

"I always have in the past. I'm not too worried about it."

He let the subject drop, and they rode in silence, music filling the car's interior as the miles rolled away. Something seemed to be on Jed's mind, but he wasn't talking about it. Every subtle attempt on her part to draw him out was met with a pleasant change of subject.

Her lips firmed. Maybe sledgehammer tactics would produce better results. Not that she was at all certain she wanted to know what he was thinking. Still, she'd never been one to hide from reality. "What's bugging you? Spill it."

"Huh?"

"You've been like a dog with a bone since yesterday. Well, not my dog. He chomps them down in no time. More like one of those fluffy little toy dogs, nibbling around the edges of a giant femur."

He turned and stared.

"Jed!"

A horn blared.

With a jerk, he swerved back into his own lane. "Sorry. I wasn't trying to kill us. I was trying to wrap my mind around your analogy." His brows nearly met above his nose. "Are you calling me a poodle?"

"If the rhinestone collar fits…"

"Aren't you the funny one. Do you want to explain what the hell you're talking about?"

"Ever since you returned with the masking tape and smelly dog yesterday, you've been lapsing into sullen fits. Whatever's on your mind obviously isn't pleasant. Are you sick of hanging out with me?"

"What? No. Why would you think that?"

"What should I think? You sure aren't talking. Have I done something you don't like—other than ask you to paint?"

"Of course not." Pressing down on the accelerator, he blew by a semi on a straight stretch of highway. "It's not you. It's me."

"Oh, my God! Are you kidding? Do people really say that?"

He pulled back into the right-hand lane before turning with a frown. "Say what?"

"What do you think? *It's not you. It's me.*" She rolled her eyes.

"It *is* me. Kane made some comments about my lack of gainful employment and easy come, easy go lifestyle. Hell, he did everything but tell me it was time to grow up." His fist smacked against the steering wheel. "What my brother said—or didn't say—has been bugging me."

"Oh." She hunched down in the seat. "I feel like an idiot."

"Why would you feel like an idiot? You have a real job. Well, sort of." He grinned. "Actually, taking pictures for a living isn't your average nine-to-five, nose-to-the-grindstone employment either."

"I'm a fool for making *your* mood all about *me*. A little self-obsessed, don't you think? As for my career, I spent years paying my dues to get to this point. Who says work has to be nine-to-five to be real?"

"You know what I mean. You've made a few comments about my penchant for having fun."

"True, but I wasn't implying anything negative about how you make your living. Work *should* be fun." She shrugged. "If I had to describe you in five words, settled or stable wouldn't make the list. Fun would. So would interesting, charming and helpful."

"That's only four words. What's the fifth?"

"Hot. Definitely hot."

His gaze met hers and held. By the time he looked away, heat had crept up her neck to bloom in her cheeks. She rolled down her window.

"Stable is overrated. Unless you need a place to put a horse." Jed tapped the steering wheel.

Claire let out a breath. "I'm beginning to think you're right."

"Kane has my best interests at heart, but he should mind his own business. That's what I'm going to tell him the next time I see him." He sat up a little straighter and jetted around a slow moving camper, sliding back into his lane just ahead of a string of oncoming traffic.

She pried her fingers off the door handle. "Speaking of horses, I should wear blinders like they do when I travel with you."

His brows shot up. "Why?"

"You drive the way you live your life—on the edge."

"You're perfectly safe. My judgment and reflexes are excellent." His voice softened. "I'd never do anything to hurt you."

She pressed one hand to her chest. "I hope not."

\* \* \* \*

Jed strolled down the beach with his hands stuffed in his pockets, missing…Scoop. God, something must be wrong with him. Still, almost everyone on this stretch of sand had a dog tugging at the end of a leash except him, making him the odd man out. He'd never had a problem with his own company in the past. Why now? Maybe it was the thick fog putting a damper on his mood since he had no other conceivable reason for feeling lonely. He'd only dropped Claire off a half-hour ago, for Christ's sake.

When an ugly mongrel raced toward him, barking enthusiastically, leash trailing behind him, he stopped and crouched down to pet it. Something about the droopy ears and long snout struck a chord...

"Wylie?"

The dog sniffed his hand. Glancing up, he scanned the scattering of afternoon strollers. A woman in running shorts and a T-shirt with a wind breaker tied around her waist jogged toward him, a smile lighting her bright green eyes.

He stood and held out his arms. "Grace!"

"Fancy meeting you here." Kane's sister-in-law hugged him back before stepping away. "If you were going to be in town, why didn't you call?"

"Last minute decision. Anyway, I never know if you're here or in Seattle, but I'm glad we ran into each other. Or rather, Wylie ran into me." He grinned. "I swear that dog gets uglier every time I see him."

She scowled before a wide smile slipped out. "Yet for some reason he still likes you. What're you doing on the beach all by yourself?"

"Killing time before I pick up a friend. We're going out to dinner later. You and Travis should join us. You'll like Claire."

Grace rubbed her arms and shivered. "Has hell frozen over? You're offering to introduce *family*—okay, extended, almost family—to a woman? I thought you were as bad as I used to be about mixing relatives with pleasure."

"Your sister marrying my brother doesn't make us related."

"If we see each other on holidays, it's close enough. Sure, let's do it. I'd love to meet this woman. Travis and I don't have plans, and I could use a night off from wedding preparation." She pressed both hands to her head and moaned. "Tell me my mother won't disown me if we elope. If I have to listen to one more conversation about centerpieces and veils and china patterns, I may shoot someone. Namely, myself."

He shook his head and laughed. "The very reason I've never been foolhardy enough to propose to a woman. What does Travis have to say about it?"

"He tells me to do whatever I want. Weddings are all about the bride."

"Smart man."

Her eyes narrowed. "How does your friend, Claire, feel about weddings?"

"Right now, she'd definitely be against. One of her ex-boyfriends wants her back and keeps leaving wedding crap and notes as some sort of weird enticement. The guy must have a screw loose."

Grace flipped long, brown, wind whipped hair over her shoulder. "Has she told him to drop dead?"

"She would, but we're not sure which old boyfriend is responsible. We've been narrowing down the suspect list. Maybe I'll talk to Travis about it tonight to get the opinion of a professional P.I."

"While you do that, I'll chat with Claire about anything but weddings since it's a sore subject for both of us. Where do you want to meet?"

"We've been camping, so I promised her a nice dinner. How about Poseidon's down on Fisherman's Wharf?"

"Yum. One of my favorites." She laid a hand on his arm. "Uh, are you sure we aren't crashing your evening? This woman of yours might be less than thrilled about having extra company on a date."

"She won't mind. Claire's the friendly sort, and you two will have plenty in common. It'll be fun."

"If you're sure?"

"I am."

"Then, we'll see you tonight. Is seven okay? Travis has a late appointment with a client."

"Sounds perfect."

"See you then." Bending to grab the end of the leash, Grace ran down the beach with the dog trotting at her side.

When she disappeared into the encroaching fog, Jed glanced at his watch. Claire should be finishing up her meeting soon, and he wanted to be on time to pick her up. With a smile, he headed back the way he'd come.

# Chapter 15

"You don't mind that I asked them to join us, do you? Grace is always entertaining, and Travis is a cool dude."

Claire tipped back her cocktail before pasting a smile on her lips for Jed. "Of course I don't mind."

*Good thing no one left any sharp objects lying around...*

"They're running late." He slid off the barstool. "Wait. Spoke too soon. There's Grace now."

Claire turned on her seat to face the door. A stunning woman smiled up at the man who followed her into the restaurant. He returned her gaze with eyes full of love. And maybe a touch of lust. Claire was willing to bet most men who looked at Grace Hanover did it with sex on the brain.

When Jed waved, the handsome, dark-haired man guided his companion through the maze of small tables toward the bar. Grace hugged Jed briefly then turned to Claire. The woman's eyes sparkled with interest as she gave her an up and down glance. Apparently Claire's go-to little black dress passed muster. Approval registered in the smiling curve of her lips.

"I can see why he lit up when he talked about you." She held out her hand. "I'm Grace Hanover, soon to be Barnett."

Claire gripped the offered palm in a firm shake. "Claire Templeton. It's nice to meet you."

"Is it? I told Jed you might not like us busting in on your date. He assured me we weren't, but what does he know? He's a guy. Dense as a rock like most of the species when it comes to what women want."

Claire managed a smile. Exactly what she'd been thinking and hadn't had the guts to say to his face. Maybe having dinner with this woman whom Jed obviously admired wouldn't be so bad after all.

"Hey, I'm not dense."

Grace patted his arm. "How about thick?"

"Funny." He laid a hand on Claire's arm. "Travis, meet Claire. Do you want to have a drink here or at the table?"

Travis gave her a warm smile. "Let's see if they can seat us. I'm starving."

Once they were settled at a table overlooking the fog-shrouded bay and had ordered a round of drinks and appetizers, Claire leaned back in her chair. Travis held Grace's hand where a big, shiny diamond was prominently displayed. Beside her, Jed's attention focused on the view out the window, and she couldn't help wondering if he was having regrets. *Does he wish he was the one holding Grace's hand?* She'd never been the jealous type. Now wasn't the time to start.

Claire forced a pleasant tone. "Congratulations on your upcoming wedding."

"Thanks. We're thinking about eloping."

Travis gave his bride-to-be an amused look. "Grace is thinking about running away to get hitched. Since I don't want to piss off her mother, I'm complying with orders."

"Easy for you since they're all directed at me." When the server returned with their cocktails, she lifted her glass and sipped. "While we're on the subject of matrimony, Jed, tell Travis about Claire's wedding stalker."

"Stalker?" Her fiancé's brows drew together. "That doesn't sound good."

"It's pretty weird." Jed pulled his gaze away from the window and swirled the ice in his vodka tonic. "One of Claire's past loves has been leaving trinkets like cake toppers along with notes to remind her of a promise. The last gift was sexy lingerie. Apparently, he wants her to make good on a vow to marry him."

Travis planted an elbow on the table and leaned toward her. "Have you contacted the police?"

Claire blinked. "No. What would I tell them? There's been no threat. The whole thing is freaking me out a little, but I'm not afraid. Not really."

Travis's frown deepened. "Is this man escalating?"

She shrugged. "His notes are worded a little more strongly each time. Accusing now rather than upbeat the way they were in the beginning."

"I don't like it. Go to the police and get a restraining order against this guy."

"That's the problem. We don't know who he is." Jed reached toward the plate of pepper poppers the server delivered. His eyes watered as he chewed and swallowed. "Could be one of two men. We'll confront them both when we get back to Shady Bend. Maybe the lame-ass will confess."

"Neither is the violent sort. I'm sure if I explain I've moved on, he'll stop." Claire picked up a pepper. "Let's talk about something else. We're supposed to be having a fun evening, and I'm not in any real danger."

Grace licked one finger. "Yum. I love hot food." She glanced over at Claire. "I'm relieved you have Jed around. Don't try to face this man down on your own. I made that mistake once and am lucky to be sitting here."

"We saw the article in the paper about the assassin." Jed took a swallow of his drink. "I'm glad they locked that psycho up for good."

"He pleaded insanity, but he's smart. My guess is he'll convince the doctors at the mental facility he's sane, and some judge will release him before he turns thirty."

Jed reared back. "*You're kidding.* The freak's a trained killer. He kidnapped you."

"The system doesn't always work the way it should. We'll see what happens, but he's locked up for now at least."

When the server returned with crab cakes, they placed their dinner orders. Travis lifted one of the appetizers onto his plate. "What do you do Claire?"

"I'm a nature photographer for *Rugged America.*"

"Very cool." Grace set down her fork. "What're you working on now?"

"A pictorial of lighthouses and sea creatures. That's why we're in the city. I needed to meet with my editor to get her approval for the story."

Grace turned toward Jed. "What about you? Have you made any decisions about work next summer?"

"Nope." He scowled. "Kane's been on my case about my lack of gainful employment. I don't need another lecture."

"Your brother's just concerned about you."

"I'm a big boy. I'll figure it out."

Travis cleared his throat. "That reminds me. An old buddy of mine mentioned something the other day that made me think of you. He's sending his son to a two-week adventure camp in July. A friend of his runs it. The kids spend half their time at the ocean and the other half in the mountains camping. It's a wilderness training thing. I guess they offer different locations to keep it fresh. The company is based out of Seattle."

Grace shuddered. "Sounds like torture to me. I've never been a fan of camping, but Rachel would have loved it when we were girls."

"I bet a lot of kids would love a camp like that." Claire munched on the last popper.

"I know I would have." Jed smiled as the cocktail server approached. "Anyone want another round?"

Travis shook his head. "A client offered to take me sailing first thing in the morning, so I'll pass. Ladies?"

Claire pushed away her empty glass. "Two's my limit, and we had one at the bar earlier. I'm a lightweight. Right now I need more food."

"That's because you're tiny." Jed responded to the pretty brunette's questioning glance with a head shake. "I guess we're good with drinks."

Their meals were served a few minutes later and the conversation lagged while everyone dug in.

Claire twirled linguini with clam sauce around her fork and inhaled the heavenly aroma. "The food here is ambrosia. Ralph's Diner isn't going to cut it for me after this."

"I don't know." Jed glanced up from his plate. "I could live on his pancakes."

Grace forked a shrimp into her mouth and licked her lips. "As delicious as this is, nothing beats pizza."

Travis gave her a pitying look. "You're warped."

"I know."

By the time they'd finished their dinners and paid the bill, Claire was willing to forgive Jed for scraping their romantic date in favor of a foursome. Full of excellent food and mellowed by Grace's entertaining account of how she and Travis had met, she tucked her hand through Jed's arm as they left the restaurant. When she shivered in the cool night air, he pulled her close.

Grace stuffed her hands in the pockets of her wool coat. "You're not driving north tonight, are you? The fog is thicker than chowder."

Jed shook his head. "No, I booked a hotel room."

"We have a spare bedroom if—ouch!"

Grace removed her elbow from her fiancé's ribs. "Sounds like you're all set then." She smiled at Claire. "This was fun. I hope we'll see you again soon. Maybe Jed can drag you along to my sister's for Thanksgiving."

When he didn't respond right away, some of her pleasure in the evening evaporated as the chill in the air crept in around her heart. Jed lived for the moment. Committing to a date two months in the future definitely wasn't his style.

He cleared his throat. "I'm too stuffed full of seafood to think about turkey." He shook Travis's hand and gave Grace a hug good-bye. "Don't stress over your wedding. When is it, by the way?"

"If we don't run off to a tropical island to tie the knot before then, December."

The expression in her eyes when she met her fiancé's gaze twisted Claire's heart.

"We don't want to wait any longer than we have to, but my mom was adamant she needed a few months to prepare."

Travis gave her shoulders a squeeze. "The day can't come soon enough for either of us. Good night, Claire. See you, Jed."

After they strolled away, Claire sighed.

"What?"

She looked up into his puzzled gaze and shrugged. "I've never been deeply in love like that. They're lucky."

He took her hand and rubbed his thumb across the back. "I guess they are. Love and commitment aren't subjects I've given a lot of thought."

Her chest tightened, but she didn't respond. There was nothing left to say.

\* \* \* \*

Jed dropped their bags, shut the hotel room door and laid his hands on Claire's shoulders. She glanced up and smiled, but the sparkle in her eyes that always sent a quiver sliding through him was absent.

"Everything okay?"

She looked away to slide her arms out of her coat. "Why wouldn't it be? I had fun tonight. Travis and Grace are great."

"Yeah, they are." He tossed her coat over the back of a chair and shrugged out of his jacket. When he laid it on top of hers, the soft leather slid to the floor. Stepping over it, he took her hand to pull her toward the bed. "Sit. Tell me what I did wrong. As Grace pointed out, I'm a little dense about what women are thinking."

She leaned her head against his shoulder. "You didn't do anything wrong. Maybe in the beginning I wasn't so happy to have our romantic evening turned into a group affair, but I got over my irritation. It's not your fault you're clueless. Probably a missing gene or something."

The floral scent of her hair filled his senses. Breathing deep, he struggled to keep the conversation on track. "Agreed. I'm an idiot. Sorry."

"Don't be. I liked getting to know your friends. But I did sort of wonder if you still have a thing for Grace."

Taking her chin in his hand, he tilted her face until he could see into her eyes. "Is *that* why I feel a chill in the air?"

"She's beautiful and funny and—"

"*Engaged*. You're beautiful and funny, too. Jesus, Claire, I'm not carrying some kind of freaking torch for Grace. Never was. We're pals and sort of related by marriage. That's it."

"You're sure?"

"Of *course* I'm sure."

She smiled, humor glimmering in the blue depths of her gaze. "I believe you. Your acting skills aren't good enough to fake that kind of indignation."

"Thank God for that. So, do you want to make out first or just get naked?"

She laughed. "We could do both, get naked then make out."

"I like how you think." He pulled her onto his lap and kissed her, taking his time, tasting the hint of raspberry tart they'd had for dessert. The way she settled against him with a wiggle of her hips made him forget everything but the woman in his arms.

Pushing strands of silky hair out of his way, he lowered the zipper of her dress. It slid down her backbone, not stopping until his hand reached the rounded curve of her sweet—

A giggle erupted in his ear.

"That tickles."

His fingers slipped even lower, cupping firm flesh. "How about that?"

Her breath hitched. "That just makes me want to rip your clothes off."

Grinning, he kissed the side of her neck. "I'm not stopping you."

With a shove to his chest, she pushed him backward onto the bed and straddled his hips. "Think I'm going to turn down an invitation like that?" One hand slipped the buttons through their holes before parting his shirt with excruciating slowness to push it off his shoulders. Her fingers glided over his chest, pausing on one flat nipple. "Not a chance. I like being in control, knowing exactly what's going to happen next."

His heart raced, the pulse drumming in his ears. "Yeah?"

"Yeah." She unbuckled his belt, lowered the zipper on his pants then stroked a path across his abdomen, leaving goosebumps pebbling his skin.

Sweat broke out on his brow as he sucked in a harsh breath. He was pretty certain he might die if she didn't speed up the process. "You're killing me."

"Good."

He nearly choked. "Is that nice?"

A wide grin and a wicked twinkle in her eyes was his only answer. Rising up off his lap, she gave his slacks a tug. When he lifted his hips, they slid along his thighs. Her gaze dropped and held. He glanced down to where his briefs tented like a teepee.

Her chest rose then fell on an exhale. "Goodness. I guess we need to get the party started."

He dragged his gaze away from the hint of cleavage. "You've got my vote."

With a backward scramble, she stood beside the bed. His eyes widened as her little black dress slipped off her shoulders and fell to the carpet.

Purple panties hardly worthy of the name and a matching lace bra covered her most interesting parts.

"Wow."

"I thought you liked the pink ones best."

"Pink. Purple. Rainbow stripes. I'm not picky about underwear." He swallowed. "Not when you're in them."

Her thumbs stroked down her hipbones and caught the elastic edges. "And when I'm out of them?"

He tried to answer, but his tongue stuck to the roof of his mouth. A croak emerged.

High black heels thumped onto the carpet. Purple silk and lace followed. Jed's vision blurred as the blood pounded in his head. Both heads. He gulped air.

When he bent forward and reached for his shoes, Claire swatted his hand. "I'm in control. Remember."

He nodded and lay back down. "Got it."

An eternity passed while she pulled off each of his shoes, his socks and the slacks still bunched at his ankles. When he grabbed the elastic waist of his briefs, she frowned.

His hand fell away. Nothing could have been sexier than her prim expression—which was the only thing she wore.

"Let me."

*Breathe, idiot, breathe.* "Okay."

When her hand brushed against him as she pulled off his underwear, he jerked and very nearly exploded. Teeth gritted, he fought for control.

Her smooth skin slid against his as she climbed on the bed to lie full length on top of him. She kissed the side of his neck then brought her lips around to meet his. Wrapping his arms around her back, he returned the kiss, easing his tongue into her mouth.

When Jed was forced to come up for air, he pressed his forehead against hers. "Have I told you how much I love...being with you?" The words he'd meant to say stuck in his throat.

*Do I love her?*

When she came down on top of him, enclosing him within her, he nearly cried. If the emotion sucking every rational thought from his head wasn't love, it was so damn close he couldn't tell the difference.

Eyes closed, her mouth opened on a gasp as she rose above him and pressed down hard. "I...love...this."

He surged inside her. "Me, too. More than I can say." Wrapped up in the magic of Claire, he stopped trying to think and let himself fly.

\* \* \* \*

He scrolled through the photos, one after the other, his hand shaking on the mouse pad. Some were older. A whimper escaped as he stared at a photo of Claire sunbathing on a lounge chair on the patio behind her cottage, a bikini top lying on the ground next to her. He'd pushed his camera lens through the thick hedge hiding her from admiring eyes to get that shot. Some were more recent. Claire bent over as she pulled on a pair of green panties, her ass so firm and fine. She should have been more careful. A pervert could have been peeking through the crack between the curtains of her motor home instead of him.

He clicked on the photos he wanted to print and placed the order. As he opted for express shipping, he winced. The price was horrendous but worth it. Claire wouldn't be able to ignore his next gesture, and he couldn't afford to wait any longer. This time she'd know for sure he wasn't joking. Fervently, he hoped it would make her as hot as the anticipation was making him.

After pulling his credit card from his wallet, he completed the order. That job finished, he clicked back to the picture folder. So beautiful. So very, very beautiful. But looking at Claire's image on a computer screen wasn't enough. Only the flesh and blood woman could satisfy his needs. Hearing her laugh. Seeing her smile. Touching her…everywhere.

With a moan, he slid his hand into the front of his pants. Until she was there beside him, he'd have to make do with pictures.

# Chapter 16

"You're sure you want to do this alone?" Jed fisted his hands on his hips and scowled. "Remember what Grace said about confronting your stalker by yourself. You might set him off, and then God only knows what he'll do."

"If you're hanging around, Ian will clam up and get defensive. He doesn't like you very much. In order to get answers, I need to talk to him one-on-one." Claire picked the keys to his SUV up off the table. "Anyway, I won't be alone with him, not that I believe Ian poses a threat. The other scientists will be at the camp with us."

"That's the only reason I'm letting you go."

She stopped at the door to the motor home and turned. "I make my own decisions. Sleeping with me doesn't give you the right to order me around like I'm a brainless child."

"I didn't mean it that way." He ran a hand through his hair and sighed. "Aren't I allowed to be worried? I care about you."

"You can express your concern without acting like a Neanderthal. Or a Bigfoot." She summoned up a sweet smile.

Some of the anxiety faded from his direct blue gaze, and he grinned. "Who says Bigfoots…feet…whatever aren't poster boys for women's lib. Their females might run the show."

The tension between them dissolved with the silly banter, and her smile grew. "Good point. If I see one while I'm out there, I'll be sure to ask who wears the pants in his family. In the meantime, I'm going to sit down with Ian and have a rational conversation. If he's the one who left the nightie and other stuff, I'll make sure he understands his gestures aren't appreciated."

"You don't believe he's guilty of obsessing over anything but Sasquatches." His eyes narrowed. "If you did, you wouldn't be so calm about confronting him."

"No, I don't think he's the one. But I'll ask him anyway, and his reaction will tell me everything I need to know. He's not great at hiding his feelings, either."

"What's that supposed to mean?"

Claire pushed open the door. "Nothing. It was a compliment. With you, I always know exactly where I stand."

"I would hope so." Stepping across Scoop who was sprawled on the motor home floor, he tilted her chin with a gentle touch then kissed her, slowly and thoroughly. "Come right back afterward. Please. I'm going to worry until you return safe and sound."

She nodded. "Since you asked nicely, I will."

The drive to the scientists' camp seemed endless, providing way too much time to dwell on Jed's phobia when it came to making a commitment. The night before—for about two whole seconds—she'd held her breath, anticipating a declaration of love. It hadn't happened, and she'd responded with equal ambiguity. Not that she doubted her feelings for him. Pretending they were a simple mixture of affection and lust wasn't working any longer. The emotion turning her inside out could only be love. Her heart jumped whenever he was near, and she melted into a puddle of yearning at his most casual touch. When he walked away, the glow that warmed her from the inside out went with him. *Stupid. Stupid. Stupid.*

Gritting her teeth, she bounced down the rutted track, going faster than she should. When a deer bounded across the road in front of the SUV, she slammed on the brakes. The strap of the seatbelt dug into her breasts. Biting down hard on her lip, she rubbed her chest and waited for her heartbeat to quiet. The deer was probably in the next county before she finally eased off the brake to continue.

*Pull it together, Claire.* She needed her wits about her to face Ian. Not that she believed he was responsible for the harassment. Running into a Bigfoot was a lot more likely, and that sure wasn't going to happen. Problem was she couldn't imagine the perpetrator as Dallas either. Still, *one* of them had to be guilty.

When she pulled into the clearing several minutes later, she wouldn't have recognized the spot from her previous visits. Gone was the big, canvas shelter along with two of the small tents. A lone ATV was parked beneath a towering fir tree. Once she turned off the car engine, the silence was broken only by an occasional squawk from a blue jay. A little unnerved, she pulled the keys from the ignition, opened the door and stepped down.

"Hey, Claire."

With a yelp, she turned to face Ian as he walked out of the forest. "You startled me. Where is everyone?"

"Lee and Margaret left for good. Bart went into town to buy some groceries to tide us over."

"The two of you are staying?"

"Only for a few more days. The vandals have been at it again, and we've made very little progress in the last week. The results of our foray deeper into the forest were discouraging with fewer signs of habitation out there than in the areas closer to camp." His gray eyes clouded. "The others have given up. Bart plans to leave soon, but I may stick around for the rest of the week."

"I'm sorry your retreat was a bust. What about your equipment?"

"We packed up the stuff needing repair, and Lee took it with him. The asshole saboteur won. I won't throw good money after bad by replacing the cameras yet again. My intent is simply to sleep out in the woods for a few more nights and hope I get lucky."

"Stranger things have happened, I suppose."

Dropping his backpack to the ground, Ian took a couple of steps forward. "Speaking of strange, your message was a little odd. What do you need to talk to me about?"

Claire drew in a breath and glanced around the empty clearing before meeting his gaze. Impatience filled his eyes. Not exactly the emotion of a man in love hell bent on luring her back into his life. She opened her mouth then shut it.

"Spit it out, Claire. I don't have all day." He grimaced. "Actually, I do, but I've other things more worthy of my attention than your petty troubles. Did your editor fire you for not getting a Sasquatch photo? Bart mentioned you were looking for me while I was out in the field. Sorry, but I'm not going to be able to help you."

She stiffened and stepped back. "When did you become so bitter? I swear I don't even recognize the man I loved and admired so much all those years ago." She eyed him up and down. "What a shame. That guy was a better person."

He closed his eyes for a minute and rubbed his temples. "What did you come out here to ask me?"

"I have my answer. I won't waste your valuable time." She jerked open the car door. "See you, Ian."

He slammed it shut. Her heart pounded as he crowded her against the side of the vehicle. Turning with her arm thrust out, she tightened her fist around the keys with the business ends sticking through her fingers.

"Back off."

His eyes widened as he retreated a couple of steps. "Sorry. I didn't mean to scare you. Jesus, are you *afraid* of me?"

The bewilderment in his eyes alleviated most of her fear. "Maybe a little. We're alone in the middle of the woods, and you're so...angry."

"I'm frustrated and more than a little pissed. I shouldn't have snapped at you, though, and I certainly didn't intend to frighten you." He backed up several additional feet. "I'd never hurt you. I hope you know that."

She nodded. "Let's forget about it. We both overreacted."

"You came out here for a reason. What was it?"

Her gaze dropped. "After this, I feel like an idiot even bringing up the subject. I knew you weren't the one, but—"

"The one, what?" Concern shown in his eyes as a bit of the caring man who'd once held her hand for hours while she fought through a bad case of food poisoning emerged. "Tell me what's wrong."

She let out a breath. "Someone's been...stalking me. Leaving gifts and notes. They allude to a promise I supposedly made. Whoever the guy is, he wants me back."

"You thought it was *me*?"

"Not really." Her voice took on a defensive edge. "But there aren't a lot of candidates whom I once promised to marry to choose from. You were hurt and furious when we split up. I had to at least ask."

His chest heaved as he let out a breath. "Are you in danger from this man?"

"I don't think so." She hunched one shoulder. "I hope not. If it isn't you..."

"It isn't." His voice was flat and hard. "I put our brief marriage behind me years ago. I'm not harboring any stupid romantic fantasy that we'll get back together—or a plan for revenge. I'm not saying seeing you again didn't hurt a bit. The memories you've stirred up certainly aren't all pleasant. However, I'm far more upset by the results of our research than I am over a long-dead marriage that never amounted to much to begin with."

"I believe you." She sighed. "Truly, I find it difficult to credit I'm so memorable someone would go to these lengths to regain my affection."

"I'd say the guy is a few cards shy of a full deck. Some people might call me crazy for believing in Bigfoot, but I'm not that kind of insane."

She smiled. "No, you're not, but neither is anyone else I ever dated. Unless he hides it awfully well. Now I really am going to get out of here. Take care, Ian. I wish you all the best."

"You, too." He hesitated for a moment before continuing, "Is that Jed guy still hanging around?"

"For now he is."

"Good. I might not respect his type much, but I'm sure he'll keep you safe."

Her eyes burned as she drove away. She didn't love Ian—didn't even like him anymore—but she had once. Leaving him standing in the clearing, a defeated slump to his shoulders, firmly slammed the door on a chapter of her life she hadn't thought about in a long time. Right now any good-bye hit hard. A precursor of greater heartache to come.

When a pickup approached on the track ahead, she dashed the tears from her eyes and maneuvered to the shoulder of the road to wait for the vehicle to squeeze past. Instead, the driver pulled abreast and stopped.

"I was hoping I wouldn't miss you."

She smiled at Bart. "How'd the grocery shopping go?"

"We're all set for a couple of days, and then I'm afraid I have to head home. I'll take a rain check on helping with the painting or whatever other project you have going."

She leaned an elbow on the open window. "I was just telling Ian how sorry I am your retreat didn't produce better results."

"Maybe our expectations were too high. We set ourselves up for disappointment." He cleared his throat. "It wasn't a complete waste of time. We wouldn't have met if I hadn't come on this admittedly odd adventure. I'll have a little free time tomorrow. Would you like to have lunch together?" His hand shot up, palm out. "Don't turn me down yet. I'm aware you're involved with Jed. This would be strictly friendly, a chance to get to know each other a little better. You can't have too many friends, right?"

Claire was willing to bet not many women said no to this man. He oozed a harmless brand of charm.

"No, but—"

"No buts. Who knows when either of our circumstances will change. There's no harm in getting better acquainted before I leave, is there?"

"I guess not."

"Great. Will one o'clock work for you? I'll pick up some sandwiches, and we can meet at the park in town."

"I suppose…"

"See you then." His pickup pulled away, leaving a plume of dust in its wake.

Coughing, Claire rolled up the window then grinned. Not a bad strategy. Bart hadn't given her time to turn him down. When she thought about it, there wasn't a good reason not to have lunch with him. As he'd said, a simple, friendly meal. Right after she confronted Dallas.

According to Theresa, her old high school boyfriend was expected back from his hunting trip tonight. Imagining Dallas was the one who'd left the nightie and the notes twisted her stomach into knots. Shady Bend wasn't big enough to avoid people, so she'd likely face him on a regular basis. Which meant the upcoming discussion would have to be handled with finesse if she didn't want to struggle with awkwardness every time they crossed paths on the street or she needed to buy a handful of nails. After her conversation with Ian, finesse was definitely beyond her capabilities. Maybe by tomorrow she'd be able to pull herself together and broach the subject of his *gifts* with a little tact.

* * * *

Jed cocked his head as the rumble of an engine sounded from the driveway. Had to be his SUV. He needed to take the old beater in for a tune-up. Or replace it, but the idea of making a car payment each month lacked appeal. Climbing off the ladder, he set the roller in the paint tray and headed toward the hall.

He'd tried not to worry about Claire—and failed. As the son of a cop, he was well aware seemingly normal people snapped for no apparent reason all the time. Life was often full of surprises, and most of them weren't of the *you just won the lottery* variety. Just the opposite. His feet thumped against each step as he ran down the stairs. By the time he reached the yard, he had to get in line behind Scoop to greet her.

She finally shoved the dog away and smiled in his direction. "I'm back."

"So I see." She looked…better than good. The only sign she'd been in a struggle was the dirty paw print marring the yellow material of her T-shirt over her left boob. He forced his gaze upward. "How'd it go with Ian?"

"He's not the one."

"You're sure?"

"Not a polar bear's chance in purgatory." The up-tilt of her lips wasn't much of a smile. "He's not harboring any lingering affection for me. I'm perceptive enough to know when a man is interested. Ian isn't. I'm pretty sure he doesn't like me any more than I like him. He has no respect for what I've accomplished with my life, certainly no admiration. Maybe there's a touch of resentment because I left him all those years ago, but that has more to do with his self-image than with any feelings toward me."

Every word rang with conviction. Jed didn't doubt her insight for a minute. "We'll cross him off our list, then. Which means—"

"Dallas is the one." The light in her eyes dimmed as she reached out to stroke her dog's ears. "I'll talk to him in the morning."

"I don't suppose you'll let me tag along?"

She shook her head. "It'll go better if I'm alone, but I'll make sure there're people in the vicinity. I don't expect him to freak out and drag me off into the forest or anything, but I'm fine with taking a few commonsense precautions. Just in case."

Something in her tone set off a warning bell. He stiffened. "Exactly what happened with Ian?"

"Nothing. A little attack of nerves on my part. Turns out Lee and Margaret already left the area, and Bart was in town shopping. Ian is beyond pissed about their Bigfoot hunt turning into a fiasco, and his anger scared me a little. He backed off the second he realized he'd frightened me."

Jed's fists clenched. "I should go out there."

Stepping forward, she gripped his arms. "No, Ian's just frustrated not dangerous, but his reaction made me realize I really don't know these men very well. My relationship with Dallas was with a boy. He's a man now, and I'm sure he's changed as much as Ian has. I'll be cautious when I approach him."

He pulled her against his chest and wrapped his arms around her. "Good. If something happened to you…" His stomach tightened.

Her gaze rose to meet his. Hope? Expectation? Need? Emotions he wasn't sure he understood flashed through her eyes. He still hadn't figured out exactly what she was feeling when she looked away.

"You're just afraid you'd have to keep Scoop."

"There're worse fates, I suppose. The mutt's growing on me, but I'd prefer to keep you around." He dropped a kiss on the top of her head. "I'm almost finished painting the tower bedroom. Oh, the contractor showed up while you were gone. He had a couple of points to clarify then said he'd have a final estimate on your list of repairs soon."

"Great. I'm sure you were more useful answering his questions than I would have been. Do you want to take a break or finish painting the bedroom first?"

"How about I finish while you make us a picnic lunch? A hike in the fresh air sounds perfect after breathing paint fumes all morning."

"Deal." Reaching up, she caressed his cheek, then pressed a kiss to his lips. "Thanks for all your help."

"You're welcome. Claire?"

"What?"

"Is everything's okay?

"Of course. Why wouldn't it be?"

He wasn't sure he believed her. "Are you upset Dallas is the one who's been bothering you? You seem—I don't know—subdued. Not your usual upbeat self."

"Maybe a little upset. I don't like thinking he has a...problem. But I'm confident we can work through it. Maybe Theresa will help. I know they're close."

Relief lightened the weight pressing down on him. The niggling feeling that he was the reason for her downcast mood evaporated. "Maybe Simms should talk to a shrink. The guy has some real issues."

Her brow furrowed. "I can suggest it."

"But you don't think he will?" His uneasiness returned.

"I doubt it. Dallas was never a fan of talking about his problems. He always kept everything bottled up inside—"

"Until he exploded? Shit. I think we should call the cops."

"No." She shook her head, her hair brushing his chin. "He was never violent. Usually he just did something stupid to let off steam. Once, when he and his dad had this big argument over a math grade, he drank half a bottle of tequila." Her nose wrinkled. "God, was he sick. But when the agony of the hangover wore off, he felt better and hashed it out with his father. He agreed to do some extra credit work, and everything was good between them afterward."

Jed snorted. "So you think he'll go get drunk then get over you just like that?"

"I hope so. Dallas was always willing to listen to a reasonable suggestion once he got over his initial anger."

"If he doesn't, I'll be here. One thing's certain, the asshole isn't going to get anywhere near you. That's a promise."

# Chapter 17

Claire climbed out of the SUV and shut the door behind Scoop after the dog jumped to the ground. Dallas's home had seen better days. Not much more than a shack set on the edge of the forest. A toothless old man in a rocking chair with a shotgun across his lap and a homemade still in the backyard wouldn't have been out of place. She laid a hand on Scoop's head. When the clerk who'd answered the phone at the hardware store told her Dallas wasn't coming in until later in the day, she'd decided bringing the dog along for company might be a smart move. With the nearest neighbor not even within shouting distance, she was glad she had.

Dense fog shrouded the cabin as she approached. Jamming her hands in her jacket pockets to ward off the chill, she headed up the dirt path to the front door. Claire hadn't told Jed she was confronting Dallas in his home instead of at the hardware store. If he could see her now, he'd go ballistic. Her footsteps echoed and Scoop's nails clicked on the porch floor. Raising her hand, she hesitated then knocked on the solid wood portal. When no one answered, she pounded a little louder.

The door jerked inward. "What the hell? I'm not buying—Claire?"

"Hi, Dallas. How was your trip?"

"Good. I got a big buck." He stepped back and waved an arm. "Sorry, I thought you were a salesman or something. Come in. The place is kind of a mess." He kicked a pair of dirty socks under a chair as he passed through the main room. "I just made coffee. Do you want a cup?"

"Sure." She glanced back. "Uh, my dog?"

"He's not going to hurt anything. Let him in."

"Thanks." After shutting the door, she followed Dallas to the kitchen. Her shoes stuck as she walked across the worn linoleum to the bar counter and stepped up onto the rung of a metal stool.

Turning, his gaze followed her progress. "I spilled orange juice earlier. Guess I need to mop." His chocolate-brown eyes were red rimmed.

Wearing a pair of old sweats and a ripped T-shirt, his face was covered with stubble. "Clearly, I'm not at my best. We got in late last night."

"I should have called first, but your employee said I'd probably find you at home. Theresa texted me your address."

He set a mug full of coffee and a milk jug on the counter then turned to grab his own cup. Taking a gulp, he leaned one elbow on the Formica surface as he faced her. "Did you need to see me for a reason, or is this just a social visit?"

She stirred milk into the fragrant brew before sipping cautiously. "I do have something to discuss." When she opened her mouth, words she hadn't intended came out. "Are you okay? If you need help with anything…"

He straightened. "I look like shit because I got four hours of sleep last night. Mandy took me to the cleaners in our divorce, so I live in a rat hole. Other than that, I'm fine. I let my life go to hell after she left town with the kids, but I'm getting things back on track. Theresa's keeping an eye out for a good deal on a better place. Until she finds something I can afford to buy, I don't want to waste a lot of money on rent."

"Oh. That makes sense."

"So, despite appearances, I'm actually doing better than I have in a long time. I don't need any charity. Now, what did you want to talk to me about?"

Wrapping her hands around the warm ceramic mug, she met his gaze. "I have a problem. Someone who probably has the best intentions in the world is scaring me a little. I was hoping to straighten out the situation."

"Is it that Jed, guy?" His voice deepened. "You want me to get rid of him for you?"

Her eyes widened. "No. No! I'm not talking about Jed. This is a man from my past."

"Ian. The guy's a weasel. I hate his type, coming into our town to act all superior with their fancy degrees while they hunt for a Bigfoot. The idiots don't know the first thing about tracking animals." His lips curved in a satisfied smirk. "This group didn't find squat, and now they're leaving with their tails tucked."

She sat back and sipped her coffee. "You really aren't a fan."

An eye roll was her only answer.

She brushed a few toast crumbs left on the counter into a pile while choosing her words. "I thought maybe Ian was…the one. I talked to him yesterday, but he isn't."

"The one, what? What're you talking about?"

She'd hoped with a little coaxing he'd come right out and admit he was the person who'd left the notes. *No such luck.*

Taking a breath, she let it out slowly. "I'm talking about the wedding trinkets you've been leaving. It's sweet you still care about me so much, but we aren't going to get back together. Our lives are just too different for anything between us to work."

A frown creased his brow. "You think I don't know that? Jesus, I'm not stupid. Wait a minute, wedding trinkets? I don't get it? Someone left you gifts?"

If Dallas was faking confusion, he should have been on stage earning a fortune. His bewilderment was almost palpable. She'd been so sure he was responsible...

"If you think I've been harassing you, you're wrong." Hurt clouded his eyes. "Damn, we were so tight all those years ago. Don't you know me better than that? I don't play games with women, and I sure as hell wouldn't play them with you."

"He said I promised. It's not like I've talked about marriage with a whole bunch of men. You, Ian, and Ross. That's it."

He reached for the coffee carafe and topped off both their mugs. "Ross who?"

"McGregor. We were engaged once, but Jed and I already tracked him down. He's on the East Coast. It definitely wasn't him."

"Then Ian—"

She shook her head. "No, he has absolutely no interest in me. I'm one hundred percent certain of that."

Dallas held up his hands. "Well I sure as hell haven't been bothering you. What exactly did this guy do?"

"He left notes and little wedding favors and cake toppers. And a nightie. That one bothered me the most. The notes made it clear he's waiting for me to live up to my promise to marry him."

"Sick freak."

"Or just lonely and a little desperate." Her voice softened. "I'm not blaming him. I just want him to stop."

"Oh, my God! You still think I might have done it." He slammed down the mug. "Is that how you see me, lonely and desperate?"

Scoop left the corner where he'd been licking something off the floor and walked over to her side. His butt hit the ground with a thump as he eyed Dallas. Claire rested her hand on his head.

"I don't know what to think. If you aren't responsible, then who is?"

"Hell if I know. You must have dated other guys."

"A few. No one serious. No one who wanted to *marry* me."

He laughed, but the sound held little amusement. "Are you really that naïve? I can name at least three guys in our graduating class who would have put a contract out on me if they thought you would have given them the time of day with me out of the picture. Good God, Claire, there could be dozens of guys out there who have a thing for you. All it would take is a warped mind to twist something you said into a vow of commitment."

Cold crept through her, chilling her bones. She rubbed her arms as she stared at him. "If that's true, it could be anyone. Someone I went on one date with or the homeless guy I handed a dollar to on a street corner."

"I think you should call the police."

She forced herself to breathe. "He hasn't threatened me."

"Do you want him to? If you ignore him, he may up his game."

"Oh, God." Holding her head with both hands, she tried to think.

Dallas touched her shoulder. "What does Jed say?"

"We both thought it was you. He was concerned, but I assured him I could handle the situation, that you weren't going to turn into a monster and chop me up into little pieces to feed to a bear."

His smile in response to her drama took away some of the numbing cold. She reached for her coffee cup and swallowed the contents. The heat kept her teeth from chattering.

"I'll do anything I can to help. I do care about you, but I'm not your stalker."

"I believe you. I didn't want it to be you, but it would have been easier. Now…now I don't know what I'm going to do."

Concern darkened his eyes. "Maybe he'll get bored and quit. How long since he left the last gift?"

"Almost a week." Hope stirred. "Instead of escalating, it's possible he'll give up if I keep ignoring him. For now, I guess I'll do nothing. I'm safe with Jed."

Dallas picked up the mugs and turned to place them in the sink. "That's good. I suppose I should go take a shower and get ready for work."

Claire slid off the stool. "I'm sorry I thought you were the one harassing me. You're right. I should have known better."

He shrugged. "I can see why you had to ask. Take care of yourself, and be sure to let me know if I can help in any way."

She forced a smile. "Thanks, I will. See you, Dallas."

"Bye, Claire."

Outside, she glanced around the yard. Thick fog obscured all but the largest objects. Was the movement in the trees to her left a branch swaying or a person ducking out of sight? Heart working on overdrive, she ran to the SUV and wrenched open the door. "Get in, Scoop."

The dog leaped up onto the seat then moved to the passenger side when she gave him a shove. After climbing in behind him, she started the engine, relieved when the door locks clicked into place.

She glanced over at her pet. Tongue hanging as he leaned against the window with eyes half closed, he appeared the picture of relaxation. *Wouldn't he sense danger?*

"I'm sure there's no reason to freak out. Still…" Clamping her teeth together, she backed the vehicle out of the driveway then headed down the road. It had been bad enough thinking someone she knew was watching her. Having a stranger follow her every move was infinitely worse.

Unless it wasn't a stranger. Maybe it was the man who rang up her groceries at the supermarket. She'd smiled at him the last time she went through the check-out line when he asked how her day was going. Or it could be someone she'd worked with at a past job or dated a couple of times or sat next to in her psychology class.

Braking when she reached the main road, she swore. Going home wasn't an option. She'd promised to meet Bart for lunch. Was he the one? Had she run into him at the U2 concert she'd attended in L.A. how many years ago and just didn't remember? Maybe he'd seen her on the beach the next day and liked the color of her bikini.

"Stop it!"

Scoop opened his eyes and barked.

"Sorry, boy." Drawing in a breath, she clenched her shaking hands around the wheel and pulled onto the highway. She wasn't going to imagine a predator behind every bush, in every man who said hello. She wasn't going to start distrusting perfectly nice men who only wanted to have lunch and a conversation. At least she was going to try not to.

When she arrived at the small park across from the high school, Bart was waiting. He waved as she and Scoop approached.

"You brought your friend." His blue gaze scanned her from head to toe. After he'd finished his perusal, he smiled.

"I did. You'll have to keep a close eye on your sandwich." *Instead of on me.* "He's pretty sneaky."

"Good to know." He patted the spot beside him. "Have a seat. I hope turkey on wheat with all the trimmings is okay."

"Perfect."

Claire dropped onto the picnic table's bench while Scoop wandered off, nose to the ground. Sitting next to Bart instead of across from him was probably smarter. If the doubt and suspicion she was trying so hard to hold at bay showed in her eyes, he wouldn't see it.

"How's the painting coming along?"

She unwrapped the sandwich he handed her. "We're nearly finished with the upstairs. Painting isn't my favorite thing to do, but the results are tangible and rewarding. How about you? Did you camp in the woods with Ian last night?"

"You've got to be kidding. The fog was like a wet blanket. At this point, he's on his own in his martyrdom to capture a Sasquatch on film. We've dismantled all the stations, so it was just Ian with his trusty handheld camera out in the dripping trees. He didn't even take a pup tent with him, said he was afraid it'd scare off any foraging Bigfoot. I left camp before he got back."

Claire shook her head when he offered her a bag of chips. "Why didn't you leave with Lee and Margaret?"

"I had some notes to finish writing up, and I'll be swamped at work the second I return. I figured I might as well wrap everything up here before going back."

*Did I expect him to admit he stayed because of me?*

"Did you finish your reports?"

"I ran out of battery on my laptop. The girl at the sandwich shop let me plug in my computer to recharge. I'll have the final drafts finished by this evening. Actually, I thought about getting a motel room then decided to give our Bigfoot hunt one last shot tonight. If the fog clears, I may even sleep in the ferns with Ian. Tomorrow, I'm out of here."

"Oh." Claire chewed slowly and swallowed then wiped her fingers on a napkin. "I guess I won't see you again then."

His teeth flashed in his still tanned face. "Never say never. I'm not giving up on Bigfoot. I may come back up this way again. Our research wasn't faulty. This is a prime area for a sighting, but we were unlucky. Maybe the Sasquatch in the region have temporarily migrated. The unusually dry summer could have affected their behavior patterns. If I do make another trip north, you can be sure I'll look you up."

She pasted on a bright smile and turned to face him. "It's strange. From the minute I first met you, I felt a...connection. You seemed familiar somehow. I don't suppose we ran into each other sometime in the past. I moved around a lot when I was growing up and later travelled all over for work."

Little laugh lines appeared at the corners his eyes. "A man wouldn't forget meeting you, Claire. There's something about you..." He smiled.

"Let's just say you're memorable. You have a likable quality along with an upbeat humor and a truly fine uh...derriere that I would never forget." He wadded up the paper wrapper from his sandwich and dropped it in the bag. "Good to know you're so comfortable with me, though."

She *was* comfortable. Bart exuded laid-back charm. Imagining this man sneaking around her motor home to leave wedding trinkets was about as likely as Scoop turning into a show dog. When her mongrel flopped at her feet then turned on his back to roll with paws waving in the air, she smiled and let herself relax. Her detective skills sucked. She'd quit trying to trip up her lunch companion—who surely wasn't guilty of anything other than admiring her ass—and finish her lunch without giving herself indigestion.

"Since you're so comfortable and all, I don't suppose you'd ditch Jed to give me a proper send off this evening. I could be persuaded to rent that motel room instead of sleeping in the woods with very little effort on your part."

Her grin broadened. "Thanks for the glamorous offer of a night out at a no-tell motel, but I'll have to pass."

He shook his head and sighed, yet the smile remained. "I figured it was worth making the suggestion. Maybe next time." Bart reached in his back pocket to pull out a bulging wallet then searched through the compartments to withdraw a business card. "Call me once you've ditched Jed."

Her hand closed around the piece of cardboard. "You're so sure I will?"

"You're a smart woman. I'm certain you'll come to your senses sooner rather than later. The guy isn't good enough for you."

She reared back. "Why would you say that?"

"No drive and ambition. You have both."

She pressed her lips together. "Jed has more going for him than you think."

"I hope so for your sake, *if* you keep him around."

She dropped the last of her sandwich in the bag, her appetite gone. "You don't think he'll be the one to dump me?"

His eyes widened. "Now why would he do that? No way. From what I've seen, the guy might be all about having fun, but he isn't stupid."

"Uh, thanks, I think." She scooted a few inches away and reached down to scratch Scoop's belly.

Bart stood. "I get the impression our lunch date is over."

"I think so." She rose to her feet. "You're a great guy. Under different circumstances I might have taken you up on your offer, but as it is, I think I should go."

He stepped closer then bent to brush a kiss across her cheek. "So be it. You have my number."

"Yes, I do."

Scoop scrambled to his feet and followed her as she walked away. Pausing, Claire turned and smiled. The fog had lifted while they ate, promising a clear evening ahead. "I'll keep my fingers crossed for you tonight. With any luck, you'll end up bunking with a Bigfoot."

He gave a shout of laughter at her joking comment. "Gorgeous blonde or big, stinky Neanderthal. What a choice."

"I know which one Ian would pick."

"Your old pal has a screw loose. I don't. Take care, Claire."

# Chapter 18

Waves rolled onto the shore as Jed and Claire walked along the beach. Sunshine sparkled on the water, and overhead seagulls squawked and circled. Scoop raced ahead then stopped to sniff a pile of seaweed. The afternoon was perfect—except for Claire's mood. She seemed ready to jump out of her skin.

Jed touched her arm. "You wanted to walk, so we're walking. Are you going to tell me what happened this morning?"

She pushed her hair out of her face and squinted toward the horizon. "Apparently, we've been all wrong about my stalker. Dallas isn't the one harassing me, either."

Stopping, he turned to face her. "Are you certain about that? It's pretty obvious the man still has feelings for you."

"Maybe, but they aren't deep seated and all consuming. I actually think he and Theresa might start something once they've both worked through the old pain over her husband's death and his wife's abandonment. Any emotion he's harboring for me is more of a lingering memory than an active pursuit."

"Sounds to me like you've put some time into that analysis."

"I did. After my lunch with Bart, I just sat in the car and thought about whether or not I was letting myself be fooled. Was I missing something? I came to the conclusion Dallas was right. The man pursuing me isn't someone I know. He's just a whack job who fixated on me for whatever reason and is living in a fantasy world of his own making."

Anger heated his blood. Everything after *lunch with Bart* was a jumble of words he'd have to decipher after he cooled off. "You had lunch with Bart? You were out on a *date* while I was painting your dammed guest bedroom?"

Emotions flashed in her eyes. Dismay followed by uncertainty that turned into irritation. "No one held a gun to your head and made you paint. If you'll recall, I suggested you go do something fun for a change."

"Why, to assuage your guilt?"

Her hands fisted on her hips. "Why should I feel guilty? It was lunch in the park, not some clandestine meeting in a sleazy motel, although he did suggest one later."

Jed turned away and started counting. He was up to twenty-eight when she interrupted.

"Last time I checked, our relationship was based on friendship and sex. No promises for the future, and I sure as hell haven't heard any declaration of love." Her voice cracked.

He heard the break, the pain she couldn't hide, but the words were out of his mouth before his brain shifted into gear. "Is this your attempt to force me into a commitment?"

She turned and ran, her tennis shoes pounding the sand. He sprinted after her. When he caught up, he wrapped both arms around her and hauled her back against his chest. She struggled and kicked, connecting with his shin. Pain ricocheted up his leg.

"Let go of me!"

"No. Damn it, stop kicking. I'll be lucky if I can still walk."

Her struggles ceased, and she bent over his arm. A sob escaped before she clamped one hand over her mouth.

Hurt far deeper than the ache in his leg filled his chest and stole his breath. He dragged air into burning lungs. "I'm sorry. Really, really sorry."

"You should be!" When he eased his grip, she spun around and dashed tears off her cheeks. "You think I don't know what we have is temporary? You think I haven't been *waiting* for you to walk away? I'm not stupid, Jed. I know the score, and trying to change you when you aren't ready for any kind of life adjustment would just make us both miserable."

"God, you make me sound like a total asshole. Is that what you believe, that I'm using you and intend to leave with no thought to your feelings?"

He closed his eyes and fought to hold his anger in check. When he opened them, Scoop leaned against her leg, eyeing him with a look that doubled his pain.

"Christ, even the dog thinks I intend to hurt you. I have feelings, too, you know."

She nodded. "I think you care—a lot." The indignation in her voice had disappeared, and her shoulders slumped. "But not enough to want to change."

"Why should I have to?"

"You shouldn't. Which is why, although walking away might not be easy for you, you'll still do it."

He opened his mouth then shut it. He couldn't argue. Despite the fact he was pretty certain he loved her, he wasn't ready to turn into his dad, working his life away to support a family. Placing fun way, way down the list of priorities and somehow never getting around to it until retirement. He was thirty-five years old. Being forced into that kind of mold for the next three decades scared the shit out of him.

Claire stood before him, eyes bleak, her hands clenched in the dog's fur. The ache in his chest twisted deeper.

"What do you want me to do?"

"I think it's time for you to go. I kept telling myself it'd be okay. We'd have a good time and build some great memories together, that it couldn't possibly hurt any more to end things later rather than sooner. Turns out I was wrong."

"Can we talk about this? I don't want to lose you." Taking her arm, he led her over to a big piece of driftwood. "Sit. I have a few concerns, not the least of which is your safety."

Leaning back, she crossed her ankles in front of her and pressed her lips together. "I'm not sure I'm capable of having a rational conversation right now. It's been a hell of a day."

"Let's start with that before we get stuck in another emotional quagmire. You said something about Dallas being right before I went all righteous caveman on you. Care to explain?"

She sighed. "We talked. I told him I didn't blame him for leaving the notes and gifts. His confusion couldn't have been faked. So we hashed it out, and he made a good point."

Jed wanted to pick up the hand clenched on her thigh but was pretty sure she wouldn't appreciate the gesture. Reaching down, he grabbed a stick and hurled it toward the ocean. Scoop took off in hot pursuit, sand spraying up behind him.

"What was his point?"

"This man alludes to a promise I made. Obviously, he's a little disturbed or he wouldn't be leaving nighties and candles in my RV. Maybe he's actually a lot disturbed and completely imagined my vow to marry him. Maybe he hears little voices in his head, and one of them happened to sound like me. This guy could be anyone from a complete stranger I passed on the street to the man who delivered my mail to a blind date I foolishly let my old roommate set me up with back in college."

When Scoop dropped the stick at his feet, Jed threw it again. "I guess that makes some kind of weird sense. We've been assuming there's logic behind his actions."

"Exactly. I'll admit I freaked out a little and started wondering if it was Bart. He's certainly shown he's interested in me."

Jed turned to stare. "Then why did you go to lunch with him?"

Her gaze remained firmly fixed on the sand. "He caught me off guard yesterday. Then I thought maybe I could elicit some kind of confession over sandwiches."

"Did you?"

She shook her head. "He's not a loon. Actually, he's a lot like you but with more focus."

Jed let the insult pass. He deserved more than that feeble jab. "We'd better contact the police. If this man's crazy, he's also dangerous."

"What're they going to do? I'm pretty sure the local law enforcement's budget doesn't stretch to babysitting me."

After wrestling the stick out of Scoop's jaws, Jed hurled it down the beach. "Well, we have to do something."

"I *am* going to do something. I'm going to take a little trip up to Crescent City to photograph the first lighthouse on my list. Maybe I'll stick around for a few days to take marine life photos, too. He—whoever he is—won't have a clue I went up there. I'll make sure no one follows me out of Shady Bend."

His heart ached. "Sounds like you intend to go alone."

"I hadn't initially, but it's probably best."

"What about after you come home?"

"Maybe he'll get bored and quit."

"Maybe he won't."

Scoop's sides heaved as he ran up and dropped the stick on his foot. Jed winced and swore beneath his breath.

Claire finally looked him in the eye. "If you keep taking your frustrations out on that piece of driftwood, you're going to give my dog a heart attack."

"The dog will survive. I'm worried about you. I don't want to leave you alone." He ran a hand through his hair. "I don't want to leave you, period."

She stood and walked slowly toward the water. Blond hair whipped in the breeze, and her windbreaker flattened against her back with each gust. Every slow, purposeful step took her further away. After a minute, he rose and followed.

"Maybe we can compromise."

She glanced over her shoulder. "That would be fine if we weren't so far apart to begin with. What do you want, Jed?"

For once, the words flowed easily. "I want what I have now—but with you added to the mix. I want to work and play and have you beside me while I do both."

"On Donner Summit?"

"Ideally. At least for the winter. I wouldn't mind spending summers at the beach."

She stuffed her hands in her pockets. "Here in Shady Bend?"

He hesitated. "I don't know what I'd do here. I have to support myself."

"So do I. I travel where I need to for each project. I'd be willing to spend time in the mountains when I could. I can be flexible to a point."

"So maybe we could make it work."

Her eyes told him she wanted to believe him—but didn't.

"For a while, but then what? I don't want to be a nomad. I want a home base. In time, I want a family. I guess I just want normal."

His throat squeezed tight. Normal might as well be a noose of responsibility.

She touched his arm. "Normal is everything you don't want. I get that."

"So we kiss and say good-bye? Jesus, Claire." He could barely choke out the words.

"Maybe we both need a break to think about it. I'll call when I get back from Crescent City. I'm sure you have things you need to do in the meantime."

He had plenty of things to attend to, starting with chopping a winter supply of wood. "What about your stalker?"

"Let's not do anything right now. If he leaves another note after I get back, I can re-evaluate my options, maybe call the police then. I'm hoping he'll quit."

He snorted. "Freaks like that don't stop until someone stops them."

"I need a break from…everything." Her eyes darkened. "Please don't push me. I'll make some decisions when I get back."

"Okay." He wanted to argue but was pretty sure she'd shatter into pieces if he did. Fine china dropped on the pavement. For now, he'd let her have the space she needed. Didn't mean he'd give up. Didn't mean he'd give in.

Maybe they *both* needed a break.

* * * *

Claire's eyes burned as she knelt on the bed to pull back the curtain. Jed's tent was set up on the other side of the yard beneath the big fir tree. After they'd eaten a meal in strained silence, he hadn't even asked where she expected him to sleep. Probably for the best. She wasn't sure she could have turned him down.

Was she a fool for blowing up at him then dragging their relationship into the misunderstanding over Bart, which could have been easily settled? She let the curtain fall and flopped back onto the bed. Maybe, but the discussion was long overdue...and had ended exactly as she'd feared. Better to know for sure than to play *what if* games. Ripping away a bandage with a swift jerk was preferable to slowly peeling it back at the edges. The pain was sharp but didn't last as long.

If she thought the platitude enough times, she might even start to believe it.

The digital clock taunted her throughout the night. When she finally crawled out of bed at six-thirty the following morning, her lids scraped across eyes grainy with lack of sleep. After throwing on a robe and grabbing jeans and a T-shirt to change into, she let Scoop out of the motor home then crossed the dew covered grass, shivering in the early morning chill. A hot shower gave her a burst of energy she feared would soon fade.

After drying and slicking on a layer of vanilla scented lotion, she reached for her bra, only to realize she hadn't brought one with her. With a shrug, she dressed and ran a comb through her hair. Grabbing her robe, she pushed her feet into a pair of flip-flops then opened the bathroom door...and ran straight into Jed. Her nose pressed against hard pecs covered with warm skin. She sucked in a breath. He smelled a heck of a lot better than her lotion.

"Whoa, there." His hands settled on her shoulders. "I was just about to knock to see how much longer you'd be."

"I'm finished." She swallowed and backed up an inch. "Where's your shirt?"

"I didn't bother putting one on. What's the point when I'm just going to take it off to shower?"

Her gaze dropped. At least he'd *bothered* to put on a pair of pants, even if they did hang low on his hips with the top button unfastened. She stepped back then flattened against the doorframe as he squeezed by.

"Uh, I'll go make breakfast. Eggs, pancakes or cereal?"

His blue eyes were slightly unfocused when he finally raised them to meet hers. "Eggs, over easy."

She glanced down. Erect nipples poked against the soft material of her T-shirt. Her cheeks heated. "Okay, eggs coming up."

He stroked the side of her face with a finger. "They aren't the only things coming up. I don't suppose..." He jerked his thumb toward the shower.

"I can't." Her voice hitched. "I want to." She closed her eyes and forced herself to breathe. "I really want to, but I can't. We're on a break, remember."

"Seems like we could start our break in an hour or two."

She shook her head. "I'll go make breakfast." Pushing past him, she ran down the stairs and through the front door. The cold breeze slapped her in the face and knocked a little sense into her. She'd made the right decision even if it felt like the wrong one.

Twenty minutes later, Jed knocked on the RV's door and pushed it open just as she slid perfectly cooked eggs onto a plate beside bacon and toast. His hair was still damp from the shower, but at least he was fully dressed. After handing him his breakfast, she cracked two more eggs into the pan and caught the second round of toast when it popped.

Brushing against her back, he reached for a mug from the cupboard to fill with coffee before taking a seat. "You didn't have to go to so much trouble."

"No trouble." Grease splattered as she flipped the eggs.

He laid down his fork. "Are you sure about this, Claire? I could still come with you."

She sat across from him with her food. "I'm sure." The first bite of toast stuck in her throat. With an effort she swallowed it down.

Jed broke off a piece of bacon and tossed it to Scoop. "Will you at least call me?"

Positive any verbal response would end on a sob, a quick nod was her answer. They finished eating in silence.

He rose to place their plates in the sink. "I'll wash these."

"No, I've got them."

His expression hardened. "In that case, I'll finish packing my stuff. Doesn't seem like there's much point in leaving any of it here."

When the door shut with a thud, she gripped the edge of the table so hard the laminate surface creaked. One whimper escaped before she dashed tears from her cheeks and attacked the dishes. Water sloshed and silverware clattered. The coffee mug Jed had used slipped through her fingers to shatter against the edge of the sink. When the broken pieces blurred before her eyes, a second whimper slipped out followed by a third.

Scoop pushed his head against her thigh and whined.

"Sorry, baby." Dragging in a breath, Claire closed her eyes for a long minute. When she opened them again, her hands were steadier as she picked up the ceramic pieces. A half hour later, the motor home was tidy and ready for travel. There was nothing left to do but tell Jed good-bye.

Letting the dog out, she followed him to the SUV. Jed slammed the back door of the loaded vehicle and turned. Reaching out, he rubbed Scoop's ears.

"All ready to go?"

She nodded. "Looks like you are, too."

He reached in his pocket to pull out a set of keys. "I locked up the house for you. What about the contractor?"

"I called Theresa to tell her I was leaving for a few days. She'll field any questions. Since he's starting with the outside first, he can still keep to his schedule." She lifted the keys from his palm.

Jed turned his hand over and closed it around her wrist. With a tug, he brought her up close against his chest. His sober gaze met hers. "This isn't good-bye."

"I know."

The other hand tilted her chin. "I don't think you do." He lowered his head to kiss her. When he finally pulled away, a little smile tilted the edges of his lips. "I'll give you some time, but I'll be back. You can count on it."

# Chapter 19

Good God, the woman was never going to shut up! All he wanted was to pick up his package, not wait around while the old biddy behind the counter asked questions about the teenage daughter of the customer in front of him, a stupid chicken recipe and—

"I heard Claire Templeton is fixing up her great-aunt's house. Is she going to move into the place or sell it?" The postmistress handed the dark-haired woman a book of stamps and took a twenty-dollar bill in exchange.

"Claire's staying in Shady Bend. She already hired a contractor for the major repairs and has been doing a lot of interior painting herself."

"Wonderful." The relic passed back a handful of change. "I bet you're glad. I know you two were close back in high school."

The woman stuffed dollar bills in her wallet along with the stamps. "I'm looking forward to having my old friend around, although she just left for a few days to take photographs for another article she's working on."

He stiffened. *Claire's gone? Where the hell did she go? Shit. Shit. Shit.*

"Oh? Where'd she go?"

"She's photographing Northern California lighthouses for this story, starting with Battery Point up in Crescent City."

The postmistress pushed rhinestone decorated glasses up her nose. "That's a pretty one. It's been a few years since I was up there, but I remember walking out to the lighthouse at low tide."

"I'd better go." The woman glanced over her shoulder with an apologetic smile. "I'm holding up your line."

Since he was the *line*, he felt obligated to respond. "That's okay."

"You take care, Theresa, and tell Claire I said hello the next time you see her."

The woman left, and he stepped up to the counter.

The postmistress smiled. "Now, what can I do for you, young man?"

"I'm expecting a package, general delivery. The name's—"

"I have it right here." She turned, cutting him off, and stretched on her toes to reach a padded mailer on the shelf behind her then placed the envelope in front of him. "Only one general delivery package came in today. Is this yours?"

He glanced at the label. "Sure is. Thank you."

"You're welcome, and thank *you* for your patience while I chatted with Theresa. Have a nice day."

"Don't you need to see my ID?"

"Oh, I suppose I should." Her gaze swept past him, and she smiled. "Well, hello Ralph. Shouldn't you be in your kitchen for the lunch rush?"

He pulled his wallet out of his pocket.

The postmistress waved a hand. "Take your package. I trust you."

Clutching the envelope to his chest, he passed a stout, grizzled man as he left the building. Once on the street, his fingers traced the outline of the photos inside the padded envelope, and his breath came a little faster… until he remembered.

He smacked the side of his vehicle. Claire was gone. Still, she wasn't out of reach. He'd always find her no matter where she went. Her little disappearing act might delay implementing his plan for a day or two, but no longer. Pulling open the door, he slipped onto the seat. A road trip was in order. North to Crescent City.

\* \* \* \*

Jed brought the axe down with enough force to send the two halves of the round sailing ten feet. Grabbing the next one, he hefted it into place and raised the axe again. *Crack.* The wood split beneath the blow.

So, maybe he was taking his frustration with Claire out on the pile of lodge pole pine. The good news was he'd have his winter supply of wood split in no time at the rate he was going.

Had she called him the previous evening to check in? No. *Crack.* Had he spent half the night wondering if everything was okay? Damn right. *Crack.* At ten-thirty he'd given in and called her. Her cell went straight to voice mail, and she hadn't bothered to respond to his message. Damn woman. *Crack.*

When his ring tone trilled, he dropped the axe, narrowly missing his booted foot, to snatch the phone from his pocket. Not Claire. His shoulders slumped as he answered.

"Hey, Kane."

"Hey, yourself. I hear you had dinner with Grace and Travis the other night. You still on the coast?"

He sat on the upended round he'd been using as a chopping block. "No, I'm home. Got here late yesterday afternoon."

"How does Claire like your cabin? According to Rachel...wait, she wrote this down so I'd get it right." Paper rustled, and a clunk sounded in his ear. "Sorry. I dropped the phone. Rachel says Grace thought Claire was perfect for you, and you'd be a fool to let her get away. Don't mess this one up."

"Is that all?"

"It's all she wrote down."

Jed grinned. "Why didn't Rachel just call me herself?"

"She was going to, but I told her I needed to talk to you anyway. She made me promise to relay her message verbatim."

"Claire isn't here." He rubbed the back of his neck. "We're taking a break."

There was silence for a moment before Kane spoke. "Who instigated this...break?"

"She did. We had a conversation about life goals, and...well..."

"You made it clear you didn't have any."

"Hey!"

"Sorry. What did you tell her?"

"The truth. I like my life the way it is. She's looking for something a little more normal. Normal was her word, not mine."

"Too bad. Grace thought Claire might be the one you'd change for. At least that's what she told Rachel. I'm pretty sure there was a lot more along that vein, but I tuned out when the baseball game came on."

"And you wonder why I'm not married."

"The Giants were playing. Anyway, I like being married. Just yesterday...never mind. Bet you'd like it, too, if you ever gave a woman half a chance."

Jed snorted. "You said you had a reason for calling other than to nag me about my love life."

"Right. Dad's going to Palm Springs with a couple of his golf buddies and their wives and the widowed friend of one of the ladies. I didn't want you to worry if you tried to reach him and he didn't answer his phone."

"I've told him a hundred times to get a cell phone—"

"But he says he only spends time at home or on the golf course—"

"And he doesn't want anyone interrupting his golf game—"

"So he doesn't need one." Kane's laugh echoed through the line. "I guess we've both heard that speech too many times to count."

"When does he leave?"

"Tomorrow."

"I'll call him tonight." His head jerked up. "Did you say widowed lady somewhere in there?"

"Yep. I think Dad's dating her. When he mentioned this woman, Deirdre Maxwell, his voice was—I don't know—soft. Weird, huh, thinking about him with someone other than Mom?"

The ache that always started in his heart whenever he thought about his mother tweaked a little—but no worse than usual. "It's been five years. Good for him."

"That's how I feel. I know he's lonely, despite what he says."

"So who's this woman?"

"He calls her Dee. He didn't say much, but I…well I—"

"Oh, my God, Kane. Did you run a search on her or something?"

"Hey, you never know these days." The defensive edge in his brother's tone eased. "She has a clean record, not even a parking violation. Her husband died three years ago of a heart attack. She has a couple of grown daughters, and her retirement benefits are a lot more substantial than Dad's, so she isn't after his pension."

"You're a piece of work. Does he know you—"

"Of course not! Don't say a word about it. He'd be pissed."

"I'm pretty sure Dad can take care of himself, not to mention he's an excellent judge of character." Jed kicked a piece of bark. "Unbelievable. Did you check out Claire while you were at it?"

"Why would I bother? We both know your track record." He paused. "You're right about Dad's ability to read people, but men don't always think straight when they're falling in love."

"You've got that right. I was actually considering compromising my principles before Claire got pissed and told me to go home."

"Good for Claire."

He kicked a bigger chunk of wood and winced. "Whose side are you on, anyway?"

"Yours. That's why I care when I hear you've ditched a woman who has the potential to make you happy."

"She did the ditching. Not me."

"Semantics. Your fault entirely, I'm sure."

He rose to his feet. "Maybe. Do you have anything else to badger me about? I was in the middle of chopping wood."

"By all means, chop away."

Jed stuffed the cell back in his pocket and picked up the axe. Kane didn't know squat about what made him happy. Just because—

The phone rang again.

He pulled it out and glanced at the display then let out a sigh. Apparently Claire was still ignoring him.

"Hi, Dad. I was going to call you this evening."

"I'm glad I reached you. When I talked to Rachel a few minutes ago, she told me you're up in the redwoods."

"Not anymore. I'm home, at least for a while. I just got off the phone with Kane. He mentioned you're going to Palm Springs."

"I'm looking forward to playing a few rounds of golf on some new courses."

"Kane also said you're taking along a...uh...lady friend." Jed rolled his eyes. What did you call the woman your seventy-year-old dad was dating?

"Dee. She's pretty and smart. We enjoy each other's company."

"I'm glad."

He assumed the rush of breath in response was a relieved sigh.

"I wasn't sure how you'd react. I haven't dated anyone special since your mom..."

"Dad, it's been five years since we lost her. You have a right to be happy."

"I won't pretend I haven't been a little lonely, even though I tried not to complain to you and your brother. A man has to find his own way past grief in his own time."

"Well, I think you should get out there and enjoy yourself."

"I intend to. Oh, I wanted to give you my number so you can reach me if you need to while I'm gone. I broke down and bought a cell phone."

Jed dropped the axe then jumped back. "You're kidding?"

"No. Dee told me I was acting like a stubborn mule. I guess some changes are for the best. Did you know you can play games on these things?"

He smiled. "You called from the house phone. What's the cell number?" As his dad recited, he typed it into his phone. "Got it."

"Good. Rachel and I had quite a talk. She said you're seeing some woman who used to live on our street when you were kids?"

"Claire Templeton. Do you remember her?"

"Dinky little blond girl who followed you around one summer?"

"Yep. We met by chance and camped together for a while down on the coast. She's still little and pretty and smart and funny..."

His dad's laugh warmed his heart.

"Sounds like you care about this girl."

"I do, but I don't think it's going to work out."

"Why not?"

"She's ready to settle down."

"And that's a problem?"

Jed turned his face up to the sky and closed his eyes. "I'm not big on settling."

"The word has different meanings. I'd be the first to agree you should never *settle* for something—or someone—if it's not what you want. But settling into a new situation and finding comfort in it, now that can be a good thing."

"Like you're doing with your friend, Dee?"

"Uh, I was thinking about the cell phone, but with Dee, too. Both are new and different. Both will take some getting used to since I'm set in my ways. But once I have, I may find life a little easier and more rewarding."

"I'll keep that in mind. Kane should take lessons from you."

"Oh? On what?"

"Giving advice. He said basically the same thing but, unlike you, managed to piss me off in the process."

His dad's chuckle rolled through the phone. "Brothers are good at that." He cleared his throat. "I just want happiness for you. What works for Kane or me might not be right for you. Your brother always has his feet on the ground. You're like a kite on a string, blowing whichever way the wind takes you. I just don't want you to miss out because you're being a stubborn mule like your old man."

"I'll keep that in mind. Have fun on your trip, Dad."

"I will. Love you, Son."

"Love you, too."

He clicked the phone off and pushed it into his pocket. Turning, he glanced at the giant pile of split logs and the rounds still waiting. "To hell with it. I'd rather go for a hike."

Leaving the axe where it lay, he headed for the cabin to change. Hiking was a whole lot more fun than splitting wood, and as everyone kept pointing out, having fun was what he did best."

* * * *

Claire hunched down to get the perfect angle and clicked. Zooming in a little closer, she took several more shots then glanced toward the shore. "Crap." She scooped her notes and the rest of her gear into the backpack and slung it over her shoulder. The tide was coming in. If she didn't hurry, she'd be stuck out on this rock for hours.

The Battery Point Lighthouse perched on an island connected to shore by a narrow strip of land when the tide was out. At high tide, a boat was necessary to reach the place. Visitor hours ended at four, and it was long past that now. She'd pushed her luck with the tide, waiting until all the tourists left so she could sneak Scoop over to the island. With the dog splashing in the sea surge beside her, she ran along the path and only got her tennis shoes a little wet before she reached the shore.

Making her way down the beach, she stopped periodically to take pictures of the little white building with the red roof near the giant cypress tree. The place was a photographer's dream. The problem would be choosing which shots to use in her article. Satisfied with her day's work, she put away her camera and glanced down at the dog. "Now what?"

He answered with a sharp bark before running off to sniff a bunch of mussels adhering to a rock at the water's edge. Claire slowed her pace. What was the point in hurrying when she had nowhere to go? No one would be waiting when she returned to the RV. For dinner she could eat out alone or cook a meal in the motor home with Scoop for company. A long sigh was caught by the breeze. Her heart ached with missing Jed.

*Better get used to it.*

Not that he hadn't tried to reach her. She'd listened to the messages he'd left too many times to count before deleting them. *Fool.* If she had half a brain, she would have erased them without indulging in the temptation to moon over the sound of his deep voice.

"Lame. Lame. Lame." Jamming her hands in her jacket pockets, she trudged onward. When a sand crab skittered across the beach in front of her, she paused to pull out her camera. She got one shot off before the animal disappeared into a hole.

Was this all her future held? Happiness over a single moment captured in time. If she broke down and accepted what Jed offered, her life wouldn't be much different in the long run. A series of poignant moments with no plan for the future to hold them together. Not to mention a gnawing ache in her stomach as she waited for him to move on to a new adventure.

Her steps took on purpose as she turned back and headed toward the parking lot. She couldn't face another lonely evening in the motor home where everything reminded her of Jed. What she needed was a distraction, preferably one with lots of noisy strangers and maybe a bowl of clam chowder. A friendly woman from the campground had recommended a restaurant out on the dock. The place sounded a whole lot better than her own company.

"Let's go, Scoop."

He bounded over to her then led the way up the winding path toward the motor home, only to stop when he reached the edge of the parking lot. A low growl rumbled in his throat.

"What's wrong, boy?" She stroked his quivering back.

No strange dog was in sight, and he was usually friendly enough with other animals. With a shrug, she moved forward.

"I need to change my clothes. Then you get to hang out in the RV while I go eat. Maybe we'll take a moonlight walk through the campground afterward if the fog holds off." She dug out her key on an eye roll. "Who needs a man when I have you to love?"

Claire pulled open the door and stepped inside. A scream ripped from her throat, followed by another and another and another…

# Chapter 20

"This is exactly how you found it?" The police officer crossed his arms over his barrel chest and gave her a long look through cool gray eyes.

A shiver shook Claire. She pulled her jacket tighter around her and nodded. "Once I got over the initial shock, I backed out and shut the door. The dog hasn't even been inside. Then I called 9-1-1."

Turning, he took his time surveying the interior of the motor home. "Looks like something an old boyfriend or a jealous lover with a grudge might have done. Maybe trying to embarrass you—or turn you on. Entice you back."

Her cheeks burned. Standing outside the RV, she could only see part of one photo taped to the back of the passenger seat. From his position in the doorway, the cop was getting the full effect of the pictures plastered all over the interior.

"It's not an old boyfriend. We eliminated all of them."

Officer Edelman's head snapped around. "What?" The word echoed like a rifle shot.

"I tried to tell you this isn't the first time someone's broken into my motor home. But what he's done here is a lot worse than before, which is why I called the police." She let out a breath. "It's a long story, and I'm cold. Do you mind if I put on a warmer jacket?"

"I can't let you disturb the scene until it's been processed, but you can sit in the squad car if you'd like."

"No, thanks. I—"

Footsteps slapped the pavement as the younger of the two responding officers hurried across the parking lot. "I talked to everyone I could find in the vicinity and checked with homeowners in the nearby houses. No one admits to seeing anyone lingering around your vehicle." He stopped beside her and held out a hand for Scoop to sniff. "Guess you should have left this big guy in your RV. I doubt anyone would have been brave enough to mess with him."

Instead, she'd ignored the sign about no pets and taken him with her to the lighthouse. "Hindsight's a…well, you know." She tried to stop her teeth from chattering. "I have a heavy jacket in the closet near the bed. If you could—"

"Hernandez, get her a blanket out of the car. No one's going to touch anything in this place before the techs get here."

"How long will that be?"

"They should arrive shortly, but it'll take a couple of hours to process everything."

When Officer Hernandez returned with a wool blanket, she smiled her thanks and wrapped it around her shoulders then grabbed her backpack and moved away to sit on the raised curb.

He followed. Kind eyes gazed down at her.

*Is this man old enough to be a cop?* With that baby face, he looked like a sixteen-year-old who worked out. Maybe he was in training.

"Once the team gets here, we can take you back to the station to get your full statement. Normally we'd handle a B&E ourselves, but the nature of the photographs turns this into something more serious. Edelman wants a thorough investigation and interview, just to be on the safe side." He turned to glance out over the gray expanse of ocean. "At least you'll be warm while he questions you. The fog rolled in fast this evening."

"A half hour ago it was gorgeous."

"You know how it is on the coast."

When the older officer called him back to the RV with a barked order, Claire let her shoulders slump. The brave face she'd pasted on after she got over her screaming attack fell away. All those pictures…

Scoop pressed against her and whined. She leaned her cheek on his warm fur and clenched her fists beneath the blanket. Wishing Jed was there beside her wouldn't make him magically appear. Her fault. She'd been the one who was so sure she was safe from her stalker. That she could do this alone….

Nameless. Faceless. She couldn't begin to imagine what kind of pervert had taken all those pictures. Sunbathing at her old cottage. Dressing in her motor home. A blurry shot of her in the shower at some campground she didn't even remember. Wait. There'd been a long, narrow window high up on the brick wall of the showers in Yellowstone. She'd set her earrings on the ledge and nearly forgotten them. That was…her brow wrinkled… three years ago. Maybe four. This freak had been following her around for a long time. There were pictures of her in Lake Tahoe and Yosemite and the Colorado Rockies. Pictures from Death Valley and Moab and... no, none from Hawaii. He hadn't followed her to Hawaii.

As bad as they were, the photographs weren't even the worst part. He'd thrown back the covers on her bed to make it up with red silk sheets and left handcuffs on the table, along with a whip and a few other objects she assumed were assorted sex toys. A shudder wracked her as she drew in a ragged breath. *Sick freak.*

*Bet your boy toy doesn't know half the things I'll do to you on our honeymoon. I'll make you feel so good. Time's almost up!*

Every word of the note taped to the refrigerator was burned into her brain. She whimpered and pressed harder against Scoop's side. The dog turned to lick her face as a van rolled into the parking lot.

Thank God. All she wanted to do was give her statement then go... where? A motel. She couldn't face the motor home again tonight. Would they take all the pictures and other...stuff...as evidence? Would the officers let her retrieve a change of clothes and her toothbrush? Scoop would want his dinner even if she didn't.

"Ma'am, we can go now." The baby-faced cop approached.

She nodded and stood to follow him to the patrol car. The older officer joined them, lips still clamped in a tight line, and waved his partner toward the passenger side. She'd be willing to bet the kid never got to drive.

When Edelman opened the rear door, she hesitated. "Scoop?"

"Damn. I forgot about him." The senior officer frowned. "I'll call animal control to pick him up."

"What? No!" She dropped to her knees to clasp her arms around Scoop's neck. Tears threatened, and she blinked to hold them back.

Hernandez regarded her over the roof of the car then turned his gaze on his partner. "Can't we let her bring him along, just this once? I'll deal with him at the station."

The hard gray gaze softened as he turned back to face her. "I suppose he can ride along."

She let out a breath then pushed up off the pavement. "Thank you." After her dog leaped inside, she climbed in beside him, feeling like a criminal trapped behind the mesh partition.

The two men talked about last night's baseball game as they cruised down Front Street then made a left turn onto a side street. Away from the view of the ocean, the town looked grim beneath a shroud of fog. Or maybe it was just her mood. They passed a bank and some other businesses then slowed to pull into the parking area behind the police station. The older cop let her out when they reached their destination since the door wasn't operable from the inside.

Hernandez gave her an encouraging smile, took the leash from her then led Scoop away. After Edelman checked in, she followed him down a hallway to a room with a scattering of metal desks and file cabinets. He pointed to a straight-back chair beside a desk cluttered with a collection of dirty coffee mugs and an array of framed snapshots before he dropped onto the cracked, fake-leather chair behind it. She would have guessed he was a neat freak. Yet another bad judgment call on her part.

After jiggling his mouse to bring the computer to life, he clicked a few times then glanced over with fingers poised above the keyboard. "We'll start with your personal information. Full name, phone number, address."

She stumbled over the last one. Thanks to Great-aunt Agatha she didn't have to admit to being homeless. She was pretty certain the man opposite her wouldn't have been impressed.

"Now, let's go over the sequence of events again. Start with when you arrived in town."

Claire repeated every detail of her time in Crescent City from pulling into the campground the previous afternoon to making the 9-1-1 call a little over twenty-four hours later. Then she went through it again.

"All right, now I want to hear about these other incidents. You didn't report them?"

Claire shook her head. "They seemed completely harmless at first. I thought the man responsible was an old boyfriend. I was certain I could handle the situation myself. Except it wasn't someone I know."

Edelman shot her a hard glance. "Let's just stick to the facts, not your interpretation of them. When did the first incident take place?"

A half hour later, Claire wondered why no one had recruited this man to interrogate terrorists. Surely they'd break beneath his unrelenting gaze. Did he ever smile?

"You mentioned your friend, Jed, was around for most of these incidents. Can I get his full name and contact information please."

She hesitated. "Jed isn't involved. He's been more concerned this... person would prove to be dangerous than I was. After the last time with the nightie and candles, he didn't want me to go anywhere alone."

The cop glanced up from his keyboard. "Then why did you?"

"We sort of had a fight."

His brows shot up. "And it never crossed your mind he could be the one harassing you?"

"No, it isn't Jed."

"But you thought it might be one of your other ex-boyfriends."

"I considered it. However, Ross is in Connecticut, so he's definitely not the one. Ian has no interest in reviving a long dead relationship, and Dallas…"

"Yes?"

"I'd know if Dallas was lying to me. He's not responsible."

"I'll need all their names and addresses."

Claire sighed then provided what information she could. The officer had a computer in front of him. She was pretty sure he would ferret out the specifics.

"Why are you smiling?"

She straightened. "Was I? Probably because I was imagining Ian's reaction when he gets a phone call from the police. He's the only person I know who frowns more than you do."

Something that might have been a snort of humor escaped before he pressed a hand over his mouth and coughed. "Let's move on. Jed's surname?"

"Lafferty. He lives up on Donner Summit. I don't have his address, but I can give you his cell phone number."

"Go ahead."

She recited it. "Jed had nothing to do with this, honestly. Anyway, his brother is a sheriff, and his dad is a retired cop."

"Just because his family is in law enforcement doesn't mean your friend isn't a pervert. Where does the brother work?"

"Kane lives somewhere near Napa."

The man typed for a few minutes then sat back in his chair. "You're sure you're telling me everything exactly the way it happened?"

"Of course I'm telling you everything. Do you think I'd make this stuff up? It sounds crazy enough as it is."

The gray eyes turned almost silver beneath dark brows. "Maybe after you and your boyfriend had a fight, he wanted to make some kind of point with the photographs. Or perhaps he got a little kinkier than you liked, and it scared you."

Fists clenched, she shot up out of the chair. "No!"

"Sit down. Please."

Claire dropped back onto the seat and let out a long breath. "That isn't what happened."

"We'll look into all the information you've provided."

She pressed her hands hard against her thighs. "Thank you. Can I go back to my motor home now?"

"Let me check on the team's progress."

He stood and walked away only to disappear into an office. The door shut behind him.

Officer Hernandez left the desk where he'd been since he returned without Scoop and offered her a commiserating smile. "Edelman can be kind of a hard ass, but he's smarter than any cop I know."

"He's wrong about this. The person stalking me may be an acquaintance, but he isn't someone close to me."

"He'll make some calls and contact the police in Shady Bend to update them on the situation. While you're in town, we'll keep an eye on you. You'll be safe enough."

She shivered. "I don't think I can sleep in my motor home tonight. I'd like to get a few things then check into a motel."

His deep brown eyes filled with compassion. "Maybe you should call a friend or relative. Talk to someone. It might help."

"I don't know anyone around here." She stood when Edelman exited the office. "I'll be fine. I just need some time to pull myself together."

"They're finished. Everything the man left in your vehicle has been bagged and taken as evidence." The older cop eyed the rookie. "You can take her back to the RV or wherever Miss Templeton would like to go."

She forced a smile. "Thank you. I appreciate your help."

He nodded. "I'll be in touch."

Night had fallen while they were in the police station. After retrieving Scoop from the kennel where he'd been languishing, Officer Hernandez opened the car door to let the ecstatic dog jump onto the rear seat before she climbed in beside him. Leaning back against the headrest, Claire stroked her quivering pet and let out a long sigh.

"Tired?" He glanced at her in the rearview mirror.

"Drained. I want to go to bed and wake up to find out this was all a bad dream."

"That'd be nice. Just click your heels and say, 'There's no place like home.'"

Except she didn't want to be transported home. She wanted Jed.

"We can stop to get you something to eat."

"No, thanks." She shook her head. "Seeing those pictures effectively squelched my appetite."

"You should still eat something. We can swing through a drive-up window and get a burger."

Her stomach churned. "Ugh."

He glanced back again through the mirror. "Vegetarian?"

"No, but I don't do fast food."

"How about a burrito? You'll think you died and went to heaven."

"I guess that's preferable to the alternative. All right."

He drove through town before parking in front of a shack down near the harbor. "I know it looks bad on the outside, but the food is first rate. Trust me on this. Do you want beef or chicken?"

"Chicken."

"Be right back."

A fog horn blared, deep and mournful, as she waited and wondered what Jed was doing. Pulling her cell from her pocket, she scrolled through the missed calls. One from Theresa. One from her mother. She'd call them both later. No new ones from Jed. She couldn't blame him for giving up on her.

The car door opened. "Here you go." Hernandez handed her a bag. "I had them double wrap the burrito in foil to keep it warm while we collect your stuff."

She reached for her backpack. "What do I owe you?"

"It's on the house. My sister owns the place."

"Well, thanks. It smells unbelievable. I love Mexican food."

He got in, backed out of the parking space, then drove to the lot where she'd left her RV. Letting the car idle, he turned to face her. "You still want to go to a motel?"

"Yes. No." She took a deep breath. "Screw that creep! I'm not going to let him call the shots. Anyway, I can't avoid the motor home forever. It's the only transportation I have at the moment."

A streetlight illuminated his flashing smile. "I like you, Claire. You're a tough chick, even if you do look like one of those porcelain dolls my niece keeps on a shelf."

"I don't break that easily, but I wouldn't say no if you offered to go in there first. Like the lion, I need a dose of courage right now."

"Unlike the tin man, you have plenty of heart. Let's go see what sort of mess the techs left in the place." He turned off the engine, opened the door and stepped out of the car to open her door.

She was slow to release her seatbelt. By the time she stood on the pavement, he'd let Scoop out and was waiting in front of the RV.

"Do you have the key? They locked it up."

Digging the key ring out of her backpack, she handed it over. His palm closed over hers, giving it a light squeeze. "Everything will be all right."

"I know. I'm just a little nervous."

After unlocking the door, he pulled a flashlight from his belt and went inside. Scoop followed. When the dog sat in front of his food bowl and whined, she smiled and joined them.

The officer switched on the battery powered light over the sink. "Not too bad. They dusted the place for prints, so you'll need to do a little cleaning." The photos were all gone. So were the sex toys and the sheets. Her bed was a tangled mess of covers. They'd taken the note as well. She let out a sigh of relief.

"I'll definitely stay here tonight. Well, not here, here. I'll go back to the campground."

"I'll follow you over then swing by a couple times before my shift ends." Gratitude filled her. "Thank you."

"No problem. Did you get your burrito?"

"I put it in my backpack."

He stepped past her as she edged toward the driver's seat. "Don't worry. I'll be right behind you, and I'll make sure we're not followed. Claire?"

"Yes?"

"The officer who relieves me will drive by a few times, too."

"I think I love you."

He laughed. "That's what they all say. Try to get some sleep. Maybe I'll see you again tomorrow if we have any news to report by then."

"I'll keep my fingers crossed."

The short drive to the campground was highlighted by Scoop's pathetic moans. Apparently he was in serious danger of starvation. Once she'd parked in her site, the patrol car cruised through the campground twice before leaving.

Claire fed Scoop then tackled the bed, putting on fresh sheets and blankets. Finally she wiped down the table and kitchenette area before sitting to eat her burrito. Officer Hernandez hadn't exaggerated. With her appetite restored, she savored every delectable bite.

Scoop's evening walk was straight to the restroom and back. She sighed in relief when he lifted his leg over a bush almost immediately. No way was she taking a leisurely stroll through the dark campground tonight. Back in the motor home, she tugged all the curtains tightly together across the windows before changing into an old pair of sweats. Her cell sat on the table. She picked it up and turned it over.

She wanted to call Jed. God, how she wanted to call him. Hear his voice. Listen to him tell her she'd be okay. Tears threatened, and she forced them back. She refused to cry. Refused to break down because some pervert had invaded what was essentially her home and touched her things. Had spied on her when she wasn't aware she was being watched. She wouldn't cry even though she ached for the man she loved.

Turning off the phone, she set it down, rechecked the lock on the door, rubbed Scoop's ears then crawled into bed despite the fact that it wasn't even nine o'clock yet. She tucked her knees to her chest and closed her eyes. A single sob escaped.

It was going to be a long night.

# Chapter 21

For the love of God, where the hell had he left his cell phone? Jed jabbed his hand through each of the pockets in the jackets hanging on the rack by the door for a third time. Nothing but lint, a gum wrapper and a used tissue. He tossed the debris into the garbage then rummaged amongst the dirty breakfast and lunch dishes still on the counter. Muttering under his breath, he stalked to the bathroom, slamming the door against the wall when he pushed inside. The only thing out of place was a razor and a can of shaving gel left by the sink. He hadn't been in the bedroom since he got up that morning. Wait. Yes, he had. He'd changed before heading out to hike off his frustration. Hunting through the clothes dropped on the floor, he came up empty. The only thing under the bed was a lone sock with a cobweb attached to the toe.

When his stomach growled, he slammed the door into the wall again then went back to the kitchen to cook dinner. He'd discovered the phone wasn't in his pocket about four miles into the hike. On the way home, he'd kept an eye on the trail, but twilight cast dark shadows through the woods long before he reached the cabin. He'd check again in the light of day, and until then, drive himself crazy wondering if Claire had ever returned his calls.

After throwing a potato in the microwave, snapping some green beans to boil and seasoning a steak, he went outside to light the grill. While the coals heated, he wandered further into the yard and turned his face toward the star filled sky. Was Claire camped somewhere near the ocean, listening to waves crash on the beach and looking up at the moon glowing softly in the darkness? Was she missing him as much as he missed her?

A muted ring broke the silence.

"Well, I'll be a son of a bitch!" He ran toward the woodpile, but the sound stopped before he reached it. Turning, he headed full bore back into the cabin to grab a flashlight out of the junk drawer he'd left open.

Taking the steak with him, he tossed it on the grill on the way to the pile of split logs. As he flicked the light over the ground, he kicked through the woodchips until a gleam of silver reflected in the beam.

Swooping down, he grabbed the phone and checked the display. Six missed calls. Holy hell! He usually didn't get six calls in a week. After pausing to flip the steak, he went into the cabin where he could see what he was doing. None of the messages were from Claire. *Damn woman.* There was a missed call from a number he didn't recognize with a 707 prefix, which he was pretty certain covered all the northernmost counties along the coast. Had Claire called him from a phone other than her cell? That made no sense. The other five calls were from Kane. He listened to the first message.

*Where the hell are you? Call me.* He clicked to the next message. *Damn it, Jed, pick up your phone.* A quiver of fear shot through him. Had something happened to Rachel or one of the girls? Maybe his dad…he pushed a button and paced to the window.

"Jed? Jesus, it's about time."

"I misplaced my phone. What's wrong?"

"Where are you?"

"At home. I told you that earlier. *What's wrong?*"

There was a pause before his brother spoke. "A couple of hours ago I got a call from a police officer up in Crescent City. He couldn't reach you and had a few questions."

Jed's heart stopped. He gripped the windowsill and prayed. "Did something happen to Claire?"

"She's fine. Honestly. *And* I think I convinced this cop you aren't a complete pervert. The officer—I have his name here…Edelman—finally gave me a few details, but I had to pry them out of him."

Jed pressed his forehead to the glass pane and breathed. "Thank God. What happened?" His nostrils twitched. "Shit." He ran to the door and threw it open.

"What?"

"I burned the crap out of my steak." He flipped the charred meat onto a plate and turned off the grill. "Tell me what happened."

"Some deviant decorated Claire's motor home with half-naked pictures of her. He also left some sex toys. She was upset and called 9-1-1, but the officer said she'd calmed down by the time she left the station."

Jed kicked the door shut. "I'm going to freaking kill the bastard when I get my hands on him."

"Yeah, well, the cop thought the bastard might be you. Claire said it wasn't, but he didn't believe her after she mentioned you'd had an argument."

He set the plate on the counter then turned off the burner beneath the beans with his free hand. His shoulders slumped. "I'm going to drive up there."

"Tonight?"

"Hell, yes, tonight."

"It's after nine o'clock, and that has to be an eight-hour drive. I don't want you to fall asleep and kill yourself or someone else on the highway. Anyway, you're upset. Not a good combination coupled with a long road trip."

"*I'm* upset? Imagine how Claire feels."

"Violated. That's the way most people react after a home invasion. But her trauma doesn't make it okay for you to do something stupid."

"I'm going to hang up now and call her."

"Jed—"

"I'll call you back after I talk to her, okay?"

"I guess it'll have to be."

He disconnected then punched in Claire's number. It went straight to voice mail. He gritted his teeth and waited until her cheery message ended.

"I heard what happened, and I'm worried. I know you're pissed at me but please call."

He laid the phone on the counter and stared at the burned steak. His stomach rolled. Whooshing out a breath, he picked up the cell again to call Kane.

"What did she say?"

"Nothing. Her phone's turned off."

"I called the police station after I hung up with you. They're driving by her campsite on a regular basis tonight. She'll be safe, Jed."

"I still want to be there."

His brother's voice deepened. "I get that. If it were Rachel…" He cleared his throat. "Why don't you drive down here tonight? You can get a few hours of sleep then head out early in the morning. You'll be a little closer that way."

Jed ran a hand through his hair. He'd been up since six, chopped wood all day then gone on an eight-mile hike. He was flat-out exhausted. He knew his brother was right, but—

"What good are you going to be to her if you arrive at five in the morning? She'll still be alone most of the night, and you'll have to sleep once you get there. *If* you get there."

"Fine. I'll choke down this piece of burnt leather, pack then hit the road." He glanced around. "Maybe clean up a little so I won't face an infestation of cockroaches when I come back. I should be there in three hours tops."

"I'll leave the key on the ledge above the door, and Rachel will make up the hide-a-bed in the living room for you. She's worried, too."

"Tell her thank you for me. I don't know if I'll see you in the morning because I'll be out of there well before sunrise. I appreciate this, Kane."

He hung up and tried Claire again with the same frustrating results. With a string of obscenities, he drained the beans and dumped them on his plate then pulled the potato out of the microwave. He'd force down the meal because he needed the energy. Even if it killed him.

\* \* \* \*

Jed woke slowly then jerked away from a blast of stinky breath. "What the hell?" Stretching out an arm, he snapped on the end table lamp.

Daisy, Rachel's golden retriever, sat next to the sofa sleeper. Her tail thumped the floor. Closing his eyes, he flopped back against the mattress.

When the dog whined, he rolled over and buried his head beneath the pillow. But only for a minute. Sitting up, he swung his legs off the side of the bed and snatched up his phone. Nearly five o'clock. He should thank the damn dog for waking him.

He didn't bother pulling on pants before heading toward the front entry. When he opened the door, the dog shot out into the yard. Yawning, he scratched his chest and stretched. Bending from side to side, he cracked his back. He'd had four solid hours of sleep on a lumpy mattress. Better than nothing.

After dressing in the jeans and shirt he'd worn the night before, he let Daisy back in then went straight to the kitchen. He'd make coffee and grab something to eat for the road. A glance at the digital clock on the stove told him it was still too early to call Claire again. If she'd turned her phone back on in the night, he didn't want to wake her.

"You're up early."

Jed swung away from the sink holding the coffeepot full of water. Wearing a pair of gray sweatpants and an old Hanover Vineyards T-shirt, his brother leaned against the doorframe. His hair, a darker shade of brown than Jed's, stood up on one side. Blue eyes regarded him with concern reflected in their depths.

"Daisy woke me."

Kane scowled at the dog. "Nice going."

Her feathery tail waved as she walked over to her food bowl and stared at it. Kane rolled his eyes then pulled a bag of kibble out of the pantry.

Nuggets rained into the bowl while Jed poured water into the tank and flipped on the coffee maker.

"Did you ever reach Claire?"

He shook his head. "No."

"Did you call Officer Edelman back?"

"I'll speak to him in person when I get to Crescent City. I should be there by noon if this damn coffee maker would brew a little faster."

Kane came over to put a hand on his shoulder. "Staring at it won't help."

"Probably not." He propped himself up against the counter. "Sorry I woke you."

"You didn't." He hesitated for a long moment. "You look like shit. Want to talk about it."

"What's there to say? I shouldn't have left Claire alone. It's my fault that pervert got to her again."

"I thought she kicked you out?"

"She did, but I chose to go. I could have flat out refused. I was so damned worried about giving up a little of my freedom, I let her convince me she'd be fine on her own." He turned to open a cupboard door, shut it, opened a second one and pulled two mugs off a shelf to plunk down on the counter. "I knew better. I told her this creep wouldn't give up."

Kane waited until Jed poured coffee into a cup then took the pot from him. "How long have you and Claire been hanging out together?"

"I don't know. A couple of weeks I guess."

"That's not very long. Why do you feel she's your responsibility?"

"I don't. She's super independent, irritatingly so at times. But..." He sipped and frowned. "I care. A lot. I'm sure as hell not going to sit back and let someone harass her."

"Are you in love with her?"

He glanced away from his brother's knowing gaze and walked to the pantry. Coming back with a bag of bagels, he sliced one in half to slide into the toaster. "Maybe I am."

"Then why won't you fight to keep her in your life? Christ, Jed, don't be an idiot."

"Hey! I didn't argue too hard because she was right. The last thing I want is for us to wind up resenting each other. She knows what she needs to be happy, and so do I."

"If that's true, why are you running to her side the second she's in trouble?"

He jerked open the refrigerator door, hunted through the shelves then pulled out a package of cream cheese. "Because I can't *not* go."

"You're just prolonging the inevitable."

"That's what Claire said when she told me to go home." He scowled as he spread white cheese over the bagel. "I hate it when you're right."

Kane drank from his cup, grimaced then added a shallow spoonful of sugar. "Are you hoping she'll change her mind about you? If you run to her rescue, will she decide you're a responsible adult ready for a commitment?"

"Doubtful. She's a little smarter than that."

"I like this woman already." Rachel crossed the kitchen to make a beeline for the coffee pot, her robe flapping around bare legs. "But I'm in love with whoever made this."

Jed grinned. "That would be me. If you dump your husband, I promise to quit obsessing over Claire."

She laughed and gave him a hug. "No, you wouldn't."

He eyed Kane over the top of his wife's head. "You're way too pretty for him."

"Maybe, but he puts up with my girls. I think he likes them more than I do most of the time. You don't even want to know what Lark did last week."

"You're right, I don't. I'm pretty sure if I ever have a sixteen-year-old daughter, I'll simply lock her in her room until she turns thirty."

"That's an idea."

Jed drank the last of his coffee and picked up the bagel. "Thanks for letting me crash here last night, but I have to go."

Rachel patted his arm. "Drive carefully." Her green gaze caught his and held. "Do you want my advice?"

"Please. You're prettier *and* smarter than Kane."

"Go with your instincts. They won't steer you wrong. When you're ready to make a change, you'll know. It's your life, and you have to live it the way you want. Sometimes that means making hard choices."

"Thank you. That's what I've been trying to tell everyone, but no one listens."

As he passed his brother, Kane reached out to pull him in for a back slapping hug. "Call if you have any problems with the police up there. I'll do what I can from here."

"Thanks." He drew in a breath and kept walking. Right now, all he cared about was reaching Claire. Once he saw she was okay with his own eyes, he might be able to relax. Then, and only then, would he think about all the advice everyone seemed hell bent on giving him. And make a few decisions, including one that just might break his heart.

\* \* \* \*

Her phone was ringing when Claire turned off the water. Grabbing a towel, she wrapped it around her middle, scooped up the cell and pushed the connect button with a slippery finger.

"Hello."

"Are you okay?"

She dropped onto the wooden bench outside the tin shower stall, wet hair dripping down her back. Jed's voice did more to warm her than a heat lamp.

"I'm fine. I thought you were the police calling me with news."

"Sorry to disappoint."

"You didn't. I mean…" She let out a shaky breath. "I was going to call you back, but it was so early I didn't want to wake you."

"I've been driving for two hours already."

Juggling the phone, she tried to dry off with the damp towel. "Oh, where to?"

*Is that sound his teeth grinding?*

The faint noise stopped. "Where do you think? Crescent City. If I don't get pulled over for speeding, I should be there in about three more hours."

"You're coming here?" Warmth spread from her dripping head down to her toes curled against blue rubber flip-flops.

"Did you think I wouldn't once I heard what had happened? Not that you bothered to fill me in. My brother called."

"Kane? How did he—"

"Officer Edelman contacted him. Apparently, he thought I was the pervert bothering you."

"I *told* him you weren't responsible. I'm sorry, Jed."

"You're sorry?" His voice rose. "You didn't do a damn thing wrong so don't be sorry." A long breath gusted through the phone. "I'm the one who failed you. I should never have left you alone no matter what you told me to do…or where you told me to go. You better believe I won't make that mistake again."

"But—"

"No buts. Look, I should probably hang up. I don't need a ticket for speeding *and* talking on my cell phone while I'm going ninety."

"Jed!"

"Where are you? Are you someplace safe?"

"I'm at the campground south of town. It's the only one, so you'll see it."

"Are the cops still keeping an eye on you?"

"I hope not. I just stepped out of the shower, and I'm naked and dripping."

Silence echoed over the line.

"Jed, are you still there?"

"I'm here." His voice took on a husky quality. "Thanks for the mental image. I won't need any more coffee to keep me wired after that."

Her breasts tingled, and heat shot straight to her core. Closing her eyes, she leaned back against the cinderblock wall. "You didn't have to drive up here, but I'm glad you're on the way."

"I'll be there soon. Stay safe."

He disconnected before she could answer. A smile spread as she finished drying off, scrambled into her clothes, gathered together her belongings, then headed back to the motor home. Nothing had changed between her and Jed, and the stalker was still out there somewhere. Waiting. *Watching?* God, she hoped not. Glancing around, she picked up her step then smiled. Despite lingering fog hanging in the trees, the morning suddenly seemed a whole lot brighter.

# Chapter 22

Damn it all to freaking hell. Lafferty was back.

After staying clear of Claire the previous night since she'd gone and called the cops—not a move he'd anticipated—he'd cruised by the campground a couple of hours earlier to check on her. Catching a glimpse of her outside with the dog, he'd thought about approaching her. Good thing his sense of self-preservation screamed *no*. Better to wait until she was down at the ocean taking photographs. The campground was relatively crowded, and if she panicked…too risky. He'd rather take his chances on a lonely stretch of beach.

Now his plan was shot to hell.

Lafferty stood close, his hands resting on her shoulders while Claire gazed up at him. The moron bent his head and kissed her.

He jerked down the gear shift and stomped on the gas. Gravel spit from beneath the tires as he swung out onto the road.

*Damn Claire.* Why'd she have to call the man and ruin everything? His hopes had skyrocketed when he realized the idiot had left Shady Bend without her. Maybe it had made him cocky, and he'd gotten carried away and overplayed his hand with the pictures. Instead of turning Claire on, they'd frightened her. Would she have reacted differently if she knew who'd taken them?

He slammed his hand against the steering wheel, and his vehicle hopped and bounced right. His teeth clenched. Too late to find out now. With Lafferty around, he wouldn't get another chance to catch her alone in Crescent City, so he might as well return to Shady Bend. Surely she'd take the rest of the pictures she needed today and leave for home by tomorrow at the latest.

He chewed on one ragged nail and frowned. Best to get far away from here, anyway. His prints were all over the pictures he'd left in the RV.

Thank God he didn't have a record. Still…no point in tempting fate by sticking around. He'd head south to wait.

No more games. No more gifts. Next time he'd simply snatch the prize and force Claire to live up to her vow.

* * * *

"We checked out your old boyfriends. Three of them have alibis."

Claire leaned back in the chair and regarded Officer Edelman across his cluttered desk. "That's all of them. I was certain no one I used to date was responsible."

"No, Ian Rutledge is still under consideration. We spoke to him early this morning. He claims he was camping in the woods, but no one was around to verify his presence in Shady Bend yesterday afternoon. The man was extremely defensive. If anyone has something to hide, it's your ex-husband." He frowned. "You failed to mention you'd been married to him."

"The marriage was annulled, so technically we weren't legally bound. Anyway, that's how Ian acts all the time. He's high-strung. You said three—"

He held up a hand to tick off the men on his fingers. "Ross McGregor was indeed in Connecticut. Dallas Sims worked in his hardware store for most of the afternoon, surrounded by customers and employees." He shot a glance toward Jed, who was talking with Officer Hernandez near the doorway. "Your friend over there purchased gas yesterday evening at a station up on Donner Summit. That clears him."

"You checked Jed's credit card records?"

"Of course."

She rolled her eyes. "You could have simply taken my word for his innocence."

"Generally, in cases of harassment, the perpetrator is someone the victim knows. I've no reason to believe this case will prove to be an exception."

"Does that mean the man who took those pictures is a casual acquaintance, a person I've spoken to a few times?"

"I'd say it's someone you know well. Either a man you dated, although not necessarily exclusively, or someone you worked with. Possibly an old neighbor. I checked with a police psychologist. She agrees this person isn't a stranger to you. His actions have been too personal."

Claire frowned. "I honestly can't think of anyone I know who would do something like this. I've dated a few men casually over the years, but our partings were amicable for the most part. I certainly can't imagine Mr. Williamson, my eighty-year-old next-door neighbor at the cottage I used to rent, following me around the country to take pictures. Anyway, some of the photos were from before I lived in Marin."

Edelman leaned forward, elbows planted on the desk. "You bring up a good point." He glanced up when Jed walked over to stand beside her. "Do you need to see the pictures again to identify when the earliest ones were taken? The person we're looking for would be someone you met prior to that time."

When Jed reached for her hand, she squeezed hard. "The shower photo was taken in Yellowstone, I think. That was almost four years ago. I'm not sure about all the locations. I didn't look closely at the pictures taped up in the back of the RV."

"I'll get the packet for you. If we can date the oldest picture, it should narrow down the suspects to someone you knew around that time." He stood and walked away from his desk, pausing to speak to Hernandez before exiting the room.

Claire shivered. "Is it cold in here?"

"No." Jed grabbed a chair to slide across the floor then sat with his knees touching hers. "Are you sure you're up to this?"

"I'll look at the pictures if it'll help." She drew in a breath. "It's just so embarrassing. I'm half naked in most of them."

"Maybe there's a room you could use that's quieter than this one." He glanced up as an officer with a drooping mustache led a sullen teen with a dozen visible piercings past them. "I'm pretty certain Hernandez will do anything you ask. The kid's totally hot for you. You're sure he didn't spend the night camped outside your motor home?"

Claire scowled. "I would have gotten more sleep if he had. He's been sweet but professional. If the man has had a few X-rated thoughts about me, it's only because he spent way too much time with those pictures yesterday. They're...disturbing."

Jed's fists clenched. "I'm going to kill the bastard who took them. The cops better find him before I do."

Edelman returned with a thick folder. "You can look at these in the conference room. There's a table you can use to spread them out to facilitate putting them in some kind of order. If we can match dates and locations in the photographs to someone in your past's vacation destinations, we'll have the creep."

"Thank you." Lips pressed tight, she stood to follow the officer down the hall. The only thing making the upcoming project tolerable was Jed's presence. If she'd had to face looking at those photos alone—

Stopping in a doorway, Edelman handed her the folder. His hard gray eyes softened. "You don't need me or Hernandez to do this job. Let me know when you're finished."

"I will. Thank you again."

Jed went inside with her and shut the door. "He's a decent guy."

"Despite the fact that he checked your credit card records?"

"I'm sure Kane would have done the same thing." His hands rested on her shoulders to squeeze. "You okay?"

Some of the tension drained out of her. "Yeah, let's get this over with." She dropped the folder on the table then handed him a notepad and pen someone had left behind. "You can take notes."

"Sure. Whatever is easiest for you."

"None of it will be easy, but let's get started."

Claire spread out the photos, cringing a few times as she did so. Her cheeks burned. When had she bought the pink bathing suit, the top of which was laying on the paving stones beside her lounge chair? Two summers ago? What about the yellow flowered one? At least she was flat on her stomach in that shot. One thing was certain, she'd never sunbathe topless again. Ever.

She picked up a picture taken of her inside the motor home. A little fuzzy, as if the photographer had zoomed in from a distance. She stood in bra and panties with her back to the window, bent slightly as she pulled something from a drawer.

"I remember this. I was debating whether or not it was warm enough to wear shorts. He took the photo about three weeks ago. It's definitely the most recent. Maybe working backward would be easier since my memory will be fresher."

Glancing over her shoulder, she dropped the picture. "Jed?"

Blue eyes flashed in a face flushed dark with color. The pen snapped between his fingers. He dropped it on the floor and threw the notepad at the wall. "I need to punch something."

She stepped closer and wrapped her arms around his waist. "Hey. Calm down. The cops won't like it if you put a hole through their sheetrock."

He held tight. "Sick freak. No one has a right to see you that way without your permission. No one."

His heart beat strong and fast beneath her cheek. The warmth emanating from him comforted despite muscles tensed for action.

"The police will figure out who's been watching me and stop him."

"They'd better."

Reaching up, she held his face between her palms. "I'm determined to do what I can to help end this. Right now I need to be objective. Identify a time and place for each photo. I can't think about who was behind the camera taking the shots."

He nodded then dipped his head to kiss her. "Sorry I lost it. Let's get the job done so we can get the hell out of here."

Reluctantly, she pulled away. "Sounds like a plan. First, go find a new pen, and while you're out there ask someone if we can number the photos on the back."

An hour later Claire was pretty certain she had the pictures in date order and each location notated. Placing them in the folder along with Jed's scrawled notes, she let out a breath. "Let's go find Officer Edelman."

Jed slipped an arm around her waist as they walked down the hall. "Then take a walk or something. I could use some fresh air."

Her steps slowed to take advantage of his closeness, drawing strength from his big, solid presence. When they entered the squad room, Hernandez rose to his feet. No one else was around.

"Something I can do to help you?"

Claire shook her head. "I finished. We left everything in the conference room."

"That's fine. I just need to ask you a few questions before you go."

She dropped onto the straight-backed chair next to his desk. "Am I going to have to repeat everything to Officer Edelman?"

The young cop grinned. "Nope. He went out on a call and left me in charge of finishing up with you."

Jed pulled up a second chair and sat. "What do you need to know?"

Hernandez glanced his way before returning his attention to Claire. "When was the oldest photo taken?"

"About five years ago. I was working for *Rugged America* and living in an apartment in San Francisco at the time."

"Were you dating anyone in particular?"

"Not really. I'd been seeing someone off and on during the summer but broke it off before the picture was taken in the fall. It's the one of me wearing a pink nightgown, standing in front of the sliding glass door at the rear of the apartment, which led to a fenced back garden area. I'm not sure how he got the picture from that angle. The only way I can figure is he climbed the neighbor's tree."

"Can I get the name of the man you were dating that summer and also your neighbor?"

"Mark Hamilton. He was a bartender at the Cliff House. We went out maybe a half-dozen times. It was never serious, and I haven't heard from him since we stopped seeing each other. I don't have his address. As for the neighbor, she was rarely home. I think she worked for an airline. Her name was Darla."

"Last name?"

"I don't have a clue. We exchanged greetings once in a while in passing. She was quite a few years older than me, and we weren't social."

"If this woman wasn't home much, someone could have entered her yard without fear of being caught."

Claire shrugged. "I suppose."

"We'll try to locate Hamilton."

"It won't be him. That was the summer I decided to learn to surf. Our only connection was a few mornings spent at the beach along with a couple of dinners. Not exactly grounds for stalking someone."

"If you remember anyone else from that time who showed an interest in you, please call." He handed her a business card.

"I will. Is that it?"

He flashed a quick smile. "I think you've been through more than enough in the last couple of days without dragging out the questions any further. Edelman will go through your notes when he gets back to see if anything stands out. Did you make that list of previous work associates he asked for?"

"I wrote down everyone I could remember. I also listed my former addresses, at least the ones since I graduated from college. My childhood consisted of one move after the other, totaling close to a dozen."

"That's fine. The stalker won't be someone you knew when you were a girl. A child predator wouldn't be interested in you now."

She shuddered. "I can't even imagine how horrifying that would be. It's bad enough as an adult, knowing someone's been watching me."

Jed rose and pulled her to her feet. "Don't think about it."

Hernandez stood and stepped around his desk. "How much longer will you be in town?"

"I was hoping to take a few more photographs this afternoon then leave in the morning. Is that okay?"

"That'll be fine. We'll pass along all our information to the police in Shady Bend. That way they'll be up to date if anything new happens."

Claire forced a tired smile. "Thank you."

"You bet. It's been a pleasure meeting you. I'm just sorry it was under such rotten circumstances. Have a safe trip home."

She extended her hand. "Thank you. We will."

The fog had lifted, and the sun shone brightly as they left the police station. Claire turned her face up to the warm rays and breathed deep. "At least it isn't foggy. I've had enough gloom and doom today."

"I couldn't agree more." Jed took her hand as they walked to his SUV. "Do you want to go down to the beach?"

She nodded. "Let's go get Scoop and my camera then see what we can find in the way of sea life to photograph. I heard a chorus of sea lions barking last night."

"Do you need more shots of the lighthouse?" He pulled the passenger door open and held it for her.

"No, I took plenty yesterday before all hell broke loose."

They drove back to the campsite to retrieve an ecstatic dog and then cruised along the coast before pulling into a turnout overlooking a long stretch of sandy beach.

She rolled down her window and leaned through the opening. "Do you hear them?"

Turning off the engine, he nodded. "The sea lions must be out on those big rocks."

"I won't get any pictures of them, but we can still take a walk. The air smells wonderful."

"Nothing like what we have in the mountains where it's so dry I get nosebleeds sometimes. Here the moisture is palpable."

"Good for the skin." She hopped down from the seat, waited for Scoop to jump out then slammed the door. "What did you do while you were at home?"

He walked around the front of the vehicle, took her hand then strolled beside her down to the water's edge. "Mostly I chopped wood. That's how I heat my cabin in the winter, so I need a lot. I also took a long hike, talked to my dad and Kane on the phone and worried about you."

Glancing up, she pushed her wind-whipped hair out of her eyes. "You didn't need to stress over me."

"Turns out I did." He stopped to face her, still holding hands. "I can't even begin to tell you how angry I am with myself for leaving you alone."

"Not your fault. I asked you to go."

His grip tightened. "I'm not ready to walk away from you. I don't know if I'll ever be ready to walk away from you. Can we please try some kind of compromise?"

Claire stepped closer to lean against his chest. His arms came around her in a tight hug. Nothing had changed. Certainly not Jed. Chances were she'd still end up with a broken heart somewhere down the line. But she didn't know how it could possibly hurt worse than letting him go right this minute.

Nodding, she held on. "I was miserable yesterday despite taking some of the best photographs of my life. The light was perfect, and every angle was better than the last. Still, all I wanted was to share the experience with you."

His eyes were sober as he regarded her. "I hiked until I was completely exhausted because I was so angry you wouldn't return my calls. Plus, I'd had to listen to Kane tell me I'm a complete idiot for letting you go when it was obvious to him I—"

Claire's heart beat so hard she feared it might burst. "You what?"

"I love you."

Warmth seeped in to dispel the cold that had held her in its grip since he'd left. "Was he right?"

Jed's lips curved upward in a smile. "Big brother's nearly always right. It's irritating as hell. Except in this case." Holding her face between his hands, he kissed her, taking his time before finally letting go. "I do love you, Claire. We haven't been together long, but it feels like forever."

Her breath caught. "I love you, too. I know we still have issues…"

"We'll work on them." He tapped his chest. "I *have* changed despite what you may think." When Scoop raced up to skid to a stop in front of them, wet and sandy and stinking of fish, Jed dropped a hand on his head. "I never wanted the commitment or hassle of dog ownership before, but I missed the mutt almost as much as I missed you. Does that count for anything?"

Her smile stretched until her cheeks hurt. "It's definitely a start."

# Chapter 23

"Oh, my God, how cute are they?" Claire spun around. "I have to go get my camera."

The sea lions snorted and moaned while one slid from his place in the row on the dock into the water of the harbor.

"Puppies and kittens are cute." Jed grinned. "Those guys are big and smelly."

"Look at their whiskery faces. Adorable. Can I have the keys?"

"Sure." After digging the ring out of his pocket, he handed them over.

"Thanks." Making a fist, she headed toward the SUV.

Cute was her backside in a pair of skinny jeans as she jogged away from him, not the mounds of flesh lying on the dock below the restaurant. A seagull circled and squawked as she disappeared around the side of the vehicle. Jed crossed his arms over his chest and angled toward the fishing boats moored in the harbor. He tried to imagine Claire baiting a hook—

A woman's cry raised the hair on his arms and startled another sea lion into the water with a splash. He raced through the parking lot, his shoes pounding the pavement. "Claire!"

"What? Eww, gross!"

He stopped beside the SUV and let out a breath as relief surged through him. Claire struggled to pull her arm from the sleeve of her jacket. No one else was in sight.

"Why'd you yell?"

"A frigging seagull flew over and pooped on my shoulder." Her face screwed up in an expression of pure disgust. "The disgusting blob barely missed my hair."

His heartbeat slowed. "God, I thought someone had grabbed you."

Her eyes widened. "I'm sorry. Maybe I overreacted a tiny bit." She dangled the jacket from the tips of her fingers.

A white splotch marred the otherwise spotless, black material.

"That is pretty disgusting."

Leaning into the car, she emerged with a handful of tissues and wiped at the gooey mess. "No kidding, but I didn't mean to scare you."

"I'll survive. Dump the jacket and grab your camera. Another sea lion hit the drink when you screamed."

"Crap." She tossed the garment on the floor of the backseat then retrieved her camera bag. "I'd better hurry before I lose the rest of them."

The door slammed, and the remote lock beeped. Jed followed her retreating figure toward the dock.

Was this how it would be until the police found the man stalking her? He'd nearly had a heart attack imagining—he shook his head. He wasn't sure what he'd imagined. Just the thought of someone touching Claire sent his blood pressure into the stratosphere.

His footsteps slowed. A few weeks ago the gifts and notes had seemed like nothing more than a game, a mystery who-dun-it to solve. Had he really been that big an idiot to believe the freak harassing her wouldn't escalate to a dangerous level? Or were his growing feelings for Claire the reason he saw the situation in a completely different light?

With her camera in hand, she squatted down before adjusting the lens. Clicks were followed by more lens adjustments then more clicks.

She stood and rested her hands on her hips. "I wonder what they'd do if I climbed down there with them?"

"Do sea lions bite?"

Her laughing glance sent heat straight to his groin.

"They might if I rolled around in a pile of dead fish. I'm more concerned one would trip me and knock me into the harbor."

"How far are you willing to go for a picture?"

"Not that far." She turned away. "Let me put my camera back in the car, and then we can go eat."

"I'll go with you."

The restaurant was noisy and crowded, but the hostess was able to seat them at one of the long tables occupied by an older couple deep in conversation at the other end. She handed over menus encased in plastic then hurried away.

Jed raised his voice to be heard. "Not exactly the most romantic atmosphere."

"I didn't get the clam chowder I wanted last night, and another camper told me this place has the absolute best around." She glanced up at him and grinned. "Romance can come later."

He laughed then shifted in his chair as his pants tightened uncomfortably. "You might scream like a girl, but you think like a guy."

"As long as I don't look like one, I guess we're okay."

His gaze ran slowly from her sparkling blue eyes over cheeks flushed pink in the warm restaurant to the curves beneath her white, clingy sweater. "No danger of that."

When the waitress stopped by their table to fill water glasses, Claire ordered clam chowder in a bread bowl, and he requested the fish and chips. Once the woman moved away, he took Claire's hand.

"You've been pretty quiet since we left the beach earlier. Everything okay?"

She squeezed his fingers. "I've been trying to imagine who could be responsible for taking those pictures. Officer Edelman is focused on people I dated, worked with or lived near five years ago. I've been at *Rugged America* nearly a decade, but most of that time has been spent out in the field. My first editor—the one before Louise—is a man, but he was married with kids when we worked together."

"Doesn't mean he didn't lust after you in his heart."

"He left the magazine a few years ago, and I think he and his wife are divorced now. Anyway, I put him on the list, so I'm sure the police will check him out."

"What about other co-workers?" Jed released her hand when the waitress returned with Claire's hot tea and his beer. "Thanks."

"You're welcome." She shot him a quick smile. "I'll be back shortly with your food."

Claire dunked the tea bag a few times. "I don't come into contact with the other writers and photographers on staff very often, and none of them ever asked me out or showed any special interest."

"Neighbors?"

"Before the apartment in San Francisco, which was my one brief try at city living since college, I rented a place down near Half Moon Bay on the peninsula. My closest neighbor, this guy named Blue, was a hippy throwback who wore tie-dyed T-shirts and smoked a ton of weed. His girlfriend, Sunshine, lived with him. I'm pretty sure he was too stoned most of the time to even know I existed."

"Even if he was higher than a kite, the dude would be aware of you. You aren't easy to ignore—or forget."

"Yeah, right. Does he sound like the kind of person who would stalk me for five years?"

"No." He opened his mouth then shut it when the waitress arrived with their dinners.

"Can I get anything else for you? Another beer maybe?"

Jed shook his head. "I'm good."

Claire nodded and smiled before leaning over the bread bowl to inhale. "Thanks. This smells wonderful."

"Enjoy."

Jed broke off a piece of fish he dipped in tartar sauce. "Okay, so maybe the stalker isn't Blue the Stoner. How about guys you used to date?"

"Other than the bartender, there wasn't anyone else around that time. Oh, a friend set me up on a blind date with her cousin who was in town over a weekend. I nearly killed her afterward." Claire scooped up a spoonful of soup before continuing. "The guy acted like he was smarter than Einstein. Heck, maybe he was. I should have thought twice about going out with him after my friend told me he was in San Francisco for a space technology convention."

"You don't like smart men? Should I be insulted?"

She grinned. "I like ones who are smart enough not to brag about it."

He choked on a ketchup dipped French fry. "Nice distinction." Reaching across the table, he touched her hand. "Let's forget about all of this for the rest of the night. Let the police run their checks. Maybe they'll come up with something."

She looked up at him and frowned. "I keep feeling like we're missing an important point."

"The cops are trained not to miss details. Let it go and relax. No one's going to come near you tonight."

"I know, but you can't be with me twenty-four seven indefinitely. After we get home—"

His thumb stroked across her wrist. "Let's take it one day at a time."

"You're right." Her eyes darkened. "I don't want to ruin our evening together or this meal. How's your fish?"

"Excellent."

He made a funny story out of his early morning encounter with Daisy's bad breath while they finished their dinners and was relieved when Claire smiled. She'd been tense to the point of breaking all day and needed time to unwind. The one topic neither broached was their declaration of love on the beach. The feelings were too new—too fragile—and needed to be treated with care.

Stabbing the last fry into ketchup, he pushed his plate back and picked up the bill the waitress had left on the table. "Finished?"

She nodded. "I ate way too much, but the chowder was too good to waste. I'm ready to go back to the campsite and collapse. It's been a long day."

"Sounds perfect to me." Standing, he pulled out her chair then took her arm as they crossed the room to the entrance. After paying the cashier, he pushed open the door and stepped outside.

Claire shivered. "It's cold. Damned seagull."

Wrapping his arm around her to help ward off the chill, he headed toward the SUV. "I'd forgotten about your close encounter with the avian bomber."

"I didn't. I—" Her cell phone trilled from inside her purse. She glanced up, blue eyes changing to cobalt. "There's absolutely no one I want to talk to right now. Present company excluded."

"Then ignore it."

She sighed. "What if it's Officer Edelman with news? I'd better answer." She pulled out her phone and frowned at the display.

"Hi, Theresa. What's up?"

Claire listened for a minute, her face losing some of its color. Jed bent closer but couldn't hear what the woman was saying.

"No. Thanks for calling me. I'll let the police up here know the man has definitely left the area." Her voice was thick with tears. "Yeah, I'm sorry, too. No, I'll be okay. Jed's here. I'll talk to you when I get home." She stuffed the phone back in her purse.

"What happened?"

"My stalker is back in Shady Bend."

He rested his hands on her shoulders. The moon had risen while they ate and shed all too revealing light over lines of pain etched in her face. He wanted to touch them, somehow erase the creases. Frustration simmered, but he wouldn't lose control again. Damn it to hell, he'd be the rock Claire needed.

"That psycho spray-painted words on the front door of my great-aunt's—my house."

His grip tightened.

"'Broken vow. Broken heart. Payback's a bitch.' That's what it said. Ouch!"

"Sorry." He loosened his hold. "How did Theresa find out about it?"

"The contractor forgot some tools he needed for another job and went back to the house around six to get them. He found the painted message on the door and called the police to report it. Theresa said he tried my cell, but I didn't answer so he called her. It must have been while I was showering before we left for the restaurant. The timing is right, and I forgot to check my messages."

Her voice was calm and steady, but a fine tremor quivered through her.

He pulled her closer. "Let's go back to the motor home. You can make any necessary calls from there."

She nodded. When they reached the SUV, she stopped then glanced up at him. For a brief moment, her composure cracked. "Is this ever going to end?"

"Hell, yes, it'll end. Soon, Claire." He stroked her cheek, a gentle caress. "Can't you feel it? The guy is coming apart at the seams. The only thing that's going to be broken is him."

* * * *

After brushing her teeth and washing her face, Claire scrubbed the stained jacket in the sink of the campground's restroom. Tears rolled down her cheeks, and she wiped them away. Exhaustion from a mostly sleepless night combined with anger and fear had stolen the last of her strength. Jed was absolutely the only thing keeping her from a complete breakdown. As it was, the urge to wallow in self-pity ranked right up there beside a burning desire to kick the guy tormenting her right in the—

"Claire, are you okay in there?"

She glanced into the mirror at the sound of Jed's voice. "Yeah, I'll be out in a minute." With the water turned off, she squeezed the moisture from her jacket. Hopefully the bird poop wouldn't leave a stain. Not that a ruined coat was the worst of her problems at the moment.

Jed and Scoop waited outside the restroom. Holding the flashlight beam steady on the path, he led the way back to the RV. Once they were inside with the door shut, he pulled her into his arms. She leaned against him and closed her eyes.

"Want to go to bed?"

She nodded. "Yes."

"We haven't talked much about—"

A sharp rap at the door interrupted him.

"What the hell?" He released her, stepped to the window then pulled the curtain aside.

"Claire, it's Mateo—uh, Officer Hernandez. I have news."

Jed dropped the curtain and scowled. "He couldn't have picked up the phone?"

Pushing Scoop out of the way, she opened the door. "Come in."

The young cop filled the entrance. Claire stepped back and ran straight into Jed's chest. One arm came around her. Hernandez's gaze dropped then rose to meet hers. A resigned smile tugged at his lips.

"I didn't mean to disturb you, but I thought you'd want to know the police in Shady Bend took a suspect in for questioning regarding the spray-painting incident."

Relief washed over her, leaving her weak with thankfulness. "They found the man?" She pressed a hand to her chest. "That's *wonderful*. Who is he?"

"Your ex-husband, Ian Rutledge. Police discovered him on your property a couple hours after the vandalism was reported. He denies having anything to do with it, but—"

"I don't believe it." Claire felt for the edge of the table and dropped onto the bench seat. "Ian might do something stupid in a fit of anger, but this deliberate, planned attack isn't his style. Anyway, he's a busy man. He wouldn't have had time to follow me around taking pictures for the last five years."

Jed rested a hand on her shoulder. "For the most part, months separated the dates for each photo. Rutledge would have vacation time and sabbaticals for research or whatever. Look how long he's been hanging out in the woods hunting for a Bigfoot."

"The authorities in Shady Bend will look into his whereabouts during the times the pictures were taken. They'll be taking over the active investigation." The officer's gaze held steady. "I thought you'd be happy with the news."

Her shoulders lifted. "I want the harassment to stop, but not like this. I don't want it to be Ian. At one point we were…close." An ache in her chest made drawing a breath difficult. "I never thought he was responsible. Despite how our relationship ended, I can't believe he'd want to hurt me."

"Doesn't seem like this creep believes he's hurting you. In some warped way, he loves you and obviously wants you back." Hernandez shifted, his cheeks coloring. "I can understand a man being completely infatuated with you. You're—"

"Involved with me."

The cop glanced at Jed. "Maybe that's what pushed him over the edge. If this guy wants to marry her, seeing you constantly at her side has to be a hell of a blow."

Claire frowned. "I still don't think the person who planned all those notes and gifts, who took those pictures, was Ian."

"Then why was he on your property?"

"What reason did he give the police?"

Hernandez rolled his eyes. "He said he was pissed because the cops had questioned him earlier about his whereabouts after your motor home was vandalized. He claims he went to your house to tell you to get them off his back because he'd had a near breakthrough in the woods and didn't want any distractions. Claimed he didn't know you weren't home."

"Now *that* sounds like Ian. Full of demands. Focused on his work." She looked up at Jed. "Do you suppose he actually saw a Bigfoot? Seems pretty unlikely."

"If he's the one who left those pictures, he's batshit crazy. Who knows what he imagines he saw."

"Ian may be obsessed, but he isn't insane."

"Obsessed with you." Hernandez's comment left silence in its wake. Finally he turned toward the door. "I'll go. I'm sure the police in Shady Bend will be in contact once you arrive there."

Claire rose on unsteady legs. "Thanks for coming by to tell me about Ian. I appreciate it."

"You're welcome. Good-bye, Claire." He paused with his hand on the knob. "The authorities will focus their attention on Rutledge. In case you're right and he isn't guilty, watch yourself. The freak who's after you may be getting desperate...and dangerous."

Jed stepped up to put his arm around her. "I'll make sure she's safe."

"Good." The door slammed shut behind him.

He let her go then pushed a hand through his hair. "Well, that was interesting."

Stepping over Scoop's prone form, Claire brushed past Jed to sit on the edge of the bed. "Interesting isn't the word I'd choose. Horrible." Her stomach churned, and she wished she hadn't eaten all that chowder. "Sickening."

"Why?" He sat beside her, his thigh pressed the length of hers.

"I'd rather it was Blue the Stoner or my old editor or my eighty-year-old neighbor in Marin...anyone but a man I once cared about. I'm not that bad a judge of character. I would know if Ian was unbalanced because that's what this pervert is. Whacko. Looney tunes. Or, as you so colorfully put it, batshit crazy."

"You haven't spent time with him in years. Fifteen or so, right? He might have changed."

"Another point in favor of Ian's innocence. Why would he wait ten years to start taking pictures of me? It makes no sense."

"No, it doesn't. Unless he didn't wait. Could be he just pinned up the most recent photos."

She jerked back. "*That's* what was bothering me. Something kept niggling at the back of my brain. Just because the oldest picture was from five years ago doesn't mean the man didn't take more before that. He could have a whole stash of photos he didn't use."

"So then you do think it could be Ian?"

She bit her bottom lip. "I won't believe it's him until I catch him mailing out wedding invitations or booking a honeymoon. The point is, the guy responsible could be someone I knew ten years ago or twelve or whatever, not necessarily the five we focused on. That's a lot of old neighbors and co-workers, along with maybe a couple dozen different men I dated once or twice over the years."

"It would take the police a long time to check out every man you've ever been in contact with. And since they have a perfectly good suspect right in Shady Bend…"

Claire let out a long breath. "They won't even bother."

He picked up her hand to squeeze it. "Where does that leave us?"

"Screwed."

# Chapter 24

Claire bumped down the driveway and braked her motor home to a stop beside a battered green truck with a lumber rack. Leaning on the steering wheel, she studied the front of her house. No spray-painted message on the door. She'd been dreading the first glimpse for the last hundred miles or so. Her brows knit. No paint period. Someone—undoubtedly the contractor she'd hired—had sanded the front door down to bare wood.

Jed pulled up behind her in his SUV and got out. Setting the brake, Claire released her seatbelt and stood. Scoop waited beside the door, his body quivering. When she opened it, he shot through, barking and running in circles, apparently thrilled to be home.

"That's a relief. No spray-paint, and look, the porch steps have been replaced."

Sliding an arm around her waist, Jed pulled her close. "The contractor did a nice job on them. I wonder who told him to remove the message."

"Probably Theresa. She knew I was upset."

"I hope the police approved it first."

Claire glanced around the quiet yard. "I guess we should ask. Vern must be around somewhere."

They found him in the backyard, booted feet propped on a rock while he ate a sandwich. His weathered face creased in a smile as he rose from a lawn chair at their approach.

"Theresa said you'd be back this afternoon. I'm glad I finished the door first thing."

"I appreciate it." She shook the hand he extended. "Vern Edwards meet Jed Lafferty."

The older man gave Jed an up-and-down look. "I've already had the pleasure."

"That's right. You discussed repairs."

Jed glanced toward the plank and ladders set up across the rear of the house where about half the rotted shingle siding had been replaced. "Are you working alone?"

"No, I have a couple of boys helping me. They went into town for lunch. Me, I prefer to enjoy the view."

"I thought you had to work at another job today?"

He hitched his jeans up over scrawny hips then turned to face Claire. "The lady postponed. Anyway, I wanted to scrape off the graffiti. I talked to the police chief, and he said it was okay. They took pictures and whatnot last night. The story circulating through town this morning is they caught a guy lurking around the property. One of those Bigfoot fanatics. Didn't have enough evidence to arrest him, so they just took him in for questioning."

Claire stuffed her hands in her sweatshirt pocket. "The police released him?"

"As far as I know." He glanced down at the open cooler beside the chair. "I'd better finish my lunch before those boys get back."

"We'll leave you to enjoy it. The place is looking great. Thanks, Vern."

"You bet."

Jed walked beside her around the house. "He seems like a good man, bright and capable even if he isn't exactly a spring chicken."

"Vern's seventy, but the *boys* working for him are in their twenties. He came highly recommended."

"You have to like that about small towns—everybody knows everyone else's business, but they'll give you the honest truth when you ask for an opinion."

Claire flipped her hair over her shoulder. "Not to mention jumping in to help out. Bet even if his other client hadn't cancelled, Vern would have been here at dawn to sand that door."

"Probably. Speaking of lunch, I'm starving. Do we still have food in the motor home?"

She nodded. "If you're okay with tuna sandwiches. I need to go to the store later."

"At this point, I'm okay with anything that doesn't move."

After they ate, Claire downloaded the photos she'd taken in Crescent City onto her laptop and tried to organize the first section of her story. The pictures were beautiful, but as she wrote the text to go with them, her mind wandered. All the constant pounding from the rear of the house didn't help her concentration. Pressing her hands to her head, she stared at the cursor blinking in the empty space.

Her vision blurred, and she closed her eyes. Sleep had been almost as elusive the previous night as the one before that, leaving her tired and on edge. Lying in Jed's arms, his even breathing had accompanied her churning thoughts. Paramount among them was how much she cared about him, how broken she'd be without him. He'd held her close but hadn't pushed to make love. Without her saying a word, he'd understood her need for comfort rather than sex...even when he'd woken up with a raging hard-on he couldn't begin to hide.

Opening her eyes, Claire smiled. If Scoop hadn't whined to get out, she would have rolled over in his arms and forgotten all about the stalker turning her life into a nightmare.

She slammed the computer shut. Most of what she'd written was garbage. Maybe after stocking up at the grocery store, she'd suggest going for a hike. Straining her muscles was surely a better use of time than straining her brain with so little to show for the effort. Jed had volunteered to clean the upstairs after their painting marathon, giving her a chance to work. Surely he'd be ready for a break by now. Just one more reason to love the man.

Leaving the motor home, she headed toward the house and climbed the new steps to push open the front door. "Jed?"

"Up here."

She ran up the stairs, pausing at the top to poke her head into each room. The fresh colors she'd chosen perked up her spirits. All the remnants of masking tape had been removed, and the glass panes sparkled.

"Oh, my God, you washed the windows."

Jed stepped out of the master bedroom holding a wad of paper towels. "Why not? There's not much left to do in the bedrooms. I figured I'd brighten up the place by letting the sunshine in without streaks—at least on the inside."

"Thank you." She pressed a smacking kiss to his cheek. "It's a gorgeous afternoon. No fog. Let's get the shopping done and then go for a hike. I could use a little exercise."

He caught her around the waist and responded with a kiss that made her knees quiver. When he finally released her, she pressed a hand to her chest.

"I really do love the way you think." He tossed the filthy towels into a garbage bag he twisted shut. Heaving the sack over his shoulder, he followed her down the stairs. "When's the tile guy coming to start the bathrooms?"

"Tomorrow."

"On a Saturday?"

"It's the only day he had time."

"Cool. Once that's done, the upstairs will be habitable." He tossed the trash into a half-full dumpster beside the driveway before wiping his hands down his jeans.

"I can't wait. Living in the RV is getting a little old."

"It *is* a tight fit. Let's change, load up the dog and go. I'll put a cooler in the SUV for the perishable groceries." His eyes brightened. "Hey, maybe we can pick up some stuff for dinner and have a picnic under the stars. There's no rush to get home, right?"

"Right." Warmth curled around her heart. When Jed referred to her house as *home*, she could almost believe they might have a shot at a future. Together.

A half hour later, Claire pushed a cart down the aisle of Hansen's General Store while Jed chose food for their picnic at the deli counter in the back. She pulled a half gallon of milk from the cooler then let the door swing shut. Turning, she nearly dropped the carton.

"Sneak up on a person, why don't you! I almost had a heart attack."

Ian scowled. "You deserve more than a scare. The damned cops hauled me in for questioning. Me! I ought to sic my father on them to sue for police harassment."

"I'm sorry about that. I told them you weren't the one stalking me."

"Obviously you weren't very convincing."

She set the milk in the cart then gripped the bar across the front with both hands. "Why were you on my property last night?"

"Not to spray-paint your door." A vein at his temple throbbed. "They'd already questioned me about my whereabouts the previous afternoon. I went to the house to talk to you—okay, maybe to yell a little. I was pissed. How was I supposed to know you were still in Crescent City?" The angry color faded from his face. "Seeing the message painted on your door shook me. Whoever wrote that shit is a complete lunatic."

"You think I don't know that." Her voice rose. "The police aren't even searching for the man responsible because they believe it's you."

His face twisted into another frown. "They told me not to leave town. Un-freaking believable. Not that I would even if they'd let me. I saw one, Claire." His gray eyes glittered silver beneath the fluorescent lights. "I saw a Bigfoot."

Her heartbeat quickened. "You captured one on film?"

"No." His shoulders slumped. "I was sleeping out in the woods about a half-mile from camp. Something woke me, and I scrambled up out of my sleeping bag to catch a glimpse of the creature in the moonlight just as it disappeared into the trees. Big. Shaggy. Lumbering."

*Maybe a bear, not a Bigfoot.* She clamped her lips shut on the thought. No need to piss him off even more. He obviously believed what he was saying.

"I heard raised voices. Claire?" Dallas rounded the end of the aisle and glanced toward Ian. His eyes widened. "Why you—" Lunging forward, he grabbed a handful of his shirt and jerked him off his feet. Arm raised, he clenched his fist.

"No!" Claire pushed the cart aside and wrapped her hands around Dallas' bicep. "Don't hit him."

"Why not?" His grip didn't loosen. "I heard he's the bastard who spray-painted your house, the one who's been stalking you."

"Dallas, let go!"

Ian's face turned an ugly shade of puce.

"Dallas!"

"Oh, what the hell." He let go, and Ian collapsed onto the linoleum floor. Gasping for breath, the color changed from purple to an angry red.

Claire squatted beside him. "Are you okay?"

"*He* won't be. Where the hell are the cops when you need them? I want to file charges."

"Pansy boy. Man up and face me." Dallas stood over him. "What'd you ever see in this loser, Claire?"

"Me, a loser? Look in the mirror, asshole." Ian rose to his feet and grabbed the cart for support.

"Will you both please just stop!"

An older woman paused at the end of the aisle to crane her neck. After a few seconds of unabashed staring, she hurried away.

Claire ran a shaking hand through her hair. "Terrific. That lady probably just went to get the owner."

"Good. Stan Hansen will back me up when I tell him I found this piece of shit harassing you."

Taking a deep breath, she laid a hand on Dallas's arm. "I know your intentions are good, but he wasn't threatening me."

"The cops arrested him for—"

"They didn't arrest me!"

Claire's temples throbbed. "Dallas, I honestly don't think Ian was responsible—"

"Couldn't have been."

She spun around, and her mouth gaped as she stared at Preston. "I didn't know you were still in town."

He shrugged. "I came for a story, and I'm not leaving until I have one. I'll get a picture of a Bigfoot or die trying."

"Are you kidding me?" Ian took a step forward. "Have you been following me around, even after we told you to get lost?"

Preston's eyes narrowed. "You should be thankful, Rutledge. I was keeping an eye on you out in the woods while the guy harassing Claire was in Crescent City. That means I can give you an alibi."

Ian stopped. "How do you know about that?"

"I had lunch at the diner. Half the town knows about it. Augusta filled me in on all the details while I ate my burger. Her cousin has a police radio and—"

"What the hell is going on?" Carrying a brown paper bag, Jed pushed past Preston and moved in to slide an arm around Claire's waist. "Are you okay?"

She nodded and leaned against him. "I'm fine. Ian and Dallas had a bit of a misunderstanding, but we're working everything out."

"Like hell!" Ian's face still held tinges of crimson. "The man tried to strangle me."

Dallas's cheeks darkened. "I thought you were going to hurt Claire."

A throat cleared behind them. Claire turned.

Stan Hansen crossed his arms over a paunchy belly. "Do you mind moving this discussion outside, folks? You're upsetting my other customers."

"There's no reason to. We're done now." She reached for the cart. "I need to finish my shopping."

Dallas took the hint and backed away. "I just came in to grab a soda. Screw it. I have to get back to work." Turning, he walked past the store owner. A moment later, the bells over the door jingled.

"I have shopping to do, too." Preston smiled at Claire. "I'm just relieved to see you're no worse for wear after the problems you've had lately."

"Wait a minute. You aren't going anywhere but to the police station with me." Ian grabbed his arm. "If you can vouch for the fact I was out in the woods when I said I was, you have to tell the cops to get them off my back once and for all."

"Whatever. I can shop later, I suppose. See you, Claire." Preston nodded at Jed then walked away with Ian matching him step for step.

Hansen followed, and Claire slumped against the cart. "What a fiasco. I felt like the star in an Abbott and Costello routine. If I hadn't been so afraid Dallas was going to kill Ian, I would have shouted, *Who's on first?*"

Jed grinned. "Sounds like I missed the good parts."

"They weren't good. They were actually a little scary."

He rested his hands on her shoulders and kneaded. "Let's grab the rest of the groceries and get the hell out of here. You can give me all the details while we hike."

"Sounds good to me."

They finished the shopping then apologized to Stan Hansen for the disturbance before leaving the market. Jed stored the groceries in the cooler then shoved the dog out of the way to take the driver's seat. "Where do you want to hike?"

"Somewhere isolated. At this point, I don't want to see a living soul besides you and Scoop. Not even a Bigfoot."

"Huh? Since when are you a true believer?" He started the engine and pulled out onto the street.

"I'm not, but Ian claims he saw one in the woods a couple of nights ago."

"You don't think he did?"

She ran a hand through her hair and sighed. "Honest to God, I don't know what to believe…about anything."

"If Preston was out in the woods with Rutledge while the stalker was taping up those pictures, then Ian can't be guilty. Preston, either, for that matter."

Her head jerked around. "Preston? We were never more than friends. Why would you consider him a possible suspect?"

"He was a co-worker, which in my opinion makes him a more likely candidate than a casual acquaintance or an old neighbor."

Claire frowned. "I suppose, but if he was with Ian—"

"He can't be the stalker."

"Thank heavens. Preston is one of those guys who tries hard at everything…and rarely succeeds. I hope he gets his Bigfoot picture, *if* Ian actually saw one out there."

Jed turned onto a dirt track, and they bounced along in silence for several minutes. Thick trees closed in around them on all sides.

Claire frowned. "I don't think I've ever been up this road."

"It isn't on a map. I discovered it by accident a while back. Maybe it was made for logging at some point but went unused for whatever reason."

"Probably when the government cracked down on cutting old growth trees."

He nodded. "Could be."

When Jed stopped at the end of the road, Claire climbed out and turned her face up to the sky. Not much light filtered through the thick overhead branches. "Beautiful."

"Like you." He stuffed the bag filled with their dinner into his backpack. "There's a trail along the creek about a hundred yards from here, overgrown but passable."

She was still basking in his complement as she followed him into the trees. They hiked for two hours, until the vegetation became too dense to push through. Jed extended a hand to help her down the shallow creek bank then stepped carefully over rocks to cross to the other side.

"Can you make it?"

"I've got this." Leaping from the final bolder studding the creek bed, she landed next to him. "Good thing the water is low, although I'm not sure why this bank is superior to the other side."

"See that mossy patch." He pointed. "It'll make a soft place to sit and eat...among other things." His eyebrows wiggled.

Claire snorted then broke into full blown laughter. "You can't be serious. I bet it's soaking wet."

"It hasn't rained in a while. Anyway, I brought something to sit on." He dropped his backpack, unzipped it then pulled out the paper bag of food and a red wool blanket.

"You must have been a Boy Scout, always prepared."

"You bet." He unfurled the blanket. "Sit. The smell of rotisserie chicken has been driving me crazy for miles. There's potato salad, too, and brownies."

They ate while Scoop lay at their feet, drooling. Every now and then, Jed tossed him a bite.

"You're a softy when it comes to my dog."

"Maybe." He threw the chicken remnants back into the bag and bit into a brownie. "You'd watch him starve?"

Her lips curved. "Hardly. He's gained weight since we hooked up." She patted her stomach. "I have, too. No brownie for me."

His eyes darkened as his gaze ran the length of her. "If you were any hotter, I'd incinerate."

Claire's toes curled in her hiking boots. "Eat your brownie."

He set it aside and made a move toward her. "You would taste a whole lot better."

Her breath caught in her throat. "Jed...oof."

She landed on her back, the deep moss and blanket cushioning her fall. Smiling, she reached up to caress his cheek.

"Are we really going to—"

Warm lips closed over hers. Even warmer hands stroked up beneath her shirt. She shivered, wrapped her arms around him and kissed back, holding tight to everything she'd ever wanted. Emotions flowed like water in the creek, a current too strong to ever be dammed up. When he rose slightly to pull her shirt over her head, she grabbed his T-shirt hem to return the favor. Bare skin pressed together, igniting a fire low in her belly.

The words bottled up inside burst free. "I love you, Jed Lafferty. I really, really love you."

Blue eyes glowed with emotion. "I love you, too, Claire. So very, very much."

He kissed her again, tasting every crevice of her mouth while she rocked against him. His hand reached around to unclip her bra...

The underbrush shuddered and shook. The dog exploded into a frenzy of barking and tore off into the trees.

Jed jerked upright. "What the hell?"

Staring over his shoulder into the deepening twilight of the forest, Claire pressed her hands against her breasts. "Did you see it?"

"See what?"

"Something big and brown..." She dragged in a long breath. "It might have been a bear...or a Bigfoot."

# Chapter 25

"Whatever the thing was, it's gone now." Jed dropped to the blanket beside Claire while the idiot dog flopped down on her other side, panting.

She rubbed her arms through the fleece jacket she'd donned in his absence. "Did Scoop chase it?"

"Yes, but he came back…eventually. Moron." He stared off into the trees. "I didn't get a good look at the creature, but from the amount of noise it was making, the thing was big enough to turn him into mincemeat."

"I never claimed he was the brightest dog in the world, but he doesn't lack bravery."

Jed scooted closer until their sides pressed together. "It was probably just a bear."

"I know. I wonder if it's the same one Ian saw."

"Could be." He wiped a trickle of blood off a cut on his chest.

Claire traced a second, longer scratch with her finger. "You should have put your shirt on before running off into the woods."

"I was too worried about your brainless mutt." He wrapped an arm around her waist and held on tight. "You can kiss my wounds to make them better."

Her gaze jerked upward to meet his. "Uh, didn't your close encounter with a big, furry animal kill the mood?"

"Honey, my mood is indestructible. That little run through the forest just got my blood pumping. Might as well put it to good use."

She glanced down and smiled. "Is that the real reason you didn't put your clothes back on?"

"Maybe." He gave the zipper on her jacket a tug. More bare skin was revealed with each inch. "You didn't put your shirt on, either."

"No time. I wanted to cover up fast, just in case."

One hand caressed the back of her neck then moved along her shoulder. "No peep show for Bigfoot?"

She snickered then gasped as his fingers scraped down the side of her breast. "If the authorities found our lifeless, mutilated bodies, I would prefer that mine not be naked."

His lips followed the meandering path of his fingers. Her skin tasted tangy and herbal, moss with a hint of salt. Gently he pushed her back against the blanket and stretched out next to her.

"What about you?" He licked over the pointed tip of one breast to rest his cheek on her flat, quivering stomach. "How's your mood?"

"Miraculously restored." Her voice hitched on an indrawn breath as he delved beneath the waistband of her stretchy exercise pants.

"Thank God. If you told me to…take a hike, I think I'd lose my mind."

When he sat up, she emitted a squeak of protest.

"I can't pull those pants off over your boots." He reached for the left one while she attacked the right. Moments later, boots, pants and flowered panties lay on the moss. Sweat broke across his brow as he stripped off the remainder of his clothes.

Claire touched his back, kneading tight muscles as he tossed his briefs to the ground. He turned to face her, and she scooted closer to kiss the long scratches. When her tongue ran across one hard nipple, he sucked in a breath.

"Easy. I've been thinking about this moment since the second I woke up pressed against you this morning. When you jumped out of bed to let the dog out, I nearly cried."

Her eyes sparkled as she kissed her way down his abdomen. "Scoop wasn't the only one who needed to go. Moving into the house will make everything much…more…convenient." Blond hair flowed across his stomach as she moved lower with each word.

He couldn't talk, couldn't think, couldn't believe what she was doing with her mouth. He gritted his teeth to hold on.

"Claire, stop. Let me…oh, God."

He pulled her up his chest then rolled with her, pushing deep. They moved together, breathing erratic, skin damp, hearts thundering. Love for this woman welled up from deep within him and spilled over on a cry of unbearable pleasure. Spent, he collapsed with her sheltered inside the circle of his arms.

Minutes passed as the twilight deepened into darkness. The first stars glimmered in the night sky. Smiling, he pressed a kiss against her hair. "I'd have to say that was definitely the highlight of my day."

Claire raised her head. "Better than chasing bears…or whatever? Better than listening to my various exes threaten to kill each other?"

His arms tightened around her. "Oh, yeah."

"I'd have to agree it was pretty darned spectacular. At the end, lights exploded in front of my eyes."

"I think that was a shooting star."

She sighed and snuggled against him. "Did you make a wish?"

"Why would I need to? I have everything I want right here. Mother Nature at her finest...and you."

She was silent for a moment as her hand stroked across his chest. "Jed?"

The hint of worry in her tone dispelled some of his contented lethargy. "What?"

"Maybe we should talk about that, about what we both want."

Fear shot through him as she sat up and retrieved her discarded jacket. He didn't want to listen, didn't want to hear that the way he lived his life wasn't enough for her. When she pushed her arms into the sleeves and zipped up, his heart dipped and settled in his stomach. The soft fleece might as well have been a suit of armor, protecting her from...him?

"I don't want to lose you. You're more important to me than settling down and making a permanent home. If you'll have me—"

"If I'll have you?" He reached out and lifted her across his lap to hold her tight in his arms. "I'd be *honored* to have you." He squeezed his eyes shut to ward off a touch of moisture. "What about your aunt's house?"

"I can sell it. Once the repairs are made, Theresa would take care of putting it on the market. I trust her to do what's in my best interests."

"You'd do that for me?"

She held his face between her palms. "I love you."

He kissed her, his lips lingering on the soft fullness of hers. "I love you, too."

"I'd have to travel for work. That wouldn't change."

"I still have to find something that'll pay the bills once winter's over."

"Only work you'll be happy to do. I won't box you into conformity. You don't have to worry about that."

Her earnest tone poked at his conscience. She was saying everything he wanted to hear. So why was there a pain deep in his chest? Must be indigestion from the brownie he'd eaten. Except he was smart enough, now, to know that wasn't the cause.

When she shivered, he rose, still holding her. "The temperature's dropping. Maybe we should hike back."

"If I can find my pants."

The humor had returned to her voice, and his somber mood lightened as he set her on her feet. "They've got to be around here somewhere. I have a flashlight in my pack."

They dressed then loaded up the trash left from their picnic. With Claire staying close behind him, he shone the light on the rugged trail as they headed back the way they'd come. When they finally reached the road, he dropped his pack and unlocked the SUV, barely holding in a sigh of relief.

"We made it. I was beginning to wonder."

She collapsed onto the seat. "I'm officially exhausted. Remind me again why we hiked so far after two sleepless nights along with driving almost two hundred miles?"

He opened the door for Scoop, slammed it behind the dog, then climbed in and started the engine. "Because I have about as much sense as your mutt. Sorry I got so carried away."

The glow of the dashboard lights illuminated her smile, which warmed him far more than the heater emitting intermittent blasts of tepid air.

"Don't apologize. Your enthusiasm for life is one of the reasons I love you."

"Can I get you to put that in writing?"

Her laughter filled the interior of the car. "Afraid I'll change my mind?"

"You wouldn't be the first."

"Maybe not, but I hope I'll be the last."

\* \* \* \*

Claire turned slowly, admiring the newly installed tile from every angle. The large squares in swirls of gray muted the forest green walls that gave the bathroom a lagoon-like feel. She glanced over her shoulder when Jed stopped in the doorway. "Didn't this room turn out gorgeous?"

"All that color is actually sort of cool."

She raised a brow. "You sound surprised."

"I thought I'd hate it. I'm a basic white walls and natural wood kind of guy, but your wild paint scheme is growing on me. Let's hope potential buyers will be impressed, too."

Her smile faltered. "Not something I considered when I picked out the colors."

He opened his mouth then shut it and shoved his hands in his pockets. "Uh, with the bathrooms and bedrooms finished, we could sleep up here now."

"Maybe I should stop by the storage locker to pick up my bed on the way home tomorrow. The mattresses left in the house smell like mildew and sag worse than Great-aunt Agatha's—"

"What?"

"Pantry shelves." She grinned. "What did you think I was going to say?"

"You don't want to know, but that's not why I stopped you. Home from where?"

She smacked the side of her head. "Geez, I still haven't told you. I started to and then was distracted by one of Vern's workers. My editor called. She wants me to complete the lighthouse story pronto. Apparently one of the other photographers bailed on a project due the end of the week because of a family emergency."

"Don't you have three more lighthouses left to photograph?"

"I'm going to drop Pigeon Point and stick with the ones north of San Francisco. If this article is popular, Louise suggested doing a follow-up piece on the lighthouses further south sometime next year."

"Sounds like a plan. So, where're we going?"

"You don't have to go—"

"Yes, I do. I won't risk sending you off alone again."

She gave a quick nod, pleased by his insistence. The thought of going anywhere alone set her nerves on edge.

"First, Point Cabrillo south of Fort Bragg. Then, Point Bonita, which is just north of San Francisco Bay. If we get an early start, we can make it a one-day trip and still have time to grab the mattress since the storage place is right off the highway." She rolled her eyes. "Unless the weather chooses not to cooperate, and the lighthouses are completely fogged in. It's supposed to be nice tomorrow, though, so I'm crossing my fingers."

"Sounds like a fun day. Busy, but fun."

"I hope so. Oh, I called Theresa. She thinks it's best to wait until the work on the house is completely finished to list it. That way she can plan an open house to showcase the place in style." She glanced down to draw a finger along the edge of the tile grout before raising her gaze to meet his. "Theresa wants to push for the week before Thanksgiving. Vern is pretty sure he'll have it done in time."

Little lines appeared between Jed's brows.

Claire drew in a breath. "Don't worry. We won't have to stay here until then. Once I make some final decisions about the kitchen so Vern knows exactly what to do, we can head for your cabin. I know you must be anxious to get back." She straightened her shoulders. "In fact, maybe we shouldn't bother with the bed. We won't be here that much longer."

"We'll get the mattress. There's no reason to rush off." The lines deepened. "Are you sure you're okay with this?"

She nodded. "Everything will be fine."

He was quiet for a minute. "Vern needs a couple more bags of mortar to finish up the repairs on the chimney. I told him I'd run into town to get them. Do you want to come with me?"

"I can't. I have to crop the pictures I've taken so far and finish the text for my story. Louise is freaking about this deadline, and I don't want to disappoint her."

"You still have to shoot the other lighthouses—"

"Yes, but I can create the whole layout and just leave space for the missing pictures. I have plenty of animal photos to work with now, thanks to that sea otter swimming around in the kelp yesterday."

He grinned. "It was a hell of a lot cuter than those sea lions. I'll leave you to it, then. You'll be safe enough here with Vern and his workers around."

She gave him a gentle push toward the stairs. "Go. I'll see you later." Turning for one last look at the completed bathroom, she let out a sigh, snapped off the light then followed.

*  *  *  *

Jed wheeled the cart loaded with mortar up to the checkout counter and pulled out his credit card, wincing a little as he handed it to the clerk. He'd be overextended if he didn't cut back on expenses before winter. Time to buckle down and think about what he was going to do in the spring.

"You can just charge it to Claire's account, you know."

He turned to face the man behind him. "Hey, Dallas."

"I assume the mortar's for her house."

"Yes, but—"

"That's why she opened an account. Vern's been charging supplies to it instead of adding a percentage to help keep her costs down."

The bells over the door jingled as a dark haired woman pushed through it. Glancing their way, she smiled. "Well, hello, Jed."

"Hi, Theresa." He returned the card to his wallet. "Claire mentioned she'd spoken with you earlier."

"What did she say? Should I be worried?" The realtor walked over and stopped beside Dallas. "Did I push too hard?"

"What are you talking about?"

"The house. When she said she wanted to sell it, I was bummed at first. Having Claire here in Shady Bend has been fun for both of us. Then my realtor radar took over, and I got excited about the listing."

He took the receipt from the clerk and pushed the loaded cart out of the line. "Isn't that a good thing?"

"You'd think, but the more I talked, the quieter she got. Does she really want to sell?"

Rubbing a hand across the sudden ache in his chest, he frowned. "She says she does. I've asked her a couple of times."

Theresa's brown eyes darkened, and her lips pressed tight. "When Ian wanted to get married on that stupid ski trip, she agreed because, at the time, she loved him. It was only after the fact she admitted it had been a huge mistake."

Dallas took Theresa's arm to guide her out of the way of a man carrying a bundle of doweling. "Sounds like Claire. I almost persuaded her to give up on Berkeley to join me at the community college. She wised up in time, but I think her parents and the school counselor helped convince her she had to go after her dreams."

Theresa frowned. "So, why'd she change her mind about keeping the house?"

Jed's gaze dropped beneath the woman's unrelenting stare. "I didn't suggest she sell, if that's what you're thinking."

"I'm not accusing you of anything, and I'm happy to list the place for her. I just want to make sure she won't regret it in the long run."

"I'll talk to her again."

She smiled. "You're a good guy, Jed. I know Claire cares a lot about you, and she'll try like crazy to make you happy. Until she gives too much of herself and reaches the breaking point. I'd rather not see that happen."

"Me either." He nodded. "I'd better get the mortar back to Vern. He'll be waiting."

"Tell Claire I said hi." Theresa tucked her hand through Dallas's arm and headed toward his office beside him.

Jed pushed the cart outside. After opening the rear gate, he dumped the bags, one at a time, inside. The vehicle rocked under the weight. He slammed the door closed to lean against it. The minutes ticked by before he pulled out his phone and scrolled through the contacts. He pushed a button and waited.

"Travis? Hey, it's Jed. I was wondering if you'd mind giving me a phone number."

# Chapter 26

Jed walked out of the recreation center in Fort Bragg with a bounce to his step and a renewed sense of purpose. The rec supervisor, the third one he'd spoken with, had been just as enthusiastic about his proposal as the others he'd approached. *If* he could produce the proper permits and insurance, the centers would be happy to advertise his summer wilderness camping program for kids along with facilitating signups. Each director had assured him there would be plenty of interested participants. Now all he had to do was organize itineraries and make schedules, round up a couple of interns to help control the kids and... He stopped beside the SUV to rub his temples.

Paperwork was his nemesis. When he'd reached Alex Conner, the man Travis had mentioned who operated a similar program out of the Seattle area, he'd warned him about the administrative headaches involved. The man had been more than willing to share his expertise—as long as Jed agreed to stay in California. Not a problem. The whole point of the endeavor was to stick close to Shady Bend and recruit campers from the surrounding towns. With luck and hard work, he'd create a business for himself here on the coast that would give purpose to his summers *and* be fun to boot. More importantly, Claire would be able to keep her house.

A win-win situation—if he could pull it off.

He yanked open the car door then sat on the edge of the seat while he tried her cell. Again. When voice mailed picked up, he scowled.

*Where the hell is she?*

He hadn't wanted to let her go alone to photograph the lighthouses, but after speaking with Alex, he'd understood the need to get organized fast. As he'd pointed out, parents wanted to nail down their kids' summer camp schedules well in advance so they could plan family vacations around them. There was only so much he could do from the Sierras this winter, so moving on the project now was critical. He couldn't afford to wait until spring to get started, and one of the rec supervisors he'd needed to talk to was heading out of town the next day.

So he'd made up an excuse, albeit a lame one, about Kane wanting his help to repair a fence after a drunk neighbor had run into it the night before. The story wasn't a complete lie. The drunken idiot *had* taken out the fence, and Kane *had* called to vent about it. Jed fully intended to tell Claire the truth—just as soon as he had all his ducks in a row. There was no point in getting her hopes up if the idea didn't pan out.

*If only she'd answer her damned phone.*

His cell rang. He smacked his elbow on the edge of the door then swore as he juggled it to glance at the display.

*Thank God.*

"Claire, are you okay?"

"Of course I…still…Point Bonita…going to…pictures…sunset…"

"I can barely hear you." He gave the phone a shake.

"…service sucks…stay down here tonight…"

"Claire, call me back. I can't understand you."

"…hike out late…don't want to drive…home tomorrow morning."

He gritted his teeth. "Damn it. I should have gone with you. I don't want you spending the night somewhere by yourself."

"…perfectly fine. I'm not…danger. No one knows where…"

"Claire? Are you still there? Claire?"

"…here. Don't worry…try call…later. Why don't…stay…Kane's… come home tomorrow, too?"

He sighed. Now was obviously not a good time to explain. "Are you sure you won't drive home tonight? Damn, I should never have let you go alone."

"No…fine…call...this evening. Love you."

He clicked his phone off and smacked the steering wheel with his fist. "Shit!" Maybe he should just drive down to…where? She was at the lighthouse now, but by the time he got to Point Bonita, she might have already left to find a campground.

He let out a long breath. She was safe. He'd stayed behind her for a good ten miles this morning just to make sure no one else was following them. If someone from her past had somehow caught up to her, she would have seen him while she was taking photographs at the two lighthouses. Driving down to Marin for the night only to turn around to come home in the morning in separate vehicles didn't make a whole lot of sense. He started the engine and glanced at the time on the dashboard clock. He had one more appointment at the rec center in Willits, and he'd barely make it on time as it was without breaking a few speed limits. Maybe Claire would have better service by the time he finished. He could talk to her again and make a decision then.

\* \* \* \*

Claire eased down on the shutter release just as the sun sank below the horizon on a blaze of orange and crimson, perfectly highlighting the Point Bonita lighthouse on its rocky perch along with the suspension bridge leading out to it. She'd taken the tour earlier in the afternoon during visiting hours then found a spot on the trail back with an absolutely perfect view—and waited, and waited, and waited. Her phone call to Jed had been a failure. All the rock outcroppings blocked the cell tower signals, and the reception was horrible.

Damp and stiff from hours of inaction perched on moss-covered rocks, she stored her camera then stretched to limber up before hiking back to the parking area. Thank God she'd left Scoop with Theresa. He would have gone crazy cooped up in the motor home for all those hours. Not that she'd planned to stay out at the lighthouse for quite so long, but the lure of a sunset shot had been irresistible.

Camping somewhere nearby for the night only made sense. Tiredness sapped her strength, and the daypack hung heavily from her shoulders. Trudging up the trail, she let out a huge sigh when she reached her motor home, all alone in the small lot. Tension tightened her muscles as she unlocked the door.

No one was around. Imagining stalkers in the shadows of a bush swaying in the breeze was pure foolishness. Still, she started the engine, switched on the headlights and pulled out onto the road without wasting any time. Her first priority was food since her stomach had been growling for the last couple of hours. Second was another phone call to Jed to ease his anxiety before he did something stupid like driving down to find her. *Impulsive and unnecessary, but thoughtful like the man himself.* Once that was settled, she'd find a place to camp.

Choosing a Mexican restaurant close to the highway, she parked and went inside. Heat and a blast of mariachi music hit her along with the appetizing scent of spicy food. Her stomach growled again. The pretty young hostess seated her then handed over a menu before filling her water glass and setting chips and salsa on the table. Claire thanked her, scanned the contents of the menu then ordered chicken enchiladas when the server stopped beside her booth.

"Something to drink?" The man's teeth gleamed beneath a neatly trimmed moustache. "The bartender makes a killer margarita."

"I'm fine with just water." As tired as she was, if she drank a margarita, someone would have to haul her out from beneath the table.

He nodded and left. Claire retrieved her cell from her purse and pushed the redial button. The sound of Jed's deep voice sent a shot of heat through her that rivaled the salsa.

"Where are you?"

"A Mexican restaurant outside Sausalito. The chips are so fresh they're still warm."

"I'm jealous. Should I drive down there to meet you?"

She crunched and chewed. "From Vine Haven? Uh, I don't think it'll take them that long to cook my dinner."

Silence stretched across the airwaves.

"Jed?"

"I'm not actually in Vine Haven."

"I thought you were going to stay with Kane tonight?"

His breath whooshed in her ear. "I never was in Vine Haven."

Her hand stilled over the chip basket. "Oh?"

"I lied."

"Why?" She leaned against the seatback. The loud music that had seemed so cheerful before grated on her nerves.

"I made a few appointments I had to keep. I think this is going to work."

"What's going to work?" Her fist clenched. "What the hell are you talking about?"

"A plan for summer employment. I didn't say anything before you left because I didn't want to disappoint you if the people at the rec centers laughed in my face. I'm trying to set up a summer camp program for kids. Everyone I talked to today liked the idea. They think it'll be popular."

She frowned. "You mean in the mountains? Did you drive back to your cabin?"

"No, on the coast. I'd center the program in Shady Bend and arrange wilderness camping trips in the redwoods and along the ocean. The focus would be on survival skills in addition to outdoor adventure and plain old having fun."

"But—"

"You could keep your house. We'd stay there all summer and fall, at least when I'm not knee-deep in kids, and live at my cabin during the winter." His voice dropped, sounding almost hesitant. "If you wanted to. I know how much having a home base means to you. I hope this would give you that sense of…I don't know…belonging somewhere permanent. I want you to be happy."

Tears smarted in her eyes. "You did this...for me?"

"For both of us. I would have told you in person, but I couldn't keep it to myself any longer. What do you think?"

The server returned to slide a plate full of enchiladas and rice onto the table in front of her. She blinked back more tears and smiled.

"Uh, are you okay, miss?"

With a sniff, she nodded. "Yes. Everything is perfect."

"Claire?"

"Sorry. The waiter just delivered my food."

"Then I should hang up to let you eat."

She picked up her fork then set it down again and rubbed a hand across damp cheeks. "Do you know how much I love you?"

"Almost as much as I love you." He paused. "Are you crying?"

"Maybe a little. Thank you for knowing what was in my heart, even when I didn't want to admit it to myself."

His voice deepened. "I really, really want to kiss you right now. Maybe I will drive down."

"Jed, no. It's too far. I'll get an early start and be home by mid-morning."

"Are you sure? There aren't any strangers lurking around? If you don't feel one hundred percent safe..."

"I do. I haven't seen anyone I recognize or who even looks a tiny bit familiar at any of my stops today. No one's following me."

"Thank God. In that case, I guess driving down there—"

"—would be a huge waste of time and gas."

"Where are you going to camp?"

"I'm not sure. I'll probably drive a few miles and stop in either Novato or Petaluma. Now I wish I hadn't waited for the sunset shot, even though the picture I took was spectacular. If I wasn't so tired..."

"Don't even think about it. I don't want a call from the highway patrol because you crashed the motor home."

"Fine. Did you pick up Scoop from Theresa's?"

"Yes. Maybe I'll take him for a moonlight walk. Not exactly the evening I'd prefer, but we all have to make do."

She grinned. "He'll appreciate the gesture. Good night, Jed, and thank you. What you've done means more than I can say."

"You can thank me properly. Tomorrow."

She put away her phone but couldn't stop smiling. Digging into the enchiladas, her energy levels rose with each bite. By the time her plate was clean, her fingers tapped along with the festive music.

Three and a half hours wasn't such a long drive. She'd be home before midnight if she left right now. Dropping a handful of bills on the table for a tip, she headed over to the hostess station to pay her bill. With excitement buzzing stronger than a bee in a flower patch, sleep would be impossible anyway. Might as well drive.

Jed would be so surprised when she slipped into bed…crap. She'd intended to pick up the mattress from her storage locker. Screw it. She'd rather sleep on the hard floor with the man she loved than on a cloud of feathers all alone.

No contest.

\* \* \* \*

Jed threw a stick for Scoop then tipped his head to gaze up at the stars. Was Claire doing the same and thinking of him? He pulled out his cell, the urge to call her again strong, then shoved it back into his pocket. It was after ten o'clock, and she'd admitted to being exhausted. He didn't want to wake her if she was already asleep.

Warmth filled him, remembering her tear-choked voice as she'd thanked him. What an ass he'd been, agreeing that selling her great-aunt's home was the smart move. Selfish didn't begin to describe him. His driving need to maintain a carefree lifestyle had caused her unnecessary pain. Turned out, all he'd needed to do was open up to new possibilities, ones they could both embrace, instead of stubbornly holding his ground. He really had been a thoughtless jerk. Lucky for him, Claire was an understanding and forgiving woman. He was damned fortunate.

When the dog dropped the stick at his feet, he bent to retrieve it. With a grunt, he heaved it down the beach.

Everything would be perfect just as soon as the police figured out who was harassing Claire. Worry for her was eating a hole in his gut, and he was sick of harboring the nagging fear. He'd stopped by the police station when he got back from his appointment in Willits to find out if they'd made any progress, but the chief hadn't revealed squat. Still, something in his tone gave Jed the impression they had a suspect…

He pulled his phone out again to punch in his brother's number. Kane answered on the first ring.

"Did you find out anything?"

"Have a little patience, for God's sake. Gathering information takes time. I did talk to the chief in Shady Bend like you asked. He was a little more forthcoming with me than he was with you."

His grip on the phone tightened. "And?"

"He wouldn't give me a name, but he did say they had their eye on an old co-worker of Claire's. Until they've established the man's whereabouts when a few of those photos were taken, he won't reveal anything more. The chief did admit the suspect looked promising."

"Why the hell wouldn't he tell *me* that?"

"It's still an ongoing investigation. He only gave me that much information out of professional courtesy. But, I did a little checking on my own using the list of Claire's co-workers and neighbors you sent me. Seemed obvious to me which man they were checking out."

"Who?"

"Preston Meyer. The guy's been in Shady Bend for weeks. The most likely suspect is usually the guilty one."

Jed let out a breath. "Of course I thought about Meyer being the stalker, but Claire said they were just friends. Nothing more. Ever. They didn't even date, so what possible reason could he have for believing she'd broken her promise to marry him? I still think it's Ian Rutledge, even though Claire doesn't and Preston gave him an alibi."

Kane snorted. "The last thing you worry about is motive. Who knows what a crazy person is thinking. All I care about is opportunity."

"I suppose you have a point."

"Anyway, Meyer could have lied about the alibi."

"Why would he? There's no love lost between those two. Ian has shut him down more than once when it came to getting his Bigfoot story."

"Frankly, I think it was a lame attempt on Meyer's part to throw the authorities off his trail. If they believed his story about being with Rutledge, then he'd be in the clear for the incident in Crescent City."

"You don't believe him?"

"No, I don't. I'd bet my badge it's either Meyer or Rutledge. If you toss out the alibi, both had opportunity. It makes no sense to hunt for another man on Claire's list when they have two viable suspects right there in town. I suppose they wanted to make sure no one else who'd been close to her in the past was in the vicinity. Unless another man turned up on their radar, I'd focus solely on those two since her old high school boyfriend's alibi is solid."

Jed rested a hand on Scoop's head when the dog dropped the stick and whined. "Still seems like Rutledge is the son of a bitch after her."

"Maybe, but I did a little checking on Meyer. The guy's at loose ends. No home. Last known address was from six months ago. No current employment."

*Jannine Gallant*

"What?" The dog yelped, and he released his grip on his fur. "Sorry, boy." He drew in a breath. "What the hell are you talking about? Meyer works for *Nature Exposed*, has for years. That's where Claire met him, when she was on staff at the magazine."

"They fired him eight months ago. From what I can tell, the man lost his home a couple months later and has been living out of his car."

"He said he was in Shady Bend for a Bigfoot story." Jed frowned. "He told Claire he hoped getting a photograph of the creature would send his career to the next level."

"Maybe that's true. Maybe a shot at salvaging his career is part of his motivation for being there, no matter how remote the possibility. Claire's just an added bonus. Or Claire was always the primary goal, and a Bigfoot picture is the bonus. Do all these crazies actually believe in Bigfoot?"

"I really think they do. Well, hell."

"What now?"

At the amusement in his brother's tone, Jed straightened and gave the stick a final toss. "Ian irritates the crap out of me. I wanted it to be him. Now I'm not so sure. Preston lied, which tells me he has something to hide."

"Just to be on the safe side, I'd keep Claire well clear of both men. You can't be too cautious. The guy stalking her is a freaking nutcase."

"Don't worry. I will. Just as soon as she gets back."

"She's not with you?" His brother's voice rose. "Where is she?"

"Photographing lighthouses. She'll be back tomorrow." He kicked a clump of seaweed strewn across the sand as his gut knotted. "She's safe. We were careful."

"I hope so. Jed…"

"What?"

"Call Claire. Tell her to be extremely cautious. If either of those men comes anywhere near her, tell her to get the hell away from him as fast as she can."

"I will. Thanks for your help."

"You bet."

Jed disconnected then checked the time displayed on his phone. Nearly eleven. He'd let her sleep and call first thing in the morning. Early. Before there was even the tiniest chance that she'd be on the road. Hopefully by then the police would have enough evidence to make an arrest. No matter whom the stalker turned out to be, Claire would be safe.

Which was the only thing that really mattered.

# Chapter 27

Claire yawned so wide she feared her jaw would crack. "Stay awake. Stay awake." She'd been repeating the words for the last half-hour, hoping her new mantra along with the loud rock blasting on the radio would keep her from drifting off. Only a few more miles to go....

"What the heck?" She stomped on the brake and prayed as the motor home lurched to a stop just short of the waving figure. What kind of idiot stood in the middle of a dark highway? Was the guy crazy?

He'd flung up an arm to cover his eyes in the glare of her headlights, but something about his posture was familiar. She rolled down her window and leaned out. "Preston?"

"Claire? When I saw the motor home, I had a feeling it was you." He stepped around to the side to gaze up at her, a wide smile lighting his face. "That guy, Vern, who's working on your house, told me you'd left town for the day when I got to talking to him in the grocery store. Thank heavens you came home when you did."

"What's wrong? What're you doing in the middle of the road?"

"My battery died." He pointed toward a turnoff where the rear of his van was just visible in the moonlight. "Since the evening was so beautiful, I hiked into the woods to do some star gazing, hoping to get lucky and maybe spot a Bigfoot."

She frowned. "You hiked from here?"

"There's a trail of sorts. Anyway, I got back late and discovered I'd left my parking lights on. Stupid, I know, but it was still light when I headed out, so I didn't notice. My battery's completely dead, and it's not easy to sleep right beside the highway even though the traffic is spotty."

"Do you want me to give you a jump start?"

"Would you? I stopped a few other cars, but people were nervous about helping a stranger at this hour. Can't blame them, I guess."

"No doubt. I would have freaked out a little if I didn't know you. I'll pull up beside your van."

He stepped away, and she drove the RV forward to the side of the road, setting the brake when she was in position. "How's that?"

"Perfect. Can you come hold the hood up while I hook up the jumper cables? The prop bar is broken."

After unfastening her seatbelt she stepped to the door, opened it and jumped down. "What a pain. Car trouble is the worst."

He glanced over, eyes bright in the glow of the headlights. "My luck's never been great, but that may be changing."

"Good to hear." She paused beside him. "Ian wasn't imagining things, then? Do you expect to get that photograph after all?"

"Something I want even more. Sorry, Claire, but this is the only way." His arm lifted, a metal bar clutched in his hand.

Fear slammed into her as she stepped back and dodged to the side. *Too late.* Pain exploded in her head as she fell into blackness.

\* \* \* \*

Scoop's frantic barking dragged Jed out of a deep sleep. He struggled to hold onto an image of Claire dancing naked in the moonlight with a Bigfoot, swaying to and fro.... The dream faded into wakefulness, and he groaned.

"Damn it!"

Struggling up out of his sleeping bag, he staggered to the bedroom window where the dog stood, paws propped on the sill.

"There better be a freaking bear out there, not a squirrel."

Rubbing his eyes, he blinked and peered through the gray of dawn. A police cruiser pulled to a stop beside his SUV. The door opened, and a uniformed cop stepped out. In a frenzy of barking, Scoop rocketed out of the room. Moments later, nails scraped the front door, grating on Jed's raw nerves.

"Shit. Shit. Shit." Grabbing his pants, he pulled them on to run down the stairs. He reached the door just as a knock sounded. "Down, Scoop!" Kneeing the dog out of his way, he jerked open the door.

The man on the other side lowered his raised fist. "I'm Officer Boylston with the Shady Bend police department. Is Claire Templeton available?"

"She's out of town until later today. Can I help you? Is this about the investigation into her stalker? Did they arrest someone?"

The officer, who was probably close to Jed's age with close cropped dark hair and a wicked scar down his left cheek, frowned. "When I called in the abandoned vehicle and the registration turned up Miss Templeton's name, the chief updated me on the harassment case then sent me here to check on her. There's been no arrest yet. You are?"

"Jed Lafferty, her...friend. Damn it, Scoop. Back off." He held the door wide. "Come in. What abandoned vehicle?"

The cop eyed the dog with a cautious glance. "A motor home. The vehicle was parked by the side of the road about five miles from here. I stopped to tell the occupants they couldn't camp there, but no one was around. When the plate came back registered to Miss Templeton, the chief got worried."

Fear rose in Jed's throat, tightening until he couldn't breathe. He pressed a hand to his bare chest to drag air into starving lungs.

"You okay? Maybe you should sit down."

He gripped the doorframe. "What happened? Where's Claire?"

"We don't know. There were tire tracks next to the motor home. Possibly she parked beside another vehicle and left with the driver."

"Did you try calling her cell phone?"

"Of course. It went straight to voice mail, which is why the chief sent me out here to find her."

"Son of a bitch!" Jed released the door and dug both hands into his hair. "No way she went willingly with some stranger—anyone for that matter. She would have called me." He pulled his cell from the pocket of his jeans and checked the display. No missed calls. No new messages. He dialed her number and waited. When voice mail picked up, he slammed his fist into the wall. "Claire, call me right away. I'm worried."

"Take it easy. We're checking into a few possibilities."

He turned on the cop. "What possibilities, exactly? I know the chief has a suspect. Preston Meyer. Is he the psycho who took her?"

"Look, I'm not at liberty to—"

"Screw procedure!" When Scoop growled, Jed rested a hand on the dog's head and unclenched his other fist. He wouldn't be a lot of help to Claire if they tossed his ass in jail for punching a cop. "Fine. I'll call the chief myself. Better yet, I'll head straight down to the station. I'm going to *live* in his office until he tells me everything he knows about Meyer, and then I'm going to hunt down Ian Rutledge just to make sure that nut case doesn't have her."

"Suit yourself." The man's lips curved in a brief smile. "I don't envy the chief his morning. By the way, he mentioned having the motor home towed back here instead of to the impound lot. Hope that will make things a little easier once we find her."

The officer turned to walk back to his car. Jed pressed his forehead against the smooth wood of the door to steady his breathing. He wouldn't—couldn't—panic. Before he went anywhere, he had to put on shoes and a shirt, grab his wallet and keys. Running up the stairs, he yanked his cell from his pocket to press a button.

"Kane, I need your help."

\* \* \* \*

Claire blinked and moaned as she dragged the world into focus despite the throbbing ache behind her temple. With care, she pressed fingers to a lump the size of a walnut and winced. Trees shifted and blurred around her as she struggled to sit up. When nausea threatened, she bent double and swallowed hard, over and over.

"Take it easy. You have quite a bump. Would you like a couple of aspirin?"

Conquering the urge to vomit, she glanced up at Preston. "What I want is to go home."

"First we need to talk." He sat beside her on the sleeping bag. Brown eyes filled with remorse studied her. "I'm sorry I had to hit you. I couldn't risk a scene on the highway in case someone drove by."

"What do you want? I thought we were friends. Why would you do this to me?"

"Do you think I liked hurting you?" He slammed his fist down on the padded nylon surface. "All I wanted was for you to keep your word. We made a vow."

Cold shivered through her, and she wrapped her arms around her middle. Obviously her old pal had completely lost it. "What vow?"

Where in the name of God was she? A glance in any direction revealed only thick forest. They were in some type of shelter made of branches and moss surrounded by tall ferns. No sign of his van. Nothing but endless redwoods and Douglas fir, rhododendrons, huckleberries and thimbleberry bushes. They might be two miles from civilization…or twenty.

*Did he carry me here?* The man might look as scrawny as a scarecrow, but she didn't weigh much.

"You honestly don't remember?" Hurt reflected in his eyes. "Even after all my reminders?"

*Don't piss him off.*

He didn't seem dangerous, just sad. Surely the somewhat pathetic guy she'd known for years didn't intend to hurt her?

*He already has. Keep your guard up.*

"I'm sorry, but I don't. Maybe you could simply tell me instead of playing games."

"I wanted *you* to come to *me*. I wanted you to *believe* we were meant to be together."

"Preston…"

"You'd had a few drinks that night, but you weren't drunk. Maybe that's why you don't—"

"How many?" She winced and held her head. "Uh, I'll take those aspirin."

He pulled a standard white pill container from the front pocket of a backpack leaning against the shelter wall and shook two tablets into her palm before handing her a water bottle. She swallowed them, drinking slowly, then splashed a little water on her face. Wherever they were, the place was well equipped with a camp stove, cooking gear and a second sleeping bag. Her gaze slid away, and her stomach lurched.

"How many what?"

"Drinks. How many drinks did I have?"

"Three."

Her eyes widened. "Three! And I didn't pass out? I *never* have three drinks. I'm a total lightweight when it comes to alcohol. No wonder I don't remember anything. When was this?"

"You didn't seem that drunk to me." He shrugged. "Ten years ago. We went to a bar after work. You'd just had it out with Ross and dumped his sorry ass. Remember that?"

Recollection stirred. Sitting at a booth in a dimly lit bar across from Preston, drinking strawberry daiquiris in an attempt to drown her sorrows. Ugh. Maybe that's why she never touched rum. She'd been madder than hell at Ross, and depressed. Really, really depressed. Lonely. Thinking she'd never find a decent man who'd treat her right. Who would love her and only her. Preston had bumped into her when she was leaving the office and offered to buy her a drink and let her vent. The rest was a blur.

"What happened?"

"You cried a little. I held your hand. Then we made a promise. We agreed if we were both still single in ten years we'd find each other and get married. It was a solemn vow."

*He's been stalking me for ten years because of a drunken promise?*

"Surely you didn't take a vow like that seriously?"

His eyes clouded, and the mobile mouth twisted into something ugly. "You swore. I kept my end of the bargain and found you. Now you need to keep yours."

"You want me to marry you because of something I said in a moment of grief-induced stupidity aided by way too many daiquiris?"

"It wasn't stupid. I'd wanted to ask you out for a long time, but you were with Ross. After your breakup, I didn't want to be just a rebound guy. I wanted forever. You haven't been in another serious relationship, at least not engaged or anything, since Ross. I know since I've kept up with your life."

Anger simmered. "Taking pictures of me when I didn't realize anyone was watching is your idea of keeping up?"

His scowl deepened. "Not for the first five years, I didn't. After that, I could see you were waiting for me, too. I didn't want to push, so I stayed in the background. I bided my time until the ten years passed."

She clenched her fists at her sides. "I'm in a relationship that matters now."

"Too late. Time was up before you met Lafferty." He pushed to his feet to stand outside the entrance to the shelter. His shoulders rose and fell in a long sigh. "Anyway, he's not good enough for you. He doesn't care about you the way I do."

"This won't work between us. I love Jed."

He spun on his heel, eyes flashing. "Does *he* want to marry you?"

She bit her lip.

"Ha. I didn't think so. The guy's a player, just like Ross. Soon you'll realize the truth. Once I convince you, once you understand how happy we'll be together, we can go back to your house." A wide grin stretched his lips. "Everything's going to work out just the way I'd hoped. I'll get the photograph I need to get my job back, and I'll have you." Worry lines marred his brow, and the smile slipped. "Is that too much to ask?"

She scooted against the rear wall of the shelter and pulled her knees tight against her chest. "No, it isn't. I see your point. You're the one I should be with, not Jed."

"Don't lie to me!" His voice rose in a screech. "Do you think I'm stupid? I know you don't believe me yet, but you will. You will."

Her head throbbed, painful enough to make her whimper. She pressed her lips tight to hold back the sound. This wasn't the mild-mannered, goofy man she'd known for years. This man just might hurt her—again. It wouldn't take much to push him over the edge...

She searched for something non-threatening to say, something to bring him back from a sheer drop into madness. "I'm hungry. Do you have any food?"

His eyes cleared. "Sure. We can make breakfast. Pancakes? Eggs?" He smiled. "I went shopping and have everything you could possibly want. Just name it."

\* \* \* \*

Kane slammed the door of his Jeep and crossed the yard toward the house. Jed met him halfway. The grim expression on his brother's face didn't promise good news, but he asked anyway.

"Did you learn anything?"

"The chief updated me, but there wasn't a hell of a lot to tell. Ian Rutledge is in the clear. The idiot tripped and fell, slicing his arm open on a tent stake yesterday. He spent most of the night in the emergency room down in Fort Bragg waiting to be stitched up."

Jed let out a slow breath. "So the son of a bitch who has Claire is definitely Preston Meyer."

"Looks like it. The police got a warrant and tracked his financials for the last six months. He made charges to his credit cards that match times and locations when Claire's stalker was busy snapping pictures of her. They put an APB out on his van."

Jed clenched and unclenched his fists before stuffing his hands in his pockets. "That broken-down relic should be easy enough to spot."

"You'd think, but so far there's been no sign of the vehicle."

He stared up at a seagull circling in the clear blue sky and did his best to rein in his temper. "The freak could have taken her anywhere! What if he parked the van in a garage or an old barn? Or left the area completely. Hell, they could be in Oregon or Washington by now, or on their way to Mexico."

"He'd have to pay for gas." Kane rested a hand on his arm. "No new charges on his cards since yesterday at the grocery store here in Shady Bend. No cash withdrawals from his accounts, which are mostly overextended. My guess is he's holed up with Claire somewhere close." He pointed toward the forested hills rising along the Eastern horizon. "Somewhere out there in the redwoods."

"Hell if I'll wait for them to run out of food to come into town. I don't want Claire spending another night with that bastard." He closed his eyes and rubbed a hand through his hair. "If he touches her…"

"Look, you said her stalker wants to marry her. He's living in some fantasy world of his own making, but he won't hurt her unless—" He turned, eyes shadowed with worry.

"Unless what?"

"Unless he's pushed. Unless he has no other choice. If Claire plays it cool and doesn't aggravate him, she should be okay. At least for a while."

"Claire's smart. She won't do anything stupid. She knows Meyer, and she's good at decompressing tense situations."

"Then trust in her ability to keep herself safe until we find her."

"How're we going to do that?" He flung out an arm. "There are hundreds...no *thousands*...of acres out there. How the hell are we going to search them all?"

"We'll start with what's accessible from old logging roads and trails. He had to park the van somewhere. The chief is organizing a search." Kane nodded toward Scoop. "You think the dog could sniff her out if he got close enough?"

Head buried in a gopher hole, Scoop dug furiously, tail wagging.

Jed frowned. "I don't know. Claire said there's a little hound in him. I don't know if it's *bloodhound*, but it's worth a try."

"Bring the mutt and a backpack with water bottles, energy bars if you have them and a couple of flashlights. I don't know how long we'll be out searching. We'll start wherever you think best. You know the area a lot better than I do."

Jed nodded. "I'll be ready in a couple of minutes. Make sure you bring a jacket. If the fog rolls in, we'll freeze our asses off."

He collected his gear, hands shaking as he loaded his pack. They had to find Claire. He drew in a ragged breath. He couldn't live without her. Didn't want to. Blinking back scalding tears, he wiped a hand across his face, wishing he'd told her that the last time he saw her.

When he returned to the yard, Kane gestured toward the Jeep parked beside Jed's SUV. "We'll take mine. That thing can go pretty much anywhere. Load up the dog."

"Fine." He held the door open for Scoop. "Let's start near the Bigfoot camp. Meyer spent a lot of time out there, and it only makes sense he'd choose someplace familiar."

"Now you're thinking smart." His brother's blue eyes held compassion. "Keep it together. We'll find her. First, though, I have to eat. I missed breakfast and lunch, and I need fuel. My guess is you do, too."

"I can't stomach food right now." His voice sounded harsh, even to his own ears. "I don't want to waste time."

"We'll grab sandwiches to go." Kane's tone was firm. "Tell me where to get them."

"Shit." He closed his eyes and rested his head against the seatback. "The market in town has a deli counter in back. Turn right at the second stop sign."

Jed waited in the Jeep with the dog panting over his shoulder while Kane hurried inside the store. When a knock sounded on the window, he nearly jumped out of his skin. Dallas stood beside the vehicle. Pushing open the door, he stepped onto the sidewalk.

"I saw you drive by the hardware store. Is it true Preston Meyer kidnapped Claire?"

Jed crossed his arms over his chest. "How did you find out?"

"Hell, half the town probably knows by now. Where'd he take her?"

He shrugged. "The police aren't sure. They think he's holed up in the woods somewhere, so they're setting up a search. My brother and I are heading out to look for her as soon as he grabs something to eat."

Dallas tipped his head to stare down at the cracked cement. "I might know where he's holding her."

"What!" Jed grabbed his arm. "Did you tell the cops?"

"No." Dallas shook him off. "I want to help Claire, but…"

"But what? Jesus. That freak could be doing *anything* to her."

"Look, I saw Meyer out in the woods once. He was coming out of a shelter that was damned hard to see, and I dodged behind a tree because…"

Jed stepped closer. "I swear to God, if you don't—"

Dallas raised his hands, palms out, and scowled. "I was the one messing with the equipment those pansy-assed, pseudo-scientists set up, okay. I don't want their type here. What do you think would happen if they actually caught a Bigfoot on film?" His chest heaved. "All hell would break loose, that's what. Officials would try to capture one and put it in a zoo or study it or some other asinine crap." His eyes darkened. "I saw one once. I say leave them in peace since they aren't hurting a soul. Keep the mystery alive."

*Is everyone crazy?* Jed took a breath. "I don't give a *damn* about what you did to the equipment or about the ultimate fate of Bigfoot. I just want to find Claire."

"If you'll keep your mouth shut, I'll take you to the spot. I just need to get my truck."

"Then get it." Jed turned away as Dallas ran down the street.

Kane headed toward him carrying a paper sack. "Who was that?"

"A friend of Claire's. Good news." He let out a whoop and slammed his hand down on the hood of the Jeep. "Dallas knows where to find her."

# Chapter 28

*What next?*

Afternoon had settled in, warm and sunny. A rarity in the redwoods, but Claire couldn't appreciate it. The breath squeezed from lungs that tightened painfully as she thought about the night ahead. How long would Preston be content to play the part of her good buddy? He'd certainly tried to bring *normal* to a situation fraught with tension. All she could do was follow his lead.

*As if I have any other choice.*

He'd made a major production of pulling a long, shiny hunting knife out of the sheath at his hip to sharpen a stick he used to toast a bagel over the camp stove flame. The dull gleam in his eyes told her he wouldn't be afraid to use it if she did something stupid. Escape was still a possibility, but not one she'd risk unless pushed.

"Rummy." He slapped his hand over her discard. "You aren't concentrating, Claire."

She dropped her cards. "Sorry."

He scooped up the rest of the deck and tapped them into a neat stack. "Maybe we need to find a new way to occupy our time." Sliding closer, he pressed his leg against hers.

Her heartbeat quickened. "Cards are fine. I'm tired after…everything that's happened, but I'll try to pay more attention."

"Let's talk instead. Did you like the gifts I left for you?"

*Do I engage him in his lunacy or shut him down right now? Come on, Claire, think. Steer him in a different direction. Use your head. Don't make him angry.*

His cheeks flushed as his gazed dropped from her eyes to her breasts beneath a thin T-shirt. She reached for the jacket she'd removed when the shelter heated beneath the midday sun.

*Or horny.*

"The cake toppers were cute. I've always loved dogs. What about you? Do you like animals?"

"I had a cat for a while. She got outside one day, and the neighbor's teenage son ran over her. The little bastard."

"I'm sorry."

"Yeah, I didn't like feeling so raw and angry afterward. Like I wanted to kill that kid even though it was probably an accident like he said. I didn't get another cat." He pulled out his knife and rubbed it along the jean-clad length of his thigh, up and down, back and forth.

Claire shuddered. *New topic.*

"You mentioned getting your job back."

He returned the knife to its sheath as a sneer twisted his lips. "I didn't tell you before, but they let me go at *Nature Exposed*. After all those years of loyalty, my idiot boss explained I wasn't producing to their standards." He snorted. "As if that rag has any standards."

"It was probably time for a change anyway. You'll find something better."

"Damn right." He pushed the hair off is brow. "Once I have a photo of Bigfoot, every magazine in the country will want me. You could put in a good word for me at *Rugged America*. We could work together again, just like old times. Except better." He touched the hand resting on her knee. "This time we'll be a real couple."

She forced herself to remain still, not to jerk her hand away. *Keep him happy.* "I could talk to my editor."

"That'd be great. Of course with a Sasquatch picture in my portfolio, your boss will snap me up in a heartbeat."

Curiosity eased some of her fear. "I would imagine. Have you actually seen one?"

"I saw something a couple of days ago. So did Rutledge. He's dead certain it was a Bigfoot. Whatever I caught a glimpse of was big and brown and moved fast. I just saw a blur as it disappeared into the trees, but if it was a bear, it was huge."

The spirit and enthusiasm she'd always admired in Preston were back, shining in his eyes, masking the madness. Maybe he hadn't completely lost it. Maybe he'd listen to reason if she approached him from the right angle.

"I don't want to distract you from your purpose. Perhaps you should focus on getting the photograph and reestablishing your career first. Once you're back on your feet—"

"No." The word snapped like a broken branch. "I've waited ten years for you. I won't wait any longer."

His smile sent a chill through her.

"It wouldn't be fair to you, either. You deserve the wedding of your dreams…and a honeymoon you'll never forget."

The quick trip to sanity was over. She dragged in a shuddering breath.

"Do you want a big reception or something small and intimate? Maybe we could get married out here in the woods." He rose to his feet then reached for her hand. Pulling her out of the shelter, he tilted his head back. "Look above you."

After a cautious glance at the reverence reflected in his eyes, she did as he asked. High overhead, sunlight sifted through the feathery tree branches, casting a lacy pattern of shadows on the forest floor. Birds chirped a continual chorus. The woods were a place of beauty to stir a person's soul. Her heart ached to share the moment with Jed. Not the sad, deluded, *dangerous* man at her side.

"The trees create a cathedral more spiritual than anything man could ever build. What do you think about holding the ceremony here?"

"How far are we from town?" She turned in a slow circle. "I don't see a path. How would our guests get here?"

"We're only about a half-mile front the scientist's base camp and maybe a hundred yards from the main trail. I followed an old animal path that's pretty grown over, but we could clear it for better access."

Was that narrow break in the underbrush the trail? If she could get a decent head start… "It certainly is beautiful today. Of course you never know when it'll be foggy and cold or pouring rain this close to the coast."

"True. We'd be taking a big risk to plan an outdoor wedding, but the payoff might be worth it." Stepping up behind her, he wrapped his arms around her waist to pull her back against his chest. His cheek rested on her hair. "I've been dreaming about this for so long."

Her heart thudded, and her breath came fast as the blood in her veins chilled. Surely by now Jed was looking for her. Please God, he'd find her before…before she had to take her chances against the hunting knife pressed into her side. Before the trembling urgency in the man holding her overrode the last of his restraint.

"Let's go back into the shelter." His whispered words brushed her ear.

"I don't suppose you have a cribbage board." Her voice squeaked, high and tight like a rubber band ready to snap. "I'm better at playing cribbage than rummy."

"No more cards. No more talking." The hard ridge poking against her backside wasn't the knife. "We're going to practice instead."

She swallowed, her throat so dry she could barely speak. "Practice for what?"

"Our honeymoon."

\* \* \* \*

"Where's this freaking shelter you saw? I thought you knew where you were going?" Frustration simmered to a boil when Dallas slowed yet again to stand with his hands on his hips, scanning the thick vegetation to the side of the path.

"Easy, Jed." Kane rested a hand on his shoulder. "He's doing his best. We found where Meyer hid the van, so we know they're close."

"I'm pretty sure I left the path somewhere around here. It's hard to be certain." Dallas squinted into the fading sunlight. "I know it was a short distance past the station the scientists had erected. I ran up the trail then dived into the bushes when that woman, Margaret, turned up and nearly caught me vandalizing their camera stand."

"How far off the trail did you go?" Jed drew in a breath and let it out slowly. "Approximately."

Dallas frowned. "Maybe a hundred yards or so."

"If we yell, Claire might be able to hear us."

Kane shook his head. "If she hears us, so will Meyer. Without knowing his state of mind, we can't risk pushing him over the edge."

The pulse throbbed at Jed's temples. "No, we sure as hell don't want to chance that. What're you looking for?"

Dallas straightened. "There was a break between the salmonberry bushes. I saw it and crashed through. It wasn't much of a path, completely overgrown."

"Maybe Meyer covered up the entrance after he hauled Claire to his hideout." Kane nodded toward Scoop. "What's the dog sniffing?"

Tail wagging, he stuck his head in a thicket of huckleberries and let out a woof. A bushy tailed squirrel scurried out the other side and ran straight up a fir tree. The dog bounded over to plant his paws against the trunk and whine.

"Furry damned comedian. I told you he wouldn't be much use."

"Maybe I ran farther than this before I left the trail. The adrenaline was pumping, so I was moving pretty fast." Dallas turned away from the dog's antics. "Let's keep going."

Tension strung along Jed's nerves as they walked. Claire's need for him thrummed with each beat of his heart as an underlying urgency settled over him like the encroaching fog.

"Wait. That might be the place." Dallas hunched down and spread apart the bushes. "Looks like an old animal path. The ferns are bent."

"We can check it out." Jed plunged into the thicket, arms outstretched to ward off tree limbs. Surely they had to be nearby.

"What was that?"

At his brother's sharp question, he stopped and strained to hear. A stick snapped. Bushes rustled. "Something up ahead. Maybe Claire—"

"Sounds bigger than a woman." Dallas pushed up beside him and frowned. "Whatever it is isn't on the trail. The noise is coming from somewhere ahead and off to the right. Maybe a bear."

"We'll keep moving and hope we don't surprise it."

Kane rested his hand on the butt of his weapon. "Will a bear attack?"

"Black bears try to avoid confrontation." Jed reached down to grab Scoop's collar. "As long as the dog doesn't go after it, we should be fine."

"Look at his fur stand up. Whatever it is sure as hell isn't Claire." Dallas gestured. "Should we let the man with the gun go first?"

Jed rolled his eyes. "He won't shoot me by mistake." Arm up to protect his face, he pressed ahead.

A scream ripped through the forest sending up a flock of starlings.

The hair rose on Jed's neck as panic flooded through him. "Claire. Claire!" Head down, he sprinted through the forest, praying he'd reach her in time.

* * * *

Wrenching against Preston's hold on a scream of sheer rage, Claire swung out, slamming her elbow into his throat. His arms fell away as he choked and gasped for breath.

"Bitch!"

She raced toward the narrow gap between the trees. Branches slapped her face. Behind her, a string of vicious oaths turned to footfalls pounding the earth in long, ground-eating strides. A whimper slipped from her throat. If he caught her…

A hand brushed her back, tangled in her hair. She jerked away and cried out as strands ripped from her scalp. "No. No. No." Her toe caught the edge of an exposed root. Arms flailing, she stumbled forward and kept running.

Her attacker slammed into the ground behind her with a thud and a moan. The bushes shook as a growl echoed through the forest. An unearthly wail sent a rush of goose bumps across her skin. Claire risked a single glance over her shoulder and caught a glimpse of a creature with shaggy, brown fur on the trail beside Preston. When he screamed again, she turned away. Blood pounded in her ears and roared through her brain. Rounding the trunk of a giant redwood, she smacked into something hard, and screamed and screamed and screamed…

"Claire. Claire."

The voice reverberated through her mind. Warm hands gripped her arms and shook gently.

"Claire, honey, are you okay?"

She blinked as the face over hers swam into focus. Jed's worried blue eyes gazed into hers. A bloody scratch ran down the side of his neck. She tried to nod, tried to force words of reassurance from her throat.

"She's in shock." Another face appeared behind his with identical blue eyes, the same concerned expression. "Get her out of here while we check on Meyer."

Strong arms lifted her against his chest. Dallas brushed past to follow the man who had to be Jed's brother.

"Is she all right?"

"I hope so. God, I hope so."

Claire closed her eyes for a few precious heartbeats, breathing in the scent of the man she loved, gathering strength from the arms holding her close, forcing the images burned in her brain to the far corners of her mind.

"I'm okay."

He stopped and bent to kiss her, a soft brush of his lips across hers. For a moment, he rested his forehead to her brow then let out a long, haggard breath.

"Hold tight. We'll get the hell away from here before we talk."

A persistent whining drew her attention. Turning her head, her lips curved. "Scoop."

"The mutt's sticking close, not that he was any use tracking you."

Her smile grew as her head fell back against his shoulder. "No, he wouldn't be."

They'd reached the main path and were halfway to the scientist's base camp when Claire shook off the lassitude sucking the energy from her. "I can walk. Honestly." She clutched his shoulder. "I don't know why I freaked out like that. Preston…" She swallowed. "Is he…"

"Listen. Do you hear the sirens? Kane must have called for backup."

The tinny wail grew louder.

"Maybe that means he's still alive. I should have gone back to help him despite everything he did, but—"

Scoop growled low in his throat seconds before footsteps echoed on the path. Jed lowered her to her feet then pushed her behind him. His tense body relaxed when Dallas appeared around a bend in the trail.

His breath huffed out. "You okay, Claire?"

"Preston didn't hurt me." Her voice caught. "What happened to him?"

"Physically, he seems to be okay except for a huge lump on his forehead from falling face first on the ground and some claw marks on his back. He'll have scars from those. He was ranting like a loon about a Bigfoot holding him down while you ran away, but Kane thinks he's concussed. Who the hell knows what really happened." He shuddered. "Freaked me out just listening to him, though."

"The bear or…whatever…didn't maul him?"

"Not except for the one swipe. That's bad enough. Kane's keeping a close watch on him until the police get there." His eyes darkened. "Did you see the animal that got him? Was it really a Bigfoot? The thing was gone when we reached him."

Claire shook her head. "I can't say for sure. The creature was big and brown, but I only got a quick look from behind while I was running, scared out of my mind and not thinking straight. All I know is it was furry."

"Maybe the crazy-ass bastard was just ranting, then." Dallas glanced toward Jed. "You remember our deal. Not a word about how I knew where to find Meyer."

"I won't say anything. Neither will Kane."

With a nod, Dallas jogged down the path and disappeared into the trees.

"What was that about?"

"I'll tell you later. The police should be at the basecamp by the time we reach it. They'll have a lot of questions."

Claire sighed. "I expect it'll be a long afternoon."

\* \* \* \*

Kane stopped the Jeep in front of the house but left the engine running. Jed helped Claire out of the backseat after the dog leaped to the ground then wrapped an arm around her. When she leaned against him, his arm tightened.

He glanced over at his brother. "You're sure you won't stay the night?"

"No, I have to work in the morning." Kane's gaze swept from Jed to Claire and back. "Anyway, I think you two need some time alone."

Jed nodded. "Thanks for dropping everything to come when I called."

"You would have done the same for me. Claire, I hope the next time I see you will be under better circumstances."

She responded with a tired smile. "They couldn't be any worse."

He laughed. "Good point. See you, Jed." With a quick, three-point-turn, he disappeared down the driveway into the night.

Claire took two steps and stopped. "My motor home's here."

"The cops were trying to be helpful." He urged her toward the RV. "Do you want to sleep in it or in the house?"

"I'm so wiped out I could probably sleep on a rock, but I'll take the bed. First, though, I want a shower."

Jed turned her to face him. Holding her face in his palms, he kissed her, slowly and gently, with a depth of feeling that twisted her heart.

"Tonight, you can have anything you want."

She touched the scratch on his neck, stroked his cheek. "All I want is you."

His gaze heated.

"And a shower."

With a laugh, he opened the door to the motor home. "Get your stuff. I'll meet you in the house. I have a couple of things to take care of first."

A half-hour later, Claire rubbed vanilla-scented lotion into her blessedly clean skin then slipped a purple silk nightie over her head. Tonight, Jed deserved a lot better than an old T-shirt or sweats. After toweling her hair dry, she combed it away from her face then frowned into the steamy mirror. Wiping away the fog with the towel, she studied the scratches and bruises she'd collected in the woods. The wounds would fade. She could only hope the memories would, too.

Pushing open the door, she stepped into the master bedroom and drew in a sharp breath. A mattress covered by a brightly patterned quilt that must have belonged to her great-aunt lay in front of the fireplace where flames crackled and popped. All around the room, candles cast a soft glow. Stretched out on the quilt waiting for her lay...Scoop. The dog rolled over and moaned, sticking all four feet up in the air.

She covered her mouth but couldn't hold back a chuckle.

Jed slipped up behind her and wrapped his arms around her waist. "I'm going to kill him. Off, you damned clown. You're ruining the affect."

With a grunt, the dog scrambled to his feet and sauntered from the room. Jed kicked the door shut.

Claire turned to slide her arms around his neck. "You're a true romantic." She grinned. "Who would have thought?"

"Certainly not me. You bring out a side of me I didn't know existed. The best side."

"How did you—"

"I dragged the mattress in from the motor home. We really, really have to get a bed in here." His fingers stroked along the side of her neck. "Vern finished the mortar work on the chimney, so we won't burn the place down. I used scrap lumber for the fire and raided your aunt's kitchen pantry for candles."

"Impressive." She touched his damp hair. "All that and you still had time for a shower in the other bathroom."

"I thought about joining you..."

"Maybe you should have." She kissed him, rubbing her hands up and down his bare back, slipping her fingers beneath the waistband of his briefs.

With an indrawn breath, he lifted her into his arms and carried her to the mattress, kicking back the quilt to reveal lavender sheets. Gently, he laid her down and stretched out beside her.

"I was scared out of my mind I might lose you." Jed punctuated each word with a kiss.

"The whole time I was in that shelter, all I could think about was getting back to you. I knew you'd find me."

He held her tight, his heart beating in rhythm with hers. "I didn't save you. Bigfoot did. Or a bear. Whatever. We'll probably never know for sure since I don't believe any of Meyer's ranting statements. The guy is out of his mind."

Closing her eyes, she pressed her face against his chest. "I feel sorry for Preston. I wonder what made him snap. I never would have guessed he had such...problems. Maybe he was a little different, but—"

He pressed a finger to her lips. "He'll probably plead insanity and hopefully get some much needed help. The nightmare's over."

"Thank God."

"The future is ours."

She raised her head to look into his eyes. "You meant what you said about living here part of the year?"

"I'd do anything to make you happy, but this will make me happy, too. I know we can work everything out."

"I know we can too. For now—"

"Forever." He kissed her, stroked a scratch along her cheek. "I don't want to live without you. Not ever."

Tears welled in her eyes. "Honestly? You're sure."

"Truly. Completely." He touched the moisture on her cheek with his lips. "The timing could be better, after the whole wedding stalker thing, but I can't wait. Will you marry me, Claire? Will you give me forever?"

Pure joy surged up to fill her and spilled over in a wide smile. "For better or worse?"

"Better. Always."

"With you, life will be everything I ever wanted." Wrapped tight in his arms, she kissed him. "I can't wait to get started."

# Meet the Author

Write what you know. **Jannine Gallant** has taken this advice to heart, creating characters from small towns and plots that unfold in the great outdoors. She grew up in a tiny Northern California town and currently lives in beautiful Lake Tahoe with her husband and two daughters. When she isn't busy writing or being a full time mom, Jannine hikes or snowshoes in the woods around her home. Whether she's writing contemporary, historical or romantic suspense, Jannine brings the beauty of nature to her stories. To find out more about this author and her books, visit her website at www.janninegallant.com.

Be sure not to miss Jannine Gallant's thrilling Who's Watching Who series!

# EVERY MOVE SHE MAKES

*No matter where she goes, he knows her every move...*

Long ago, Rachel Carpenter was a glamorous soap star. She gave it all up to move to Napa Valley with her daughters to open up a bookstore near her family vineyard. Her life is safe and dependable, until she encounters Kane Lafferty at a wilderness camp in the rugged High Sierra. A burned-out police detective struggling with his own demons, Kane is instantly attracted to Rachel. And like Rachel, he isn't sure if he's ready to open up his heart. But everything is about to change...

Someone is watching from the darkness. A fanatic obsessed with Rachel for years has decided to claim what he believes is his. It will be up to Kane to not only protect his new love and her family, but to uncover the identity of the stalker before it's too late for all of them...

Lean more about Jannine Gallant at
http://www.kensingtonbooks.com/author.aspx/31646

# Chapter One

"My baby has pink hair." Rachel Carpenter planted her elbows on the table and held her face in her hands. "No, I take that back. Not pink. Magenta. Her beautiful, blond hair is magenta."

Her sister smiled from across the table, the green eyes they'd both inherited from their mother sparkling with amusement. "Magenta is a lovely color."

"Did I mention she cut it, too? Her hair is short and spiky. She looks like a punk rocker."

Grace Hanover covered her mouth but couldn't hide a smile. "I bet she still looks cute, even with short, magenta hair."

"Of course she does. Lark would be beautiful bald." Rachel let out a deep sigh and poked at a scallop on her plate. "I don't know what to do with her. She's so rebellious and angry all the time. She's only fourteen, for heaven's sake."

Grace reached across the table to squeeze her sister's hand. "Lark is too smart to do anything really stupid."

"Her actions lately haven't shown a lot of forethought. I'm worried about this new friend of hers. Rose is the one who talked Lark into dyeing her hair. Rose's hair is Day-Glo orange." Rachel pleated the napkin in her lap. "Why did Bryce have to go skiing that weekend? He might have been a lousy husband, but he was good with the girls."

"The avalanche was a freak accident—one that wouldn't have happened to him if he'd taken the girls to Hawaii like he promised." Grace's tone hardened. "Oh, no, his current bimbo wanted to hit the slopes instead." She tossed long, brown hair over her shoulder with a sharp flip of her wrist. "Too bad you wasted over ten years of your life on the bastard before you finally divorced him."

"They weren't wasted. He gave me three beautiful daughters. You and I both know Bryce was a cheating idiot, but the girls loved him. They miss him so much. Jade and Ivy are adjusting, but Lark broods. She's been seeing a therapist. The woman assures me she'll come around eventually."

"There you have it. Your daughter just needs more time. Eat your dinner."

If only Rachel could dismiss her worries so easily.

They dined at her favorite restaurant on Fisherman's Wharf. Through the window, the sun cast a golden glow over San Francisco Bay. To their left, the majestic span of the Golden Gate Bridge stretched northward. Farther out in the bay, Alcatraz stood sentinel on its lonely rock.

"How's work? Do you have a full staff for the summer?"

Rachel turned to face her sister. "I think so. Ellen and Chandra are still with me, and I hired a new guy, Tim."

Grace's eyes held a challenge. "How about a quick fling with a young stud?"

"Very funny. I would never hit on an employee. Anyway, I think Tim's gay, and I don't date college boys."

"You don't date anyone."

"Let's not go there. It's your turn for the hot seat. Who's the new guy you're seeing?"

"Nolan Marconi. He's Italian and very intense."

"What does he do?"

"Believe it or not, he's a cop, a detective with the SFPD. Cops usually hate investigative reporters as a rule." She sipped her wine and smiled. "But this one seems to like me—and not just in bed."

Rachel covered her ears. "Too much information. Geez, Gracie, some things should remain private."

"I'm trying to motivate you. Live a little. At thirty-five, you probably still have a few good years left."

She ignored the direct hit. "Am I going to meet him before he goes by the wayside like the legions of men you've dated before him?"

"Yep. He's picking me up when his shift is over." Her eyes brightened. "In fact, here he comes now, and he has someone with him. Talk about hot." She fanned a hand in front of her face.

Rachel glanced over her shoulder. Two men approached, and more than one woman in the crowded restaurant gave the pair a lingering look. They were definitely worth a second glance. One was of medium height with a rangy build. With his black hair tied back in a ponytail, he was movie-star handsome. The other man stood well over six feet and looked like he spent some serious time in the gym. Chestnut hair brushed the collar of his shirt, and sharp blue eyes didn't miss a thing. When his gaze landed on her, Rachel sucked in a breath. Her sister was right about the hot factor.

Grace greeted the black-haired man with a lingering kiss.

"Grace, this is a friend of mine, Kane Lafferty." The detective's gaze never left her sister's face. "Kane, this gorgeous creature is Grace."

"Nice to meet you. Nolan and Kane, say hello to my big sister, Rachel Carpenter."

"It's a pleasure." Nolan reached across the table to shake her hand. "Grace has told me all about you."

"That can't be good." Rachel turned to the man at his side and smiled. When he grasped her hand in his large, warm palm, a tingle jolted through her. The last person she'd felt that kind of chemistry with was her ex.

Kane's brow creased as he released her hand. "Rachel Carpenter... Why does that name sound familiar?"

"Not because you saw it on a rap sheet." Grace scowled. "Her husband was Bryce Carpenter."

The frown cleared. "Of course! I was a huge fan."

Nolan nodded. "Everyone on the force was a fan. With that amazing arm, he led the Niners to some incredible victories. What's not to love?"

"Plenty, but we won't get into it. Have a seat, gentlemen." Grace pointed to the empty chairs. "How about a drink before we leave?"

Despite the temptation to stay, Rachel lodged a quick protest. "I really shouldn't. I have a long drive, and it's getting late. The girls are home alone with Lark babysitting."

"Don't be a spoilsport. You've been nursing the same glass of wine all evening. The girls are fine. Lark is fourteen, and Mom and Dad are practically a stone's throw from your house."

Her sister was right. She was just making excuses, and it wouldn't kill her to be social for a change. "I guess one small drink won't hurt."

"Darn straight. Enjoy yourself while you can. Summer vacation is just around the corner. In a couple of weeks, you'll want to run screaming away from your children."

"Probably." Rachel turned when Kane took the seat beside her. "Do you have a family?"

He shook his head. "Just an ex-wife. No kids. Look, I didn't mean to crash your evening."

"You aren't crashing anything." Nolan tore his attention away from Grace. "Kane and I ran into each other at the station, and I asked him to join us."

"The more the merrier." Grace waved to catch their server's attention. "What does everyone want to drink? I think I'll have a cosmopolitan."

After they ordered, Rachel restarted the conversation. "Do you two work together?" Her gaze wandered from Kane to Nolan and back. Strong was the word that sprang to mind. Kane had a jaw carved out of rock, and those shoulders… She squirmed in her seat. A broad set of shoulders was her secret weakness.

"We're both homicide detectives." Nolan draped his arm over the back of Grace's chair and twirled a lock of her hair around his finger.

"Right now I'm on a…vacation of sorts." Kane's fist clenched on the tablecloth. "I'm headed up to the mountains in the morning for some camping. Hopefully a couple weeks spent under the stars will clear away the cobwebs."

Before Rachel could ask what he meant, Nolan spoke up.

"Which is why I insisted he join us. Anyone who plans to commune with nature for more than a night deserves a civilized send off."

Their server delivered the drinks.

Rachel took a sip of her Irish coffee. "Where're you camping?"

"My brother runs a wilderness camp on Donner Summit called Granite Lake Retreat. There're cabins to sleep in, and all the food is provided for the guests. He offers nature hikes and canoeing, that sort of thing. I volunteered to give him a hand until the rest of his summer staff arrives."

Rachel smiled. "Sounds like fun. I haven't been camping in ages."

"My sister actually enjoys sleeping in a tent." Grace shuddered. "She hikes for fun. If I'm on vacation, I want a luxury hotel with a gym."

"I'm with you there, babe."

"You two are soft." Rachel shook her head. "You're missing out. Nature is good for the soul."

"You didn't tell me you had a crazy sister." Nolan gazed into Grace's eyes.

"I try to keep it a secret. A whacko in the family might reflect badly on the rest of us."

Kane raised a brow. "How many of you are there?"

"Five." Grace rolled her eyes. "We have another sister and two brothers. It was always a battle for the bathrooms when we all lived at home."

"That's nothing." Nolan tapped his chest. "My mama raised seven boys and two girls."

"I thought having one brother was more than enough." Kane swallowed the last of his cocktail. "I'm sorry to break up the party, but I really should go. I still have to pack, and I want to hit the road early to beat the morning traffic."

"Me, too." Rachel pushed back her chair. "It was nice meeting you, Nolan." She turned to face the man beside her. "I hope you enjoy your vacation."

"I'll walk you to your car."

"Thanks, but it's a bit of a hike. I couldn't find any parking close by."

"All the more reason to have an escort. Are you ready to go?"

"As soon as I pay the bill." She stood and swooped to retrieve the folder from the approaching server.

"I'll get the drinks." He pulled his wallet out of his pocket.

"Don't be silly. You're our guests, right, Grace?"

"Right. Let her pay. She always gets her way in the end, so you may as well save the argument."

After Rachel handed the young man her credit card, he retreated, nearly bumping into an older woman hovering nearby. The woman stepped around him with a broad smile.

"It is you! I told my husband I couldn't be mistaken. I said, 'Ted, that's Jordan Hale.' Sure enough, I was right. Honey, would you mind signing an autograph. I adored you before you fell off that cliff and drowned." The woman paused for breath and pulled a notepad from her purse.

Rachel pasted on a smile. "I'd be happy to."

"Make it out to Mary Cooke, with an *e*, please. And can you sign it from Jordan Hale and then your real name? I can't tell you how thrilled I am to meet you in person. I don't know why those horrible writers had to go and kill you."

"Here you go, Mrs. Cooke. It's always a pleasure to meet a fan who still remembers me."

"Thank you, dear. Why you're just as nice as you were on the show." The woman backed toward her own table. "Wait until I tell Mildred. She's going to be green with envy."

Rachel laughed. "Tell Mildred I said hello." When the server returned with the credit card slip, she signed it.

Nolan looked from Rachel to Grace. "What was that all about?"

Kane's brow creased. "Yeah, why did that woman call you Jordan Hale?"

"Because that's who she was back in the day. My sister was Jordan Hale, seductress extraordinaire on *Days of Desire*." Grace grinned. "Pretty cool, huh?"

Rachel shook her head. "Neither of them looks like a soap fan, so I doubt they know what you're talking about."

"Don't be such a sexist. Plenty of men watch soap operas. After all, the women are hot. Why shouldn't men watch them?"

Nolan scowled. "Grace, what the hell are you rambling on about?"

Rachel took pity on him and explained. "I was on a soap opera while Bryce and I lived in New York. You might remember he played for the

Giants before he was traded to San Francisco. Anyway, my character's name was Jordan Hale."

Kane pushed his chair in and stepped closer. "That was, what, a dozen years ago?"

"Soap fans have long memories, and mine was a popular character. I had quite a following back then."

"You still get recognized, though not as often since you cut your hair shorter." Her sister studied her and tapped one manicured nail on the table. "Jordan Hale looked a lot younger than you do."

Rachel rolled her eyes. "Thanks, Gracie. Remind me to break out the support hose."

"I don't think you're ready for a nursing home yet." A smile tugged at the edges of Kane's firm mouth. "Shall we go?"

She nodded. "Good night, Nolan. Grace, I'll talk to you soon."

"You certainly will." A speculative gleam lit her eyes. "I'll expect a full report."

Kane guided Rachel through the restaurant with a warm hand against the small of her back. "What did your sister mean by that?"

"Nothing. Grace is just being Grace. She's a nut." Rachel's cheeks heated. She knew full well what her sister had meant. Unfortunately, Grace had seen her attraction to Kane and was undoubtedly hoping for a juicy end to the evening. As Rachel wasn't in the habit of jumping into bed with relative strangers, her sister was doomed to disappointment.

"Where'd you park?" Kane waited for her response as they stepped out into the brisk spring air.

"Down the Embarcadero." She shrugged on the sweater her mother had knit her the previous Christmas. "I suppose you're in the opposite direction."

"No, I'm that way, too." Taking her arm, he led her around a crowd of people who'd stopped to listen to a street musician.

The clear, clean notes of his saxophone followed them as they strolled down the brick-paved sidewalk. The moon was out, a silver orb shining over the bay.

She tilted her chin. "Look at that sky."

"Beautiful, isn't it?"

Rachel nodded. "I'm glad I don't live in the city anymore, but I do miss nights like these."

"Where do you live?"

"Up in Vine Haven, north of Napa."

"I know the area, lots of rolling hills and grape vines. What do you do there?"

"I own a combination bookstore coffee bar. The town has enough of a tourist trade to survive, but not enough to ruin the small town atmosphere."

"I think I've been there. Years ago, my ex-wife dragged me through Napa County on a wine-tasting tour. Is there a small winery in Vine Haven?"

Rachel smiled. "Only the best one in Northern California, but I may be a teensy bit prejudiced. Hanover Vineyards belongs to my family. I grew up there, and my father and brother still run the vineyard and winery. We offer tours on the weekends."

"Oh, yeah? So you moved back to the family homestead after your husband died?"

"Actually, the year before. Bryce and I were divorced when he died in the skiing accident."

"I remember hearing about that. I don't imagine living with a professional athlete was easy."

"There were some negatives." Bitterness edged her voice, and she forced herself to relax.

"Cops make lousy husbands, too. Just ask my ex-wife."

"You seem like a good guy. What happened?"

"The usual. I spent more time at work than I did with her. Diana is a very nice person, and she's a fighter. She stuck it out for five long years before she finally gave up. I guess she came to the conclusion I wasn't going to change."

Rachel stopped walking and looked up at him. The breeze blew her hair across her face. One strand caught at the corner of her mouth, and Kane reached out a finger to free it. Her breath stuck in her throat as she struggled to remember what they were talking about.

"Did you want to change?"

"Not really. I was younger and had a lot to prove."

"And now?"

He ran a hand through his hair. "I'm not sure anymore, but I do need a break."

"Did something happen?"

His expression closed. "Yeah, something happened." After a moment's hesitation he took her arm to lead her forward. "I don't know why I'm boring you with my problems. How did we end up talking about me?"

"I have that effect on people. Something about me makes everyone I talk to want to spill their guts."

He grimaced. "I'm not the only one? There's a crowd of needy jerks bending your ear? Terrific."

"Mostly just family." She gave him a teasing poke to lighten the mood. "I'm no psych guru, and even if there was a crowd, I'd say you're unique."

"Hardly. I'm just one of a million divorced cops. You may want to warn your sister we're bad relationship risks before she gets too involved with Nolan. Not that he isn't a great guy."

"I'm sure he is. Anyway, I'd be more inclined to worry about him. Grace discards men faster than empty pizza boxes."

Kane grinned. "Your sister seems like quite a dynamo."

"She is. When God passed out inhibitions, he skipped Grace and gave me a double dose."

"I doubt that. Anyone who was a soap star can't have too many restraints."

"Ask my oldest daughter. She'll tell you all about them. Here's my car." Rachel stopped beside her red SUV.

"I rest my case. Inhibited people don't buy red cars."

"I chose the model, but I let my girls pick the color. They take after their aunt."

He smiled, his rugged face lit by an overhead streetlight. Kindness—and pain—was reflected in his eyes. Lines radiated from the corners of his lips, and creases marred his broad forehead. He looked like a man who'd seen the darker side of humanity and was worn down by the experience. It took all her willpower not to reach up to stroke his cheek.

"It was nice meeting you, Rachel Carpenter. More than nice."

"I hope you have a wonderful time camping. I must admit I'm a little jealous."

"You should come up. My brother's retreat is a great place for families. I bet your girls would love it."

"Jade and Ivy probably would, but Lark's another story. Anyway, I imagine the camp is fully booked for the summer."

"It is for July and August, but I think there's space left in June. People tend to wait until it's warmer to go camping in the Sierras. It can be pretty cold at night this time of year. I wouldn't be surprised if there's still some snow left around the lake."

"In other words, pack a warm sleeping bag."

"You've got it. If you decide you're interested, Jed has a web site. Look up Granite Lake Retreat on the Internet, and you can get the phone number to make a reservation."

"I'll think about it." She let out another sigh before she could stop herself. "I'd better go. The drive isn't getting any shorter standing here." She touched his arm. "Thanks for walking me to my car. I know you're anxious to get home."

"My pleasure, and it wasn't out of my way. I own the Jeep parked three spaces over. Anyway, it's not safe for a woman to be alone on the street this time of night."

"True, more's the pity. Good night, Kane. Maybe I'll see you again sometime."

He enclosed her hand in both of his, and a tingle shot through her.

"I certainly hope so." He hesitated then released her. "Drive carefully."

She unlocked her car door. "Careful is my middle name."

Made in United States
North Haven, CT
25 August 2023

40721980R00157